Dear Reader:

In April 1831, her grace  widowed son, Lord Julian, daughter, Miss Sophie Wilkie she was twelve years old, silent him. He doesn't want to go. H .... if not persuasive, and Julian reluctantly accompanies her to London to meet the young lady. And he knows that whatever happens isn't going to be good.

Lord Devlin Monroe, Julian's nephew, is very fond of his intriguing vampire persona in society: he delights, he frightens, he brings on delicious shudders. He's enjoying an extraordinarily pleasant bachelor life until Miss Roxanne Radcliffe and her niece, Miss Sophie Wilkie, appear in London society, and suddenly he finds himself wondering how he could have enjoyed midnight alone.

Julian and Devlin must discover what really happened three years earlier when Julian's first wife, Lily, was found dead. If they don't find out the truth, their lives could be ruined. And there is another, even more perfidious danger that lurks in the shadows, waiting.

I hope you enjoy *Prince of Ravenscar*. Please visit my website, www.catherinecoulter.com, and come to my Facebook page, www.facebook.com/catherinecoulterbooks, for up-to-date information, contests, reader chats, and lots of fun. Do e-mail me at readmoi@gmail.com and tell me what you think of the book.

Enjoy,

Catherine Coulter

"The prolific Coulter balances this tale's serious themes and tone with humorous moments and a charming secondary romance between Devlin—Julian's half nephew and best friend, who is so pale it's rumored he is a vampire—and one of Sophie's relatives, Roxanne. Fans of Coulter's popular Sherbrooke series will be thrilled by this latest addition." —*Booklist* (starred review)

Praise for *The Valcourt Heiress*

"An engaging medieval romantic suspense starring two fascinating lead characters . . . The story line is fast paced from the moment Merry sneaks out of the castle and never slows down . . . Fans will enjoy Catherine Coulter's exciting thirteenth-century thriller." —*Genre Go Round Reviews*

"With an unpredictable plot and characters readers will root for, Coulter delivers a tale of magic, mayhem, and true love." —*BookPage*

"Everything an historical romance fan could want: A compelling hero and heroine, historical descriptions that make you feel like you traveled back in time, nasty bad guys who get thwarted in the end, evil that gets defeated by good, and a romance . . . Coulter is one of the genre's great storytellers, and does weave an intriguing story that will quickly captivate a reader's interest and keep it until the final page . . . There are surprises, emotional moments, and triumphs. Along with compelling protagonists is a support cast of characters that become real as soon as you meet them. The mysteries that Coulter weaves through the story, as well as the relationship between Garron and Merry, will capture and keep a reader's interest." —*New York Journal of Books*

"Coulter returns to her historical roots with a fast-paced tale of medieval intrigue and high-stakes danger . . . Coulter's colorful characters and distinctive voice should carry readers through to the end." —*Booklist*

PRINCE

of

RAVENSCAR

{A SHERBROOKE NOVEL}

Catherine Coulter

JOVE BOOKS, NEW YORK

THE BERKLEY PUBLISHING GROUP
Published by the Penguin Group
Penguin Group (USA) Inc.
375 Hudson Street, New York, New York 10014, USA
Penguin Group (Canada), 90 Eglinton Avenue East, Suite 700, Toronto, Ontario M4P 2Y3, Canada
(a division of Pearson Penguin Canada Inc.) • Penguin Books Ltd., 80 Strand, London WC2R 0RL,
England • Penguin Group Ireland, 25 St. Stephen's Green, Dublin 2, Ireland (a division of Penguin
Books Ltd.) • Penguin Group (Australia), 250 Camberwell Road, Camberwell, Victoria 3124, Australia
(a division of Pearson Australia Group Pty. Ltd.) • Penguin Books India Pvt. Ltd., 11 Community
Centre, Panchsheel Park, New Delhi—110 017, India • Penguin Group (NZ), 67 Apollo Drive,
Rosedale, Auckland 0632, New Zealand (a division of Pearson New Zealand Ltd.) • Penguin Books
(South Africa) (Pty.) Ltd., 24 Sturdee Avenue, Rosebank, Johannesburg 2196, South Africa

Penguin Books Ltd., Registered Offices: 80 Strand, London WC2R 0RL, England

This is a work of fiction. Names, characters, places, and incidents either are the product of the author's
imagination or are used fictitiously, and any resemblance to actual persons, living or dead, business
establishments, events, or locales is entirely coincidental. The publisher does not have control over
and does not have any responsibility for author or third-party websites or their content.

PRINCE OF RAVENSCAR

A Jove Book / published by arrangement with the author

PUBLISHING HISTORY
G. P. Putnam's Sons hardcover edition / November 2011
Jove mass-market edition / November 2012

ISBN: 978-0-515-15115-2

JOVE®
Jove Books are published by The Berkley Publishing Group,
a division of Penguin Group (USA) Inc.,
375 Hudson Street, New York, New York 10014.
JOVE® is a registered trademark of Penguin Group (USA) Inc.
The "J" design is a trademark of Penguin Group (USA) Inc.

PRINTED IN THE UNITED STATES OF AMERICA

10 9 8 7 6 5 4 3 2 1

ALWAYS LEARNING   PEARSON

To my beloved Kaitlyn.

You will help many people throughout your life

with your skill, your kindness, and your caring.

And that is a good thing.

Catherine

PRINCE

of

RAVENSCAR

~⇒ *I* ⇐~

Near Saint Osyth
On the Southern Coast of England
MARCH 1831

The night was as black as the Devil's dreams, not even a ghost of a moon, not a single star to pierce through the thick rain clouds.

It was a perfect night.

Julian tethered his sixteen-hand bay gelding, Cannon, to a skinny branch of a lone bent oak tree and made his way carefully down the steep narrow winding path to the hidden cove, a trek he'd made countless times in the years before he'd left England. It was good to be back. He slapped his arms against the cold, the wind off the channel slamming against his thick coat, wheedling in to cozy up to his bones. Down, down he went. When he finally reached the shadowed overhang in the cliff, he lit the lamp and held it up, flashed it three times, a signal he himself had established many years before.

Three answering flashes of light came five minutes later, some fifty yards offshore. Two boats were moving closer now with every passing second. Soon they'd be close enough for him to hear the oars dipping rhythmically through the water. Julian felt his blood pump faster, as it always did with the ever-present threat of excisemen suddenly appearing over the edge of the high cliff, waving guns and yelling. He could only hope the bribes his man Harlan had put into place held, though to his knowledge no one even knew about this small hidden cove.

No matter how you dressed it up, smuggling—*free trading* always sounded high-flying and righteous—was still against the law. And smuggling would continue until those idiots in the government finally did away with the high import duties. Would they ever see reason? Julian hoped it would take the old curmudgeons a while, since he'd enjoyed the midnight hide-and-seek since he was sixteen, when Sergeant Lambert had introduced him to the adventures of smuggling. Teas, brandy, tobacco, China rice, gin—it didn't matter, he did it all. Every time Julian walked down to this beach, he thought of Lambert, who'd died the way he'd lived, all flash and excitement, charging forward, his bayonet fixed, a yell coming from his mouth when a howitzer shot had exploded at his feet. Julian remembered falling to his knees, tears flooding down his face as the mayhem continued around him, searching, tearing at the bloody ground, but there'd been nothing left of Lambert. Julian knew someone had dragged him away from where Lambert had died, because he remembered Wellington buffeting his shoulder, telling him to carry a message to his left flank. It was demmed important, move! And Julian had run faster than he ever had before.

He still wondered how he'd managed to survive Waterloo with only one sword gash, in his left shoulder. Blessedly, his memory of those long hours that became days blurred with the battle blood and screams and death, and with Wellington's voice, yelling orders, always encouraging, even at the end of the day, when exhaustion sapped everyone's will.

His mother had asked him once about Waterloo, but evidently the look on his face had stopped her in her tracks. She simply pulled him against her and said nothing more about it. But she'd been very proud when the Duke of Wellington himself had sent a commendation to the sixteen-year-old Julian.

Until Julian had left England three years ago, every June seventeenth he'd visited Sergeant Lambert's empty grave at his farmhouse near Saint Osyth. Julian was certain Lambert's spirit knew he was using his favorite smuggling cave, and perhaps he occasionally slipped through from the other side to watch Julian bring in his boats. *Is there smuggling in Heaven, Lambert?* Why, he'd asked Lambert on the eve of Waterloo, couldn't men ever be content? Because greed and envy and jealousy were sewn into the very fabric of a man's body, Lambert had said, and spat.

So quickly the future became the present, and the present became a collection of memories, some bringing a smile, others still with the power to smash you with despair. Would he die in the next war, blown apart, as Lambert had died at Waterloo? Witness what was happening in Europe, revolution everywhere, and death and destruction, and always there was hope that something good would come of the violence. He wondered if this was ever true.

"All's well, Captain!"

He smiled and walked down to greet Cockeral, a madman, some whispered—but only out of his hearing.

He stilled. He'd heard something, he knew it. Excisemen? He held up his hand for quiet, and Cockeral and his men fell flat beside the boats.

Someone was there, watching, waiting, Julian knew it. But what? Who?

Time passed. They unloaded the cargo, mostly brandy and tea this time, and stored it in the hidden cave. Julian listened but heard only the wind.

When he fell exhausted into bed an hour before dawn, he knew in his gut his prized hidden caves were no longer a secret.

❧ 2 ❧

THE PRINCE RETURNS

Ravenscar
Near Saint Austell, Southern Cornwall
APRIL 1831

Corinne threw her arms around him, hugged him close, and breathed him in. He smelled of a wild wind and a storm-tossed sea. His face was darkly tanned from months spent striding the deck of his ship, and his eyes were alight with pleasure. He looked fit and healthy and splendidly male. *Her son.* She'd thought of him every single day he'd been gone, savored his letters, most arriving each and every week, and she'd worried, but he hadn't wanted her to come to Genoa, where he'd lived. Too dangerous, he'd written.

She stepped back, her hands still clutching his arms. "At last you're home, dearest. Ah, three years, Julian, three whole years—but now you're here safe and sound. Come and sit down, and I will serve you tea, just as you like it, a tiny squirt of lemon, nothing more. Oh, dear, you haven't changed, have you?"

"Not about how I like my tea, no, I haven't." Julian lightly laid his palm on his mother's soft cheek. She looked not a day older than she had when he'd left her on that miserable stormy Tuesday, only two days after Lily's funeral. Her eyes and hair were nearly as dark as his, but unlike him, her complexion was fair. "You're still as beautiful as when I left you three years ago."

"That is very kind of you to remark upon, dearest." She studied his beloved face for a moment, so very beautiful he was, and she could see some of herself in him, the way his eyes shined when he was pleased, how he threw back his head when he laughed. Did he look at all like his father? She didn't know, she'd never seen a portrait of her husband as a young man. She supposed there was a portrait hanging at his ancestral home, Mount Burney. She'd sometimes wondered if the father had resembled the son when he'd been young, if he'd had Julian's habit of tilting his head when he listened, if he'd usually thought before he spoke, if he'd been as beautiful as his son. Such a pity Julian's father had been old, white-haired, but never stooped, no, the old duke had stood straight as a sapling until his death, and he'd had most of his own teeth when he'd breathed his last breath.

"Three years, Julian," she said again. "I hope you have—" *Recovered from your grief* hung in the air, unspoken. "That is, how are you feeling, dearest?"

He grinned down at her. "I am fine, Mother. Three years is a long time, too long, truth be told. I am very glad to be home. No, I do not still mourn Lily, but I miss her. I suppose I always will."

Corinne looked up when the drawing-room door opened. "Pouffer! There you are, tea and some black cake for my returned prodigal."

"Yes, your grace," Pouffer said, his old eyes on Julian, but he bowed grandly in both their general directions. He gave another wide grin to Julian, so happy he was to see him at last.

"Ah, Prince, I was remarking to Mrs. Trebah that you look as grand a gentleman as even the sternest critic could demand. She agrees, though she only saw the veriest glimpse of you."

"Thank you, Pouffer." Julian's earliest memory of the Ravenscar butler was from his third year of life—he'd rolled a ball against Baron Purley's feet, and Pouffer had bowed to the baron as grandly then as now, scooped Julian up, rubbed his head, stuck him under his arm, and carried him out, Julian yelling for his ball. Pouffer had little hair now, only a white tonsure circling his head. As for Mrs. Trebah, the Ravenscar housekeeper, she'd been here even longer than Pouffer, come when the old duke had been a mere seventy, five years before he'd married Julian's mother.

"Come and sit down, Julian."

Julian hugged his mother once more and gladly accepted her fussing over him. She gently slipped a thick blue satin pillow behind his back, positioned the hassock directly in front of his wing chair, and even lifted his booted feet. He was laughing. "Enough, ma'am. I am not used to being so spoilt."

"I am your mother, I will spoil you as much as I like. Now, while we wait for Pouffer to bring in sustenance, I will tell you we must leave for London very soon."

He looked at her blankly. "London? But I just came from London."

"You went to London? Already?"

"Well, yes, I had business with Harlan."

"Ah, well, Mr. Whittaker and business, that is very different. No, dearest, I mean *London,* as in *the Season.* You did turn thirty-two last month—although you were not here to celebrate your birthday—and in my disappointment, I downed an entire bottle of champagne. I drank so many toasts to your beautiful self I was flat in my bed all the next day. It is past time you were wed again."

The words burst out of her in a torrent. Julian raised a black brow at her as he pulled his watch out of his waistcoat pocket. "I have been home exactly ten minutes, Mother. Perhaps we can wait to leave for London? Perhaps in a day or two?" Past time for him to wed again? What was this?

He found himself looking around the vast drawing room, giving his mother time to marshal her arguments, always entertaining, always worth waiting for. "I like what you have done with this room, Mother, the blues and cream shades suit it nicely, and the Aubusson carpet is magnificent."

"I am glad you admire the carpet, since you paid a substantial number of groats for it."

"As for London, you're right, Mother, I was there only a few days. As you said, I spent most of my time with Harlan, reviewing all Ravenscar expenditures, tenant profits, repairs to be done, crops to be adjusted. You've done an excellent job, Mother."

"Well, none of the stones are crumbling away, all our tenants are content—well, several of them would complain even if God himself were to take tea with them. Actually, since you wrote detailed instructions to me every single week, it required little thought on my part." She paused for a moment, gave him a fat smile. "Did you not notice the score of palm trees—so very *tropical* they look, and so very distinctive—and the silver maple and oak trees I had planted along the drive? And now all the bare ground is covered with heath and daffodils. They have softened the landscape, which is what I wanted. I always thought Ravenscar looked so brutally stark."

Actually, Julian had always liked the barren promontory that sloped down until the land fell away gently into the channel. "I must admit the new trees add interest. I suppose since there are no more enemies to invade our shores, Ravenscar has no more need to intimidate anyone, so the clumps of daffodils waving in the breeze add a nice romantic touch." He paused, thought of Elena, and smiled.

"Ah, Pouffer, here you are at last. Bring on the black cakes for my beautiful son. He is fair to dwindling away before my eyes."

When Pouffer grandly lifted the silver dome to uncover Mrs. Coltrak's black cakes, Julian's stomach growled.

He was drinking his second cup of tea when his mother said, "Lily died three years ago, and you left England, not, of course, to avoid scandal, since there wasn't any, but to leave the Langworths and their terrible grief, and their blame. It is behind you now, Julian."

The gentleness dropped from her voice. She became brisk. "You are not getting any younger, dearest. I will remind you yet again that you are turned thirty-two years old. You really must have an heir."

This was an interesting approach. "An heir? Why? Mother, I'm a duke's son, true, but I am only a second son, not a duke's heir. Why is it so important that I produce a male child?"

His very smart mother realized her logic wasn't sound and retrenched in an instant. "Well, what I really meant is that I have the fondest wish to be a grandmother."

Now, that was a lie that didn't bear scrutiny. He lifted a dark eyebrow. "Shall you be called Grandmama, or perhaps Nana Corinne?"

She shuddered.

"Mama, I have no desire to return to London. Indeed, I have an overdue ship from Constantinople, the *Blue Star*. I must travel to Portsmouth."

"Why? How can your being in Portsmouth hurry the ship up?"

She had a point.

She hurried on before he could muster another objection. "I miss all my particular friends, dearest. I miss attending balls and routs." She closed her eyes. "And there are many new plays to be enjoyed on Drury Lane."

And shopping, he thought.

"And shopping, naturally. I do adore shopping on Bond Street, you know."

She also adored shopping in Saint Austell, Julian thought, recalling the quantity of clothing bills that arrived punctually on Harlan's desk.

"And you need to visit your tailor. Your coat is very well indeed, for *Italian* society, but not exactly what you would want here in London, and your boots, well—"

Yes, he did need new boots, but—

She rose from the blue brocade settee opposite him, patted his shoulder, leaned down to kiss his cheek. "I truly wish to go. There has been so much rain here, and to be blunt about it, I am growing mold, not an elevating sight. It is time for a change of scene—specifically, it is time to visit London, for the Season this time, not for your wretched man of business."

Julian felt the earth shifting beneath his boots, his *old* boots. At last he was home. He wanted to settle in, manage his property, play with his spaniels on the dog run that ended at the low cliff above the beach. He knew it was time to see if Richard Langworth and his father, Baron Purley, still blamed him for Lily's death. "You really don't need me, Mama. You could as easily travel to London, open the town house, and do whatever pleases you. Why do you want me along?"

She said, with a good deal of hauteur, "Do you forget you are my son, my *only* son, and I have not seen you for three—*three*—years? I wish all of society to gaze upon your exquisite self, admit there is no finer-looking a young man in all of England, and be jealous of me."

What was going on here? He said slowly, "Don't forget the other Monroe lady, namely, Lorelei, your stepdaughter-in-law. She will doubtless be there. You know you would rather have your eyebrows plucked than have to deal with her."

His mother had thick black brows like his, and he'd heard her shriek when her maid, known as Poor Barbie, had to pluck them every week and a half.

"I shall firmly plant myself above Lorelei this time; I shan't allow her to give me the headache with her obnoxious little observations on my looks and health and how you should never have been born and how your dear father turned into a pilchard-headed old moron when he turned seventy-five, and just look what came of it—namely, me— and would you look what I did—brought you into the world. And then, naturally, she will go on and on about you, her chins quivering all the while—a duke's son, even though you should never have been born in the first place, and you're obviously deficient, since you sprang from an old man's tired seed, and not the healthy, intelligent seed of a vigorous man, as your dear father was many decades ago. Worst, you indulge in trade, and what a horror that is."

She paused to take a well-earned breath. She tapped her

long fingers against her teacup and brightened. "If I recall, Lorelei had gained flesh when I last saw her, and I haven't, and I'll wager she still persists in wearing all that purple." She gave a small shudder.

Julian said nothing.

She eyed him. "Devlin is always in London for the Season. I know his father is beginning to agitate for a daughter-in-law, since Devlin is now twenty-seven—can you believe that?—and he needs to get himself wed and set up his nursery."

"Both Devlin and I are to be consigned to leg shackles?"

She ignored that. "Really, Julian, do not concern yourself about my dealing well with Lorelei. I shall give her my most regal nod and continue on my way."

Julian gave it one more try. "As I said, you really don't need me with you, Mother."

To his surprise, her small rounded chin began to tremble, and those beautiful dark eyes of hers sheened with tears.

"All right, I see you will have the truth out of me, Julian."

3

The truth?

Before he could find out this truth, Julian heard barking outside the drawing room and rose. "I have a surprise for you." He opened the door and motioned to his valet, Pliny, to release the King Charles spaniels he'd brought back from Genoa.

Freed, the spaniels ran to him, yipping, leaping about, their long silky ears flopping up and down. They didn't jump on him, but they circled him, dancing, as he'd taught them.

He went down on his haunches and gathered them all to him. He said, pointing, "Mother, I would like you to meet Cletus, Beatrice, Oliver, and Hortense. They are a year old. You might think they all look the same, but their personalities are as different as ours. Since my estate room gives onto the dog run, that is where they'll spend most of their time."

"Ah, that is fine, dearest. Goodness, they do leap about, don't they? Look at that one."

"Cletus."

"Why, I think he would like to meet me."

Julian picked up an excited Cletus and carried him to his

mother, the other three spaniels barking madly behind him. She petted his soft hair, received a dozen enthusiastic licks.

"Cletus," she said. "I fancy you are a very well-behaved little fellow, are you not?"

Cletus wriggled free from Julian's hands, yipped and barked, and relieved himself on the Aubusson carpet.

Corinne said, "Yes, your estate room is an excellent place for these charming little dogs. Call for Pouffer, dearest, to clean up little Cletus's accident."

Soon the four spaniels were racing after Pliny, barking, tails wagging, to visit their new home in the estate room, and Pouffer was directing a maid to clean up little Cletus's accident, after which he burned two feathers to eliminate any possible odors.

"Pliny is looking well," Corinne said.

"As much as his poet's brooding soul allows," Julian said. "He should have trod the boards, I've told him. He adores drama and being in the center of it. I'm pleased, though, he didn't cry when Cletus relieved himself on the carpet." Pliny, a dapper little man of forty, blessed with a full head of white-blond hair, had been selling boots in Portsmouth and fair to starving when Julian had hired him away as his valet. *Eleven years,* he thought. He'd been so young. On the other hand, Pliny had been young as well.

His mother eyed him and spit it out. "We must go to London because there is a young lady for you to meet."

"Ah, so this is the truth you must tell me?"

"Yes. You remember Bethanne Wilkie. She was my very best friend. She died two years ago."

"I'm sorry, Mama. You wrote to me of her death. I remember her as a charming lady, always smiling."

"Yes." Corinne sighed. "I still miss her. Do you happen to remember her daughter?"

Julian recalled a skinny little girl with dark braids scraped back from her small face, tall, awkward, never saying a word in his presence. He remembered once when he'd been working at his desk, he'd happened to look up and see her peering at him from behind a curtain in the estate room.

His mother cleared her throat. "The truth is Bethanne Wilkie and I always wished to have our families united."

His stomach dropped to his dusty Hessians. He had a terrifying image of the skinny twelve-year-old gowned in white standing beside him in front of a vicar, a long veil covering her face, the beautiful Ravenscar ruby ring sliding off her small finger to land on the floor and rolling, rolling— "Good grief, Mama, she's a little girl! When she wasn't trailing after me, she was tucked against her mother's skirts or lurking behind curtains to stare at me. As I recall, I once said hello to her, and she turned pale and ran from the room."

"Little girls become ladies."

"Why have you never spoken to me of this young lady before?"

"When you married Lily, she was far too young for you. When Lily died, she was still too young, but it didn't matter, because you sailed from England for three years."

"I don't recall her name."

"Her name is Sophie Colette Wilkie. Sophie is spelled quite in the French way, since her father, a clergyman, adores the French, a people few can stomach, and rightfully so, but so he does, particularly the classical French, particularly the playwright Molière. Sophie even has a French second name—Colette."

He had no memory whatsoever of the little girl's name. Sophie Colette—it was enough to curdle his innards. Julian had come home to find peace. And instead, his mama wanted to present him with a bride named Sophie Colette? He said, "I like Molière as well."

"Yes, he is classical enough, I fancy, but I mean, who cares? Now, I have informed Sophie's father that I shall present Sophie in London at the Buxted ball Wednesday evening, exactly two weeks from today. You will be there, naturally. I understand dear Sophie will be chaperoned by her aunt, Roxanne Radcliffe, who is one of Baron Roche's daughters, and they will stay in the Radcliffe town house on Lemington Square. Since Roxanne was Bethanne's sister, she must be well advanced in her years. Bethanne always told me Roxanne preferred the country, and so I simply must travel to London to assist her in bringing out my dear Sophie." She paused, raised her dark eyes to his face, the look that always pierced him to his gullet, and had, obviously, pierced his father's gullet as well, ancient though his gullet was at the time.

He tried once more. "If you tell me Sophie Wilkie is fresh out of the schoolroom, I will board one of my ships and sail to Macao."

"I don't know where this Macao place is, but it sounds nasty and foreign. Oh, no, dearest. Since her mama died two years ago, followed quickly by her grandmother, Sophie has worn black gloves *forever,* poor child. She is well into her twentieth year, not a child at all, indeed, very nearly a spinster."

Twelve years between them, an acceptable age difference by society's norms, but too many years for him. She'd been naught but a little girl when the Duke of Wellington finally vanquished Napoléon at Waterloo. She would have no memory of what was happening in the world during his first twelve years. Julian realized he might as well batter his head against the huge stone fireplace in the great hall of Ravenscar. No hope for it. He folded his tent. "When would you like to leave?"

His fond mama wasn't a fool. She never rubbed her fist in a face when victorious unless it was that of her stepdaughter-in-law, Lorelei. She gave him a sweet smile as she rose to kiss his cheek and pat his shoulder. "Did I tell you she is a beauty? Her hair is dark brown, her eyes a light blue like a summer sky. She is no small mincing miss. Indeed, I find my eyes must travel upward a goodly distance to meet hers." She patted him again. "You are a remarkably fine son, dearest."

"Do you think, Mama, that I might have a week at home to see to estate matters?"

She patted his face. "With your exquisite brain, I believe four or five days will do the trick nicely."

He wasn't stupid. He had four days.

Julian hadn't been home in three years. Why hadn't he waited three more months, until, say, August? The wretched Season would be over. But he hadn't. He would go to London, he would meet Sophie Colette—spelled in the French way—and he would pat her head and leave her to the younger gentlemen.

4

Lord Devlin Archibald Jesere Monroe, the seventh Earl of Convers and heir to the Duke of Brabante, and only son to Lorelei Monroe, stood quietly in the doorway of his half uncle's estate room, watching him study a sheaf of papers, his concentration so profound he hadn't even heard his butler, Tavish, announce him. Devlin realized he'd missed Julian very much. Three years, it was too long a time.

Julian's black hair was standing on end, his collar was open at his throat, and he wore a linen shirt nearly as white as Devlin's face but not quite. Devlin smiled as he cleared his throat.

Julian jerked up, his pen spluttering ink on the final page of a document he was on the point of signing. He shot a glare at his half nephew. "Damnation, Dev, look what you made me do. Now Pennyworth will have to recopy this page."

"Pennyworth was last seen flirting with one of your downstairs maids, so your butler told me. Her name, I heard Tavish say to Mrs. Stokes, is Emmy."

Julian laid down his pen, rose, stretched, gave his nephew a lazy smile, and strode to him, hugging him close. "It's been too long, Dev. How are you?"

Devlin grinned. "I remember things were always more stimulating when you were about. I trust you have not become dull and sober in your old age?"

"We will spend the evening together, and you will tell me."

He realized Devlin was nearly his size. How could he have forgotten that? He clasped his shoulders, studied his face. "You look as pale and healthy as the last time I saw you. No, since it's been raining interminably, you're paler than I remember."

Devlin laughed. "I worship the rain. I chant for its coming, since I must maintain my otherworldly vampire persona."

Julian remembered that at eighteen, Devlin had become enthralled with some ancient manuscripts he'd read at Oxford and decided that being a vampire would amuse him. It had. Devlin, Julian thought, made an excellent vampire.

"Would you like a brandy, or do you need to drink some blood?"

"Do you know Corrie Sherbrooke once offered me her neck at midnight?" He laughed again. "It was only six months ago. I remember once when I rode with her in the middle of a sunny day, I took a huge risk and didn't wear a hat. It must have been a wager, I don't recall."

"You did not burn up. That is a relief. So she wed James Sherbrooke, did she?"

"Yes, last fall."

"I remember the Sherbrooke twins. Didn't all the ladies consider them gods?"

"Curse James, he does look like a bloody god, the bastard."

Julian said, "I've got something better than brandy or blood." Julian walked to the sideboard and held up a crystal decanter. "Whiskey from the wilds of America."

"I hear it is a nasty drink," Devlin said.

"Here, give it a try."

Devlin eyed the whiskey. "You insist on forcing me to burn out my stomach?"

Julian laughed. They clicked their glasses and drank.

Devlin felt the brutal fire all the way to his heels, but he wasn't going to cough. He nearly turned blue, the effort was so great, then he lost the battle and wheezed until Julian, grinning like a bandit, smacked him hard between his shoulder blades.

"You are my elder," Devlin whispered. "You should protect me, not torture me. Give me brandy, Julian."

Once he'd drunk some of Julian's very fine Spanish brandy—Gran Duque D'Alba, no less—he was able to collect himself and sit down, his color restored, but since there wasn't much color at all on Devlin's face, Julian couldn't tell. He crossed his legs and swung a booted foot.

Devlin said, "My mother told me this morning she received an impertinent missive from your upstart mother informing her that you were home at last and she would be in London for the Season, you as her escort. I was pleased. It really has been too long. I'll say, the thought of dumping insults on your mother's head perked my mother right up. Your mother is well, Julian?"

"My mother is always well. I was dragged here to meet a young lady, the daughter of my mother's bosom friend, Bethanne Wilkie is her name, now dead, and thus the daughter has been in black gloves and not as yet had a Season. Her name is Sophie, spelled in the French way, you know, and thank the good Lord she isn't fresh out of the schoolroom, else I would flee to Scotland to hunt grouse."

"How old is Sophie, spelled in the French way?"

"Twenty, but that is still too young for me."

Devlin grinned. "As long as men must insist on not wedding until they're in their dotage, young wives will continue to flourish. It is said they are more malleable."

"What idiot said that?"

"Still, twelve years between husband and wife isn't anything out of the ordinary."

"It is to me," Julian said.

Devlin laughed again, stretched his arms behind his head, and regarded his step-uncle. "Do you remember when you and I sailed to the Isle of Wight in your yacht *Désirée* and those drunk young men from Oxford plowed into us?"

"I do, although they were about your age, as I recall."

"Possibly, but I was more mature, more governed in my habits. In any case, do you remember that one very young girl we saved when she got tossed overboard?"

"I remember. What was her name?"

"Giselle, quite French, she told me, as she coughed up water all over my shirt, like your French Sophie."

"What happened to her? You never said in your letters."

"Ah, I brought her to London. We quite enjoyed each other for a time. She is now in Plymouth, I believe."

Julian rolled his eyes. "Trust you to save a girl and take her to bed."

Devlin said in his world-weary voice, "Do tell me your point, old boy."

Julian laughed, couldn't help himself. Three years had made a difference in his half nephew. Devlin was more sophisticated, he supposed, much more confident, at ease in his world. He realized he loved his half nephew and quite enjoyed his vampire affectation. How strange life was, he thought. Julian's very old father had married his very young mother, produced him, and he'd instantly become the half uncle to the future Duke of Brabante. As for Devlin's mother—the evil witch Lorelei, according to Julian's mother—he found her amusing and blessedly predictable in her bone-deep dislike of him. He said to Devlin, "I daresay she considered you a fine protector."

Devlin said, "It is always quite nice when there is only a question of recompense involved between a man and a woman. Now I will take you to my tailor and boot maker. You are in grave need of polishing up, Julian, before you meet this Sophie, spelled in the French way."

5

London
Radcliffe Town House
16 Lemington Square

Roxanne Radcliffe bounded out of her chair when her niece, Sophie Wilkie, appeared in the doorway to the drawing room.

"My dear girl, you are hours late. I've been so worried!"

Sophie tossed her cloak to Mint, the Radcliffe butler, whose mouth pinched at such careless behavior in a young lady. He'd traveled from Allegra Hall with Miss Roxanne to attend her during her upcoming travails in this huge city that was a cesspit of both wickedness and delight. He'd said to Mrs. Mifflin, the Allegra Hall housekeeper, and his occasional mistress, "I fear it will be a proper travail, what with that wild sprat, Miss Sophie, ready to turn her poor aunt's hair gray."

He had assured Lord Roche that he would protect Miss Roxanne with his life. He recalled Lord Roche had nodded gravely and thanked him. He did not know, however, that Lord Roche was quite certain that if such an unlikely occasion should arise, it would be Roxanne to protect Mint, who was of a very modest size, unlike his mistress. Mint watched

Miss Roxanne skip like a wild sprat herself to Miss Sophie and embrace her.

"Oh, goodness," Sophie said, "I forgot how wonderful you smell. What is it? Jasmine with a hint of lemon?"

Roxanne laughed. "Yes, a hint. What delayed you?"

"A carriage wheel broke outside of Marleythorpe, but let me tell you, I quite enjoyed myself at a local inn—the Screaming Gander—drinking lemonade. Well, mayhap there was a minuscule dollop of brandy mixed in, made me shiver all the way to my toes and laugh at everything the owner, Mrs. Dolly Grange, said to me. She joined me, but I fear there was more than a dollop of brandy in her glass. Do you think Cook could prepare this sort of lemonade? No matter, ah, it is so good to see you, Roxanne. Why would a gander scream?"

"Doubtless she was being pursued by a lusty goose."

Sophie laughed, hugged her aunt again, then danced around the Radcliffe drawing room, her full skirts a beautiful kaleidoscope of greens. She untied the ribbons beneath her chin and gently laid her very new and stylish green crepe bonnet on a chair. "It is so good to be with you. At last I am to be presented. I had wanted to be with you a fortnight ago, as you know, but my father was overset by some local matters—ah, you know how he is—"

Roxanne knew exactly how he was.

"—but that's not important now. I'm here to dance until there are holes in my slippers, and"—she looked utterly wicked—"I can flirt and flutter my eyelashes and slay all the gentlemen within ten feet of me. What do you think?"

"I think at least fifty feet, and slaying is always a fine idea."

Sophie blinked, laughed. "Ah, I forget. You don't ever wish to take a husband." She shot a look toward Mint, hovering in the doorway, her lovely pale green velvet cloak still spilling over his arm, no expression at all on his plump face. She had no doubt he was paying close attention to everything they said, and gave him a little finger wave. "Do you know, even the rain feels different in London?"

Roxanne smiled and shook her head. She said to Mint, "I know Mrs. Eldridge is at sixes and sevens, but perhaps she has some tea and cakes?"

Within ten minutes, the two ladies were seated on a lovely blue-and-cream striped brocade sofa, their skirts spread out around them, drinking oolong tea and savoring apricot tarts that tasted like heaven.

Roxanne saluted Sophie with her teacup. "Did you know your mama gave me lessons on how to flirt with my eyes on the morning of my sixteenth birthday?"

Sophie stared at her, mouth open. "My mother gave you eye-flirting lessons?"

"Yes, indeed. I also remember her waltzing you around the drawing room. You were shrieking so loud, your grandfather came marching in demanding some 'demmed' quiet. Of course, he stayed to waltz. Do you remember that visit?"

Sophie said, "Oh, yes. It was so exciting, since Mama never waltzed me around our drawing room at home. And Grandpapa, such fun he was. I thought he was taller than a tree. Do you know, I don't think Mama ever waltzed around the drawing room with Papa? Actually, I can't imagine Papa ever dancing. I don't think he believes it proper. Do you think she ever flirted with Papa with her eyes?"

"Who knows?" Roxanne sipped her tea and kept a smile on her mouth. Reverend William Wilkie, that officious prude, would condemn waltzing and all those performing that lewd act to the far reaches of Hell. Indeed, she'd heard him denounce waltzing to her own father. How could Bethanne have wanted to marry him? So many years she'd spent with him. At least she'd had Sophie. Thank the good Lord Sophie had her mother's looks as well as her good nature, and as far as Roxanne could tell, nothing from her father. That must frost the old hypocrite.

Sophie raised her eyes to Roxanne. "I miss Mama, Roxanne. She always loved me completely, no matter what mischief I ever got into. Do you know when she was dying, she apologized to me that I would have to wait a year to make my come out?" Sophie burst into tears.

Roxanne pulled her close, rubbed her hands up and down her niece's back. "I know, love, I miss her as well."

She's a grown woman now, Roxanne thought, *no longer a child,* yet she felt decades older than Sophie, even though a mere seven years separated them. When Sophie had dried her eyes, Roxanne said, "You've grown into a splendid woman, Sophie. I am so happy to be here with you."

She watched Sophie gather herself, watched her ease her mother in the bittersweet past. She patted Sophie's hand. She looked, Roxanne thought, fresh and innocent, and so beautiful it would make gentlemen's teeth ache. The cut of her gown made her waist look the size of a doorknob, emphasized by a wide, dark green belt. The sleeves of her gown weren't as large as the fashion dictated this season, but still formidable. Her hair was styled with the requisite ringlets cascading in front of her ears, a high pouf of hair twisted atop her head and fastened with green ribbons. Such a style made Roxanne look like an idiot, but Sophie could be bald and it wouldn't matter. She was a beauty, like Bethanne, and her nominal dowry wouldn't make any gentleman withdraw, Roxanne knew it. She wore the small pearl earrings Roxanne had given her.

She looked, Roxanne thought, perfect.

"Remember how short Mama was? And Papa never gained many inches himself. But then I simply would not stop growing. Papa now looks up at me. He says I am too tall, that no gentleman will want a maypole. Then he says this Season is a waste of time and his groats, and I should stay at home and immerse myself in spiritual lessons. When I asked him what spiritual lessons I particularly needed, he could only mutter about making jams for the poor. I told him no one particularly liked my jams, that indeed, Mrs. Pipps, the innkeeper's wife, had accused me of trying to poison her, and he left the room."

Had Reverend William Wilkie been here at the moment, Roxanne would have kicked him. What a tiresome fool he was, but it sounded like Sophie could hold her own with him. It was thanks to Bethanne there was money for Sophie's

Season, and Roxanne's father had reminded Reverend Wilkie of this fact several times to ensure he didn't spend it on himself. She said, "Your grandfather is the tallest gentleman in the north, and God blessed us with his height." She leaned close and whispered, "Papa told me a good height can work wonders to depress a gentleman's unwanted pretensions. It is a lesson I took to heart. So, my dear, always stand tall, keep your shoulders back, and prepare to look down your nose at all the gentlemen congregated at your slippered feet."

That made Sophie laugh. They were indeed of a height, Roxanne thought, and both had the slender build of Roxanne's mother, but there all similarity ended. Roxanne's hair was a deep red. Where did that come from? Sophie's father had wondered, his deep voice bewildered. Her skin was white as new snow, not a single freckle to give interest to all that white, not even on the backs of her knees. Her eyes were a dark green, filled with mysteries and shadows, one of her beaux had once whispered in her ear. He'd tried to kiss the same ear and earned a clout.

Sophie had an olive complexion, like gold dust had been sprinkled on her by a benevolent fairy at her birth, Roxanne had always thought, and her eyes were the light blue of a cloudless sky. As for her hair, it was a rich, deep brown that would become streaked with sunlight in the summer, since Sophie was a great walker.

"It's been two years since I last saw you, Sophie, and look at you, quite the young lady, no longer a girl."

"I am told by every well-meaning lady of my acquaintance that I have left girlhood well behind. Indeed, according to Mrs. Beaver, our blacksmith's wife back home, I am fast approaching spinsterhood and must hie myself to the altar before that dreaded fate befalls me."

"Then with my advanced years I am a spinster indeed, nearly wobbling on my cane."

"You don't have a cane!"

"It is only a matter of time—a very *short* time—so the well-meaning ladies of *my* acquaintance tell *me*. Now,

Sophie, this Season is about you, not me. I have no desire to give myself over to marriage, you're right about that. Why bother? I can think of not a single reason why a man would be needful to me. I could support myself if the need arose. Nor do I need the protection a husband supposedly provides, since Father taught me all sorts of useful tricks to discourage the most presumptuous of gentlemen." Roxanne tapped her fingers against her chin. "That is not at all to the point. I am the odd one, so you will disregard what I say about marriage. I foresee you will find an excellent husband."

"What sorts of things did Grandfather teach you?"

Roxanne hugged her. "Later, Sophie. First we must make plans. Oh, yes, I have received six letters from her grace, Corinne Monroe, the dowager Duchess of Brabante, informing me that since I am basically a nobody from nowhere and don't know anything, she will assist me to bring you out."

Sophie rolled her eyes, then felt guilty. "She and Mama were such good friends. I haven't seen her since Mama's funeral. But I remember her voice very clearly; she never stopped talking and laughing. She thinks you're a nobody? How strange. I hope she will not be overbearing, Roxanne."

Of course she will try, as I will try not to shoot her. "I hope she will tell me stories about your mama. I never knew Bethanne all that well, since she was so much older than I was, but I remember whenever our mama said her name—*Bethanne*—she would nearly sing it."

Sophie gulped and quickly ate another apricot tart. "Her grace will doubtless be kind to me because of Mama. She can chaperone me whilst you are dancing your slippers off. Ah, so many gentlemen will want to dance with you, Roxanne, to look close upon your beautiful hair, and wonder what you are thinking, since your eyes never give you away, not like mine do."

Roxanne waved that away. "I did not think this through. Gentlemen might not be needful to me in the everlasting sense of the word, but, on the other hand, one cannot waltz alone. Now, you need but a bit of seasoning to learn to hide your thoughts. You will begin tomorrow evening at the

Buxted ball. I believe her grace is visiting us tomorrow to make certain you will be presentable."

Sophie laughed. "Well done. I swear to be perfectly well behaved. Now, tell me what sorts of things your father taught you, Roxanne."

A dark red eyebrow shot up, and Roxanne, grinning wickedly, leaned close. "Well, the first thing he taught me was to carry a stiletto in my sleeve, or slip a small penknife in my glove. Your grandfather has marvelous taste, you know. I always seek his approval before I have any gowns made, so when I showed him several styles that interested me, he remarked that the sleeves were so enormous I could hide a brace of pistols in there as well as a dozen knives."

"Could I have a knife, Roxanne? Just in case?"

"Why not? If any gentleman goes over the line, we will discuss which of us should give him a nice sharp prick."

⊷ *6* ⊷

Until Eve arrived, this was a man's world.
—RICHARD ARMOR

Buxted Ball
Putnam Square
APRIL 16, 1831

Her grace, Corinne Monroe, the dowager Duchess of Brabante, tapped her fan on her son's arm. "Julian, look at that tall gentleman standing by the potted palm. It is Richard Langworth, is it not?"

Julian followed his mother's finger and nodded. "Yes, it is Richard." He hadn't seen Richard while he'd been home, and now he was here in London. Had he followed him?

Actually, Julian wished he were anywhere but London. He didn't know which he dreaded more—meeting Sophie Colette or speaking with Richard. His yacht, *Désirée*—now, that would be the thing. He could sail to the Hebrides, visit the Viking stone huts, and wonder whether, if he'd been born a Viking, he would be dead by the age of twenty.

Corinne said, "I have seen him and his family only at a distance since Lily's funeral. In short, they have avoided me. He doesn't look happy. Do you think he still blames you?"

Oh, yes, he will always believe I murdered his beloved sister, no matter what I say. "I doubt Richard will be unpleasant to either of us, since there are at least two hundred people here tonight. Ignore him."

The ballroom was too hot, he thought, but he wasn't about to drink the iced champagne punch, knowing one glass could fell an ox, and that felled ox would then immediately want another glass. *Sophie Colette,* he thought, and started to cast about for escape plans, when his mother tugged on his sleeve and pointed her fan. "It is about time. There she is—Sophie Colette Wilkie, my dear. Is she not stunning? Look at that rich dark brown hair, the color of mink, I thought this morning when I saw her—like her mother's, and those magnificent blue eyes, so brilliant and sparkling, don't you think? As for that beanpole next to her, it is her aunt, Roxanne Radcliffe. As you can see, even from here, she didn't have the good taste to be older, as she should have been. I had quite counted on her being older, if you know what I mean."

"No. What do you mean?"

She gave him a look that clearly said, *How can you be such a dolt?* "She will doubtless try to steal the attention from Sophie. It is too bad, and I should have told her so when I saw her. Alas, I am too kind, and since Bethanne was her sister, kindness seemed the appropriate thing. Don't you think the gown Sophie is wearing is very flattering? Does not the term *princess* come to your mind when you look at her?" *Since you are a prince, it is fitting,* but Corinne didn't say that aloud, knowing Julian would hoist up his eyebrow and stare at her. Best not to overdo; she didn't want to put him off. He was a man, after all, and in her experience, for an idea to be worth anything, it had to spring from a male brain.

"She looks well enough," he said.

Actually, Julian had to admit Sophie Wilkie had a well-nigh-perfect figure, and a lovely face, topped with dark brown hair—mink, his mother had said—all poufed and ringletted. How many hours, or days, did it require to achieve such a style? *A princess?*

To counter the scale, and to test the waters, Corinne added, "She is dreadfully brown, though. I hadn't counted on that."

"I quite like the golden complexion, Mother," Julian said, but he was looking at Roxanne Radcliffe. He'd never seen such incredible red hair, piles of the stuff, full and rich, worn in thick plaits atop her head, pale pink ribbons threaded through the stack, a plain and simple style that suited her. Her skin was very white, like a new snowfall over the Gallatin Mountains, as white as Devlin's face. Her gown was pale pink, matching the ribbons in her hair, the skirts full, gauzy stuff that made his fingers itch, her white shoulders bare, small puffed sleeves falling off those shoulders, as they were meant to. He was surprised the pink so suited the opulent red hair, but it was a perfect complement. He said, "Your Sophie Colette is quite as tall as her too-young beanpole aunt."

Corinne frowned. "I have to admit it, Julian, I was quite surprised to see that Sophie had grown to such an unflattering height, not that I remarked upon it to her, of course, since I doubt there is anything to be done about it. It is a very good thing you are so tall, so she will not have to stoop. Still, I cannot like it. No gentleman likes a girl to stare him right in the eye." She paused for a moment, studied his face. "Tell me the truth, my dear, are you too revolted?"

"Not at all. I will not get a crick in my neck waltzing with her." Julian prepared himself. Once he'd met the girl, once he'd waltzed with her and made inane conversation about all the dark clouds covering the half-moon, he could leave this damnable jewelry museum with all the dripping candles and the score of potted palms, Richard Langworth still standing beside one of them, watching, ever watching, and walk in the cool night air to the docks, see if he could find any men from ships coming from Constantinople. He'd spoken again to his man of affairs, Harlan Whittaker, but there was still no word on the *Blue Star*. As for the most recent shipment of smuggled goods, Harlan was pleased to tell him they'd added a goodly number of groats to their coffers.

He was aware his mother was talking nonstop, but he'd learned to nod in agreement while his mind sailed a continent away. But for the moment, his brain was focused on

Roxanne Radcliffe, as she gracefully made her way through the crowd, steering Sophie toward them.

He said, "She is too young to be a chaperone. Perhaps you can mentor both of them."

"She is not *that* young, Julian. She is a spinster, she told me so herself. She also said she wasn't on the hunt for a husband; indeed, she said she had no interest whatsoever in any man, that this Season was all for Sophie. If she was telling me the truth, which I must doubt because I'm not stupid, then she is wise. I mean, look at all that red hair. Who would admire hair like that?

"Oh, dear, there comes my blasted daughter-in-law. Why does God send Lorelei to plague me this soon? Have I committed a sin of which I am not aware? I daresay it would have to be a very *grievous* sin," she added, and sighed. "It is a pity I snubbed Mr. Dinwitty so thoroughly, a very *godly* man, and no doubt this is my punishment."

"Gird your loins," Julian said, and stepped away, for he'd seen Devlin waltzing past with a lovely young lady, the patented ironic smile on his mouth, a dark eyebrow slanted upward. He'd nodded to Julian.

The two ladies had nearly landed.

So had his sister-in-law, Lorelei, the Duchess of Brabante. He saw his half brother the duke sheer off when he saw his wife's destination, and make a straight trajectory toward the card room. What would he do there? Cleveland never gambled. But of course Julian knew the answer—his grace had no intention of witnessing a possible bloodbath between his stepmama and his wife. Wise man.

His mother clutched his sleeve.

Julian nodded to his sister-in-law. "You are looking well, Lorelei," he said. "A lovely gown you're wearing. The purple satin is regal. I saw Devlin. He should be coming over when the waltz ends."

Her grace, Lorelei Monroe, looked him up and down. "Why are you not out sailing on one of your merchant ships, Julian, or perhaps stacking up coins in your countinghouse?"

An immediate attack, no shallying about for Lorelei.

Julian gave her a lazy smile. She was older than his own mother, and she looked it, knew it, and it galled her to her toes or her purple slippers.

He said, the smile still on his mouth, "A man can never have too many coins to stack, I always say. You are a shining light tonight, ma'am, the purple suits you admirably. All other ladies dim in your presence, with the exception, of course, of my mother."

"Young man, my shine comes from within, all remark upon it. Your compliments began splendidly, but they died quickly. And coming from you—her spawn—I know they must be lies, no matter how you slither around with very nice-sounding words. What are you doing here? As to that, what are you doing here, Corinne?"

The ladies landed.

Corinne ignored her daughter-in-law and stepped forward, immediately enfolding Sophie in her arms. "Ah, dear Sophie, how very beautiful you look. Your lovely gown— when I looked at your gown this morning, I knew it would suit you to perfection. You look so like your dear mama. She would be so very proud of you." And her grace, the dowager Duchess of Brabante, gulped down tears.

Sophie found herself patting the dowager Duchess's back and staring helplessly at Roxanne.

Roxanne said matter-of-factly, "Sophie is indeed a vision, your grace."

"Which grace?" Lorelei Monroe turned her dark eyes on the lady with her common red hair.

"Are you a grace as well?" Roxanne asked, her voice guileless.

Not for an instant did Julian believe her ignorant, not with the deviltry in those green eyes of hers.

Lorelei drew herself up. She was impressive; all remarked on it. Many feared her, as was proper. She would depress this redheaded baggage. "I am the Duchess of Brabante, young lady. This one here"—she gave a curt nod toward Corinne— "isn't. She is naught but a dowager Duchess, and she never would have been even that, had my dear father-in-law not lost his wits in his dotage and married her, and would you look at the result of that?" Her eyes flicked toward Julian.

Corinne was so used to this litany of insults, they bounced off her lovely yellow sleeves. She said, "Actually, Miss Radcliffe, the both of us are graces, and his grace never lost his wits. He was thrilled when Julian was born. Now, let me make you known to everyone."

Corinne made the introductions, gave Lorelei a look to dare her to be nasty, and was promptly taken up on her dare.

7

Lorelei said, "I do not know either of you, but I must question your affiliations, seeing that you are here with this one. You are both too tall to be pleasing. As for your hair, Miss Radcliffe, the less said the better. You," she continued to Sophie, "are passable, I suppose. I very much like your hairstyle, though it renders you even taller.

"Ah, here comes my dear son, the Earl of Convers, you know. He will become the Duke of Brabante when his father sheds this mortal coil."

"Which I hope will not be for a very long time," Devlin said, laughing, and kissed his mother's white cheek—not as white as his, even powdered—and turned to the young ladies. "Ah, so you're Sophie Wilkie. Julian has told me all about you."

"Your mama told me all about you, sir," Sophie said, but it took a moment for Devlin to turn his attention to her, since he was looking at Roxanne. He'd never before in his life seen such glorious hair. Well, he'd seen red hair, actually. Alexandra Sherbrooke, the Countess of Northcliffe, had beautiful red hair, but the red of Roxanne's hair was different.

Corinne was frowning a bit when she said, "Sophie, my dear, this is his lordship, Devlin Monroe."

Devlin kissed her wrist as he bowed. "I'm Julian's nephew."

Julian said, "More accurate, he is the madman who tried to kill us both on my yacht some years back."

"I have constantly advised you to keep your distance from this *person,* my son," Lorelei said. "He may be your step-uncle, but he is much too dangerous for you, too wild and unpredictable. I do not wish for such a connection for you. And he simply fell off the face of the earth for three years."

Julian laughed. "It really was your son, madam, who nearly rammed us into another sailboat, this one filled with drunk young gentlemen. We all survived the encounter; Devlin survived it very well, he has told me."

"Unfair, Julian," Devlin said. "They nearly rammed us; I was trying to steer clear of them. You are purposefully disremembering. Miss Wilkie, it is a pleasure to meet you." He looked at Roxanne, straight in her green eyes. "Ah, and you are the elderly spinster companion Julian told me about. Perhaps I may fetch you a warm shawl? Or perhaps I may bring you a chair so you may rest? A cane?"

Roxanne looked into that far-too-handsome pale face and grinned like a bandit. "I very much like to sail. Unfortunately, all my life I have been landlocked, well west of York, you know, and my father is afraid of the water, having nearly drowned when he was a boy. I thank the good Lord for delivering up a very cordial gentleman with a lovely sailboat in Brighton." And she eyed Julian as she shuddered with pleasure at the memory.

Julian stared at her, fascinated. "You said all that without a single pause. I am impressed, ma'am."

Roxanne gave him a regal nod that still held wickedness. Sophie determined to practice it in front of her mirror. "You are too facile with your praise, sir, but it is true, we all have our little talents. At least some of us do." Roxanne studied the man Corinne wished Sophie to marry. He looked like a pirate, dark, too dark, at least in comparison to Devlin Monroe, his half nephew. He did have wit, though, and wealth. Still, Roxanne could not like it. He was too old for Sophie, it was as simple as that. An even greater age difference was more common than not, but still, this man *knew* things, he'd experienced things no young lady should know about— maybe even things at her advanced age she shouldn't know about—and that made her shiver. He was far too handsome for his own good, and probably a conceited buffoon.

Devlin remarked, "Does that ability to speak without breath develop with age, ma'am?"

She laughed, simply couldn't help herself. "I found when I was a little girl I detested periods for the simple reason that a period signals the end, and who wants to be forced to end when one is speaking witticisms? I recall my father telling me this from my earliest years.

"I have been wondering which of us has the whiter skin, sir. I have always found a mash of strawberries and a drop of lemon to be efficacious. What do you use?"

"Since we live in England, a land whose climate is as soggy as its morals, I do not have to think of it overly. However, when the sun chances to show itself, I become very fond of shade trees."

"The chestnut?"

"I find the oak to be superior, ah, except there is the willow, the royalty of shade trees, I have found. Unfortunately, the willow prefers to hang about country ponds, so it is difficult."

"So you laze about beneath willow trees and chew on water reeds?"

"I much prefer lazing about at midnight. Now, I believe I must dance with the young lady."

Roxanne watched him bow over Sophie's hand, gracefully draw her from Corinne's side. He arched an eyebrow at Corinne.

Corinne, horrified, said, "But you are not the right one,

my lord. It is Julian—" No hope for it. Corinne shut her mouth. She saw Lorelei was frowning ferociously, and that brought a complacent nod.

Roxanne watched Devlin Monroe and Sophie walk to the dance floor. She hadn't realized Devlin Monroe was as tall as his uncle. Even though he was more Sophie's age, she could not approve of him, either. He was a hedonist, the sort she couldn't abide, and a poseur, what with his dead white face. Willow trees! But he was amusing, and he had indeed sharpened his wit on her. He would give Sophie experience in dealing with a quick-witted gentleman. Surely there was no harm in him. She said, "It is rather warm in here. I think I fancy some of that lovely punch." As she lifted her hand to take a crystal flute, filled to the top with the moral-wrecking punch, Julian lightly placed his hand over hers, gave her a small bow. "Miss Radcliffe, will you dance with me?"

"*Hmm*. Punch or a waltz?" She laughed, placed her white hand on his black-coated arm, and off they went to the dance floor.

He said in her ear, "You do not wish to indulge in the punch, ma'am. It is rumored ladies quickly lose their moral compass with but one glass."

"Really? And gentlemen? How many glasses does it require for a gentleman to lose his moral compass?"

"Nary a one."

"Perhaps it would not be such a bad idea to be rendered insensible to the mayhem brewing between your mother and the duchess."

"I have been gone from England for three years. I return to find nothing changed. I have never seen them come to blows, though I think they might both enjoy it." He took her into his arms and swept her into large spinning circles.

"Oh, this is lovely." And Roxanne laughed, twirled, swirled in great circles, and admired how they never crashed into other couples, so good was he at steering her aright. Yes, a man was needful for a waltz.

Corinne stared after them, aware that Lorelei was looking at her with steel in her eyes. "You will not fob that creature off on Devlin. She is a nobody, I doubt not, and too tall. Do you hear me?"

Corinne turned to ask with great interest, "Why do you think she's a creature and a nobody?"

Lorelei retrenched. "You wouldn't want a pig in a poke for your precious son, now, would you? I see it all now. This girl is an heiress."

"That is an interesting conclusion, Lorelei. Do you really think that is true?"

"Ha, you do not fool me. Who is she? I have never heard of a Wilkie before of any account at all. Where is she from?"

Corinne smiled. "Perhaps she is a creature, perhaps she is a nobody, a veritable adventuress who will wed with your son. Wouldn't that be something?"

"How old is she?"

"I forget."

"I do not like this, Corinne. You are toying with me, and all of it with a false smile. Were I that girl's mother, I would be chagrined at her behavior."

"Be happy, then, that you are not," Corinne said, flicked her fingers at her mortal enemy, and walked to greet a long-time friend. She had a fancy to waltz herself, and Amelia always surrounded herself with eligible gentlemen. Surely there would be a gentleman to please her, dance and flirt with her, and ply her with glasses of the lovely punch.

8

4 Rexford Square

Devlin Monroe said, "Do you know, Julian, my mother actually called on me this morning? I came down for breakfast, and there she was on my doorstep, rather standing right there in my entrance hall. Ponce was so affected, poor fellow, he was nearly tripping over his tongue and his feet, trying to steer her into my drawing room. If my mother comes here to hunt me down again, do consider hiding me in one of those large cabinets from China. A snifter of your excellent Spanish brandy wouldn't come amiss. Please, no more whiskey."

Julian, who'd been reading about the schooners built in Baltimore, rose and poured both of them some brandy. After he clicked his glass to Devlin's, he said, "You are too large to fit in one of the cabinets. They are from Japan, not China. So your fond mama is worried that Sophie Wilkie is after your title?"

"That's it, but not really. First, she demanded to know who the chit is, claimed it was perhaps possible she's a fortune-hunting hussy. Then she did an about-face and demanded to know if she was an heiress, and that's why her hated stepmama-in-law—namely, your mother—wouldn't tell her a thing about her."

"You dangled her on your string, didn't you?"

Devlin laughed. "I hinted she might very well be an heiress, since your mother was after her for you. She was perfectly willing to believe it, and huffed out of my house. What do you think?"

"Since my mother was laughing up her sleeve at breakfast, I fancy that is exactly what happened. I danced with her as well."

"Ah, well, your mother does want you to marry her. I approve; she is charming, quite lovely, and has wit beneath that beautiful hair of hers. An heiress makes it all the better."

Julian sighed. "I agree that Miss Wilkie is graceful and amusing. However, as I told you, she is twelve years my junior."

"Oh, come on, Julian, who cares about years?"

"Look at the difference in age between my mother and my father—talk about lunacy."

"You can't consider it lunacy when you are the outcome of that union."

Well, Devlin had a point there.

Devlin said, "My grandfather was well into his seventies, was he not, when he begat you, or you were begatted."

"I believe I was begotten. And my mother was an ancient eighteen-year-old."

Devlin said, "Ah, I see it now. You fear a young wife will dance on your grave when you depart the earth, dish up all your money to a wastrel husband who will find her within six months of your demise."

Julian said, "On the other hand, twelve years isn't all that great a number. Mayhap I wouldn't cock up my toes before she did."

Devlin spewed out brandy, he laughed so hard. "Look, Julian, you do not have to marry this girl, so stop worrying about years. Let's go riding; you've spent enough time reading those journals, whatever they are."

Lemington Square

I think Devlin Monroe is very creative," Sophie said, chewing on toast heaped with strawberry jam, and added, "As for his ancient half uncle, the one I am evidently supposed to marry, I found him a bit on the stiff side."

"How do you know about that?"

"How could I not know his mother wants me to marry him? Everyone was talking about it."

"His lordship—stiff? Oh, no, Sophie, I found him vastly amusing, mayhap even more amusing than his nephew."

"You should know, since you waltzed with Julian Monroe three times, Roxanne. Three times! His mama's eyes were slits, since he is supposed to focus his interest in me, but it was obvious he preferred you."

Roxanne sipped her black India tea. "Was it really three times? No, you must be mistaken. I remember we finished the second waltz, but before we could remove ourselves from the dance floor, another started up. We merely continued the same one, so to speak. He has no interest in me, Sophie, nor do I have any in him. As I told you, I have no use for a husband. I rather hope you do not fancy him, because he is too old for you. Why do you say he is creative?"

"Who is creative?"

"His lordship, Devlin Monroe, the earl. You said he was creative. What do you mean?"

Sophie leaned forward, lowered her voice to a whisper. "Do you think he could be a vampire, Roxanne? I heard lots of talk about that, and saw ladies give delightful little shudders. He is so pale, and he spoke of learning to waltz on a black windy night in the private garden outside his father's estate room. Do you not think that unusual? Perhaps creative?"

"Most of all, he prefers the willow."

"What?"

"The willow offers the most shade from the sunlight, he

told me. It is all an affectation, Sophie. He likes to shock people, to make them shiver, I daresay, with his white face and all his little vampire remarks. Did he eye your neck?"

"Oh, goodness, I wonder if I should wear a high collar when I am with him?" And Sophie laughed.

Roxanne said, "Speaking of Devlin, after I danced with him he introduced me to another couple before bringing me back to Corinne. His name is James Sherbrooke, Lord Hammersmith, and I'll tell you, Sophie, he is the most beautiful man I have seen in my life. His new wife was stylish and pleasant, pretty, certainly, but nothing like her husband. I could have been content to stare at him the rest of the night. Then Lady Hammersmith smacked Devlin's shoulder. He gave her the sweetest smile and asked her if she still preferred that paltry viscount she'd married, who, he felt honor bound to point out, would never be a duke. I wondered if there had once been something between them.

"Then, while Devlin and Lord Hammersmith were conversing, Corrie—she insisted I call her by her first name, since Lady Hammersmith quite battered her down and made her nauseous, since she was breeding—well, she pulled me aside. She leaned close and asked me if I had yet offered Devlin my neck at midnight. I wanted to laugh, but I managed to hold my countenance and tell her I was already too pale and could not afford to lose any more color." Roxanne paused, pleased with herself. "She was the one who laughed. As I said, her name is Corrie Sherbrooke, and I fancy we will see her again. I would like you to meet her. You will like her. Even if you don't, you can kindly ask her to bring her husband when she visits, then you and I can stare at him. Do you know, I have a feeling she is well used to this."

"I saw him," Sophie said. "I didn't know who he was, but looking back on it, I realize now it must have been him. I saw four young ladies were forming a circle around him, making it smaller and smaller, but he saved himself with no muss or fuss, merely nodded to a gentleman and eased past them."

Mint appeared in the doorway. In his arms, he held a huge vase brimming with red roses. "Excuse me, Miss Roxanne, but I must tell you the drawing room is stuffed with flowers, and we must now consider other localities. Do you have a preference?"

"Since the bouquets were sent to Miss Sophie, Mint, then she must be the one to decide."

"I should say the male offerings balance between the two of you, Miss Roxanne. These lovely blooms are for you."

Roxanne raised a brow. "Who sent these?"

"Ah, let me see. How odd, the bouquet is not from a gentleman. The card is signed Corrie Sherbrooke."

Roxanne threw back her head and laughed. "She is an original, Sophie. Mint, let's place those lovely roses right here on the dining table, that's right, in the very middle. Sophie, I've a fancy to visit her soon, all right?"

She paused, drummed her fingertips on the table. "Do you think it impertinent were we to ask to have her husband present?"

⊷ 9 ⊷

The only reason some people get lost in thought
is because it's unfamiliar territory.
—PAUL FIX

Lemington Square
THE FOLLOWING MORNING

"The Duchess of Brabante demands to see you, Miss Sophie."

"How odd," Roxanne said, and chewed her final bite of toast. "I was expecting the duchess later. She *demands,* Mint? What do you mean she *demands* to see Miss Sophie?"

"You are thinking of her very charming grace, the dowager Duchess of Brabante, Miss Roxanne. This is a duchess I have never seen before. She is a very forceful female, I might add. I have placed this duchess in the drawing room."

"Oh, dear, is she wearing purple, Mint?"

"A cartload, Miss Roxanne."

"So it is the current one—Lorelei, isn't that her name, Sophie?"

"Oh, yes. I thought it a lovely name until I realized a battle-ax was wearing it. What can she want with me, Roxanne?"

"We will soon see." Roxanne folded her napkin carefully and laid it gently beside her plate. She opened the door to the kitchen and called, "Mrs. Eldridge, the breakfast was lovely, thank you." She heard a deep booming voice say she was pleased. Roxanne still couldn't get over that voice coming out of the tiny Mrs. Eldridge.

Roxanne hummed as she straightened the lace at her throat, tweaked one of her braids back into place. Sophie was looking at her, a dark eyebrow raised. "Oh, I see, you want to make her pay."

Roxanne turned to smile at her. "Let her cool her heels for a bit, whip her up into a purple froth. Hold still, Sophie, you have some toast crumbs on your sleeve."

By the time the ladies walked into the drawing room, Mint behind them, Sophie realized she was no longer so terrified.

Roxanne said quietly, "This is our house, Sophie. Contrive not to forget that, all right?"

The Duchess of Brabante was standing by the lovely white Carrera marble fireplace, tapping the toe of one purple slipper, an exact match of the deep purple of her morning gown. She occupied about twelve feet of space, Roxanne thought, so many petticoats was she wearing to hold out that purple tent.

Both Roxanne and Sophie smiled and each gave her a lovely curtsy.

The duchess didn't move, merely began tapping her fan against her palm in beat with her slipper.

"You have kept me waiting. I am not used to such behavior. You will not do it again."

Roxanne said easily, "The demands of one's stomach cannot be ignored, your grace. How may we serve you at this very early morning hour?"

"It is not that early," the duchess said. "I am here to see this one, not you."

Roxanne never let her smile slip. "You must consider us a matched set, your grace, rather like the two nymphs that stand side by side on the mantel. My father gave them to my mother when they were first married. Do not think them lovely? Ah, well, won't you be seated?" Would the sofa hold all those skirts?

Lorelei Monroe wasn't happy. She took one look at Sophie Wilkie—such a silly name, mayhap even a common name. "I understand you rode in Hyde Park with my son yesterday afternoon from three o'clock until five o'clock. I demand to know the meaning of this."

Sophie said, "Devlin allowed that since it was overcast, your grace, not a dollop of sun in sight, he could forgo his hat and raise his face to the heavens without fear. I assure you there is no need to be alarmed. His lovely pallor is intact."

"Of course his pallor is intact! My son has no real fear of the sun; it is all an amusement to him. I want you to tell me exactly who you are, missy, and you will do it right now and to my satisfaction before you sink your teeth into my son the earl, who will be a duke, eventually. He is not for the likes of you—at least, I do not think he is." She paused, drew herself up. "I must know who your family is before I make the final determination. That other Monroe woman would not tell me. She teased me, evaded my very civil questions; her rudeness quite appalled me. So you will enlighten me. Now."

"*Sink my teeth into him?*" Sophie said. "I believe it is Devlin who thinks of teeth sinking."

"You will cease your impertinence. My son is not a vampire. As I told you, playing the vampire amuses him."

"Do you know he asked me to look at his eye teeth to see if they were at all pointed? I swear to you, your grace, I assured him they were not. However, I believe he was disappointed."

The Duchess of Brabante stared at her. Roxanne eased down into a wing chair opposite the duchess, and motioned for Sophie to sit in the matching chair beside her. When they were both settled, Roxanne said matter-of-factly, "Sophie is in London for her first Season. Her father is Reverend William Wilkie of Willet-on-Glee in Surrey. The alliteration is amusing, don't you think? Ah, I thought you already knew that, your grace."

"Don't be smart with me, Miss Radcliffe. That is not at all what I meant."

"Then what do you mean, your grace?"

"Very well. You force me to be blunt. Is this one an heiress?"

"Wherever did you get that idea, your grace?"

"I will have an answer!"

Sophie smiled. "My financial affairs are no one's concern, your grace. Can you imagine my asking you to tell me your husband's yearly income? I would not be so rude, I assure you."

"When you are the mother of a much-sought-after son, Miss Wilkie, you are forced occasionally to be rude, not that I would ever stoop to that, of course. I am simply asking an interested question which perforce must involve me. I must know if that other Monroe hussy is toying with me, setting up my precious son for a mighty disappointment. I will not let that happen, do you understand me, young woman? I will know the truth of your situation." She rose to her feet, and it seemed to Roxanne that purple splashed into every corner.

"Actually, your grace," Sophie said, all calm and collected, "that other Monroe woman, as you call her, was my own mother's best friend. I believe she wishes me to wed her son, not yours. Does that relieve you?"

"Julian has no need to marry again. I knew his first marriage was doomed, in fact, I told him so, and since she died, I was perfectly right. My dear son tells me Julian has no intention of finding himself another wife. There is no reason for him to propagate in any case, since he will not have a title. It is to be hoped his line will begin and end with him, since it should never have been begun in the first place."

What a dreadful thing to say, you old besom. Roxanne paused for only a moment, tenting her fingers and tapping them against her chin. "Do you know," she said, limp as a lily pad, "Devlin told me he finds Sophie exactly to his taste. He tells me she is amusing and beautiful, and her lovely inches add to her appeal—"

"When would my dear son tell you anything, Miss Radcliffe? It is not you who have been hanging about him, it is this one, who, I believe now, is indeed an heiress, since

Corinne wants her for her son. So I will know the truth. Are you an heiress?" A large finger covered nearly to the knuckle with a mammoth sapphire ring pointed at Sophie.

Roxanne continued as if Lorelei had never spoken. "And he much admires Sophie's lovely complexion, all golden and rich, the perfect foil to his glorious pallor—"

"Enough, Miss Radcliffe! You are impertinent. I will not have it. You"—she shook her beringed finger again at Sophie—"you will answer me now. If your answer is not satisfactory, you will stay away from my son."

Sophie gave her a sweet smile. "As I said, your grace, my situation is none of your affair."

"This is not to be borne!" The duchess flounced out, head up, shoulders squared, her immense net bonnet with abundant bunches of purple grapes quivering, looking like a regal purple ship under full sail. She whipped about in the doorway. "You are an heiress, aren't you?"

When the two ladies only stared at her, she yelled at Mint to open the door so she could leave this den of iniquity. She was not, she boomed, in a voice more penetrating than Mrs. Eldridge's, pleased.

"Well," Roxanne said, after they heard the front door close, "that was entertaining. Let the old battle-ax stew on that. An heiress or not an heiress, that is the question. Let's go to Hookham's; there is a new novel I have heard about."

M y lady, the two young female persons I believe you
told his lordship you found vastly amusing at the
Buxted ball are here to see you," Willicombe said, bowed,
stood back, and ushered Sophie and Roxanne into the lovely
classical drawing room, filled with sunlight, a valuable com-
modity on any day in England. Willicombe bowed deep
again to Corrie, this time at a different angle, not out of
respect, she knew, but to allow the sunlight to shine off his
bald head.

"Thank you, Willicombe," Corrie Sherbrooke said, and
rose quickly, too quickly. "Oh, dear," she said, and dashed
to a covered pot behind a wing chair in the corner of the
room and threw up.

Roxanne started forward, but Willicombe raised a hand.
"Pray be seated, ma'am," he said, and walked in his stately
way to where his mistress was on her knees, heaving. He
poured a dollop of clear liquid into a glass, eased down
beside his mistress, and held out the glass and a handkerchief. "When you drink it down, my lady, you may have one
of Cook's special biscuits."

"I hate you, Willicombe."

"I know, my lady, I would most assuredly hate me as well, were I to be hugging the chamber pot as you are. Drink this wondrous potion. It will set you back on a fine course. Who knows, you may steer straight into the wind for several hours before you again crash into the shoals."

"I am not a bloody boat, Willicombe."

"No, indeed, my lady, but if you were, you would be a lovely yacht, similar to his lordship's *Esmerelda,* whose sails billow so prettily in the wind."

Corrie Sherbrooke's eyes nearly crossed. She wiped her mouth, then took the glass, gave it a look of loathing, and tipped it down. She sputtered and coughed. "I have downed that nasty stuff, now give me my biscuit, Willicombe, before I clout you."

Without a word, Willicombe handed her what looked like a piece of a scone.

After a minute of silent chewing, Corrie drew a breath and allowed Willicombe to assist her to rise. She sent a dazzling smile to Roxanne and Sophie, both still standing by the door.

"Such drama I provide, and all on your first visit. Hello, Miss Radcliffe. Ah, you must be Miss Wilkie."

Roxanne said, "Yes, this is my niece, Sophie Wilkie. Sophie, Lady Hammersmith."

"A pleasure. Do call me Corrie, both of you. I am very pleased you are here."

Sophie said, "That is very kind of you. Believe me, it was not our intention to make you sick. Goodness, perhaps we should take our leave."

"I should be alone in the world if everyone were to leave me when I got ill. The sickness comes and it goes. My mama-in-law assures me I have but two more weeks and all the pots can be packed away—until the next time."

Sophie stared at her, clearly appalled. "You wish to have a next time?"

"I should shoot myself if I believed for a minute I should wish for a next time. However, my husband, James, tells me he is assured by my physician, a sadist in Harley Street named Silas Legbourne, that the good Lord wipes away a lady's memories of all the unpleasantness of childbearing."

Sophie said, "How utterly unfair. Are you sure this physician knows what he is talking about? Oh, dear, I just thought of Mrs. Masonry back home. She has birthed ten children. Oh, goodness, after all that, how could you possibly have any memories left in your head at all?"

Willicombe cleared his throat.

"Yes, Willicombe?"

"Dr. Legbourne assures all of us, my lady, that a readjustment of a lady's memories in this instance is critical to humanity, that if it were not the case, then the world would empty itself of people quickly enough, what with the excessive croaking that goes on. So, he concludes, ladies must forget all their travails in order to further produce replacement human beings to fill our world."

Roxanne said to the plump little man with his perfectly round bald head, "You have made an excellent point. But would it not lead one to inevitably conclude that ladies are then responsible for all wars and famine and general misery in the world?"

Willicombe recognized the light hand that had delivered the lovely irony, but before he could reply in equally stunning irony, Lord Hammersmith appeared in the doorway, took in his wife's pale face and the two ladies who looked, he thought, equal parts bemused and horrified, and said, "Good morning, ladies. Corrie, you look ready for a bit of brandy."

All female eyes followed him as he walked to the sideboard, lifted a lovely crystal carafe, and poured his wife a dollop of brandy. He wrapped her white hands around the snifter and watched her drink it down, shudder when the heat landed in her belly. He then took her arm and led her to a high-backed pale blue chair. He said over his shoulder, "She is nearly herself again. My mother's potion and Cook's scones always work wonders."

He leaned down and kissed his wife's forehead.

All it took was for Corrie to look up at him and she forgot about smashing him for getting her into this fix. She loved him too much, she supposed, and was, she realized, quite ready to forget her travails, which didn't say much for her brains. She managed a sneer. "You wouldn't sound so calm, so very bored, if you were the one lurching toward chamber pots in every single room in this bloody town house."

"Of course not," he said, "but I am not the heroine here, you are." He patted her cheek and turned. "Willicombe, she drank down my mother's potion and ate her reward scone?" At the profound bow, James added, "Magnificent shine this morning, Willicombe. Now, you are Miss Radcliffe and Miss Wilkie, are you not?"

We are no more than six feet from him, Roxanne thought, staring into those unbelievable violet eyes, which, she saw, held concern for his wife and good manners toward his doubtless unwanted guests.

"Yes, we are," Sophie said, and to Roxanne's eyes, she appeared unaffected by this god of a man. "I agree, Corrie is a heroine. However, I believe we have come at a particularly bad time. We will take our leave."

"Oh, no," Corrie said. "I am feeling quite fine now. Willicombe, please fetch us some cakes and tea. James, will you remain, or have you an engagement?"

He eyed her, seemed reassured. "I am meeting Father at Signore Ricalli's. Mother might be there as well. She told me she needed to polish her fencing skills. You've never seen her fence, Corrie, she's really rather good, fast as a flea, hops around my father, makes him curse and laugh. Try not to throw up on your slippers, sweetheart. Your maid told me three pairs have already been sent to the dustbin."

"I simply can't figure out how I manage to do that, I mean, my skirts stick out a good five feet," Corrie said, and took a quick look at her favorite Pomona green slippers. Not this time, thank the good Lord.

"You have big feet."

She threw a pillow at him, which he plucked out of the air not six inches from his perfect nose. She said, "There is no reason to tell our guests all of my defects on their first visit. Now, after I have given you your heir, I should like to polish my fencing skills as well."

"Why not? I like your feet, they're substantial, they can waltz for hours, and I imagine they will support your growing weight."

"Your wit fells me, James." She threw another pillow at him when he laughed. He caught it as well, and tossed it back to her, smiled at all the ladies, and walked out of the drawing room, whistling.

"Sometimes I want to clout him," Corrie said, smiling comfortably at both of them. "But he makes me laugh, you see, so what am I to do?" She sat forward in her chair, eyes sparkling, yet she'd been violently ill only five minutes before. "So tell me what you think of my vampire."

Truth be told, Roxanne would have rather spoken at great length about Corrie's husband, couching her interest in questions about his lordship's work in astronomy, but it was not to be. Roxanne gave it up. "Ah, Devlin. He does enjoy shocking people, curdling their innards when he talks about otherworldly bloodletting, giving them little frissons of dread when he looks pointedly at their necks. All in all, I should have to say I find Devlin Monroe vastly amusing. How long has he been playing this role?"

Corrie said, "I heard he read some ancient books at Oxford. There was a drawing of a vampire, and he decided he'd make a better bloodletter than the monster shown—he'd be more discreet." She laughed.

Sophie said, "Was he not one of your beaux before you married Lord Hammersmith?"

"Mayhap, but not really, if you know what I mean. I met Devlin when I came to London last fall for my practice Season. Unfortunately, I was not granted much of one, since—well, a number of strange things happened to spur James and me into marriage."

Sophie said, "Lady Klister confided in me that Devlin was brokenhearted when Lord Hammersmith got kidnapped and you went haring off after him and were ruined and thus forced to marry him, not Devlin."

"Marry Devlin? That brings strange sorts of images to the mind, doesn't it? As for Devlin being brokenhearted, that is doubtful, since James told me he keeps three mistresses—yes, indeed, *three* mistresses—and all at the same time—at least he did last fall. I am being scrupulously honest here, since my husband assured me it was critical to our child's future sense of morality."

Roxanne was riveted. "*Three* mistresses? *All at the same time?* Are you certain about this? I mean, how could any gentleman have the time to go from one to the other to the other to the other? It is absurd. Surely it is one of those male sorts of exaggerations."

"To the best of my knowledge, James has never lied to me. He said I couldn't marry Devlin because when I found out the mistresses were still in the picture, I would kill him and then be hung, and he didn't want me to end up dead because of Devlin's excesses. I, of course, told him since Devlin is already dead, being a vampire and all, I couldn't be hung."

Roxanne was shaking her head. "I simply can't believe it. *Three,* Corrie? As in three separate and different mistresses?"

Corrie gave a merry laugh. "Can you imagine? Three mistresses and a wife? The man would die of exhaustion, don't you think?" Corrie tapped her fingers on her chair arm. "Forgive me for being indelicate. Since you are not married and do not know of marital sorts of things, I shouldn't be speaking of—ah, but James—well, never mind that. I have known Lord Hammersmith since I was three years old. I know all his habits, good and rotten. Since the scales tip in his favor, I have no regrets. However, I envy both of you. You can sow wild oats until the bucket is empty, whereas I must be a proper wife and become fat." She burst into tears.

Roxanne quickly rose and walked to sit beside Corrie, and pulled her into her arms. "It will be all right." Pat, pat,

pat. "Surely your husband does not have all that many rotten habits, and since you know all of them, you must also know how to punish him when he backslides into them. There is another thing about your husband—you can also simply sit and look at him, and surely that would bring great pleasure."

Corrie pulled back. "Forgive me, it's not the thought of being wedded to James that makes me weep, it is the babe. I burst into tears upon being presented to his majesty the king. He was quite without a word to say. My papa-in-law told his majesty the babe, even unborn, was so overcome in his presence, he made his mother weep.

"You cannot imagine the ruckus that caused. My papa-in-law laughed for a good week. About my husband, you're right, Roxanne. I particularly like to look at him when he's sleeping. Every contrary sin he's committed during the day simply disappears when the candlelight flickers over his lovely self. I try and try, but I can only remain angry with him when I am at least one room away."

"Not strange at all, I should think," Roxanne said. "You feel all right now, Corrie?"

"Oh, yes, it comes and goes, as I said. Now, that is quite enough about me. I want to know about you and Sophie."

Roxanne said thoughtfully, "I was considering staking Devlin out in the sun, to see what happens."

Corrie sputtered her tea, wiped her chin, and grinned. "What an amazing idea. How I wish I'd thought of it. When can we do it?"

Sophie laughed. "How about I suggest to him that he take me out on the Thames at the Marksbury garden party on Saturday? I will feed him a sleeping draught and row back to shore. The three of us will remove him to a far part of the gardens and stake him out."

"It will rain on Saturday."

Roxanne stared at Corrie. "How do you know?"

"My mama-in-law told me it is an unbroken law of nature that it always rains when an alfresco luncheon is planned. She told me once she announced a date for an alfresco party, then changed it at the last minute. She said it hadn't mattered—English nature wasn't fooled—it poured buckets."

"I think we should be optimistic," Sophie said. "If my optimism is misplaced, we will simply postpone the staking until a bright, sunny day. What do you think?"

"I think we are mad," Corrie said happily, rubbed her hands together, and laughed until she suddenly paled and ran into the corner and threw up.

"I'm coming, my lady," they heard Willicombe call from outside the drawing-room door.

"I wonder," Roxanne said later, as their carriage bounced along the cobblestones, "if we should remove Devlin's coat and shirt."

Sophie said, "I wonder if he is as finely made as his uncle Julian."

"Or Lord Hammersmith," said Roxanne, and shuddered delicately.

II

Marksbury Manor
On the Thames
SATURDAY AFTERNOON

"It is such a lovely warm day," Sophie said. "Look yon, my lord, the sun is emerging from behind those lovely fluffy white clouds. I swear I do not smell any coming rain. What do you think?"

Devlin Monroe looked from the drawing-room window to the sprawl of well-manicured gardens that gently sloped down to the water, where pleasure boats were tethered to a long narrow dock, awaiting young ladies and eager young gentlemen. White tents dotted the landscape because there was always the expectation of rain. Devlin looked at Miss Sophie Wilkie's lovely dusky complexion. He raised his finger to stroke down her smooth cheek. She started, stared at him for a moment, then took a step back.

"My apologies. Your beautiful face was there, and my finger wouldn't be denied. Yes, look, the sun is now coming out. Amazing. Are you certain you wish me to row you on the Thames? Perhaps I should prefer if you rowed me."

"Since I have practically lived in boats all my life, I should be delighted to row you, my lord. You can wear a hat and carry an umbrella. A black one, so you would not be mistaken for a lady with very short hair and a parasol, in mourning black."

A brow shot up. "As an insult, that was fairly comprehensive, Miss Wilkie. Now I must row you, my manhood demands it."

She gave him a sweet smile, but there was something in that smile, he thought, something he didn't particularly trust, something wicked. He studied her. "Would you like to tell me what mischief you are brewing, Miss Wilkie?"

"Oh, look, my lord, there is Corrie Sherbrooke. All alone, standing in full sun. Shall we say hello to her? Or would you wish I call her to come inside?"

"Only if James isn't in the vicinity."

"Why ever not?"

"He does not appreciate me, I fear, ever since I asked Corrie's uncle for his permission to wed her."

"Goodness, I wouldn't appreciate you, either. Corrie told me you found her amusing, nothing more."

"Ah, last fall was an interesting time. A pity you couldn't have been here to witness all the drama. Corrie is an original. And now she is expecting a child. James did not waste any time."

"That strikes me as being a rather indelicate disclosure for my innocent ears, my lord."

"If you were really listening, you would have heard the whiff of sarcasm in my voice. In short, Corrie was forced to marry him. It was a pity, but she appears resigned to her fate."

"Do you really think so? Let me see. James looks like a god, his form is close to divine, he is ever so smart, and I've watched him laugh and jest with her. Do you really think she has resigned herself to this appalling fate?"

"Your own use of sarcasm is wasted on me. It is only ladies who are prone to flights of fancy, Miss Wilkie. Beautiful? A man would think James Sherbrooke and his twin, Jason, to be good sorts, nothing more than that until they cheated at cards, for example."

"He has a twin?"

"Yes. They are identical. However, Jason has moved to America. Baltimore, I believe, is the name of the provincial city where he now resides. Unlike his brother, Jason is horse mad."

"And do they cheat at cards?"

"To the best of my knowledge, no."

"Then men must admire them as well?"

"There is no need to go that far. Now, let us say hello to Corrie, see if perhaps she wishes to throw up behind one of Lady Marksbury's prize rosebushes."

Sophie and Devlin Monroe, hat back on his head, his umbrella tucked under his arm, walked out into the gardens overflowing with laughter, endless gossip, extravagant jewels, and champagne goblets in every beringed hand. Devlin eyed his mother across the wide Marksbury lawn, saw she was well pleased with Viscount Earswick's ponderous attention, and that was what counted. He hadn't realized his mother found crop rotation so invigorating. She looked very impressive today in her purple satin gown with sleeves the width of a tree trunk. As for his sire, the duke was probably down at the Marksbury stables, eyeing Lord Markham's new bay gelding he himself had wished to buy. Mayhap he would drop a warning in Lord Markham's ear, since he knew his father was perfectly capable of having the gelding stolen right out of the stables.

Devlin wanted to speak to Julian but didn't see him. He'd said he might show himself if he couldn't find anything more amusing to do with his Saturday afternoon, which he probably had. Then Julian had asked Devlin about Miss Wilkie, an eyebrow raised. "The chit pleases you, Dev?"

"Like Corrie Sherbrooke, she is an original. I fancy to give her some attention, at least for a while. No need to pour it on, however."

"She seems a good sort of girl, so perhaps you should consider pouring it on in liberal amounts. Your father is right. You are now twenty-seven, time to wed and produce an heir for the succession. Life is terribly fragile, Devlin. A man can die in a moment."

Devlin looked at his half uncle closely. "You are morose today. What are you thinking? Has something happened?"

And Julian told him about his smuggling run and how he knew that there'd been another there, observing them bringing in the gin and tobacco. No more shipments until Julian found another landing site, a pity, for this one had served well before he'd left three years earlier. He imagined Harlan would have suggestions.

Devlin Monroe smiled now at Sophie. "Miss Wilkie, I fear my mother has seen you. Yes, she is dismissing the aged roué who was doubtless encouraging her to rotate her barley crop more frequently. She still does not know whether to despise you or nab your fat purse."

"Even if I were an heiress, I think she would still despise me, since my mother was best friends with her own stepmama," Sophie said. "How odd that sounds when Corinne is younger than your mother. I am not, you know—an heiress, that is. My father is a vicar, the younger nephew of Viscount Denby."

"Yes, I know exactly who you are. My mother had only to ask me, but she never does. I cannot imagine why she wants an heiress in the family. Well, every parent wants their off-spring to fatten the coffers. But the truth is I have no need to wed an heiress, since the ducal boat sails nowhere near the River Styx. Even the thought of marrying an heiress—no, I thank you. They tend to be unpleasant, from my experience, full of conceit and their own worth, and double chins abound."

She said, "Roxanne is an heiress."

"Ah, well, that settles it, then," he said.

"Settles what?"

He gave her a flick of the finger against her cheek, simply couldn't help himself, and walked away from her, raising his black umbrella over his head. Sophie watched him meet his half uncle, who had appeared around the corner of the house. The two men fell into close conversation. What were they talking about? They seemed so serious. Was something wrong? Had something happened? How to get Devlin to row her on the Thames?

Sophie grinned and walked to where Corrie stood,

staring with intense concentration at Lady Marksbury's rosebushes.

As for Devlin, he and Julian had moved to stand at the top of the grassy slope of the Thames embankment, watching several small pleasure boats move smoothly through the calm water, rowed by young men eager to impress. Devlin said, "I know you're worried about the *Blue Star*. Have you any word of her?"

"It's not only the *Blue Star*. And no, I haven't heard a word."

"Then what is it?"

Julian eyed his half nephew. He said, "I remember not long ago when you believed what your mother told you: I was naught but an interloper, an adventurer out to destroy your legitimate family—in short, an unwanted disgrace, your grandfather's most striking mistake in an otherwise long life of uprightness and common sense."

Devlin laughed. "You're right, Julian. All my life, my mother dinned in my ears that you were a bastard in everything but name. My father never said a word against his own father or against you. Then I finally met you when I went up to Oxford at eighteen. Perhaps it would have taken longer to appreciate you if I had not been desperate. Even if you were everything my mother said, you were there, and you appeared quite competent."

Julian laughed. "I'd wanted to meet you for some time, and here was my unknown half nephew, who'd gotten himself into a proper mess. I remember I was proud of you, even though you should have run rather than face down three bullyboys bent on breaking your head."

"You know what really won me over? Your teaching me how to fight dirty. It is a fine thing, Julian. Did I tell you a cutpurse tried to bring me down two years ago on Boxing Day? I was no more than a dozen steps away from my own town house when he leaped out from an alley, knife slashing." Devlin paused, smiled big. "I, myself, dragged him to the watch after I'd given him a good pounding. Now, you have distracted me. What is it, Julian?"

12

J ulian debated with himself, then said, "Richard Langworth was at the ball last night, looking at me like he
wanted to stick a knife in my gullet."

Devlin nodded. "I saw him, too. However, he made no
move toward you or your mother, as least that I saw. Is he
still of the same opinion as he was when Lily died?"

"He evidently is, given the death look in his eyes last
night. I had hoped he would recall he'd known me to my
heels—but apparently any recollections on his part didn't
change anything. He obviously still blames me. I also saw
him looking at you as well, and there was an expression on
his face I well recognized.

"I believe he might hurt you to get to me. Stay away from
him, Devlin." Julian saw immediately that this was the
wrong approach. Never tell a man to keep away from danger;
he will always do the opposite. "What I meant to say—"

Devlin slashed his umbrella through the air. "You will
never be a diplomat, Julian, nor do you have my facility with
words, which means you said exactly what you meant to say.
I will be careful, I promise you. What I cannot grasp, knowing

you as I do, is how he can believe you murdered your wife, his sister. Good Lord, Julian, he's known you all your life. Surely he knows you would never harm a woman, much less your wife of six months."

Julian's voice was emotionless. "One deals with what one must. The sun is very bright today, Devlin. You are wise to hold the umbrella over your head."

"You're right. I don't wish to take any chances. Now, about Richard Langworth—"

"No, I will say no more about it. I merely wished to warn you." Julian turned to stare toward a large covered barge lumbering downriver in the distance. He wondered at the cargo. Something very heavy, mayhap something smuggled. It warmed his heart to think of goods coming into England with no excessive import duties.

"Good Lord," Julian said, more to himself than to Devlin. "It was Richard who followed me to Saint Osyth. He's the one I sensed was watching my men bringing in my goods."

"You've already had a smuggling run? This soon?"

Julian shrugged. "I wanted to see if it was still enjoyable. It was."

"Then you will have to change your landing spot," Devlin said. "You could ask me to go along, you know." He saw Julian stiffen. "I see. You still think I'm a puling lad who has to be protected."

"No, you are a future duke."

"Wellington was already a duke when he fought at Waterloo. Had I been with you, I could have circled back and cornered Richard."

Julian said nothing at all.

"Oh, to the Devil with you. Very well. Would you care to row Sophie Wilkie on the Thames? She asked me to row her, but the sun is very strong today. You know how the water reflects the harsh light on your face."

Julian cocked a black brow. "My mother would be pleased to see me in the young lady's company. But it is not to be—I will say it again, she is too young for me, and that's the truth of it, but she appears a good sort, Devlin. You might consider doing the rowing of the young lady. Keep well covered, keep close to shore, and sing love songs to her. What do you think?"

"Perhaps if the day were cloudy." He shrugged. "You are still dark as a Moor, Julian. Perhaps I could provide you with a hat?"

Julian was smiling as he left his half nephew, the umbrella held firmly over his head, which also had a hat sitting on it, looking out toward that same laden barge.

Julian spoke briefly to his mother, then, perversely, asked Sophie Wilkie to take a turn in one of the pleasure boats.

Her face was a study in consternation. "No! What I mean is—well, I—oh dear, that is—"

He saw her shoot a look toward Corrie Sherbrooke and Roxanne Radcliffe, who had their heads close, and now they were looking toward him. What was going on here?

He said slowly, "You wish only Devlin to row you?"

"Why, yes, I much enjoy his company, you know. But I quite fear I am not now in the mood for a good rowing. One's feelings and desires shift and change quickly, don't you know?"

The wide guileless smile put him on instant alert. "Try out the truth, Miss Wilkie. I promise you my feelings won't be hurt." Chagrin—he saw it now, writ clearly on her expressive face. "You wish to have Devlin—ah, I see, you want to see if he would burn to ashes in the sun, is that it?"

"I would never want him to burn up! As to his even being a vampire, you know very well it is all fiction, based on legend; there is no truth to it at all. Devlin simply enjoys amusing himself at other people's expense. All that would happen to him is a sunburn."

"Then why did you wish him out in the sun?"

"It is not that—I simply prefer him to you."

"A blow," he said, and flattened his palm over his heart. "I lied. I am hurt, cut to the very quick. You do realize, of course, that even though your mother and mine were bosom bows, there is no need for you to feel pressured to marry me, nor I you. You may prefer whomever you wish to prefer. Consider me in the way of being a kindly uncle. If you have questions or concerns about gentlemen you meet, why, you may confide in me. I will pat your shoulder and give you guidance. What is this? You look ready to explode, Miss Wilkie. Your eyes are nearly crossed."

She poked him in the chest with a nanny's finger. "A kindly uncle! Of course I don't have to marry you; no one ever said I did. It is patently absurd."

He heard Roxanne Radcliffe laugh. He looked back at Sophie's red face. "I see," he said slowly, "there is a plot brewing. I'll wager Corrie Sherbrooke is a part of it."

"I have no idea what you're talking about, my lord."

"I see it all now. All of you want to get Devlin out on the water. You claim you don't wish to fry him. Then what is your plan?"

"You have quite ruined everything," Sophie said, and flounced away. He liked the cut of her gown, the way she moved. Her figure was quite nice, indeed, and even though she wore enough petticoats to sew a tent, he could still see the graceful motion of her hips. He was reminded he hadn't visited Marlene in three days.

What were the ladies planning to do to Devlin? He should have warned his nephew about them, in addition to Richard Langworth. He saw Roxanne Radcliffe walk his way, only to be stopped by Mr. Ludley Owen, a singularly kind old gentleman who had a great collection of silver and gold Japanese chopsticks.

A shadow cast itself beside Julian.

"What a paltry little poseur you've got for a half nephew. Imagine such a foppish creature as the future Duke of Brabante."

Speak of the devil. Julian turned slowly. "Richard. I assume you're here because you knew I was attending?"

"No, I fancy to sample some of Lady Marksbury's salmon patties. My father tells me they're the best in London."

"I was not aware of that. Keep your distance from Devlin Monroe."

"Keep my distance from the vampire? You are afraid he would try to take me down and suck my blood?"

"If he did, he'd probably be poisoned. Keep your distance. This is between you and me. Devlin has no part in it. Do you understand me?"

Richard Langworth's laughter sounded in Julian's ears as he walked toward Lady Marksbury's buffet table, where a platter of salmon patties was piled high.

⇥━○ ○━⇤

Two hours later, Julian was naked in Marlene's frothy white bed, kissing her silly as he covered her. His last thought before he fell into a stupor was *What had those witches planned to do to Devlin?*

13

Radcliffe Town House

Roxanne drummed her fingertip against middle C over and over again until Sophie called out, "Roxanne, if you don't let that poor note rest, it will run like a flea from the keyboard. Come, what is wrong?"

Roxanne raised her finger. "Sorry. I was thinking about a gentleman I met at Lady Marksbury's party. His name is Richard Langworth. I asked Lady Bottsby who he was—she knows everyone—and she told me he was the son of Baron Purley of Hardcross Manor in Cornwall. Near Saint Austell, she said. She tapped my arm with her fan and counseled me to take care around him, for he was something of a mystery, and who knew what he was really like?

"Then I saw him speaking to Julian. I moved closer and listened. There wasn't much said, but I felt anger toward Julian coming off him in waves. He means him ill. And Julian knows it. He all but threatened Devlin, mocking him about being a poseur and the like, and Julian warned him away."

That snagged Sophie's attention away from the narrow band of yellow satin she was stitching into the curve of her new cottage bonnet. "I believe we are all poseurs, depending on the company we're in. I wish I could think of something vampiresque to make me more interesting. So you don't know anything more about this man, Roxanne?"

"No, but I have a fancy to find out. I think I should like to stake him out, find out what mischief he's brewing."

"Lady Bottsby said his country house was near Saint Austell?"

Roxanne nodded.

"That is where Ravenscar is located as well. If they grew up near each other, then they've known each other forever. What could have happened?"

"We will ask her grace." She heard Roxanne heave a big sigh, strike middle C again. She said, "I wish we'd been able to stake out Devlin."

"If you'd asked him directly to row you," Roxanne said, looking up, "he couldn't have refused."

Had she asked him directly and he'd sidestepped her? Sophie couldn't remember. He was smoother than a river rock.

Roxanne said, "You know, in the long course of things, I can see Devlin doing only what he wishes to do."

Sophie concentrated on snipping off a pale pink thread. "You should have asked him, Roxanne."

"Me? It's you he caresses with his voice when he speaks to you, Sophie."

"Caresses? Me? Goodness, I've never noticed that. He merely touched my cheek, probably practiced flirting on his part. I think he likes me because I'm not as white as he is and thus make the perfect foil. Whereas you, Roxanne, you are in the nature of competition, with your yard upon yard of white skin."

Roxanne said, eyebrow arched, "You want to stake me out now?"

They laughed together, but it wasn't long before Roxanne was again tapping notes on the pianoforte.

Mint said from the doorway, "It is her grace the Duchess of Brabante—the dowager duchess—in other words, the one you would wish to see."

Roxanne rose from the pianoforte. "Thank you, Mint. Your grace, how lovely to see you. Won't you have a cup of tea with us?"

Corinne tapped her foot, stared hard at Sophie surrounded by her sewing. "I want to know why you aren't making at least a small push toward my son, Sophie. He was with his mistress; one of my acquaintances saw him emerge from her lodging—it was the middle of the afternoon! He must have gone directly from the Marksburys' garden party to her. If you were encouraging him at all, Sophie, he wouldn't be straying in such a dreadful manly way. How he found her so very quickly, I do not know. He has been in London only a sennight. He obviously met her when he was here before meeting with Harlan Whittaker, his man of business."

Roxanne's eyebrow shot up. "But, ma'am, however could one of *your* acquaintances know it was his mistress's lodging?"

Corinne turned a lovely shade of pink, tossed her head. "Well, it's quite simple, really." She sat herself down on the sofa, spreading her voluminous India muslin skirts around her.

"Simple?" Sophie asked.

"If you must know, I hired a young boy to keep an eye on Julian."

Roxanne stared at her. "You mean you have your son followed? This boy reports his movements back to you?"

"You make it sound like I am a nosy mama, which isn't the case at all. Julian is, and always has been, more stubborn than his proud papa. I must see to his welfare, since he is so very careless of it."

Sophie snipped another thread, not looking up. "What is his mistress's name?"

"She calls herself Marlene Ronsard. It is doubtless a fabrication, that lovely name, and I strongly doubt she has ever seen even a stick of driftwood on the shores of France. I asked my boy—his name is Jory—if she spoke with a French accent, but he didn't know, said it didn't sound at all *furin* to him."

Corinne huffed at the two sets of astonished eyes staring at her. "I should not speak of such things in front of you, that is true enough, but you would know, so now you do. No, you shouldn't, since you are well-brought-up young ladies and you should remain as ignorant as dirt or purposely stupid on the subject of men and their lust, but you forced me to tell you, did you not? I shall have some tea now, Roxanne. Don't forget, two sugars and no milk. Dreadful stuff. I ask you, who can drink a proper tea with milk in it?"

A mistress, Roxanne was thinking a few minutes later, as she stirred sugar in the dowager duchess's tea. Did Julian by chance have more than one mistress—mayhap three, like Devlin?

When she handed the saucer to Corinne, she said, "Your grace, by any chance has Jory followed Devlin Monroe?"

Corinne took a sip of tea, nodded in approval. "Why ever should I want to have Devlin followed? He is *her* son, not mine. If Lorelei is interested, she can see to employing her own—"

"Spy?"

"What an unflattering word, Roxanne, a word that surely gives the wrong impression. Do not jest about such a thing. It is a mother's duty to be fully informed about her son's activities to ensure he is kept safe. He is safe, is he not? So that means I am doing what is needful and doing a good job of it."

Roxanne said, "Ma'am, tell us about Richard Langworth. He is tall, dark, rather fine-looking, I suppose, but not as dark or as fine-looking as your son. He could be, but he has this sneer about his mouth that is very unattractive. At least he did when he was speaking to Julian."

Corinne stiffened. "Richard Langworth is the reason I am having him followed, truth be told. Jory knows bully-boys, he tells me, real toughs who he can call quickly to protect my son."

"Why does Richard Langworth wish him ill, ma'am? Sophie told me his family home and Ravenscar are very close."

"Yes, a mere three miles separates our homes."

"Then that means this Richard and Julian grew up together?"

Corinne nodded, then she raised her hand. "This is a subject I will not discuss with you. If you wish to ask Julian—" Her voice stopped, and she knew, looking at the two young ladies, that both of them would ask him the first opportunity that presented itself. "Let me say only that Julian's wife was shot and Richard believes Julian killed her. He wants revenge."

"But why—"

"Sophie, if you and Roxanne want to know more, you must ask Julian. I will say no more."

⊷ *14* ⊷

Covent Garden Theater

Sophie looked through her opera glasses at Charles Kean striding to the middle of the stage like a short, puffed-up conqueror. He stopped, looked out over the audience, raised his hands, and declaimed. He continued to declaim, wildly gesticulating all the while. She stopped listening after the third bombast. She could feel a headache coming on. She lowered her opera glasses to her lap and looked around the theater. She was not in the majority. Most patrons' eyes were glued to the stage, all their attention focused on Kean. Wait, there was a matron in the next box rolling her eyes as Kean clapped his hand over his heart and stumbled around a bit.

Sophie looked at Roxanne when she squeezed her hand. Roxanne winked at her, then smiled as she nodded toward Corinne. She was leaning forward in her gilt chair, her eyes fastened on Kean. She looked enthralled.

Julian sat on Roxanne's left, garbed in stark black, his linen nearly as white as Devlin's face, his arms crossed over his chest, looking stoic. Roxanne leaned close, whispered, "My father told me Kean could posture better than Elrod, his prized rooster. I will write to tell him I think he may be right. Also, I do believe Kean trumpets louder than Mr. Rickett's cow Lisette when she wants to be milked."

"I would like to shoot him," Julian said. "But most appear to be enjoying his performance, which raises serious questions about the taste of our countrymen."

Corinne sent them both a look, and they subsided.

When the intermission finally arrived on the heels of a five-minute Kean invective, all but one in the Monroe box wanted to cheer.

Sophie jumped to her feet, snagged her gown, and nearly got jerked over the edge of the box. Roxanne caught her and pulled her back down.

Julian was looking at her, an eyebrow raised. "It wasn't that bad, was it? To bring on such despair?"

Roxanne said, "Tell me, dearest, that you only sought escape, not an end to it all."

"It was close," Sophie said.

Julian bit off a laugh, since his mother was looking at him. "Miss Wilkie, you would have landed in a mess of drunken young louts if Miss Radcliffe hadn't caught you. Would you like to accompany me downstairs to fetch some champagne?"

His mother said, "I heard her give you permission to call her Sophie. This was three days ago. You may do so, Julian. Roxanne, you may do as you please, since you are not the focus of—well, never mind that. I should love some champagne. One gets so parched watching a great performer." The look she gave them dared them to disagree. No one was stupid.

It was Roxanne who said, "I will go with you, sir. Sophie has the beginnings of a headache."

"I assure you there is no need to protect her from me, Miss—Roxanne. I have told your innocent young pullet to consider me a kindly uncle, a comfortable older gentleman in whom she can confide her woes."

"That is nonsense, Julian," his mother said. "You are not at all comfortable."

This guileless comment brought laughter. Corinne blinked, realized she'd uttered a witticism, and preened.

Sophie said, "My headache isn't that bad. I will accompany you to the champagne, sir."

"If I am not to be your comfortable uncle, then you must call me Julian."

Roxanne said, "Or you may call him 'my lord.' That is utterly impersonal, is it not?"

"Oh, dear," Corinne said. "You mean to say when people greet me as 'your grace,' I could be any grace at all, and it doesn't really matter?"

Roxanne grinned at her, patted her hand, and rose. "I believe I see our vampire ready to stretch out his legs, perhaps his fangs as well. Look, he is waving at you, Sophie. Why don't you wait for Devlin, and I will accompany his lordship?"

Julian cocked a dark brow at her but said nothing. They made their way down the staircase into the theater lobby, crammed with ladies and gentlemen, many of them appearing to have a great thirst, as all wanted champagne, and all wanted it now. Waiters expertly threaded their way through the throng, ducking elbows, slithering between ladies whose gowns were so voluminous they were momentarily lost to sight.

"Shall I think of you as an uncle also, Julian?"

He didn't answer her immediately. She realized he'd slipped some money to a waiter, who promptly disappeared, only to reappear with a full bottle of champagne and a half dozen glasses, cleverly held between his fingers. "Shall we follow the fellow, Roxanne?"

"Well, are you an uncle to me as well?"

"I will be your uncle if you will be my aunt, since we are both rather long in the tooth."

"What a dreadful thing to say," Roxanne said, then laughed.

"That's better. You do not wish to insult me, since I am providing the champagne. Stop licking your lips."

"It is Sophie who licks her lips over champagne. She never tasted champagne until last week, and I swear she poured half a bottle down her throat. I fear I shall have to watch to make certain she doesn't become a tippler."

"Likes the bubbles, does she?" He took her arm and deftly steered her away from a large woman covered in black lace who was on a direct collision course. "Take care, my child. These stairs are more fraught with danger than a battlefield. I was wondering how many petticoats were present this evening at the theater. Do you think if all the petticoats were piled on the stage, they would hit the rafters?"

Roxanne lightly tapped her fist against his arm. "I daresay they might make a pile so high they would spill out onto the street. Oh, dear, the waiter is escaping us."

Julian gave a soft whistle that stopped the waiter in his tracks. He turned, gave Julian a nod, and waited for them.

"That was well done. Is that a prearranged signal?"

"No, but it always works. Waiters have very acute hearing, you know. Lean close, here comes another wave of petticoats."

When they weren't more than twenty feet from their box, Julian said, "All right, tell me why you didn't want Sophie to accompany me."

She stared at her slippers.

"I am not a ravager of young maidens, nor do I plan on trying to attack her, no matter what my mother wishes, so tell me, Roxanne."

"I am worried for her. The thing is, Julian, you know too much."

A black brow shot up. He laid his hand lightly on her arm. "Nothing more than any other kindly uncle."

"All right, here it is. I think she and Devlin would be perfect for each other. They only need time together to come to this conclusion."

Julian stared at her in amazement. "Stay out of it, Roxanne, that's my best uncle's advice."

When they reached the box, it was to see Devlin sitting between Sophie and Corinne.

He saluted Julian, smiled at Roxanne. "Forgive me for being late, but my mother—well, never mind. My sire tells me the senior Kean—the great Edmund—was finally forced to act beside his son, an event that did not stir his blood, evidently, so my sire told me. The son, my sire remarks to all who will listen, is paltry by comparison, not nearly as dramatic as his father, his declamations too conservative, not enough feeling—in short, my father believes him a stick."

"If the stick showed any more feeling," Roxanne said, "I should pick up my chair and hurl it at him."

Corinne said, "Listen to me, you philistines, you are all too ignorant and too young to appreciate him. He is a master, mayhap not as great as his father, but still . . ."

No one wanted to disagree with the dowager duchess; well, everyone did, but none wanted to have her cannon aimed at him. Devlin gave Julian a lazy look. "Good evening, Uncle, Roxanne. You brought champagne, I see. So did I. With two bottles, we should be able to survive the remaining scenes without undue misery."

Corinne harrumphed.

Julian merely smiled and handed her a glass filled to the brim with chilled champagne.

"Hear, hear," Sophie said. She toasted everyone indiscriminately and drank down the glass without pause.

"I see what you mean," Julian said. "A budding tippler. Let's see how you behave." Julian handed Roxanne a glass. He watched her tip back the glass, drink down half of it, lower the glass, hiccup into her palm, and smile widely. "Do you know, Sophie, I think you and I should take one of the bottles and join Mr. Kean onstage. I've a fancy to play Sir Edmund Mortimer myself."

"Hear, hear," said Sophie again. "I believe my headache only a memory." She beamed at them all.

During the final act, Roxanne would swear Kean glared up at their box once when he was delivering his lines. Not one of them had thrown anything at him. What did he want?

Devlin Monroe did not return to his box. He sat beside Sophie, refilling her glass until, alas, the champagne was gone.

Roxanne happened to spot Richard Langworth seated in a box to her far left, between two ladies, a mother and daughter, she thought, both very comely. He was looking up at her, and he wasn't smiling. He gave her a small salute. She snuck a peek at Julian, but as before, he was staring at the stage, his arms folded over his chest. He wasn't seeing Kean, of that she was sure; he was seeing something entirely different. She fully intended to ask him about why Richard Langworth believed Julian had murdered his wife, Richard's sister. Or perhaps he was concerned about his ship that still hadn't arrived from Constantinople? He was that worried? She wondered what cargo the *Blue Star* carried.

Julian's carriage was promptly delivered because Julian told her he always paid the theater postboy a coin to make sure he had excellent placement. As the carriage rocked easily through the London streets back to Lemington Square, Roxanne said, "Richard Langworth was looking at our box. He was in the company of two ladies."

Sophie said in a lilting, happy voice, "He was probably staring at you, Roxanne. Goodness, all the gentlemen stare at you, you are so beautiful this evening. Your hair is glorious; it glows like a sunset in the candlelight. How I envy you. Don't you agree, Julian?" She giggled. "Surely an uncle would appreciate an aunt's beauty."

"Uncles are strange ducks," he said.

"This Richard Langworth," Roxanne began.

Julian merely shook his head at her.

Corinne said, "Perhaps I should speak to Lord Arthur about him."

"Pray do not, Mama," Julian said, but he couldn't help a smile. He tried to imagine Arthur Wellesley, the Duke of Wellington, receiving that request. Rather like praying to God to take away the pain of your stubbed toe. When they reached the Radcliffe town house, he said, "I will call on you ladies tomorrow, if that is convenient."

With Corinne's spy Jory doubtless on his heels, Roxanne thought, and nodded. And maybe that wasn't such a bad idea. She wanted to know more about Richard Langworth, if he posed a threat to Sophie.

Sophie was humming as Mint assisted both her and Roxanne out of their evening cloaks. She realized she was happy.

She felt light, her feet gliding above the floor. She breathed in and laughed. If it had rained, she didn't think she would have minded at all. She realized in that moment she hadn't laughed much since her mother had died.

She turned to speak to Roxanne, when Mint drew in a deep breath and blurted out, "Your sister is here, Miss Roxanne. Lady Merrick."

Oh, no, not Aunt Leah. Sophie's feet hit the floor with a solid thunk. She sobered very quickly. She hadn't seen her aunt Leah since her mother's funeral, but she well remembered her endless criticisms of Roxanne, heard throughout her life, comments not meant for her ears. She saw Roxanne had stilled.

The glorious days of champagne and laughter, she thought sadly, were over.

⚒ *15* ⚒

The next morning, Roxanne eyed her elder sister across the breakfast table. Sunlight flooded through the bow windows, haloing Leah's head, and it made her look quite angelic, which, Roxanne thought, had to give one serious pause about angels.

Leah was here, actually here, and what was one to do? She hadn't said last night why she'd come, merely kissed her sister's cheek, nodded briefly to Sophie, and taken herself off to bed. Elvira, her maid of ten years, plump and merry, followed behind her, looking exhausted, Leah's jewelry casket hugged close.

Leah had married two weeks before her twentieth birthday to a naval man who'd had the misfortune to drown five years later when the ship he captained ran aground during a violent storm off the northern coast of Portugal. The first mate had perished as well. No one was able to explain why Captain Merrick hadn't been piloting the ship during a storm or why he'd fallen overboard, much less why his sailors hadn't saved him. Like most sailors, he couldn't swim, and that surely made no sense at all.

Leah Cosgrove, Lady Merrick, had worn black gloves for twelve months, and not a day longer. She was now twenty-nine, two years Roxanne's senior, quite lovely with her nearly white blond hair, fair complexion, and a reputation as the most graceful of the three Radcliffe sisters, a vision to behold when she waltzed. And the meanest, Roxanne thought, staring at her sister calmly sipping her tea, her eyes locked on Sophie, who was picking at her eggs, keeping quiet, smart girl.

Leah said finally, her voice so sweet, it nearly dripped, "Father was worried about you, Roxanne."

What was this about? "He was? I received a letter from him yesterday. He said nothing about worry. Indeed, he hoped Sophie and I were enjoying ourselves."

"He would not want you to think he felt you were incompetent, and so he asked me privately to come to assist you with our niece."

Sophie looked ready to leap at Leah.

No, don't move, Sophie, keep quiet.

Roxanne smiled. "I don't think Sophie needs assistance from anyone. She is smart, bright, and not a fool." Excellent words, but still, she sounded defensive, Roxanne thought, a weakness her sister would exploit. She eyed Leah, wondered how she could get rid of her, decided it would take a dozen strong men to haul her away, and unfortunately she knew only two such men who might be willing—Devlin and Julian. Life, she thought, wasn't fair. Why hadn't her father warned her? Ah, he would have warned her, and that meant he hadn't known Leah was coming.

Leah said, "Well, then, I shan't have to be bothered with Sophie, since she is so smart and bright. I can shop to my heart's content, and see—never mind that."

See what?

Sophie said, "I haven't seen you since my mama's funeral, Aunt Leah. What have you been doing?"

"Doing? I have servants to *do* things, Sophie."

"Forgive me, such a stupid thing to say. How have you been amusing yourself?"

"It is difficult being a widow; one is never quite a part of things." But she was smiling, and why was that?

Roxanne said, "Farleigh's mother lives in Battlesdean, only ten miles distant from York, does she not? Do you not visit her occasionally?"

"She's old and boring, and all she can talk about is how it is the Navy's fault her poor Farleigh drowned."

"How is the Navy to blame?" Sophie asked blankly.

Leah shrugged as she picked up a slice of toast, smeared it with butter and elderberry jam, and bit in. "She claims the first mate was drunk, and a spy."

"A spy for whom?" Roxanne asked.

"Who cares? Then she accuses me of having forgotten him much too soon."

Roxanne said, "Why would she say that? You wore black gloves for a year."

"I believe she would have preferred that I wear black until I was lying in my coffin. But even that is not enough—she tells me I avoided the marriage bed so now she does not have a grandchild to remind her of her perfect son."

Sophie said, "Since your husband was at sea so much of the time, it certainly did not require much avoidance on your part, did it?"

Leah shrugged, and Roxanne realized in that instant that none of this was to the point. She also knew the reason now for the smile. She said, "You have met someone, haven't you? That's the 'never mind.'"

Leah smiled widely at both of them. "Why, yes, I have, and he is here in London for the Season."

"Does he know you are here, Leah?"

"Of course. Well, perhaps not specifically, as I had not yet made up my mind to come, since Father hadn't spoken to me about his concerns. I shall send him a note. He is a fine gentleman." She added in a very deliberate voice, "You will not flirt with him, Roxanne. He is too high-minded for such nonsense."

"Flirt with him? I don't even know him, Leah."

"You flirted outrageously with Farleigh, made him vastly uncomfortable; he told me so."

Roxanne could only stare at her sister. This was a new criticism. Roxanne couldn't imagine flirting with Farleigh Cosgrove, Lord Merrick, whose face was covered with black whiskers to protect him from the biting winds at sea. She supposed he married Leah to produce a child, which hadn't happened. Sophie was right, he'd scarcely ever seen his wife to get the job done. But this—"Why are you saying such a thing, Leah? I never flirted with your husband. If you would know the truth, I didn't even like him very much; he was very aloof, mayhap even grim, and his fingers were stained yellow from all that tobacco he smoked. Besides, as Sophie said, he was never home."

"You say that now, now that he's dead. I believe you wanted him, but he chose me."

"But I was only seventeen when you met and married him, Leah."

Leah shrugged. "You were a very mature seventeen, nearly eighteen. Even his mother remarked I was not blessed in my sister, and I was forced to defend you even though I knew it was true."

Roxanne would swear she smelled fire and brimstone in the morning room. She thought of the precious few lovely days she and Sophie had spent here in London. At home, she rarely saw Leah, who, nonetheless, lived only five miles from Allegra Hall. *It will be all right. Time will pass. Besides, what can she really do?* "How long are you planning to visit us, Leah?"

"What is this? You do not wish to have me visit you?"

No, I don't.

"As I told you, Father was concerned, and he believed I would be a good influence."

Father would choke on his soup before he'd say that.

"Am I not welcome in my own house?"

No, you are not welcome. There was no hope for it. Roxanne said, "I hope you will enjoy yourself here, Leah."

"If you have the proper invitations from the right sort of people, then naturally I shall. I will accompany both you and Sophie. Is there a ball tonight, perhaps?"

Sophie said, "There is the Caulcott musicale. I'm told there are two tenors from Milan, twin brothers, who are excellent."

"Then I shall attend with you."

Sophie said, "But you do not have an invitation, Leah."

Leah simply raised a brow and stared her down. "If your consequence isn't enough to make me accepted, then I fear I shall have to find my own friends."

That would be good, Roxanne thought, but kept her mouth shut. *Keep quiet, Sophie, keep quiet.* She'd hoped when Leah had married Farleigh she'd change, that she'd stop despising her own family, primarily her sisters, primarily her youngest sister, namely, herself, but it hadn't happened. Now, it appeared she was in love again. Mayhap this time she'd met a gentleman who would stay put once she married him, mayhap a gentleman who would make her see her sister wasn't out to sink her, mayhap a gentleman who would render her pleasant, give her a dozen children. But so far it didn't appear he'd made any headway.

She said, "I did not flirt with your husband, Leah. I will not flirt with your new beau, either. What is his name?"

Leah chewed another bite of toast slowly, thoughtfully. "I do not believe I will tell you yet. He mentioned to me that he likes keeping me to himself." Her voice was coy, like a young girl's. Goodness, what was going on here? Surely this man wasn't ashamed to be associated with a Radcliffe?

Sophie gave her a sunny smile. "It really isn't important, is it? Welcome to London, Leah. I'm sure we'll have a marvelous time."

Leah looked at the vibrant young girl at her right elbow, Bethanne's daughter—a full nine years her junior, fresh, lovely, an innocent, her smile like Bethanne's, beguiling, sweet. She said, "Bethanne wasn't as tall as you are."

"No, she wasn't, and I'll tell you, once I reached my full height, Mama didn't like it at all."

"Well, no, how could she like it? She would see it as a mistake, giving birth to a maypole."

"No, you misunderstand. She said she quite envied me my glorious height. However, you're quite right. My father didn't admire my height at all. Whenever he called me a maypole, my mother said that was true, but I was the prettiest maypole in Willet-on-Glee." Sophie smiled at Leah, and spooned down a bite of Mrs. Eldridge's delicious porridge.

Roxanne marveled. It was well done of Sophie to turn around Leah's criticism with seeming agreement. It quite left Leah without a word to say. Perhaps she could learn to do that as well.

16

The dowager Duchess of Brabante arrived at Lemington Square an hour later, to be greeted with another Radcliffe offspring. She'd heard about this one often enough from Bethanne, always in gentle measured tones, but she'd known Bethanne had considered Leah an ill-tempered fishwife. Leah, the middle sister, while very pretty, sported the beginnings of a pinched mouth. Whatever did she have to be unhappy about? She had a glorious head of hair, she was a widow, she wasn't starving in a ditch, she wasn't so old her teeth were loosening, and she didn't have to obey anyone at all. Surely that was close to heaven—she should know, since she'd been a widow since the age of twenty, Sophie's age, she thought, and wasn't that amazing? How had she felt when she'd wedded the Duke of Brabante at the age of eighteen? Had she been hopeful? She couldn't recall, but she did remember she wasn't averse to marrying him. She'd never learned what the duke had paid her father for her hand.

She was fully prepared to be pleasant to Lady Merrick, since she was Sophie's aunt and Roxanne's sister. "Come," she said, after eating three of Mrs. Eldridge's apricot tarts, "tell us the name of this paragon you will see in London."

"Very well, your grace. His name is Richard Langworth. He is Baron Purley's eldest son. I believe he has one sister. Her name is Victoria, and she is about Sophie's age. There was another sister who died. Richard told me he had no need to rent a house here in London, since his family decided to remain in Cornwall, so he has rooms on Jermyn Street."

Leah did not notice Corinne drop her fourth apricot tart on the carpet, but Roxanne and Sophie did.

"He is very handsome, his address is charming, and he sought me out at the assembly rooms on Mount Street. He told me he'd wanted to meet me because he had heard of the Radcliffe sisters of York." She modestly lowered her eyes to her soft pearl-gray morning slippers. "He told me I was reputed to be the most beautiful of the three sisters."

Sophie said, not an ounce of guile in her voice, "It was my mama who began that, you know, the Radcliffe sisters of York—everyone worshipped my mother, and then of course you and Roxanne grew up, both of you every bit as beautiful as my mama and so fun-loving, and then everyone worshipped both of you as well."

Yet again, Leah was left without a word to say.

Watch and learn. Roxanne said, "I am pleased Mr. Langworth believes you the most beautiful of the three of us, Leah, since you wish his regard," Roxanne said, and smiled, and she thought, *Why had Richard Langworth really sought her out?*

Corinne shot a look at Roxanne and said, "But this man, this Richard Langworth, surely you don't know all that much about him, my dear."

Leah said, "Yes, indeed I do, your grace. He is a man of adventure and action, a man to admire, a man who has traveled the world, seen and done so much. He is very smart, you know. He confided to me that I was his star, leading him to York. He never mentioned Roxanne's name—no wonder, since she is on the shelf now and can no longer be counted. Being a widow, however, is very different."

Taking a page from Sophie's book, Roxanne said, "You're

quite right. I'm so high on the shelf, I pray I will not totter off it. Then where would I be?"

"On the floor," Leah said.

Corinne said, "But you are not *that* antiquated, Roxanne; you are merely well into your adulthood."

Roxanne nearly spurted out some tea. "As is your son, ma'am?"

"Julian is a man," Corinne said matter-of-factly. "As a man, he will never be considered to be too far along in anything. Growing into adulthood conjures up images of maturity and common sense, and I daresay few men ever manage to achieve that.

"As it is, my Julian is only thirty-two, a prime age for a man. He is experienced, he is a treat to the eyes, and he is not an idiot. In short, he is quite the perfect age for a gentleman. Ah, I was so very young when he was born, barely more than a girl, and widowed so soon thereafter. However, being a widow has many advantages, as I'm sure Lady Merrick realizes. One is completely free to do exactly as one wishes."

Free to do exactly what you wanted. That would indeed be nice, Roxanne thought. But it wouldn't be enough for her. No, she wanted a home of her own, she wanted to love and be loved, and she wanted to share laughter with this unknown gentleman who would be there only for her. She could imagine no greater gift out of life than that. But she was twenty-seven years old. Such a gentleman had never swum into her waters, well, one had, but her father had told her he only wanted her money, and although she would have thrown herself in his arms, uncaring of his motives, the years of trusting her father implicitly had won out. In odd moments, Roxanne wondered what had happened to John Singleton. She hoped he'd found a pleasant heiress and was now the fond papa of a hopeful family.

If occasionally she was a bit lonely, she accepted it, accepted that she was probably meant to be a spinster. There had been other gentlemen; indeed, half a dozen marriage proposals had flowed in over the years, but those gentlemen had seemed somehow insubstantial, not touching her, even when she allowed several of them to kiss her. If, upon occasion, she thought of the child or children she would never shepherd into this world, she wanted to weep, but she soon got over it. Her lot was an enviable one, and she should never forget it. Thank heavens her father was a fine man, filled with laughter, with a tolerant view of his fellow man.

Sophie said to Leah, "Julian believes me a positive youngster, doubtless an empty-headed schoolroom chit. He wants me to consider him a fond uncle."

Leah looked from Roxanne to Sophie. "Since I am a widow and thus expected to be older than twenty, your grace, then mayhap your son—the perfect age—will consider me the perfect age as well."

"But what about Richard Langworth?" Roxanne asked, cup poised halfway to her mouth.

Leah said calmly, "I have learned a lady can never have too many gentlemen dangling after her. It keeps her sparkling, don't you know. As for my dear Richard, I have written him a small missive, telling him where I will be this evening. I hope he will be able to come." As she walked out of the drawing room ten minutes later, she said quietly to Roxanne, "He is mine, do you hear me?"

"But Leah, you said a lady can never have too many gentlemen—"

"Do not make me smack you, Roxanne. It has been a long time, but I remember how to do it."

"What a singular woman," Corinne said to Roxanne, after Leah and her maid left in the Radcliffe carriage for shopping in Bond Street. "I cannot like it that she is seeing Richard Langworth. I started to tell her he was a dangerous man, but—forgive me—your sister isn't at all, well, pleasant, I guess I would say, and maybe they deserve each other.

"But this worries me. Do you think he sought her out purposefully, Roxanne? That he knew of my son's connection to your family?"

I certainly do, she thought, but she said, "It doesn't seem very likely. I mean, he could find out that I would be coming with my niece to London for the Season. It's also possible he could have discovered that you, your grace, and Sophie's mama were best friends, even heard you hoped for a wedding between her daughter and your son. But all of that seems so convoluted to me.

"Since I have not attended the assembly-room balls on Mount Street in several months, it is quite possible he did indeed meet Leah there. Mayhap this budding romance is only as it appears—an innocent encounter."

Sophie said, "An innocent encounter? Come, Roxanne, it blasts one in the head with the coincidence of it."

"Whatever the reason," Corinne said thoughtfully, "he moved quickly to attach her. It appears he was successful."

"It would help, ma'am, if you told us why he believes Julian shot Lily."

Corinne shook her head.

Sophie said, "My mama always said she was blessed and cursed with her sisters. She said Aunt Leah was the curse part. I think it was one of the few times my papa agreed with her. I believe Aunt Leah once called him an advocate for the joys of Hell. He didn't know what she meant, but he was put off by her. Not that he ever appreciates a female expressing an opinion in his presence."

Roxanne wanted to curse Reverend Wilkie and laugh at the same time—an advocate for Hell—*well done, Leah,* but she didn't laugh. She stood up and shook out her skirts, said, "Leah obviously does not know what sort of man Richard Langworth is. Do you think I should make the push to detach her from him?"

Sophie said, "I cannot imagine she would believe you, Roxanne. She would think you jealous."

Corinne said, "I do not like this, girls. It doesn't bode well for bringing to fruition what I want in the full passage of time." She gave Sophie a significant look. Sophie merely smiled at her. Corinne added, "I believe I shall have to set Jory to following him. Mayhap I shall have to hire another boy."

And I, Roxanne thought, *shall have to determine what, if any, danger Richard Langworth poses to my sister. And to Julian.*

17

Devlin fired. The small white paper target fifteen feet distant burst into pieces.

"Good shot," Julian said, raised his own pistol, and fired. The paper square beside the first one exploded.

As he picked up his second pistol and fired it at the third square, Devlin said, "I saw Sophie," and missed. He frowned, set the pistol down, turned to Julian. "It draws dreadfully to the left. You win, Julian, since I missed that last one. Sophie told me the other Radcliffe sister has come to London to visit—her aunt Leah. I must say she sounded rather ambiguous about it."

"What do you mean 'ambiguous'?" Julian seated himself in front of a table that smelled of oil, waved off the attendant, and began to clean his pistol himself.

"Her name is Leah Cosgrove, Lady Merrick, widow of a naval captain, a baron, who drowned some years ago. I fancy if I knew her better, Sophie would have relieved her bile and called the woman a bitch. She said Aunt Leah was sharp with Roxanne, insulting her, really, and she didn't like it, and what did I think?"

"What did you say?"

"I said I would meet the woman and then tell her."

Julian laughed. "As you know, my mother, who has never minced matters, called her an ill-intentioned harpy. She told me about her visit with them. And believe me, Dev, that's not the worst of it."

Devlin said only, "Yes, I know. Richard Langworth is in the picture, evidently the *close* friend of Lady Merrick."

Julian nodded. "I do not know how it came about, but I am convinced it isn't a random coincidence. I believe Richard somehow discovered my mother wanted an alliance between Sophie and me. I don't know how he found out, but I will discover it."

Devlin closed his two pistols in a very old mahogany case. "Do you know, I think it's time you put a bullet in him, Julian—cleverly, of course, since you don't want to be forced to leave England."

"I shall consider it."

"Good. Now I'm off to see Corrie Sherbrooke. I want to see if she's still vomiting in the chamber pots."

As for Julian, he worked with Pennyworth until his eyes nearly crossed, worried more about the *Blue Star,* and took himself off to speak to a half dozen bullyboys Harlan had told him knew everything that happened at the docks.

He was walking toward his house when he simply felt the other man's presence. He felt his small derringer solid and loaded in his vest pocket. He slowly turned. "Richard."

"Three years have passed since you left England after Lily's funeral. Indeed, you left so quickly I didn't have time to kill you. Why did you come back? Did you possibly believe that all would be forgiven? Did you think I would forget what you did? Forget you destroyed my family?"

Julian said, his voice utterly emotionless, "I have known you and your family all my life. We grew up together. I loved Lily, you knew I loved her, you were pleased when we married. How could you ever believe I would harm a hair on her head, much less kill her, even if there was this supposed lover in the picture?"

Richard stared at him, rage narrowing his dark eyes. "You ran like the puling coward that you are."

Julian shrugged. "I ran believing I could somehow outrun my grief. But do you know, there is no place to hide from a desolation that is burrowed in the deepest part of you? Time has faded her face, the way she looked in death, but the pain is still deep. I never knew the pain of loss before, so I do not know if the pain will ever go away."

"It is your guilt that keeps it fresh, but the pain of loss, of anger at the injustice, is mine and my father's and my sister's. But you know that. You still will not admit your guilt to me, will you? There is none near to hear you, so why not?"

"I did not kill Lily."

"There was no one else, no lover lurking about. Do you believe she killed herself?"

Julian shook his head. He simply couldn't bear to think Lily could have shot herself.

"Such a lovely dark night it was at Saint Osyth."

"So," Julian said slowly, "it was you watching me and my men bring in our goods." Thank God he hadn't allowed Devlin to come with him. "I finally realized it must have been you."

"I only wish I'd known where you were going. I could have brought a dozen excisemen with me. At least now your amusement is over. You dare not risk using that cove near Saint Osyth again. If you do, I might be waiting for you."

"Once upon a time you and I went smuggling together, Richard."

"A lifetime ago. Have you heard of your ship?"

Julian said slowly, "What do you know of the *Blue Star*?"

"All know she is weeks late. Out of Constantinople, I'm told." Richard gave him a sneer, nodded, and left him, whistling.

Julian realized in that moment that Richard had planted a man on his ship, and that man had done something. He took a dozen fast steps, grabbed Richard's arm, and spun him around. He grabbed his collar and hauled him close, saw the shaving nick on his chin, the coldness in his dark eyes. "You will tell me what you have to do with my ship being late."

Julian felt the muzzle of a pistol pressing into his belly.

"That's right, Julian, if you do not release me this instant, I will blow your guts out your back."

Slowly, Julian released him and stepped back. "You obviously want to tell me, or you wouldn't have mentioned it. What have you done?"

Richard looked at him dispassionately. "I hear your mother wants you to marry Sophie Wilkie. She's a lovely little pullet, but nothing like Lily. Lily was a goddess. She didn't deserve to have you as her husband.

"Nothing to say? I heard Sophie Wilkie giggle at something Devlin Monroe said to her. She sounded happy, bless her infant's heart. She's an innocent. She doesn't have any idea what you are, does she? Yet you will draw her in, and she will end up dead."

"What do you know about the *Blue Star*?"

"Ah, I see, you're afraid I may try to attach little Sophie myself. I could, you know. What would you do then, Julian?"

Julian suddenly saw Sophie naked, Richard covering her. He said easily, "I would kill you."

"And risk being hung? My father would see to it, you know. He is not without influence, and he hates you as much as I do. He now believes you murdered Lily."

"Richard, look at me. Do you remember the first time we got drunk? It was just the two of us, laughing our heads off, then puking up your father's brandy. We sailed together on *Désirée*. We hunted together. We went to Oxford together. How can you believe me capable of killing anyone, much less someone I knew and loved all my life?"

"You are a liar, Julian. Someone saw you. No, I will not tell you who, that would sign a death warrant, wouldn't it?"

"Then why isn't Bow Street hauling me off to Newgate?"

Richard said, "I have all the proof I need."

"I see, Bow Street wouldn't believe this person, would they? Tell me, Richard, what is this proof?"

Richard leaned close, his breath hot on Julian's face. "I will make you pay. Soon you will know and understand the pain that is now woven into my life, a pain that invades my dreams."

Julian managed to grab Richard's wrist before he pulled the trigger. When the gun fired, the shot went wide. There was only one bullet in the derringer. Julian pulled Richard close again. "Listen to me, I loved her, no one else, and she loved me."

The familiar sneer marred Richard's mouth. "Time grows close now, don't forget."

Julian felt his blood run cold. "Stay away from Sophie Wilkie and Roxanne Radcliffe. Stay away from Devlin Monroe. This is between us, no one else, just us."

Richard slowly raised his pistol, leveled it right between Julian's eyes. "This derringer holds two bullets, but I shouldn't want to hang or be deported, either. Soon, Julian." He turned away, whistling again, a Navy ditty, popular on Julian's ships, actually written by Amos Toft, first mate aboard the *Blue Star*.

Julian's heart pounded hard and fast. He called out, "Stay away from Sophie's aunt Leah. Surely she cannot know what you are about."

Richard turned slowly. "That's right, Leah is Sophie Wilkie's aunt, isn't she? Fancy that. It is indeed a small world, isn't it?"

"You knew exactly who she was, and that is why you attached her."

"But how could I have known that?" He laughed. "Leah is known as the most beautiful Radcliffe sister, at least that is what she told me. Mayhap she is more beautiful than Roxanne Radcliffe. What do you think?"

"I have not yet met her."

"I believe I find Leah quite fascinating. The stories she tells me, so many of them, about her sisters and their silliness, their never-ending ill will and spite toward her—the beautiful middle sister. The only time she shuts her mouth is when she is moaning. And that is lovely, I assure you."

"You set yourself out to meet her because you knew who she was. But I wonder, how did you find out about my mother's scheme?"

"I haven't the faintest idea what you're talking about, Julian. Will you be at the Caulcott musicale this evening? You will be able to meet the most beautiful Radcliffe sister. Do you know she looks like an angel, all pale blond hair, blue eyes the color of a summer sky? Thankfully she was not cursed with the red hair of her sister—it is vulgar, don't you think?"

"Her hair is the color of the sunset over the Aegean Sea."

"So the wind blows that way, does it? And not toward little Sophie Wilkie? How very disappointed your dear mother must be."

Julian said not another word, forced himself to walk away, his own pistol still in his pocket. He wanted to shoot Richard right between the eyes. He was the better shot, at least he was once upon a time. It all seemed so long ago as to be a different lifetime.

What are you planning, Richard? To hurt Sophie? Roxanne? So that I will be hurt as you were?

There appeared to be no hope for it. The last thing Julian wanted to do was go to a musicale with twin tenors from Milan, even though his mother had begged him to attend with her as her escort. He would rather face a Spanish firing squad. But now he had no choice at all.

Did Richard's derringer really hold two bullets?

⇒ *18* ⇐

Corinne lightly tapped her Spanish fan on her son's arm, careful of the delicate spans, since he had sent it to her the previous Christmas. "You are not being at all obliging, Julian. There is Sophie, and she looks ever so lovely, doesn't she? All that glorious hair, and her blue eyes, I am reminded of spring when I see her eyes. Yes, a fresh spring day with the heavens practically glowing."

"So it isn't raining?"

She tapped him again, a bit harder this time. "Your jest is on the thin side, dearest. I really believe you should save her from her Leah, not a pleasant woman, too much spite and venom. Bethanne told me all about her, but so gently—you know how she was—but I knew what she was really not saying. I'm sure Leah made poor Roxanne's life a misery whenever she could. I remember Bethanne said once Leah always seemed eager to tear down, never to build up.

"You have five minutes before we are treated to the Milanese twin tenors. Have you met them? Lady Caulcott marched them out a while ago, showing them off to her guests. They speak no English, so all they do is bow when one speaks to them. Would you look at that, there's Richard Langworth fast approaching Leah and Sophie. I don't like this, Julian."

Julian didn't like it, either. He patted his mother's hand and managed to reach the women at nearly the same time Richard Langworth did.

"Sophie," he said, giving her a bow. "Perhaps you would care to have a glass of the wicked champagne punch? To fortify yourself for what is to come?"

She grinned. "I should prefer champagne, but I see no bubbles in my future. First, Julian, I would like you to meet Roxanne's sister, my aunt Leah, Lady Merrick. This is Lord Julian Monroe, Lady Merrick. Ah, and Mr. Langworth."

If Richard noted the sudden coldness in Sophie's voice, he gave no sign. He watched Leah extend a graceful hand to Julian, watched him bend over her wrist but not kiss it. He watched Sophie Wilkie place her hand on Julian's arm, to draw him away. Since he wasn't blind, Richard also saw the banked threat in Julian's eyes.

He smiled. "My dear," he said to Leah, "shall we take a stroll around the room before we are bolted to our seats for the musicale?"

She dimpled up at him. "I am so pleased you are here, Richard. I was beginning to wonder—"

"The moment I received your note, Leah, I changed my plans for the evening. You look delightful. Come."

Sophie watched the two of them walk toward the huge buffet table at the far end of the large ballroom, weaving their way gracefully through the crowds of black-coated gentlemen and rainbow-gowned ladies.

"He seems so charming," Sophie said. "Not showing on the outside what boils inside him." *Why does he believe you murdered his sister?* But she said nothing.

Neither did Julian.

"You came to rescue me?"

"Consider yourself rescued. Since there is no champagne, would you like me to take you to Roxanne? She is speaking to a portly gentleman who is, I believe, a longtime friend of her father's."

"Let us stroll for a bit, if you don't mind. I wish to consult my wise uncle."

"I am at your service. Something bothers you, Sophie?"

She placed her hand on his arm again and drew close. "I'm thinking perhaps I can mask my face, lure my aunt Leah onto the balcony, tap her on the shoulder, and when she turns, smack my fist to her jaw, topple her over into the bushes. What do you think?"

"That could work, since the balcony railing isn't all that high. She is so very dreadful?"

"This evening, before we left, she told Roxanne to her face that she had aged, that Leah now looked like the younger sister. Then she mentioned that yellow wasn't the best color for her, as it made her look *sallow*. Can you imagine?"

"No, yellow doesn't make her look sallow at all, but I have seen a certain shade of blue she wears that does. What did Roxanne have to say to that?"

"Roxanne laughed. She said perhaps Leah could lend her one of her own beautiful gowns and then she would look just the thing."

"That was well done of her," he said.

"Roxanne said she'd been watching how I turned Leah's insults back to her with a smile and agreement, thus spiking her guns." Sophie sighed. "However, this time it didn't work out. Leah said since Roxanne had vulgar red hair, wearing any of her stylish gowns would only make her look more slovenly. Roxanne laughed again, even though I saw her hands fisted at her sides. She acts like she doesn't care, but I know she does. Leah is not happy, Roxanne tells me, to excuse her, I suppose. Evidently, she never has been happy, even when she was a child. When I asked her what in heaven's name Leah had to be unhappy about—then and now—Roxanne couldn't think of a single thing. I think Leah was born mean.

"And now she is cooing over Richard Langworth. I really want to cosh her, Julian. Is the railing really low enough so I can heft her over it?"

"It is, my child, but your kindly wise uncle fears you must forgo retribution, as tasty as it might sound."

"I am tall. I could come up behind her; she might believe she'd been smacked by a man, her lovely Richard Langworth, for example. Then I would run away, quickly."

"It is Roxanne's decision how to deal with her sister." He placed his finger on her mouth. "If you like, I will speak to Roxanne, give her my wise counsel."

Sophie sighed. "I wonder what Roxanne would say to you if you did offer her counsel?"

"Surely she would be excessively grateful." He paused for a moment, tapped his fingertips to his chin. "Do you know, Sophie, I have changed my mind. Maybe you should sneak up behind her."

"I might," Sophie said, leaned up and kissed his cheek, patted his arm, and danced away.

"Are you Lord Julian Monroe, sir?"

He turned to face James Sherbrooke. So he'd heard him speaking and recognized his voice, had he? Well, Julian had wondered when this would happen. He remembered so clearly the night last fall at Saint Osyth when he'd smuggled in tea and brandy from France, the only time he'd come back to England in three years. And it had been only for a fortnight, staying with Harlan in his rooms on Potwin Street, because he hadn't wanted anyone to know he was here, except for the gentlemen in the ministry who'd asked him to play diplomat for England to Rome, and, naturally, he had.

"Yes, I am." He said nothing more, simply waited for James Sherbrooke to introduce himself and his wife.

Julian bowed to James but made no attempt to kiss Corrie's wrist, a good thing, since she kept her hands at her sides. She said, "You are Devlin's uncle, sir, are you not?"

"Yes, Lady Hammersmith, I am his ancient graybeard uncle."

She tried to look fierce and condemning but couldn't manage it. He smiled down at this lovely young lady, seeing the tangle-haired ragamuffin on that wild night long ago. He remembered her knee against his neck. A heroine, she was, that was what Devlin had told him. More courage than brains, Devlin had added. Could he believe she'd actually ridden a horse into a cottage, a pitchfork in her hand, to rescue James?

No, Julian would never have believed such a tale until she'd had her knee pressed hard against his own throat.

Both husband and wife were studying his face. Trying to make certain he was indeed the smuggler? He realized they weren't quite certain what to say to him now that the evil villain was standing two feet in front of them.

He said easily, "I must say the two of you look much better than the last time I saw you—both of you were filthy, your clothes torn, nearly drowned in that deluge. I see you are married and appear quite content with each other, my felicitations to you both." And he gave them a charming smile. He touched his fingers to his throat. "A sharp knee you have, my lady."

They stared at him. Obviously they'd never expected him to simply spit it right out. Corrie said finally, "We thought we recognized your voice, but it's difficult to believe that you— Lord Julian Monroe—are that wretched smuggler who would have dragged us to Plymouth if we hadn't bested you. Of course, we did just that, didn't we?" And up went her chin.

Julian laughed. "Yes, I am the wretched smuggler who couldn't take the chance you'd report me to the excisemen. Smuggling has been a hobby I've enjoyed for many years."

"But you don't have many years!"

He grinned at Corrie. "I am tempted to say smuggling runs in the blood, but alas, my sire died when I was a mere babe, so I do not know if he ever indulged." There was no need to tell them soldiers in Wellington's army had taught him all about the joys of smuggling. "Now, I would ask that the two of you contrive to forget it."

Corrie was outraged. "*Forget it?* Forget that you would have *kidnapped* us? Forget that you might have *shot* us dead if you'd wished to, or had your gnarly men *beat* us into the ground?"

James couldn't help it, he laughed. He laughed even more at her red-faced outrage. Corrie shook her fist in his face and sputtered. She looked from Julian to her husband, and her sputter turned into a laugh. Soon all three of them were laughing like the best of friends. Guests began turning to look at them.

When Julian caught his breath, he said to James, "I understand you are an astronomer, that you presented a paper to the Royal Astronomical Society on what you called the silver cascade phenomena on Titan. A fascinating description you gave, so my friend told me, since he knows I have always been interested in Saturn's moons—"

Corrie couldn't believe it when James leaned close to this man who'd held them at gunpoint, this man who'd planned to kidnap them, and now look at him—hooked like a channel bass. She said loudly, "I understand your mama wants you to marry Sophie Wilkie."

Julian said, "Alas, my nuptials to Sophie are not meant to be. I am far too old for her. My mama will survive her disappointment."

Corrie said, "James is seven years older than I. Do you believe him too old for me?"

"Seven years is, I should say, the perfect age difference. However, I am twelve years Sophie's senior."

Corrie said, "Isn't seven years about the age difference between you and Roxanne Radcliffe, Sophie's aunt? Perhaps your mama should pursue her for you instead."

"There are only five years between Roxanne and me—not enough, I fancy, to give me any sort of advantage in the marital ring."

"You do have ready answers, don't you, sir? I imagine many would believe your smart replies quite amusing. Perhaps, as Devlin's uncle, you can answer me this. Is Devlin really a vampire?"

He leaned close and said into her lovely little ear with its pearl drop earring, "He carries my blood and my lineage. My father, my mother has told me, hated the sunlight, avoided it at all costs. I shall let you draw your own conclusions, my lady," and then Julian left them, humming, until he heard one of the Milanese tenors clear his throat. The evening's torture was about to begin. He saw Roxanne walking toward Sophie, his mother in tow, and moved to join them. He looked back once to see James and Corrie Sherbrooke looking after him. He didn't believe they would inform on him at Bow Street.

19

Rexford Square

Julian refolded the letter, stared off at nothing in particular, and began tapping his fingers on his desktop. This was unexpected. What the devil should he do?

He opened the letter and read yet again:

> *Julian, it would relieve me greatly were you to visit me here at Hardcross Manor. In short, I wish to end the antipathy between us. I bear you no more ill will. If you wish to escort your mother, I should be pleased. Perhaps this upcoming Saturday would be convenient?*
>
> Your obedient servant,
> Rupert Langworth,
> Baron Purley

Julian sent the letter and a note to his mother, and took himself off to the stables to ride Cannon. He joined up with military friends who'd befriended him at Waterloo.

Lord Alfred Ponsonby, an older gentleman with a wealth

of gray frizzled hair and thick whiskers, had jerked him up by his collar at Waterloo to avoid an onrushing French soldier, his bayonet at the ready. He looked him up and down. "Fine horseflesh, my lad."

"Cannon could beat that nag you're riding, my lord."

"I'll grant you he could give it a good try." Lord Alfred turned to the other three gentlemen. "I remember the grand old man himself give Julian that name; he said Julian here was so fast he looked shot from a cannon—one that worked and didn't fall limp on the ground. And now you have transferred your name to your horse."

Everyone laughed.

Major Ramey said, "Our poor Iron Duke—beset on all sides. I fear the end is in sight for him, with the Whigs and Earl Grey waiting in the wings, but that is politics, something I abhor. When I saw Arthur at the ministry last week, he told me he'd heard you'd finally returned to England."

"The speed of gossip astounds me. I returned from Italy only a month ago. Since Lord Arthur is still the leader of England and has endless demands, I doubt not that the only time he would have free to see the likes of me is in the water closet."

❖⟾ ⟾❖

H is heart was lighter when he returned to his town house on Rexford Square, a lovely Georgian bequeathed to him by his sire, a house he quite liked because, he freely admitted, his sister-in-law, Lorelei Monroe, very much resented Julian's owning the town house and not her own dear husband, who wasn't a nobody like Julian, but rather *the Duke*. Tavish, his butler, wasn't to be seen. He strolled into the drawing room to find Roxanne Radcliffe planted in the middle of a small sofa, her beautiful pale pink skirts fanned out around her, Harlan Whittaker seated on the edge of his chair opposite her, his hands on his knees, looking anxious and smitten, both at the same time. A fine-looking man was Harlan, Julian thought, not very tall but wiry and strong, his hair a copper color that shone in the sun. Harlan was only two years older than Julian. He realized he was seeing his man of business as one would see a man who could possibly have interest in the fairer sex. Julian prayed he never looked so pathetic when he looked at a lady.

Tavish appeared at his elbow, carrying a magnificent silver tray holding a teapot and a pile of cakes. Tavish had a magnificent head of dark hair, which he pomaded straight up to give him at least three more inches in height. He was a man Julian had known and trusted as long as he could remember. Tavish and Pouffer both had been mainstays in his life since he'd been a boy.

Tavish said, a dollop of worship in his deep voice, "As you see, my lord, we have a guest, a lovely, *tall* guest, a tall female sort of guest, unusual, to be sure, but quite invigorating to see. Ah, such a waste of inches, but I am forced to admit that she does wear all those lovely inches well, don't you think, my lord?"

Julian shot a look at Roxanne, who was returning his look, hers quite limpid. "She does well with inches, yes, Tavish. On the other hand, I daresay if she didn't do well with her excessive inches, it wouldn't make much difference." He said to Harlan, "I see you have made Miss Radcliffe's acquaintance."

Talk about enthusiasm, Harlan overflowed with it. "I have indeed, Julian. She has been telling me about growing up in Yorkshire, walking for hours on desolate moors, listening to ravens caw to each other from bare oak tree branches, black silhouettes in the distance, and watching storm clouds draw nearer and nearer."

"You are a poet, sir," Roxanne said, laughing. "I am not so fluent as you. But it was a wonderful childhood, that is true enough. Hello, Julian. May I serve you tea?"

"A dollop of milk, Roxanne, thank you. Harlan, are you here to give me news of the *Blue Star*?"

"I fear not, Julian. There is still no word. I am here to deliver papers concerning the new ship you are considering adding to your fleet. I made inquiries of Lord—" He shot a quick look at Roxanne. "Well, names are not important, are they?"

"No, not in this instance," Julian said.

Roxanne handed Julian his saucer, then poured tea for Harlan and herself. "Harlan tells me he has worked for you for a goodly number of years. I inquired how goodly, since neither of you are all that aged, and he tells me you and he met in a tavern at the docks." She paused, smiled toward Harlan.

Harlan cleared his throat. "I hadn't yet told her you were there to find a miscreant who had word about valuable items stolen from one of your cargoes."

Julian nodded. "That ended satisfactorily, with your assistance." He said to Roxanne, "Harlan and I have been together for six years." Julian toasted Harlan with his teacup. "A very profitable association," he added.

"Shall I place the documents in your estate room?"

"Yes, thank you, Harlan." *Pick your tongue off the floor.* "Say good-bye to Miss Radcliffe now."

"An exquisite pleasure, Miss Radcliffe."

Roxanne inclined her head, a small smile played over her mouth. The witch was fully aware Harlan was ready to slaver on her slippers.

"I will see you tomorrow. Now, I have need to speak with Miss Radcliffe."

Harlan gave Roxanne one final pitiful look before he left the drawing room. Julian said, "Do you think it was your talk of walking the desolate moors or the caw of the ravens that did him in?"

Roxanne grinned. "Perhaps it was talk of my two pugs, Popper and Perky, who were always trying to relieve themselves on my father's left trouser leg. When I made civil inquiries after his family, and he told me he'd been cursed with six sisters, which made me pat his hand in commiseration, an image of Leah duplicated six times over in my brain." She shuddered.

Julian sat down. "Harlan was the only boy in his family. His parents and all six sisters treated him like a prince. I daresay if one of his sisters had insulted him like Leah does you, she would have been tossed out the window by her siblings."

Tavish set a platter of cakes in front of them, his rooster tail of hair standing tall and proud.

Julian waited until he'd bowed himself out. "For Christmas each year, I present Tavish with a special pot of hair pomade that comes from Naples. It shines, does it not?"

"He is a vision."

After they each selected a tart from the heaping platter, Julian said, "Are you without sense? You should not be here alone, Roxanne."

"Oh? And why is that, my lord? Must I remind you that I am twenty-seven years old, not a tender young morsel like Sophie? I assure you I could visit any number of questionable places and it not be remarked upon. Let me add that since you are the son of a duke, you cannot be considered a bad influence or dangerous to my virtue. You well may be, but it is not immediately apparent."

"Why are you here?"

She grinned like a bandit. "Your mama has begged Sophie and me to accompany the two of you to Hardcross Manor, the home of Baron Purley, the father of the slimy Richard Langworth."

Even after all these years, Julian was still surprised at how quickly his mother moved. He began to tell Roxanne he wasn't at all certain he was even going. He paused, took another sip of his rich India tea, studied her over the rim of his cup, and said, "Why, yes, I think that is a marvelous idea. You and Sophie can enjoy the pleasures of the countryside—Hardcross Manor is close to Ravenscar, only three miles distant. Have you ever visited Cornwall?"

"No, but I have heard the southern coast is vastly different from the northern, and there are very few miles between them."

He nodded. "Prepare to see palm trees along the drive to Ravenscar. I believe you will like my home, Roxanne, it is something of a castle but not really. It was quite barren, but my mother has planted greenery to soften the landscape. There are also rolling green hills, scores of barrows—"

She sat forward, all attention. "Barrows? Do you believe them burial mounds from long ago?"

"Yes, I do."

"Your mother told Sophie about Ravenscar. We are both anxious to see it, and the barrows, of course."

"Good. You could spend hours poking about whilst I—"

After a moment, she said, "Yes? Whilst you have it out with slimy Richard, who believes you murdered your wife, and his sister. Will you tell me why he is so certain you are guilty of such a horrible deed?"

He studied her for a moment. "Do you not believe I could be guilty of murder?"

She waved that away. "No, not for a moment. You see, Julian, I have come to know you. You are an honorable man, a man who once he makes a promise would never break it. You would not murder anyone, particularly your own wife."

She'd known him for weeks and believed it impossible for him to kill another person? Because he was honorable? A man who kept his promises? He felt humbled and grateful. And yet Richard, whom he'd known all his life, believed him guilty to the point he wanted him dead? Who was the damned witness he claimed knew Julian had killed Lily? He said finally, "It makes no sense for you to be completely ignorant when you will come with us to Hardcross Manor." He paused for a moment, then said, "I would assume Baron Purley knew my father, but he never spoke of him to me that I remember. I suppose I never asked, since my father was an old man when I was born.

"I spent my boyhood years in and out of Hardcross Manor, a part of the family, really. Richard and I were inseparable, then Lily grew up and I saw her with new eyes, and so we married. Richard was my best man; Vicky was her flower girl. Six months," he added, "we had only six months before she was shot, before she died." He stopped, simply couldn't bring himself to tell how he'd run into the garden to see Lily dead, blood covering her chest, how that warm sunny day had irrevocably changed all their lives. He said only, "Someone killed her or she shot herself. Neither makes sense to me, but it is either one or the other.

"I admit I'm surprised the baron wishes to make amends, to end the antipathy between us; that is what he wrote."

Roxanne felt tears burn her eyes. What had really happened? Why would a newly married young woman kill herself? Who would kill her? It must drive him mad to not know what happened. She cleared her throat. "Your mother is very surprised as well. She believes it is now obvious the baron realizes he was wrong about you, and wishes to apologize to you. Do you think this is true?"

"I don't know. Richard gave me the opposite impression. We will see."

"Well, I think it a fine idea to see what he has to say. I would like to see Richard Langworth's face when he hears of this. I wonder, do you think he will be at Hardcross Manor as well? Do you think his father consulted him? Well, no matter. How many days does it require to get to Cornwall?"

"Three days."

"We will leave on Wednesday?"

When he walked her to the front door some ten minutes later, Roxanne paused, laid her hand lightly on his arm. "Julian, this is an awful burden for you to carry, both the grief for your wife's death and Richard Langworth's belief you were responsible. I am very sorry for both." And she wondered how he stood it, the not knowing what had happened that terrible day.

He remained standing on the doorstep, watching until her carriage disappeared from Rexford Square.

He received word that afternoon that the *Blue Star,* six weeks late, had arrived in Plymouth. He was on his way to Plymouth within the hour, Cannon running like the wind.

20

Lemington Square

Corinne pulled off her lovely York tan gloves. "I know only that the *Blue Star* at last arrived in Plymouth, and my son was gone within the hour on that beast of his. We are to leave tomorrow, yet I have heard nothing at all."

Roxanne looked up from her sewing. "If Julian said we will leave tomorrow, then he will be back, ma'am. You'll see."

"But there might be trouble. It might require a lot of time for him—ah, I shall pull off my bonnet and stomp it. No, everything will be all right. Julian knows what he's about." But the dowager duchess continued her pacing, her lovely pale blue skirts sweeping over the Aubusson carpet. "His father was the same way, at least I think perhaps he was. It has been so very long, and I knew him for only a year and a half, but I do remember he was stubborn as a stoat, and if one continued to question him, he became silent as a rock. I was breeding, right away, and I do remember wanting to clout him upon occasion."

Sophie laughed, couldn't help herself. "I agree with Roxanne, ma'am. Julian will be here. I am quite interested in meeting Richard Langworth's father and sister. So he wishes to end the ill feeling? I wonder, does this end it for his son as well?"

"We will see."

The three ladies looked up to see Julian standing in the drawing-room doorway, Mint hovering at his elbow.

His mother rushed to him, pulled him to her, then pushed him away. "What about the *Blue Star*, Julian?"

He nodded to Sophie and Roxanne, who were standing next to each other, the light flooding through the bow windows, showing him for the first time the resemblance between aunt and niece—the same tilt of the head, the same winging brows.

"My ship was run aground in a storm off the coast of southern Spain. My captain sent me messages, but none got through. Repairs required nearly a month. All is well."

"Thank goodness for that," Roxanne said. "None of your men were hurt in the storm?"

He shook his head. "I was afraid of sabotage, but it was not."

"So you are now richer than Croesus," his fond mama said.

"It is close," Julian agreed, a twinkle in his eye. He smiled down at her. "I brought you a present, Mama."

It was in that instant that every person in the room fell in love with him, including Mint.

He presented Corinne with a two-foot-long rope of pearls, earrings, and a bracelet. They were fit for a princess, Mint said reverently, watching the pearls shimmer through Corinne's fingers.

"Actually, they did belong to a princess," Julian said, "a real princess named Labina Falusi. The family has fallen on hard times. I believe they wanted me to marry the princess, but I decided I preferred the pearls. My first mate, Mr. Toft, kept them with him throughout the entire voyage, since I was never sure when bandits might strike."

"And did bandits try to rob you, Julian?" Sophie asked.

He nodded. "Outside of Naples. Fortunately, they were incompetent."

"Thank goodness for that," Corinne said, sliding the pearls through her fingers.

He watched his mother loop the pearls three times around her neck, then fasten on the earrings and the bracelet. He watched her rush to the large mirror over the fireplace and stare at herself.

"You look lovely, Mama." And he saw in that moment what his father had seen when she was eighteen years old.

Corinne rushed back to him and hugged him tightly. "I love you, Julian. You drive me to madness, but never forget I love you. The pearls, they are amazing. Do you really like them?" She turned this way and that, and the pearls shimmered and glowed.

"They—you—are magnificent."

Roxanne, Sophie, and Mint admired the pearls and loved him even more when Julian asked his mother to waltz. Roxanne rushed to the piano. Sophie sat on the sofa, watching Julian and his mama in her beautiful pearls sweeping gracefully around the drawing room.

When Roxanne stopped playing, it was to see Mrs. Eldridge and three maids crowded behind Mint in the drawing-room doorway, smiling from ear to ear.

"Excuse us, Miss Roxanne, but the lovely music, all the laughter, ah, t'were lovely," said Mrs. Eldridge, her hands over her heart. "A man waltzing with his mama, 'tis a fine thing to see."

Mint said, "I will bring champagne to celebrate the safe arrival of your ship, my lord."

They drank champagne while Julian answered questions. He finally raised his hands. "That is enough. Really, all is well. I'm not certain, though, that all of you should accompany me to Hardcross Manor. I'm not certain it is reconciliation the baron seeks. I cannot believe Richard has suddenly changed his mind, particularly since he told me he had proof, so—"

Corinne interrupted him smoothly. "We have discussed it, Julian. You will consider us your reinforcements. We will not allow Baron Purley to stick a stiletto in your back. Also, Roxanne and Sophie wish to visit Ravenscar."

Still, he didn't like it. But he thought about Roxanne and Sophie alone here in London. With Richard Langworth. He gave it up. "Very well. We will leave very early tomorrow. It will require three days. We will take two carriages."

⟶⟶ ⟵⟵

On a dismal very early Wednesday morning, thick fog covering the ground, two carriages left Lemington Square.

The sun was setting on the third day when the carriages pulled to a halt in front of Hardcross Manor, sprawled atop a small rise amid rolling hills and thick maple and oak woodlands six miles east of Saint Austell, and only three miles from Ravenscar. The grounds surrounding the house were vast, covered with freshly scythed grass, smooth and green. Neat rows of flowers were beginning to burst into bloom, and trellised rosebushes stretched themselves to the sky. It was a lovely property, Julian had always thought. He realized he'd missed Hardcross, missed the baron, a man he'd known his entire life, a man he'd always admired, until—he felt the rip of remembered pain, closed it down. The past was done and over, only pain and hatred remained. And endless regrets, and questions with no answers.

He also wished they were staying at Ravenscar, but soon, he thought, soon, they would leave Hardcross Manor.

"It reminds me of the gardens at Allegra Hall," Sophie said, and breathed in deeply as she stepped to the graveled drive. "Roxanne is quite the gardener. Flowers and plants adore her."

"It hasn't changed," Corinne said, and then she added, "I wonder what Rupert—"

Roxanne waited for her to continue, but she didn't.

"I don't know," she said slowly, "but something isn't right. That letter of his, it leaves too much out, don't you think? There was only a hint that he might be nearing death, but I don't know—"

"We will see soon enough if he is sincere."

Sophie said, "Something is wrong, Julian."

He frowned but found his step was quicker as he walked up the wide steps to the front portico.

21

Time is nature's way of keeping everything
from happening at once.
—WOODY ALLEN

Julian didn't know why he was surprised, but he was.
Richard Langworth stood in the now open front door, a
fine sneer on his mouth. So this was the something Sophie
felt was wrong. She'd somehow sensed that Richard was
here. Well, his presence would certainly make things more
interesting.

"So you brought all your ladies," Richard said, sneer in
full bloom. "Your timing, as always, Julian, is impressive.
My father is anxious to see you. Since he wrote me the same
time he wrote you, I decided it best that I come." He stepped
back, saw the three ladies, two maids, and Julian's valet,
Pliny, and whistled.

Julian stepped back, allowing the ladies to precede him
into the long, narrow entrance hall.

The butler, Tegan, tall, straight, and more impressive
than King William on a good day, cleared his throat. "His
lordship instructed me to show you to the library immediately, Lord Julian. Perhaps the ladies would care to refresh
themselves in the drawing room?"

"I would like to be shown to my room," Corinne said.

"Forgive me, your grace, but dinner will be served in precisely"—he consulted his watch—"thirteen minutes. As you know, his lordship has a fondness for punctuality."

"It is more than mere fondness, Tegan, it is an obsession with him," Richard said. "However, if the ladies wish to refresh themselves, I am certain Julian can keep my father occupied."

Tegan gave a short bow to Richard, gave a longer look to Julian, and escorted both him and Richard to the library, a grim, dark room Baron Purley had inhabited and loved for forty years, a room that had, as a child, made Julian uneasy—too many dark corners where an enemy could hide.

He saw Rupert Langworth, Baron Purley, closer to seventy than sixty, seated in his favorite chair, heavy and dark with elaborate carved arms, behind a massive mahogany desk of equal years. He slowly rose. He never looked away from Julian as he said, "Richard, leave us."

Richard said, "I hope you know what you're doing." At his father's nod, Richard left the library, closing the door behind him.

"Come here, Julian, I wish to see you. It has been three years."

Rupert Langworth looked hale and hearty, as fit as Julian, his full head of white hair as thick as Julian's.

"I suppose I was expecting to see you wheezing in your deathbed, sir, bargaining with God to bring you to Him rather than to the Devil, issuing orders on what foods would be served at your funeral breakfast."

"I didn't wish to lay it on with a trowel, but I thought the veriest hint I might be dying and wanted to close my accounts was the only way I could think of getting you here, Julian."

"I believe a straightforward invitation would have sufficed. I did not come alone. My mother is with me, as well as her two protégées, Roxanne Radcliffe and Sophie Wilkie.

I had not expected to see Richard here. Are we to have a house party, sir?"

"No, it is more a funeral. We are to bury the hatchet."

"In my head?"

"No." Rupert Langworth raised a pistol and fired.

⊷ *22* ⊶

Julian's breath whooshed out as the bullet slammed into a bookshelf three feet to his left. He didn't move, merely stared at the baron.

"You see how easy it would be to kill you and end poor Richard's obsession with you."

His heart was still beating a mad tattoo. "That is true, sir, you could, but you would also doubtless hang."

"For taking revenge on the man who murdered my daughter? I don't believe a jury of my peers would find me guilty." Rupert wiped his handkerchief over the pistol, laid it carefully back into the top desk drawer, closed the drawer.

"I am tired of repeating myself, sir. You know very well I did not shoot Lily, that I would shoot myself first."

The baron said, "It doesn't surprise me that you have ice water in your veins. Your father was the same way. You couldn't frighten him, couldn't make him tremble or quake, no matter what you said, no matter what you threatened. You never knew your father—a pity, really, for you would have admired him greatly. But he was an old man when your mother became pregnant with you. When I was a young man, he was a god to me, strong and powerful, ruling everything and everyone in his sight. He spent more time at Ravenscar than he did at his home, Mount Burney. He always loved it, the way it hunkered out over the water, the way its very presence was a threat to any enemy. He once said, I remember, that if he were a house, he would be Ravenscar—solid and enduring, and fine-looking, of course."

Julian had never heard anything like this about his father, particularly from Baron Purley. His father—a foolish old man, he'd always thought him, even though his mother had never said anything of the sort to him. But Lorelei Monroe, his sister-in-law and the current Duchess of Brabante, had endlessly criticized the old duke, and he saw now her words had burrowed deep inside him, and he'd believed her. He felt something inside him move. He swallowed. He said slowly, "You said my father was powerful? Strong?"

Rupert nodded. "His physical strength, it was legend, but he also had a brain and speech that could mesmerize.

"His heir, your estimable half brother Constantine, has never seemed to have the same sense of knowing who he was and his place in the world. That sounds strange, I know, given Constantine manages his ducal estates with intelligence and fairness. No, you are more like your father than Constantine is—a foolish name, I heard your father say once, but it fit the lad. As for your name, he told me it was a right and just name for you. Do you know why he selected it for you?"

Julian shook his head.

"Julian—after Julius Caesar, an emperor over millions of souls, a man above all other men in his time, a man with vision and fortitude. He told me you wouldn't ever be a duke—you would be more. You would be a prince."

Julian knew none of this. He said, "It is disconcerting to hear myself called prince by all here in Cornwall."

"It doesn't matter. As I said, it was your father's commandment. All grew very used to calling you prince. It is what he wanted for you, and so it was. When the end was drawing near for him, he murmured, 'My son is the Prince of Ravenscar.' I see you did not know this. So your father never told your mother why he wished you to be called Prince."

"When I asked my mother if I was indeed a prince, she told me only that it was what my father called me, and all followed suit." He gave a twisted grin. "She said I was to accept it and not fret. Nothing more." He paused, shook his head. "After Julius Caesar—my father had visions of grandeur I will never attain."

"You are already making your mark in the modern world. Ah, your glorious mother. Your father took one look at your mother and fell tip over arse. He wanted her powerfully. Nothing Constantine said, nothing the duke's friends said, could make him change his mind. I believe he died a very content man. Your mother was so very young, innocent, and beautiful, maybe three pence to her family's name, but they were a rapacious lot, eager to sell her to the old man. Your father didn't care. What need had he of more money? He wanted your mother, paid her father a lot of money for her, married her, and told her family he never wished to see them again.

"When you were born, your father was happier than he'd been at Constantine's birth. As I said, you are very much like him. And like no other—you are the prince."

Julian said slowly, "You have known me all my life. Why have you never told me this before? You have never before spoken to me of my father—I believed him a foolish old man."

"Forgive me, I didn't know. Time passes so quickly and one forgets. I remember after your father died, your mother considered taking you, an infant, back to her family. Luckily, both her father and mother died of a virulent fever that struck their neighborhood. There were only cousins, none of whom she cared for, so she came to me for assistance, assistance I freely offered."

Julian said, "I asked her once about her family, but she said they were dead. But years passed, sir, yet you never said anything to me."

The baron shrugged. "One focuses on the present, on the people who must be dealt with, those who distract and confuse and create havoc. Things are different now."

"Tell me more about my father."

"It is a pity you never had the joy of knowing him, knowing how proud he would be of you. He was not only a man to admire, he was a man who saw people clearly, both men and women. Just as you do, Julian."

Julian's heart drummed slowly. He had no words, only feelings he'd thought wouldn't ever exist for him.

"I'll never forget one day I visited Ravenscar and was shown into your father's estate room. He stood in the middle of the room, rocking you in his arms, and the joy on his face moved me unutterably. 'Look at my boy, Rupert—is he not meant to do great things? He is the prince; he is my gift to the world.' His heart failed him two weeks later.

"I wish the animosity to be done with. To intimate I was nearing my just rewards seemed the only way to get you here after what happened three years ago. I have also come to realize that Richard's wound has festered, not healed."

"He wants to kill me or hurt those I care about."

"That does not surprise me. You left England, and he refused to see that you did not leave to escape your guilt, you left to escape your grief. Richard is not pleased that I invited you here to make peace, but I told him it was time he got on with things, to leave the past in the past, where it belongs."

"Will he listen? I must doubt it, for he is more stubborn than I am." He paused for a moment. "You know, your father was more stubborn than the two of us together."

Julian didn't know.

"And then, of course, there was Lily, but we will not speak of her now.

"Let us go in to dinner. My ribs are rubbing against my backbone. Also, I wish to meet Corinne's protégées, one of whom I hear you are to wed." He frowned, consulted his watch. "It is late."

"No wedding, sir."

The baron lifted a brow at this but said nothing more. As Julian preceded the baron out of the library, he turned. "I wish to know every single memory you have of my father."

Rupert said, "If you wish."

23

Dinner, Sophie thought later that night when she lay in bed next to a sleeping Roxanne, was a meal she would as soon forget. Richard had watched her closely, as if trying to see if there were any spots on her face. Then he watched Roxanne. He scared her to her toes. *Does he think Julian will wed one of us? And he wants to know where to focus his vengeance?*

There was a light knock on the door.

There was no answer. Slowly, the door opened. Sophie felt her heart drop to her feet.

"Who is there?"

"It is I, Sophie, Corinne. I could not sleep. I do not like my bedchamber, and so I came to beg a place in your bed. I asked Barbie to sleep in my bedchamber—a strange house, you know—but alas, I quickly discovered she snores. Oh, you and Roxanne are sleeping together? How did this come about?"

"I couldn't sleep, either. I am like you, uncomfortable in a strange house. The bed is very large. The three of us will fit nicely." Sophie lightly shoved Roxanne over to make room for the Dowager Duchess of Brabante. Sleeping next to a duchess, it boggled the mind. Her father had accused her of being too proud. Well, if he knew she shared her bed with a duchess, his eyes would surely goggle and he would change his opinion. Perhaps. Perhaps not.

When Corinne slipped in beside her, pulling the soft covers to her chin, she whispered, "Thank you. I tell you the truth, Sophie. I was lying there in that mammoth bed, all snugged in, listening to Barbie snore, when I heard something move near the windows. You know my chamber faces the front of the house, and there was a half-moon shining directly in, but I saw nothing. After I settled again, I swear to you I heard a rustling noise. I nearly choked dead with fear. Barbie never stirred, even when I bounded off the bed and thankfully remembered this was Roxanne's room."

Corinne moved closer and whispered, "I know someone was in my bedchamber, besides snoring Barbie. It wasn't my imagination, and it wasn't a dream, for I hadn't slept yet."

Not likely, Sophie thought, but whispered back, her voice soothing, "The three of us should be safe together, ma'am. It must be odd, being Baron Purley, knowing his son blames Julian for Lily's death. Do you think the baron still blames him?"

"I don't know, this evening he didn't seem to. However, Rupert was always shifty; one simply never knew what was behind his eyes. Rupert was what I called a worshipper, had been since he'd been only a boy. I was told he would have followed Julian's father about like a puppy if Maximilian had allowed it, even after Rupert became Baron Purley, even after he wedded and his wife birthed a son—namely, Richard.

"My husband believed Rupert was enamored of me, which is ridiculous, let me tell you. No, it was always Maximilian who drew Rupert to him, like that proverbial moth. He had no interest in me, no, indeed, Rupert did not care a fig about me, never did, still doesn't. But he wanted what was best for Maximilian's son, and so he helped me to get through the endless chores that surround one when a husband dies."

"I wondered why the duke spent more time at Ravenscar than at Mount Burney."

"Ravenscar, he told me once, was in the very marrow of his bones. It was deep in his heart and brain."

"Why do you think the baron was so drawn to the duke?"

"I don't know why Rupert loved my husband. Like a father? I don't know. It was so long ago, I was so young, and he was dead only a year and a half after I'd met him in London at my coming-out ball. It was given by my great-aunt, since my parents hadn't a sou. But with the dowry the duke gave them to marry me, they died happy, I can tell you that. Well, I suppose my cousins—their heirs—were even happier."

Sophie sighed in the darkness. She felt Roxanne warm and unmoving on her right, Corinne on her left. She realized she felt safe. She admitted it, she was afraid of Richard Langworth and the violence in his eyes, the sneer marring his mouth, and afraid of this house, where there were too many shadows. As for the baron, he'd been nothing but charming and kind to her and Roxanne. Was he sincere in his wish to end the strife? Sophie listened to the other women's steady breathing, and closed her eyes.

Roxanne rose straight up in bed and said in a chatty voice, "How I wish Devlin could have come with us. Mayhap he'll finish that dratted business his father asked him to deal with and come to us today. He would suck Richard's blood and the bounder would fall over dead, all white and empty." She fell back again, sound asleep.

Had someone been in Corinne's bedchamber? Sophie wondered. Should she tell Julian about it? She was on the point of crawling over Corinne to go to Julian's bedchamber, when she pictured Julian sleeping, sprawled on his back, not a stitch of clothing covering him. That brought a lovely hazy image to her mind, and she stilled, and wondered what it would be like if she—if she what? Leapt on top of him, kissed him silly, and then what? She would certainly like the answer to that question. She forced herself onto her back and stared up at the black ceiling for a good five minutes before she fell asleep.

Three bedchambers down the corridor, Julian dreamed he'd found his wife wildly kissing another man. He couldn't see the man's face in his dreams any more than he'd seen the man's face then, in the Hardcross gardens that horrendous day three years ago. Had there even been a man?

⇜ *24* ⇝

S ir, may I ask you something?"

Baron Purley looked up from his letter to see Sophie Wilkie standing in the library doorway. *Lovely,* he thought, and felt a brief stab of envy—for Julian? He smiled at her as he rose. "Come in, Miss Wilkie. It is quite early. Have you breakfasted yet?"

"Yes, my lord. Your cook has a fine way with baked eggs."

"It is her specialty. I trust you slept well?"

She thought of Corinne and Roxanne, both turned against her sometime during the night, and when she'd awakened, she was so stiff she creaked when she'd crawled over a still-sleeping Roxanne. "Perfectly, thank you."

"Please sit down, Miss Wilkie."

When he faced her across his desk, he said, "How may I help you?"

"I would like to know what you believed really happened the day Lily was killed."

His shirt collar was open, and she saw the pulse in his neck quicken. She waited, saying nothing more.

"I do not know you, Miss Wilkie," he said slowly. "Indeed,

I do not know what place you hold in Julian's life. My son tells me Corinne wishes him to marry you. Is this true?"

"Yes, it is true."

"Will you marry him?"

"He believes himself too old for me, sir, believes I must consider him in the way of being an older uncle in whom I should confide my girlish woes."

The baron gave a bark of laughter. So Richard had been right. "And have you? Confided your woes to him?"

"Not yet."

"Forgive me, but I can see Julian saying exactly that. Perhaps he is too old for you, though most would not agree. Mayhap he comes to that opinion because his father was so much older than his mother—more than fifty years between them. It renders him more sensitive than most men to the years that separate a husband and wife."

"He is not fifty years my senior."

"No, he most assuredly is not. So there is no question of marriage between the two of you, despite his mother's fondest wish?"

Sophie paused, shook her head. She sat forward, her hands clasped. "Sir—"

The baron sighed. "Forgive me, Miss Wilkie, but as I said in my letter to Julian, I wish to end the acrimony. Does my son? I do not know, but I will tell you truthfully, I doubt it. Richard seems even more obsessed with avenging his sister now than he did three years ago. What has changed? I do not know."

Sophie slowly rose to her feet, leaned forward, and splayed her hands on the desktop. "You say you invited Julian here to make peace. Let me be blunt. I do not like your son, sir, there are bad things lurking in his eyes. I believe he is dangerous, primarily to Julian, perhaps also to her grace, maybe to me and Roxanne. When he looks at me, I feel he would like to throw me into your very lovely lake, a rock tied around my neck."

"May I ask you why you came, Miss Wilkie?"

She eyed him, sitting there, so at ease, and wanted to kick him. She said easily, "I believe you must ask her grace about that, my lord," and walked out of the library, straight to the front doors of the manor and out onto the wide, deep stone steps. It was a glorious morning, the air a bit chilly, but there was no wind to speak of, and spring flowers scented the air. She looked toward the home wood. She knew from Corinne that the lake lay just beyond. She raced back up to her bedchamber to see Roxanne standing in the middle of the room, Tansy dressing her, both quiet as mice, since Corinne still slept.

And as luck would have it, Roxanne was dressing in a riding habit. Sophie whispered to Emmy, "Me next. I wish to go riding, too."

Thirty minutes later, both Sophie and Roxanne were at the stables, viewing the two mares the head stable lad brought out for their inspection. But Sophie was eyeing Cannon, lazily munching on oats, ignoring everything going on around him.

"I would like to ride Cannon," she said to Bicker.

"I don't think so, miss," Bicker said. "'E's a rare 'un, old Cannon is, can be sweet as a shorn lamb or mean as 'is lordship when the snit carries 'im into a rage."

"Which lordship? What do you mean, snit?"

"Ah, the baron. It be jest an old expression, if ye please, miss. Ye'll not want to ride old Cannon, trust me on this."

Roxanne watched this exchange and felt sorry for Bicker. Ten minutes later, Bicker tossed Sophie lightly onto the sidesaddle and handed her the reins. He didn't look happy. He kept looking back toward the manor. Did he want Julian to magically appear and remove Sophie from his horse's back? "Ye 'ave a care now, miss, please, ye'll not kill yerself."

"I promise I won't, Bicker. I am really a very good rider. Horses love me."

Bicker took another look toward the manor, then turned to Roxanne. "Pigeon is a sweet'um, she'll not give ye a moment's cut-up." He patted both Pidgeon and Cannon on their glossy necks and led them out of the stable.

"Ye young'uns 'ave a care, now!"

Roxanne grinned at him. She hadn't been a young'un for a long time now. As for Sophie, she laughed as she lightly kicked her heels into Cannon's sides. He shot forward. "Ah, your name, it is fitting," she sang out, and waved to Roxanne. He was, she realized, being sweet as a new-shorn lamb.

When they reached the home wood, they saw several well-marked trails. When they came out of the woods some minutes later, it was to see a small meandering lake before them, blue as the sky, the water still. There was a small dock, two boats tethered to it.

"It's a beautiful morning, the water's calm, let's row out on the lake." Roxanne was off Pigeon's back in an instant, tying her to a low-hanging maple tree branch so she could graze as she wished.

"A pity Devlin isn't here yet," Sophie said, as she tied Cannon to a yew bush. "We could stake him out. The sun is shining very nicely. Surely it would do the trick."

"What trick, exactly?" Roxanne asked, as she dipped an oar in the water.

Sophie said, "I don't know. Maybe he'll finally have to admit his vampireness is his jest on society."

"If," Roxanne said, "it is a jest," and waggled her eyebrows.

Sophie threw a cupped hand of water at her.

Once they found their rhythm, they rowed smoothly to the middle of the lake. They brought in the oars and sat back to enjoy the quiet rocking of the boat, the sounds of the birds, the occasional silver streak of a fish rippling through the calm water.

"This is lovely," Sophie said. "Not like that blasted house. There is so much bad feeling boiling right beneath the surface. Well, with Richard, it's all out there for anyone to see. But the baron? And the daughter, Victoria?"

"Actually, I was thinking about Corinne's noises in her bedchamber last night. Corinne isn't a wilting twit, Sophie; there was something in her bedchamber. Someone besides her and Barbie."

"I'll wager it was Richard Langworth. He probably was looking for Julian and found her instead."

"Richard Langworth appears to be many things, but stupid he isn't. He knows which bedchamber Julian is staying in, just as he knows which room is Corinne's and which room is mine—now ours. She could have dreamed it, I suppose, it makes sense—a strange house, and all of it on top of that delicious dinner that tasted like grated ashes in that cold, stiff, very uncomfortable company."

Sophie said, "The baron tried to keep topics light and amusing, but it wasn't to be. Too many tangled emotions swirling about at that table. As for Victoria, like you, I asked her questions, very interested and polite I was, but she said nothing at all, or just gave me nods and an occasional yes. She never looked away from her brother and father. Do you think she was afraid Richard was going to leap over the table and try to kill Julian?"

A shout went up from the shore.

They turned to see Julian and Devlin standing on the end of the dock, waving to them.

Roxanne perked right up. "Ah, it's Devlin, what a lovely surprise. He must have ridden like the wind to get here so quickly. You stay close to Julian, and I will get Devlin to row me back out to the middle of the lake. Perhaps I can get him to remove his shirt, display his manly self to the sun. That would be fun. I don't see any horses. I suppose they must have walked here."

Sophie laughed. "I hadn't realized, but do you know, Devlin is nearly Julian's size?"

"Mayhap he's a bit taller than Julian."

Sophie said, "Oh, no, Julian is by far the taller. But, you know, Roxanne, that's only the outside. They really are quite different from each other."

"As are we all."

Sophie nodded. "I wonder how Julian would feel about stretching out without his shirt so I could, well—*hmm,* observe him."

"That is rather shameless of you, wishing to see your older kindly uncle unclothed."

Sophie laughed. "Only his upper parts, and only for scientific reasons."

"Are you lying to your aunt, Sophie?"

25

Devlin was wearing a wide-brimmed black hat.

Roxanne smiled widely as she stepped onto the dock, flung out her arms. "You are a glorious sight, Devlin—you look like one of those Puritan preachers I've seen in books. Shall you open your mouth and chastise us sinners? No? It is about time you got here."

"I rode like the Devil," Devlin said, and took her hands between his. "I came as quickly as I could—consider me Julian's protector, to ensure that base scoundrel Richard doesn't try to throttle him, or the baron, either one, truth be told. As for Victoria, who knows? As for Julian, he wasn't even at the manor to welcome me, didn't arrive until I was on my way to find you two. All out of breath he was, but he won't tell me why. Since he's more stubborn than Cannon, I'll never know in this lifetime.

"You and Sophie look in fine spirits. I see you managed to row yourself very competently, which means there is no reason for either of you to ask me to do the work."

"But I should like to show you the magnificent water

reeds on the other side of the lake," said Roxanne. "Won't you row me back out, Devlin? I'm really quite fatigued."

Devlin eyed Roxanne, lightly touched his finger to her cheek. "Young one, you do not dissemble well. Perhaps you'd best not try it again with me."

"I am your age, and very nearly on the shelf. Indeed, my years are beginning to wear on me, since I am, indeed, really quite tired from all that rowing." She began to rub her arms.

"Another Kean," Devlin remarked to Julian, who was lightly stroking Cannon's neck. He had one eye on Sophie, and it wasn't a fond eye, Roxanne saw.

Devlin said, "I am the one who is fatigued, my dear. Julian and I both walked here, since some foul individual stole his horse, and he was, as I said, already fatigued from walking so quickly."

"Where did you go?" Sophie asked Julian.

Julian gave her a harassed look. "Nowhere, only a walk in the home wood to think about things."

He was lying, Sophie knew it to her stockinged feet. Did anyone else?

How can she know I'm lying? I know she does, I can see it in her eyes. Julian had brooded, albeit in his cave, not in the home wood. It had taken him a goodly amount of time to walk from Hardcross Manor to his cave by the river. He hadn't ridden Cannon, he could be seen, his presence wondered at. No, he wanted no one to know where he'd gone. He'd had to see if his boyhood cave would be an acceptable hideout for smuggled-in goods. It was perfect. He had sat on the sandy floor, leaned back against a wall, and planned out his next and last smuggling run. Time to end it all.

It was a pity.

Devlin said, "I could not very well ride with him walking beside me, now, could I? So demeaning to Lord Julian."

Julian strode up to Sophie, grabbed her arms, and shook her hard. "You stole my horse, damn you, after Bicker told you not to. You could have been thrown; you could have your damned neck broken."

"I knew I could ride him, Julian, really, there was no danger. Stop looking at me like you want to drown me. And his whinny, it smote me. I felt sorry for him. He nearly begged me to give him some proper exercise. Really, we dealt very well together."

"You twit, Cannon is *my* horse, not yours. What's more, he's mean as a drunken cutpurse. You deserve to be pulverized for this, Sophie."

She saw the pulse pounding in his throat. *Oh, dear,* he was very angry with her indeed. She supposed she deserved it, but still, she was a fine horsewoman. He should have trusted her; he should have—*oh, dear,* she had been a twit. She realized he was more scared for her than angry, scared she could have been seriously hurt. She lightly laid her hand on his arm. "I'm sorry, Julian, truly, it—it wasn't well done of me. I won't do it again. Will you forgive me? Will you not pulverize me?"

He eyed her, said slowly, "You think I'm being unreasonable? I'm not, it's just that—very well. You're forgiven."

He lightly touched his fingertips to her cheek. *She was all right, thank the good Lord.* He said, "As for that other one, Devlin, standing there looking all angelic, I fancy she wants to stake you out beneath a bright sun, to see what will happen."

Sophie rounded on him. "However would you hear such a thing, sir? It is absurd."

"I have a working brain, Sophie. Also, your plan at the Marksbury garden party set up quite a fine spate of gossip, which reached my ears very quickly."

"How odd," Devlin said, frowning, "I didn't hear a thing."

"I suppose that means more people than Sophie and I wish to see what would happen if your bare chest was exposed to the sun," Roxanne said.

Devlin said, "I should not like that at all. Sun is the enemy."

Roxanne said, "Nonsense. The warmth of the sun is delicious. Oh, dear, are you certain you must hide away from that glorious sun, Devlin? Let's just see about that," and she grabbed the black hat off Devlin's head and raced back toward the home wood, her laughter wafting behind her.

Devlin sighed. "What do you think, Julian? Should I teach her some manners?"

"She will bring you low, Devlin, pay heed," Sophie said.

Devlin ran toward the home wood.

"He is fleet of foot, isn't he? Now," Julian said, "we're alone. Do you know, I thought Bicker would burst into tears when he saw me, swore to me he'd tried to talk you out of it, but she's 'a headstrong little bickel, more stubborn than me long-sainted ma,' I believe he said."

"So, this means you still haven't forgiven me. But it's true, Julian, Cannon was gentle as a lamb. He quite likes me."

Julian handed her a carrot from his pocket. "Feed him, see if he bites off your fingers."

Without hesitation, Sophie held out the carrot to Cannon, who licked it off her palm. She rubbed her hand on her skirt. "Ah, Julian, perhaps you could ride along beside me and give me pointers if Cannon goes into a snit?"

He placed both his hands around her throat. "No, I will not give you pointers. You will leave Cannon to me."

"But—"

"You may not even lead Cannon about on a rope. I have decided you are brazen, ma'am, a baggage, and you want taming."

She closed her hands over his. "Really? I'm all that? What is a baggage, I've always wondered."

"But you understand brazen, do you not? And taming?"

"Brazen is nothing, but taming? Goodness, no, what does that mean? Does it involve whips?"

"Don't mock me, Sophie. I might stake you out beside Roxanne, because I imagine that is what Devlin is doing to your elderly aunt at this very moment."

"No, impossible. Roxanne is wily, not to mention she is very strong. Devlin doesn't have a chance of besting her."

A black satyr brow shot up. "A wager? Say, five pounds?"

"Done," she said, and shook his hand. They left the horses eating lake grass and walked back to the home wood.

They heard shouts, laughter, then dead silence.

They stepped into a small clearing to see Roxanne on her back on the ground, Devlin's black coat beneath her, Devlin holding her wrists over her head.

Roxanne was laughing even as she jerked and pulled. "Let me go this instant, Devlin, or I swear I will annihilate you. I will leave you tied down in the sunlight for a fortnight."

"That would give me an inflammation of the lung, given it will rain thirteen of the fourteen days."

"Very well, I will throw you into a moat if I find a castle. Is there one hereabout? Does Ravenscar have a moat?"

"No," Devlin said, released her wrists, and rose. He looked down at her, his arms crossed over his chest. He began to laugh. "I bested you very quickly, Roxanne. You tried your poor womanly best, but you didn't stand a chance, not against such a man as I. Do you admit I am your superior?"

"My superior? What does that mean? You're fast?"

"Fast and strong, admit it; I had you on your back in an instant."

"I don't believe this," Sophie said, and raced to Roxanne, who was now sitting up.

"You're sitting on the ground. How can that be? Goodness, Devlin's coat is even under you. However did that happen? Roxanne, how did you allow this? I made a wager with Julian! You have lost me five pounds."

Sophie gave Roxanne her hand and pulled her to her feet. "Five pounds, Roxanne. Perhaps I should have left you on the ground."

"I think it's time for a bit of retribution," Roxanne said, and jumped on Devlin. The momentum drove him to his knees, then, because he wasn't stupid, he twisted and fell onto his back, dragging Roxanne down to sprawl on top of him.

There was a moment of silence, then, "Help me, Julian. She will surely kill me, mayhap bite my neck, for she is endlessly curious. Look, she is eyeing my neck, licking her lips."

Julian, laughing, lifted Roxanne off Devlin, set her beside Sophie, and stepped back. He held up his hands. "Don't either of you attack me, for I am innocent of any wrongdoing. Devlin, get up, you look ridiculous lying there, squinting at the sunlight pouring through the tree branches."

Devlin jumped to his feet, found his hat on the ground, placed it reverently back on his head, and breathed a sigh of relief. "You're right. I felt such heat against my skin, building, building. It quite scared me to my toes."

Julian held out his hand to Sophie. "Five pounds, if you please."

Sophie looked at Roxanne, who was brushing leaves off her riding skirt. "How could you let him take you down? I told Julian you were strong—"

"You were proved wrong." Julian held out his hand, then eyed her. "Are you telling me that you are suffering penury or you don't carry money on your person?"

"Neither. Both."

"A gentleman always pays on a debt of honor, my child."

"I will pay you, for I have honor, probably more than I deserve."

Roxanne was pulling twigs from her unraveling braid, spilling bright red hair down her back and over her shoulders. She said, "Devlin was listening for my footsteps. When I stopped and turned to see where he was, he ducked behind a lovely maple. Mayhap I walked back a bit, to make sure he wasn't close, and he grabbed me from behind, threw me over his shoulder, and dumped me on the ground. In short, he ambushed me."

"You were too curious this time, Roxanne," Devlin said, considering. "At least you weren't out for blood—more's the pity."

"But his coat was lying beneath you," Sophie said. "Placing it just so—that takes time."

"He had his coat in his hands when he grabbed me. He is smart," Roxanne added, and pulled another twig from her hair.

Devlin lightly squeezed her arm. "Ah, not much muscle

at all, Roxanne, it is disappointing. You weren't much of a challenge at all."

Julian turned to see Sophie racing back through the home wood. She wouldn't dare. He waited until he heard Cannon whinny.

Devlin grinned. "You toy with her, Julian. I quite like that."

Julian waited another moment, then he whistled.

When Cannon came trotting up to him a few minutes later, a red-faced Sophie racing behind him, waving a carrot, he said, "I believe it a fine idea if you and Roxanne were to have a nice walk back to the manor. I forgive you for taking him, but I believe a bit of punishment might make a powerful point."

"You are not a gentleman, sir."

He swung onto Cannon's back, then gave Devlin a hand to bring him up behind him. Cannon snorted. "You are no lightweight, Devlin," Julian said over his shoulder. "No matter, Cannon won't have time to work himself up. We'll fetch Roxanne's horse for you."

Sophie and Roxanne stood in the clearing until the gentlemen came riding back through. Julian gave them a silent salute. Devlin merely shook his finger at Roxanne. He called over his shoulder, "Your hair is quite beautiful all long and tangled down your back. All that sinful red."

Roxanne lifted the pile of hair that hung down her back. She twisted it up, stuck it beneath her riding hat. She brushed her skirts again, straightened her jacket. "Well, Sophie, would you like to walk to that gazebo on the other side of the lake?"

— 26 —

Sophie didn't go back inside the manor with Roxanne because she saw Victoria Langworth slip behind a maple tree. Why was she hiding? Surely she could not have taken Sophie into dislike; she didn't even know her.

Sophie waited a moment, then walked resolutely to the maple tree. She called out, "Hello, Miss Langworth. It is a glorious day. Won't you come out and speak to me?"

She waited. Finally, Victoria emerged from behind the tree. She didn't move, simply stood there, watching Sophie, rather like a deer watching a hunter, wanting to spring away but frozen to the spot.

She looked very young to Sophie, in her schoolroom muslin gown, but Sophie knew Victoria to be close to her own age. Why had she not married? Why did she still dress like a schoolgirl?

Sophie said, "I rode Julian's horse, Cannon. Julian would have choked me if he could have gotten away with it. Actually, it was close. He was very angry with me. What do you think?"

Victoria didn't fidget, didn't move. Finally, she said, "I

would choke you, too, if you stole my horse. Cannon frightens me. You really rode him? You weren't afraid?"

Sophie, all good humor, walked over to where Victoria stood, swinging her bonnet by its long violet ribbons. "No, I wasn't afraid, probably because Cannon decided to humor me. He was playful, unlike his master when he found me. Do you know Cannon comes to Julian when he whistles?"

Victoria nodded. "Yes. Julian tried to teach me to whistle once, but I could not manage it."

"I could teach you."

"No, no, I am too old for that now. Father keeps reminding me that I am a grown lady and I must be mature and thoughtful. Excuse me, Miss Wilkie—"

"Please call me Sophie."

"I overheard Julian's mama speaking to my father. She said Julian was going to marry you, since your mother was her very best friend."

Sophie merely smiled.

"Julian was married to my sister, you know," said Victoria. "She loved him very much, at least I thought she did, but then she had private relations—that's what I heard the servants whispering to each other—with a man I never saw. I don't know if any of the servants saw him either. And then Lily was dead. It was all very sad."

Lily had been married to Julian only six months and she'd taken a lover? Sophie said carefully, "I think her name very pretty—Lily. I'm very sorry she died."

"She didn't die of a putrid throat, like my own dear mother, she got shot in the heart. If Lily were still alive, she would be thirty next Monday. Isn't that strange?"

"It is very strange—may I call you Victoria?"

"No one calls me that. I'm Vicky. Do you believe Julian is sorry as well?"

"How could he not be? She was his wife."

"There was something wrong between them if Lily had private relations with another man, don't you think? But I don't think Julian shot her in the heart—I saw how shocked he was when he was trying to get her to wake up. But she couldn't, you see, she was dead."

Vicky continued after a moment: "Such a beautiful wedding it was, at Saint Thomas's church in Ravenscar Village. They went to Italy on their wedding trip. How I wished to go with them, but Julian told me it wasn't what was done, and he patted my cheek. Lily laughed at me. I remember she twirled around and around in her lovely traveling gown, and I heard her whisper, 'I'm free, I'm free.'

"When they returned, Julian took her to Ravenscar, and I became the mistress of Hardcross Manor. I do a good job. Did you like the beef we had for dinner last evening? It was done precisely to my recipe. It was my mother's recipe, actually. I miss her all the time, more than I miss Lily. My father never misses her, you know. I think he's glad she died. The day of her funeral, he began humming. He hums all the time now."

Sophie wasn't pressing Vicky for information, Vicky was spitting it right out. Sophie heard herself ask, "You never saw another man, so perhaps Lily didn't have a lover; perhaps that was simply gossip."

"Then why would she spend so much time here when she was married to Julian? I mean, she was supposed to live at Ravenscar, but she spent a great deal of time with us. She said she didn't want to take my place, that she was responsible for Ravenscar, and that was quite enough. But I ask you, Sophie, if she was always here, how could she manage Ravenscar?

"I don't think she liked Julian's mama very much. She said she was a bitch. Her grace has always been kind to me, but she wasn't my mama-in-law, so maybe that makes things different."

Sophie said, "Her grace is really very nice. She is very kind to both Roxanne and me as well. I'm sure she was very pleased Lily was her daughter-in-law."

"Papa was telling me perhaps we should have a party, since you don't ignore a duke's heir, and that's what Devlin is. I've known Devlin since Julian brought him to visit from Oxford. Julian had never met Devlin before he went to Oxford. Isn't that odd? Well, that is what I heard Lily tell our father. She said his father's family wished Julian didn't exist."

"You were eavesdropping?"

"Yes, I learn everything by listening at doors or standing by the wainscoting or hiding behind draperies. I am very good at it, have been for years now."

"The wainscoting? But how does that make you disappear?"

"Oh, I simply stand very still and no one sees me, not really. I must leave you, Miss Wilkie—Sophie. I must meet with Cook to ensure she has the correct recipe for the dinner mutton. I like to decorate it with mint, you know, that's what my mama did. I mustn't forget the Yorkshire tea cakes. My father said he quite liked Miss Radcliffe's father—Baron Roche, that is—said tea cakes were his favorite, and so perhaps she will enjoy them as well. I don't particularly care for them, but that doesn't matter, now, does it? Listen, I can hear my papa humming."

Vicky left Sophie standing by the maple tree. Sophie didn't hear the baron humming, but then again, she didn't hear anything above the loud pounding of her heart.

What had Lily meant by saying, "I'm free, I'm free"?

27

Sophie ran into the manor, nearly knocking Julian over. He grabbed her arms to steady both of them.

"Sophie? What's wrong?"

"Julian, I must speak to you immediately."

He studied her face, then heard a soft rustling sound and looked up to see Vicky standing on the bottom stair step, smiling, looking from him to Sophie and back again. What had Vicky told her? Had it made sense? Frightened her? With Vicky, you never knew what would come out of her mouth next.

Fey, Richard called his sister, and then he would snort and add under his breath that she might as well be on the moon for all the good she was here on earth—the elfin child who would probably be happier dancing around an All Hallows' Eve bonfire than partaking of tea in a drawing room, sharing her life with family and friends.

What had she said to Sophie?

Julian drew in a deep breath. Vicky was still watching him, that smile still on her mouth. It wouldn't surprise him if two minutes from now, she turned into the mistress of

Hardcross and asked them in for luncheon. It gave him a headache, probably gave a headache to her brother and father as well. He remembered Lily had said Vicky was an original. Then she'd added that Vicky always knew how best to get what she wanted, and how best to protect herself. Protect herself from what, he'd always wondered, but Lily had only shrugged, said nothing more.

"Hello, Julian," Vicky called out. It wasn't her young-mistress-of-the-manor voice, it was her fey voice. "Isn't it a lovely day? I always adore a lovely day. I think Sophie does, too. It was lovely that day you found Lily lying dead in the garden, wasn't it?"

Julian said to Sophie, who was staring gape-mouthed at Vicky, "Come with me." He turned on his heel and walked toward the back of the manor. He opened a narrow door and walked into the small airless estate room, used only by the baron's steward, now an old man who slept most of the time he was here, something no one appeared to mind in the least. Julian walked to another narrow door, opened it. Sophie walked past him into a small perfect gem of a garden.

She smelled jasmine, the hint of sweet lilies.

Lilies. She shuddered.

She walked past him onto well-trodden cobblestones that wound whimsically through the small garden, creating little curves and hideaways. It was natural, all the flowers spilling over one another, different scents mingling together. It was perfect.

He said in an expressionless voice, "This was Lily's favorite place when she was a child. She created this garden herself when she was eight years old, she tended it, no one else was allowed to—even after we were married she still spent most of her time here. I see her father has maintained it well in the three years she's been dead."

Sophie slowly turned to face him. "Why did she not build a garden like this at Ravenscar?"

"She said this small garden was part of her, that she never wanted to duplicate it, even at Ravenscar."

"But she was your wife. When she married you, Ravenscar became her home."

"Yes."

"Vicky told me when Lily was in her traveling gown, ready for your wedding trip, she whirled around and around and whispered 'I'm free, I'm free.' Can you tell me from what she was now free? From whom?"

"Vicky never told me that. I wonder if she's told anyone but you. I wonder if it is even the truth, or something she merely imagined or something she made up. One must always consider all possibilities when Vicky says something provocative. Do I know why Lily whispered that, if indeed she did? No, I do not. Let's assume Lily did say that. Then that would mean Vicky picked you to tell because she had a reason to. What the reason could be, I have no idea."

"But those simple words of Lily's raise frightening questions, Julian."

He shrugged. "I have never been able to tell what Vicky is thinking, and I have known her all her life. She lurks about, always watching and listening. I imagine she knows every secret in Hardcross Manor. She has never said anything to me for or against my marrying again. She doesn't spend much time with anyone; she doesn't converse like regular people do." He wondered if she'd been hiding in her father's library when he'd arrived yesterday, hiding, listening, watching. He wouldn't be at all surprised.

"She intimated Lily had a lover, but she said she never saw him. Did the servants, she wondered. She also told me she didn't think you shot Lily in the heart, because you were too shocked when you found her. Was there a lover, Julian?" Sophie whirled about, horror in her eyes at what she'd said. The words tasted rancid. "I'm sorry, I'm sorry, that is none of my business. It's just that I want you to resolve this mess, and—"

Julian ran his fingers through his dark hair, making it stand on end. "No, I'm quite sure there was no lover. I've had to face it, Sophie, for there is no other conclusion—she shot herself through the heart. Why? I have no idea." He hit one fist against the other, then gave a brutal smile. "Or I killed her, one or the other. Both Richard and his father believe I did. I don't know about you."

She grabbed his jacket and shook him. "I have already told you I didn't for an instant believe you guilty of murder. *And of murdering your own wife?*" She shook him again. "What is wrong with you? Do you think I have rocks for brains? Stop that nonsense. Are you certain there is no one else who could have killed her?"

He smiled down at her. "I haven't known you very long, Sophie, yet you believe me innocent without knowing all the facts?"

"Of course, you moron."

"Thank you." He studied her face. "I wonder, would you defend me to the death, Sophie?"

"Probably. Listen to me, I happen to care about you. I don't want to see you hurt any more than you have already been. I drives me quite mad to think of Richard Langworth threatening you. And he honestly believes you killed your own wife, and he's known you all your life."

She looked at him, straight on. "It's time you told me exactly what happened. Can you do that, Julian? Can you confide in me?"

He said nothing for several moments, then, in an emotionless voice, "I have never told anyone exactly what I saw, what I did, but yes, I will tell you." He drew a deep breath. "I came here to Hardcross Manor that day to tell Lily I had to go to London on business, because I didn't wish to write her a letter. I heard a gunshot. She was lying over there, her skirts fanned out around her, and there was a large bloodstain covering her chest. So much blood. I remember I couldn't accept it, simply couldn't. She still held a pistol in her outstretched hand. Her beautiful hair was loose around her head, black as night her hair, and I wondered why it was down. She never wore her hair loose during the day." He paused for a moment. "I felt as though I'd walked into a nightmare. Nothing made any sense, yet I knew it didn't matter what I thought or what I did, because everything was over."

"Did you see anyone? This so-called lover?"

"No, no one was here, but Richard came a few moments later. He'd heard the shot and saw me on my knees beside her. He believed I'd shot her. Actually, I was trying to make her breathe, make her open her eyes, but she didn't."

"You said the gun was in her hand."

"Yes. Richard believed I'd placed it there. He believed she wanted to leave me, perhaps with a lover, and so I shot her." He touched his fingertips to her mouth. "Yes, you want to say Richard is quite mad to believe me guilty, but you see, there had to be a reason he could grasp. It had to be something shattering, and a lover was the only reason he could latch on to. He was wild with grief, whereas I was cold and stiff, my brain and my body frozen. Richard threw himself on her, tried to get her to breathe, just as I had, but she didn't. He was sobbing and cursing, beside himself, yet I—I rose and stood over both of them, apart from all of it, and I felt the wet of her blood soaked through my shirt. I remember I looked at my hands. They were covered with her blood from when I'd pounded on her chest, trying to make her breathe."

"Don't try to make it some sort of condemnation of yourself. You were shocked insensible. Surely when Richard recovered a bit, he knew you could never harm a woman, even one he believed had betrayed you. And Lily was his sister—how could he have thought so little of her he'd believe she'd take a lover after being married to you for six months?"

"I don't believe he really thought there was a lover, he simply had to have a reason he could understand. I was the only one here when he burst into the garden. I hadn't seen either Richard or Lily when I arrived. I simply came to where I knew Lily was likely to be."

Sophie said, "All right, if she didn't kill herself, if someone did kill her, then this person could have easily escaped, could he not? I mean, you didn't immediately go searching, and neither did Richard."

"No, not immediately."

"Let's consider this lover possibility for a moment. Can you think of any man who perhaps admired her overmuch?"

"Believe me, I've thought a great deal about that. I don't want to believe she killed herself—wouldn't that mean that I'd driven her to it?" He slashed his hand through the air. "But is the other preferable? God only knows. There was no other man. Perhaps Richard and the baron tried to believe it, but I know they couldn't. Lily wasn't that kind of woman."

"So if both the baron and Richard believed there was no lover, and they couldn't consider that she shot herself, then it makes sense they would think you killed her, is that what you're saying?"

"Yes. I couldn't bear to tell them it had to be suicide, I simply couldn't. In fact, I only told my mother that Lily had killed herself, that nothing else made any sense. I remember she said only, 'I don't know why she killed herself, Julian, but I do know something was different about her. I suspect you knew it, too.'"

Julian stopped, walked away from her again to open the back gate. She walked through the gate to find herself on the edge of a scythed lawn, and beyond the lawn was the wood. She was surprised. "I hadn't realized where we were."

"It surprised me the first time I saw it as well." He added, "Of course, I was only four years old at the time."

She lightly laid her hand on his forearm. The dark brown wool of his sleeve was soft against her fingers. "Tell me, did you ever suspect her brother, sister, or father?"

28

He walked past her to a bank of yew bushes into a small gated garden closed in by trellises and boxwood. To Sophie's surprise, it held a score of different rock formations, each artfully crafted, some large, some small, all fashioned in geometrical shapes. He walked to a bench and motioned for her to sit, then stood in front of her, looking around. He said, "Nothing has changed since the last time I was here. The baron likes to have rocks brought in and fashioned into different groupings. He fancies himself a mathematician, thus all the shapes." He paused a moment, then, "Could any of them have shot her? Yes, but why? They were her family."

"You were as well."

"I remember after we were only three weeks in Genoa on our wedding trip, she begged me to come back to England. What I didn't understand was that she wanted to come home—not to Ravenscar but here to Hardcross Manor.

"Every single day she came here. If she didn't miss them terribly, why did she spend so much time here? Whenever I asked her about it, she simply said she loved her home.

Never would she say more, and finally, I simply gave up and let her do as she wished. My mother continued to manage Ravenscar, and I was very busy at the time with my shipping interests, no excuse, but there it is. I am not proud that I spent so much time away from her, but I will admit it was easier to work, to travel to Portsmouth or to London, than watch my wife pull completely away from me. So, yes, my mother was right. There was something different about Lily, but neither of us ever knew what it was. I still don't know.

"Was I blind? Was it possible Lily did come here to meet a man? Here amongst the rock formations? You see how private a place it is. No one comes here."

"Julian, let me ask you a question." At his slow nod, she said, "Have you changed? Or are you now like you were when you were married to Lily?"

He frowned at her, cocked his head to one side. "Changed? I don't believe so. Why?"

"Because, you simpleton, how could Lily have taken a lover when you were her husband? That is impossible to believe. I mean, look at you, you are beautiful. You are smart. You make me laugh. You are—thoughtful, yes, that is it, you think things through. You are good, Julian. There isn't a mean-spirited bone in you, though I will admit you can be a superb autocrat. I know that once you make up your mind, no one can budge you—it is many times provoking, but there it is, it is simply part of what and who you are.

"I cannot imagine you did not please Lily, that you could not please any woman, particularly if you loved her enough to marry her."

He stared at her. Finally, he managed, "I'm beautiful?"

"Ah, of all the things I said about you, you picked out that one. So you're vain, as well. Yes, you are beautiful."

"Thank you."

"You're welcome; it's nothing but the truth. Is there more?"

Julian shook his head. "I don't know. I only remember I stared at Richard, shaking my head while he hurled accusations at me. Truth is, I felt nothing at all. Lily lay there dead, yet Richard was shaking, screaming that I was a murderer. I picked her up and carried her through the house, people crowding around me, yelling, crying, trying to talk to me, but I said nothing to anyone. No one tried to stop me, even Richard. I rode back to Ravenscar with my dead wife in my arms."

Sophie was shaking. She whispered, "I am so very sorry, Julian."

He nodded. "It happened three years ago this month, actually. I left after I buried her in our cemetery. It was not well done of me, but at the time I simply couldn't deal with the awful grief, and yes, the guilt. Guilt over what? Because I'd left her alone so much? Because I hadn't convinced her to tell me what was happening with her? I suppose so. I left my poor mother to deal with the rumors and gossip, Richard's threats and accusations. The baron shut himself in his library, she wrote me, and didn't come out for months. What Richard did, I don't know.

"When I came back last month, my mother told me everyone accepted that Lily had shot herself, everyone except the baron and Richard. She said everyone believed she'd had a lover and he had left her and she couldn't bear it, and that the guilt and shame led her to kill herself."

He paused. "I must say it is possible."

"You will listen to me, Julian. Believe me, no woman would take a lover when you were her husband." Sophie shook his arms as hard as she could. "It is impossible."

He lightly touched his fingers to her cheek. He even managed a smile. "Such faith in me, little one." He studied that beautiful pure face, the shining eyes, filled with the truth of his innocence, her truth. He said slowly, "You are very young, Sophie."

She reared back and punched him hard in the belly, never looking away from his face. "Yes, but I am not stupid."

"No, you're not."

"I have a special gift, I suppose you'd call it. My mother pointed it out to me when I was only sixteen. I have the ability to see things as they really are, she told me. So I will tell you now, something had obviously happened to Lily, but it had nothing to do with a lover or with some mad stranger or a disappointed suitor who happened to walk into the garden to shoot her. I don't know what worried her, but it was something profound. Did she kill herself? I don't know, I can't quite grasp it."

"Something profound? I don't think I will ever know the truth now. It's been three years. If there are answers lurking about, they are now so deeply buried, how will I ever discover them?"

"I don't suppose you, Richard, and the baron could all discuss this? Rationally?"

"Very probably not."

"Do you mind if I speak to Roxanne? She has a fine brain, and she will look at everything with a fresh eye. However, I will not say anything to anyone if you don't wish me to."

"A fine brain, you say?"

"One of the finest. Julian, you have suffered from this long enough. I will use my gift to see my way through this to the truth."

Sophie thought she saw a movement from the corner of her eye and whipped about. A shadow, she thought, something. She called out, "Who is there?"

Julian was whirled about. Sophie put her fingers to her lips.

"Who is there?"

There wasn't a sound.

But Sophie knew she hadn't imagined the movement. She saw Julian's eyes were darker than she'd ever seen them before. She smiled up at him—not all that far up—and said, "Do you know, my lord, I quite like that I am going to be your champion."

29

Sophie went on a search for Roxanne, but neither she nor Devlin was to be found. Where had they gone? It was a fine sunny day. Had Roxanne finally managed to talk Devlin out into the sunshine?

Sophie paused, hearing humming. It was the baron, and he was humming under his breath, head down. When he saw her standing in the entrance hall, the front door open, he politely asked after her health, gave her an absent smile, and excused himself.

She didn't have long to think about speaking to Roxanne, because at that moment, a carriage pulled up in front of the steps. From the carriage emerged her aunt Leah, all smiles and laughter. Richard Langworth came from around the side of the manor and started at the sight of Leah, then strode forward to welcome her.

Sophie watched Leah demurely present her gloved hand to Richard, watched him gently fold down her glove so he could lightly brush his lips over her bare wrist. He gave her an intimate smile.

"What a lovely surprise," he said. Did he really think it lovely? Sophie wondered.

Leah nearly danced, she was so excited to see him. "I simply could not bear being in London without you, Richard. Ah, what a lovely home you have. I hope you do not mind I came without inquiring as to your wishes?"

Richard was many things, but foremost, Sophie realized now, he was a gentleman. He said, "I should be an ungrateful sot if I objected to seeing you, my pet," and kissed her wrist again. Sophie was impressed. He continued to speak quietly to Leah, then gave her his arm, and together, Elvira trailing behind, he assisted her up the steps into the manor. Her maid wasn't smiling, Sophie wondered if she'd be smiling if she'd had to sit next to Leah for three days straight. No, Sophie would probably have strangled her, and buried her body behind an ancient Druid oak tree.

She had some more questions for Julian, but she'd seen him go into the library to speak to his former father-in-law, and how very odd that seemed. Had the two men reached some sort of accord? Would the baron try to dissuade his son from trying to cut Julian's throat?

So many undercurrents in this house, she thought, walking to the nether reaches of the house to see if Cook had the teakettle boiling. There were shadows and secrets. Where were Roxanne and Devlin?

⤜⟹ ⟸⤛

This is quite the oddest place I have ever seen," Roxanne said over her shoulder, and walked up to a grouping of six big rocks, each carefully carved down to sharp edges and straight lines.

"It's a hexagon," Devlin said.

She rolled her eyes. "Thank you, my lord, for continuing my education. Look, there's moss growing on the rocks, so all these groupings have been here for some time."

Devlin said, "True. Now, my girl, turn around and face me."

"Girl? Me? We are the same age, Devlin, and I shouldn't dare call you a boy." But she slowly turned to see him take off his hat and lay it carefully on a stone bench. He gave her a wicked smile as he eased out of his riding coat. She said not a word as he dropped the coat to the ground and pulled off his cravat. Indeed, she stared at him, mesmerized.

She pulled her handkerchief out of her cuff and began fanning herself. "Well, am I to see your manly self go up in smoke?"

Devlin paused, raised his face to the sun. He closed his eyes, groaned, and gave a mighty shudder. He quickly grabbed up his hat and plunked it back down over his brow. "I had every intention of pandering to your female curiosity, but alas, the sun is simply too strong for me today. Perhaps tomorrow." He pulled his cravat around his neck and shrugged back into his coat, dusted himself off. He said, "I do not trust Richard Langworth, nor do I trust his father. I distrust the manor house itself. Its corners are cold and shadowed. There are lurking secrets making the air shimmer and darken."

Roxanne was silent for a moment, then slowly nodded. "Has Julian told you of any changes in the baron or his son? Or does murder still lurk in their hearts?"

"I plan to stick closer than plaster to my half uncle. It is time for luncheon. Let's go see what the Hardcross cook has conjured up for us."

Roxanne said, "The sun has crept behind clouds. You're quite safe now, Devlin."

He grinned at her. "I thank you for monitoring the weather for me, Roxanne."

Roxanne looked up, hearing a voice she recognized very well. "Oh, dear. I do believe we have added another thick blanket of unpleasantness. I should have guessed, but I didn't." She drew a deep breath. "My sister Leah has arrived, doubtless because Richard Langworth left London."

"At least she will distract Richard. Onward, my girl, we have dragons to search out and slay."

30

A party of nine sat down to dinner that evening at precisely six o'clock, the ladies resplendent in a rainbow of colors, her grace in a striking emerald green gown that quite outshone the young ladies in their pastels. The gentlemen were garbed in severe black, their linen white as the Devonshire cream Cook presented.

As on the previous evening, the baron directed the conversation, smooth as butter, Sophie thought. Perhaps it was the addition of Leah that made things easier tonight. She was certainly filled with laughter and gaiety and gossip from London.

"I believed our guests would enjoy Cook's fine Exeter stew, Papa," Vicky said. "Pray tell me what you think."

The baron was staring at Leah, who looked very beautiful, indeed, her hair like spun gold in the soft candlelight. "I think it is very fine, Vicky." He looked back toward Leah, as if unable to help himself. "My son has told me you are the loveliest of the Radcliffe sisters."

He'd better have told his father that, Roxanne thought, a smile firmly set on her mouth.

Leah, known for her charm, something neither Roxanne nor Sophie saw much of, looked from Richard to his father. "That is kind of him. Let me say I consider Richard the finest-looking gentleman of my acquaintance. Now I see he resembles you greatly, my lord. And your house is not only impressive, it quite invites one in. Thank you for welcoming me, in spite of the surprise of it."

The baron laughed, waved a fork that held a good bite of cheese pastry. "I've always believed my son has excellent taste, my dear. Welcome to Hardcross Manor. I should be delighted to show you the gardens when my son isn't monopolizing you."

Julian saw that Vicky had a smile fixed to her face even as she slowly chewed on a bite of roast turkey. Did she even care what was being said? Julian wondered, and saw the same question in Sophie's eyes.

Julian said to the table at large, "I must leave you tomorrow to visit Ravenscar."

"I shall go with you, dearest," his mother said. "I wish to see how my vegetable garden fares."

Julian was pleased when Roxanne, Sophie, and Devlin asked to come as well. He wanted Sophie to see his home. He also wanted her to meet his four spaniels.

Everyone was shocked silent when Vicky said suddenly, "Do you know, Julian, I haven't been to Ravenscar since that day you buried Lily? May I come as well?"

31

Corinne waved toward the butcher's wife as the carriage rolled through Ravenscar Village. "Isn't this a charming town?" she asked any or all of her companions in the carriage. "Look yon at the village church. It dates back to the thirteenth century. Julian's father always saw to it that the cemetery was well maintained, and naturally, I have continued to see to it now." *Since Lily is buried there* hung in the air. Corinne continued after a moment, "He had the beautiful stained-glass windows installed toward the end of the last century. He was very proud of this village, of its people, but Ravenscar was his heart. It is a palace and a castle spun together by a drunk magician, Julian always says, but it doesn't matter, it makes you feel safe from any invaders who might land on our shores, something that seems very doubtful now in our modern times. His grace would say 'Ravenscar endures.'" She sighed. "Maximilian only wished he could endure right along with it. But, of course, no one can endure past his time, and his grace was blessed with a long life."

Roxanne said, "A castle and a palace, I like that. You said

the duke spent more time here than at his ancestral home—Mount Burney, near Colchester."

Corinne said, "He did, though, to be honest, he thought of Ravenscar as his ancestral home. He told me he'd never liked Mount Burney, a drafty old place without a whit of charm. He was frankly relieved that his son Constantine loved the place. He always preferred Cornwall, the balmy south with its palm trees, and the north as well, with its savage coastline—and all of it so very close together.

"Do you know, I have never visited Mount Burney nor do I ever wish to. His grace married me here in the local church, and here is where we lived until he died. Constantine once invited me to visit, but I declined. I knew Lorelei wouldn't be at all kind, were I to come.

"Since Ravenscar was unentailed, he was able to bequeath it to Julian." She paused for a moment. "Do you know that hereabouts Julian is called the Prince of Ravenscar?"

"How vastly romantic that sounds," Sophie said. "Prince! Goodness, what does that do to his opinion of himself, I wonder? How did that happen, your grace?"

"When Julian was a mere babe in arms, his father apologized to him that he couldn't be the future Duke of Brabante. But it wouldn't matter, he told him, because he was going to make him more important than a mere duke; he was going to make him a prince. From that day on, he would kiss Julian's tiny hand and say grandly, 'Never forget in the years ahead that you are the Prince of Ravenscar.' As you can imagine, this makes Julian very uncomfortable."

Sophie said, "I rather like it. He should, too." And she said it over and over to herself, and smiled.

Roxanne said, "Devlin owns his own home—Holly Hill, on the outskirts of Hythe, he told me. Like Julian, he very much likes to live near the sea. He told me Holly Hill was his great-grandfather's creation." She turned to Sophie. "Would you like to visit Holly Hill? Devlin said he would take us out on his boat. He said it wasn't as grand as Julian's *Désirée,* but stir up a good wind and the *Fifer* flies."

"Fifer," Sophie said. "That is an odd name for a boat."

"Devlin told me he was only five years old when his father presented the boat to him, and he didn't know what else to call it. I believe Fife was the name of his dog at the time."

Corinne paused a moment, then turned to look out the carriage window. "I do wish Julian and Devlin had not chosen to ride."

"The carriage is rather full, your grace," Sophie said. "Besides, are you telling me you would prefer to speak to gentlemen rather than very smart witty ladies? Haven't we entertained you sufficiently?"

"Oh, you are both very clever girls, as are you, Vicky. Now, Vicky, do you remember how you spent as much time at Ravenscar just as Julian did at Hardcross Manor?"

Vicky was gazing out the carriage window, seemingly mesmerized by the rolling hills interspersed with thick maple forests, but she was listening, Sophie knew it. Finally, Vicky nodded.

That was enough for Corinne. She said, "When Vicky was very young, she was in and out like both Richard and Lily. But you stopped coming, Vicky. Why?"

"I had to stop coming, you see. There was so much for me to do at home when Lily married Julian, so how could I continue to come?" Vicky turned back to the window.

That quashed the conversation.

"Surely you came to visit your sister at Ravenscar?" Roxanne asked her.

Vicky said, "There was no need. Lily spent every day at Hardcross. Why should I come here when Lily was never here anyway?"

That quashed the conversation again.

Roxanne said, "I tried to convince Devlin to ride inside the carriage with us. I even warned him that it was such a beautiful day and the sun would surely roast his sensitive self." She leaned toward Corinne. "I told him if I had to be closed inside a rolling box, then he should suffer and join us. He said he had no intention of being at the whim of a handful of ladies in a rolling box. He said he doubted we could control ourselves. I did not inquire exactly what he meant by that."

Corinne laughed. "It will be a full moon tonight. I wonder if Devlin has any special plans."

The ladies were laughing, except for Vicky, when the carriage pulled to a sharp halt, and the horses snorted and whinnied. They heard Julian shout, "Look—that is smoke!" They saw Julian jab his heels into Cannon's sides, and his gelding leapt forward, Devlin beside him. They disappeared around a curve in the road.

John Coachman spurred the horses forward.

It was Corinne who cried out, "Oh, no. It's the Queen Ann Dower House! Thank heavens there is no one living there." Flames were shooting out of the windows. There was no doubt in anyone's mind the inside would be gutted, but of course the stone exterior would remain.

A score of people splashed buckets of water on the flames, but everyone knew it was no good.

Roxanne, her head out the carriage window, felt Sophie tugging her away and obligingly made room for her.

Sophie sucked in her breath. "How did this happen?"

Corinne said from behind them, "Who would burn down the Dower House? How can it be an accident?"

"That would mean someone set it afire," Sophie said.

The carriage stopped near the Dower House. Julian pulled Cannon close. "No one knows how the fire started. It would seem I have an enemy, though I already knew that. Mother, I will be up to the house in a little while." He gave them a salute and motioned for John Coachman to continue. The carriage rolled up the wide tree-lined drive to Ravenscar. Corinne didn't point out that the palm and maple and oak trees were new. She said, "I considered living there, you know, when Julian married Lily, but when Lily said she had no wish to displace me, I continued on at the big house. A good thing I did. Look, there it is."

"It is magnificent," Sophie said. "A palace and a castle, all mixed together. Look, Roxanne, there is enough stone to empty a quarry."

Corinne said, "That huge central block was built back in the fourteenth century; the other wings have been added at the whim of succeeding generations. His grace said we didn't need any more drafty corridors, any more chambers that would serve to house unwelcome guests. He elected to modernize the family wing. There are even water closets and the loveliest airy dressing rooms. The family wing is to the left of the central core. It stretches back nearly to the sea. His grace always said he liked to smell the sea when he awoke in the morning." She paused, seeing, remembering, Roxanne and Sophie knew, then she said matter-of-factly, "He wanted to be buried here, and he was."

There were no crenellated walls, no turrets, no moat, despite the house's having been built during the age of continuous warfare. It was massive, stretching high to the heavens, a solid fierce warrior to vanquish any enemy who dared approach. Sophie said, "I can smell the sea. I agree with his grace, it is a splendid fragrance."

The carriage pulled to a halt in front of the—palace, castle—Sophie shook her head. No, it was a palace, since a prince lived here.

On the steps stood an old man garbed in stark black. "That is Pouffer," Corinne said. "He is very old, but when Julian once asked him if he wished to retire, I thought he would burst into tears. Since this is his home, both Julian and I agree he will go directly from here to heaven when his time comes. And there is Mrs. Trebah, our housekeeper, blind as a bat, has been for twenty years, but I swear to you she can smell a dust mote from ten feet. She is a dear woman. Wait until you taste Mrs. Coltrak's black cakes."

Pouffer, smiling widely with his six remaining teeth, welcomed the ladies. Then his composure disappeared and he began to wring his hands. "By all the sins of Satan, sin still abounds, your grace, did you see it? Our precious Dower House is no more, burned to the stones by some ruffians. Oh, my, will we be invaded by miscreants and burned in our bed? Begad and begorrah, 'tis too much to bear on a fine April day. Aye, I am feeling on the weedy side."

"Get hold of yourself, Pouffer, we have guests." But even as she spoke, Corinne patted the old man's arm. "Do not worry so, Pouffer, we will be fine. You know very well the prince will keep us safe. Look, I have brought you three beautiful young ladies to amuse. Ah, Mrs. Trebah, how well you are looking. Did you hear me tell Pouffer about our three guests? Yes, they are standing very near me. Now, let us go into the house." Corinne, her hand now transferred to Mrs. Trebah's arm, to ensure she didn't run into anything, led them up the dozen wide stone steps into the entrance hall.

Prince? Sophie smiled. Surely this address, used by all who lived hereabouts, must drive Julian quite mad. She liked it very much.

32

S ophie stood beside Roxanne and Vicky in the huge central entrance hall and stared upward a good sixty feet.
A gleaming chandelier hung on a massive rope to within
twenty feet of their heads. Everything shone and smelled of
lemon wax, and, oddly, there was the scent of dog, not a wet
smell but just—dog.

There were Flemish suits of armor lining one wall, a
massive open fireplace that could roast an entire cow, an
incredibly old beautiful Turkey carpet covering the stones.
It would require a dozen men to roll it up and lift it.

Corinne walked briskly to the right. "Pouffer, may we
please have some of Mrs. Coltrak's tea and saffron cake?
Come into the drawing room, girls." She took off her lavender leather gloves as she walked into a long, narrow room,
a fireplace in the middle, wide glass windows looking out
onto the front courtyard.

Vicky said, "I have always believed Ravenscar to be the
most beautiful house in all of England. I always wanted to
live here."

Then why did you stop coming here? Sophie wanted to

ask but didn't. Who knew what would come out of Vicky's mouth with that question?

Corinne smiled. "My dear, there are many beautiful houses in England. Have you ever been out of Cornwall?"

"No, but I do know what is what, your grace, and my father has given me books with drawings in them. I have read many travel journals. I have visited the world."

The ladies watched Pouffer, his shoulders back, make his stately way into the room, a huge Georgian silver tray on his arms.

"But most of all I love saffron cake," Vicky said, sat forward on the green brocade chair, and watched Pouffer closely. The old man smiled, knowing he had an audience.

Corinne said, "I can't smell the smoke here. Luckily, the wind is sending the smoke away in the other direction."

"It wafts toward the village, your grace," Pouffer said, and gave Corinne a beautiful bow, "which is a pity."

Roxanne said, "The house was nearly gutted when we stopped, the flame was that virulent. We believe someone must have set it afire. What do you think?"

The old man didn't immediately answer her, but she saw that his hands shook a bit as he served the cake. "Oh, dear, this is bad, so very bad. I do not know who could have done something so bad, miss, but there are so many cloven-hoofed young'uns about, it fair to curdles Major Dawkins's precious Glenda's milk."

Roxanne said, "Cloven-hoofed, Pouffer? You mean you have Devil worshippers here? Near Ravenscar?"

The old man slowly straightened. "Her grace will tell you, miss. They light fires in the meadows and dance and cause mischief when it pleases them to do so."

"Like what?" Sophie asked.

"Like stealing a cow's milk," Pouffer said, "or digging up vines and throwing them through windows. This is the first time they have destroyed something that belonged to the prince. Bad things coming, miss, bad things coming."

"Thank you, Pouffer. You may leave, now that you have scared the liver out of our young ladies."

Pouffer gave Corinne another magnificent bow and took himself out of the room.

"Only a fool would be frightened of the witches," Vicky said, a slice of saffron cake in each hand. "I would join them, but I don't know who they are. I have never even seen them. Sometimes I don't believe they even exist, it is all a fairy tale to frighten children. Can you imagine dancing around a fire in a meadow, moonlight spilling down to glitter off your white shift? Now, the Dower House, now it will be a romantic ruin—once the smoke smell is gone."

Witches and cloven-hoofed young'uns? How, Roxanne wondered, would they deal with a vampire in their midst? She smiled as she rose. "I believe I shall see if the gentlemen are here yet. Ma'am, I'll bring them in for tea." And she left the drawing room with her long-legged stride.

Sophie frowned after her. What was Roxanne up to?

They heard voices. When Julian and Devlin came into the drawing room, their clothes covered with smoke and ashes, their faces black, Corinne jumped to her feet, eyed both of them carefully, realized they were fine, and said, "Come over here, but do not sit down. You may drink your tea standing smartly by the fireplace."

Both men turned down the offer of tea and took themselves off to clean up. It was some time before Julian and Devlin presented themselves again to the ladies and spoke about the fire.

"There were no obvious signs that someone set the fire," Devlin said. "But we all know someone did."

Julian rose when Sophie asked if he would take them about the house—no, the palace, she corrected, and he smiled. He turned to Vicky. "You wish to accompany us? You know every nook and cranny in this pile of stones."

"No, Julian, I don't wish to walk anymore today," Vicky said, and took a small bite of yet another slice of saffron cake. "Ravenscar is not a pile of stones. There are water closets in the new family wing. Six of them, I believe. Later, I wish to inspect the ruin."

Once in the entrance hall, Devlin paused in front of a

suit of armor. "Look at this one knight, Roxanne. Can you imagine a man inside that thing? He would die of heat prostration."

"Look at this rust, Devlin. Do you believe it to be ancient dried blood?"

Sophie and Julian left them to the discussion of waging battle while entombed in armor and walked toward the back of the house.

"You still smell like smoke," Sophie said, sniffing Julian. "I suppose it will take a while to wash it all out. At least you did not burn yourself. Did you?"

He shook his head. "My valet, Pliny, does not take such a sanguine view, I'm afraid. He is currently moaning and wringing his hands, blaming me at great sustained volume for ruining a good set of clothes. He is quite enjoying the drama."

"Have him take the clothes and toss them on the embers at the Dower House."

"Destroy the evidence?"

"That's right. No proof left."

He eyed her, smiling. "A good idea."

"So everyone here calls you prince?"

He laughed. "Don't unsheathe your wit on me. I promise I have no plans to become an insufferable fat idiot who orders everyone about. To be honest, I really don't pay it any attention anymore, since everyone has called me that all my life."

When Julian paused in front of a large portrait of a gentleman in a ruff and velvet pants, Sophie said, "Pouffer says cloven-hoofed young'uns set the fire."

"I doubt that, particularly since I've never seen a single cloven hoof in the area."

"It was Richard, of course," Sophie said dispassionately. "He probably hired a local to do it for him. I really do wish to stick a blade through his gullet, Julian. I smelled dog when we came in. Where are the spaniels?"

"They're very probably in the estate room; that's where they spend most of their time. Unlike the Hardcross estate room with its small, enclosed garden, here there is no garden but rather a stretch that goes to the cliffs, walled in on either side. It's been a dog run for years. The spaniels bark their heads off as they race directly to the edge of the cliff, a very low cliff. It's as if they are daring each other to see who will get closest to the edge before stopping. No, not one of them has ever slipped over the edge, not that they would get hurt."

"I'd like to meet them. My pug died last year from extreme old age. I have missed him."

"All right." Julian turned them down a corridor that led into another wing of the house. "They're King Charles spaniels, from the same litter and only a year old. You will take care of your gown. Even though they are well behaved, you are new and thus a possible enemy. They seek only to protect me."

"Well, why not? You are their prince."

He arched a dark eyebrow at her.

They heard frantic barking before Julian opened the stout oak door. Four floppy-eared spaniels ran madly to Julian, paused, then danced around him, barking their heads off, their tails waving so fast they were blurs. They ignored Sophie completely. They were some protectors, she thought. She watched Julian tug on ears, call out names, and pet each one—scratching bellies as he accepted frantic licks. Then he rose. "Sit!" All four of the spaniels dutifully sat in a line in front of him. "This is Sophie. She is a girl, so be kind and patient with her. Say hello now. Sophie, this is Cletus, Oliver, Hortense, and Beatrice."

They didn't dance and leap around her, they lightly sniffed at her skirts, gave soft little barks, then returned to their line in front of Julian.

"Pouffer has continued to train them," Julian said. "He is magic with them. If he told them to spit out a well-cooked piece of meat, they probably would. They were learning when I left to go to London with Mama. Sit down, Sophie."

When she did, one of the spaniels jumped up and licked her hand. Soon Sophie was sitting on the Aubusson carpet, her skirts spread about her, the spaniels vying for her attention.

Julian stood by the small fireplace, his arms crossed over his chest, watching. He saw her pleasure, heard her laughter, and felt something he had no wish to feel at all move deep inside him. She was a child, nothing more than a charming, innocent child. That was it, she charmed him with her candor, her openness, her utter lack of artifice and deceit. She knew nothing of the world, of his world in particular. She was meant to be protected, to be cherished. He said, "Cletus, stop chewing on her hair."

Sophie, laughing, pulled Cletus into her arms and held him close, rocking him. "So you are Cletus, are you?"

"Let's take them out." When the four spaniels were racing hell-bent for the cliff edge some sixty feet distant, Julian drew Sophie to a stop.

"I know what you are planning, I can see it in your face. I cannot prove Richard burned the Dower House, so I do not wish you to accuse him, all right?"

"Do you know, Prince, as I believe I've said before, if I knew I wouldn't be hanged, I should delight in sticking a stiletto between his ribs."

So much for protecting and cherishing this one, he thought. He told her about his childhood here, all the dogs he'd watched race toward the cliff. He told her about Pouffer, how he loved the old man, how he'd been in his life since he'd been born. Finally, he called out, "Come, let us go back inside." All four spaniels came pelting back to them, tongues lolling, tails wagging. "You do not have to call me Prince."

"Yes," she said slowly, looking up at him. "I do."

33

Devlin said, "I prefer cats to Julian's brood of spaniels. I do not like to be licked." He paused for a moment, cleared his throat. "Well, I must amend that. I should have said I do not like dogs scouring my face. As for licking— well, never mind that. What do you think?"

Roxanne, who was pulling out a weed that threatened to choke a rosebush, looked up at him over her shoulder. "So you prefer cats to do the licking?"

"Yes, of course, cats. My two princesses, Maybelle and Penelope, are small and white, and each one so sure of her own superiority I many times have to beg them to sleep with me. But eventually they come to bed and wrap themselves around my neck, or snuggle in behind my knees."

"Wouldn't it be rather crowded?"

"Crowded? What do you mean?"

Roxanne said in a distant voice, "I have heard it said you have mistresses, my lord. What do your ladies think of your cats sleeping around your neck?"

He said, "Wherever did you hear such a thing, Roxanne?"

She heard his voice change, deepen, grow more austere.

She shrugged. "It seems to be common knowledge. You, my lord, are known as a man of the world, as well as a man of possible other worlds as well, given your avoidance of the sun."

"Isn't it also common knowledge that mistresses never sleep in a gentleman's house?"

Roxanne rose, dusted her hands on her skirts. She looked him straight in the eyes. "However should I know that?"

He waved a hand. "You are twenty-seven years old, you were raised in society, albeit the salons of York, and I don't believe you've ever even visited a convent. Ah, enough of that. I asked Sophie if you preferred cats or dogs, and she told me you worshipped cats as well. Is this true?"

"Yes. I miss Mathilda and William dreadfully. However, my father also adores cats. I wouldn't doubt they are warming him at night now that I've deserted them. Where are Maybelle and Penelope?"

He pulled her up, drew her hand through his arm. "My housekeeper at Holly Hill spoils them shamelessly both when I am there and when I am not. Let's walk to the cliff edge and observe the movement of the waves on the shore."

The breeze was balmy, the day cloudy enough so that Devlin was not constrained to wear a hat. Roxanne saw a dozen palm trees and couldn't help smiling. This place was amazing, and there was something of magic in the air. Finally, she couldn't help herself. "Do you still love Corrie Sherbrooke?"

Devlin stopped dead in his tracks, turned to face her. "Do you know, my dear, that inquiry throttles all attempts at sparkling conversation in my throat? Why ever would you ask me that?"

Why, indeed? Shutting her mouth occasionally might be a wise course to follow, but she didn't. "I believe you asked her uncle to marry her."

"Did I? That was more than six months ago. Perhaps, at the time, upon reflection, I felt compelled to give her a choice, and she made it. She is a married woman now, so revoltingly happy with James it makes me shake my head in wonder. Yes,

yes, I know he looks like a god, but who cares? Who wants a face that makes ladies swoon in your path?"

"I cannot believe you said that."

Devlin sighed. "I can't either, truth be told."

"You are not a troll, Devlin."

"No?" He cocked an eyebrow at her.

"You are even more handsome than your half uncle, and he is renowned for his good looks."

"His mother started that rumor."

She grinned up at him shamelessly.

He said, "Now, my girl, look out over the channel. It is calm today, so you know the fire was set at strategic spots in the Dower House, since there is no wind to whip up flames."

"It seems a paltry attempt at revenge," Roxanne said slowly, tasting the salt air in her mouth. "I mean, why the Dower House and not a direct assassination attempt?"

"Richard tried that in London last week, so Julian told me. But he wasn't really serious, Julian said, because he knew he'd be hanged, so I suppose, as a man of little imagination, he was forced to destroy the Dower House as a sort of token slap in the face when he knew Julian would be riding here to Ravenscar. However, I do believe this time he has pushed my uncle to the brink."

"The brink? Surely you don't believe Julian will shoot him?"

"Who knows?" He shrugged.

She wanted to punch him but managed to control herself. "Look at those stone walls. Why are they there?"

"Those are protective walls so the four spaniels aren't tempted to abscond to Land's End and chase rooks. The run leads directly from Julian's estate room to the cliffs. Well, some cliffs—they're not at all high above the beach. The dogs can dash about here, daring each other to leap off the cliff, which wouldn't hurt them, even if they leapt."

"But they don't know that."

"No."

Devlin paused for a moment, lifted his face to the cloudy sky. "Do you know, I'm beginning to believe my uncle isn't regarding your niece with an elder's indulgent eye anymore. What do you think?"

Roxanne tossed a rock over the edge of the cliff, watched it bounce on the rocks and fall onto the dirty sand some ten feet below. "I believe Julian has a fondness for her, since his mother does. Is it more? Maybe. Do you not like Sophie as well?"

"Oh, yes, she sparkles, you know. I've watched her ignore the gentlemen who have tried to attach her, not that they've had all that much time. And why does she ignore them? I wonder." He walked to the edge of the cliff and studied the beach below. He turned slowly to face Roxanne. Her vibrant hair haloed her head. He said slowly, "It is the strangest thing, but I have not visited any of my mistresses in over a week now. Do you not think that odd?"

"It is possible," she said, not looking at him, "that you are so charmed by Sophie you have no wish to indulge yourself."

"Indulge myself," he repeated. "What a quaint way of putting it. No, being charmed by Sophie hasn't anything to do with it."

A shout came from Ravenscar. It was Julian. "Devlin! My mother requests your presence."

"Ah, well, perhaps it's best, you know?"

"No," Roxanne said. "I don't know if it's for the best or not." She walked in silence beside him back toward the huge stone manor, mansion, castle, palace—she didn't know what to call Ravenscar, and at that moment, she didn't particularly care. She was twenty-seven years old, the same age as Devlin Monroe, the future Duke of Brabante. She wasn't a young miss suffering in the throes of her first Season, terrified she wouldn't gain one single marriage proposal or enjoy any gentleman's exclusive attention. No, she was a seasoned matron—well, very nearly—and she knew what was what and how men and women behaved, but this: Did Devlin admire Sophie more than Julian appeared to? She didn't know. It seemed to her, though, that Sophie hadn't suffered a single throe of anxiety. On the other hand, she was twenty years old, not a young girl of eighteen fresh out of a protected schoolroom. Roxanne loved her, indeed, she did, she was so like Bethanne. Was she too young for Julian? If so, she was the perfect age for Devlin. She sparkled?

Roxanne's heart hurt, something she recognized even though she'd felt it only once before in her adult life, with her long-ago suitor John Singleton, who had only wanted her money.

⇥ 34 ⇤

THE NEXT MORNING

Sophie stood facing Julian in his estate room, her arms crossed over her chest, the four spaniels sleeping on every available chair and the sofa—it was, in short, a dog's room. That made her smile as she gently picked up Beatrice, sat herself down on the leather sofa, and laid the dog gently on her lap. She began to lightly caress Beatrice's long, floppy ears, resulting in soft snorts of pleasure.

"She appears to like you, Sophie."

"She likes what I'm doing to her, that's all. I will say it again, since you did not appear to hear me, Julian. I do not wish to return to Hardcross Manor. Why should I? I do not like the feel of the place, nor do I like the inhabitants. I do not trust the baron. He is all smiles and bonhomie, but there is something lurking in his eyes that makes me nervous. And there is Richard. I might forget myself and try to pound him into the floor. Actually, I don't want to have to see Vicky across the breakfast table again, either.

"I want all of us to remain here at Ravenscar, not go back to Hardcross Manor. If you wish to visit, why then, it is a short ride." She paused for a moment, frowned. "As for Vicky, I was thinking she might be pretending to oddness. That way, she can say whatever she pleases, and from what I've seen, no one stops her and asks her why she's saying such ridiculous things."

"An act?" Julian leaned down and picked up Oliver, and like Sophie, he began stroking the dog's long, soft ears. "She didn't used to be so odd," he added.

"What did she used to be?"

"I remember her so clearly as a little girl, all giggles and smiles and mischief. I can see Lily scolding her for some childish misdeed, then hugging her. As Vicky grew older, though, she changed, as everyone must. I really can't pinpoint when she became as she is now, but it has been a while."

"You were at Waterloo?"

He stopped stroking Oliver's ears. Oliver yipped, and Julian began rubbing his belly. He nodded curtly, "Yes, I was. How do you know that?"

"Your mother told me about your commendation from the Duke of Wellington himself."

"You were very young at that time."

"Yes." Sophie had known two other men in her village who'd fought with Wellington at Waterloo, and neither of them wished to speak of it, either. "So were you. You were a boy. And then you went into the shipping business?"

"That's right. This demonstrates to you what a small world we inhabit—I met Thomas Malcombe, the Earl of Lancaster, in Genoa. He is very successful in shipping. He saw my enthusiasm and asked me to join him, to see if I could be of use to him, I imagine. I was. Then he helped me strike out on my own. Thomas Malcombe is an excellent man. He lives part of the year in England, in Glenclose-on-Rowen; part in Ireland; and at least three months a year in Italy. He always takes his wife and four boys with him. They're a grand family."

"So where is your small world in this recital?"

"Malcombe's wife is Meggie Sherbrooke, James Sherbrooke her cousin, the Earl of Northcliffe her uncle. Do you know, Pendragon—that is their home in Ireland—is the premier training mews for racing cats in Ireland?"

"Racing cats?" Sophie said blankly. "How does one race a cat? I can't imagine it. No, that's not possible, you're jesting with me."

"Not I. Actually, I once attended a cat race at the McCaulty racecourse near Eastbourne. Eight racing cats out of twelve actually crossed the finish line. There was betting and cheering and some fisticuffs; a tough sport, is cat racing. Thomas told me once that at the first cat race in Ireland, his dog got loose and decided to race with the cats. As you can imagine, it was pandemonium. If ever you meet the Malcombes, Meggie can tell you all about it."

Sophie studied Beatrice's soft ear. "You've done so very much, Julian. No, no, don't tell me it's because you are so ancient and you've had simply dozens of years to click up your heels and do everything imaginable—no, you started when you were only a boy—Waterloo, for heaven's sake—whereas I've only—" She broke off, sighed. "I'm whining, aren't I? My twenty years on this earth have been excellent. I've never known want or been around bad people—well, there was Mr. Jack, who strangled his wife, but he was drunk at the time and never remembered a thing. My father is a trial, but he is not rotten like Richard Langworth. Let me get back on track. To me, all the inhabitants of Hardcross Manor worry me to my toes. To Roxanne's toes as well, I think. I spoke briefly to your mother, and she thinks it a marvelous idea if we remain here until we return to London. Actually, when your mother sent you to find Devlin yesterday, she wanted to get his agreement to remain here as well."

He eyed her. "So you went behind my back."

She gave him a blazing smile. "Doesn't a competent commander always line up his supporters before he charges forward?"

He eyed her again. He knew when a person was unmovable, particularly ladies, who excelled at deciding what they wanted and getting it. He knew his mother wanted Sophie here so they would be thrown together every single hour of the day. He was getting quite used to the pitiful sighs from her whenever he didn't give Sophie his full attention. How many times would he have to repeat to her that this girl was young enough—nearly—to be his daughter, not his bloody wife?

He didn't want anyone here at Ravenscar for the simple reason that he wished to smuggle in goods one final time, and he didn't want to take any chances. He'd never before considered smuggling this close to his home—too dangerous, too many eyes—but after Richard had followed him to Saint Osyth and discovered his midnight hobby, he knew it had to stop. So one last time. No one would know, no one would find out. He'd direct in boats from the channel to row their way up the River Horvath to a small landing. His cave was very close by.

One final time.

He would simply have to sneak out, very quietly. No one need ever know. He was fooling himself—he knew to his boots that if they were here, they'd find out. He could picture Sophie listening for his footfalls at midnight, putting on her own boots and following him, Roxanne at her side, Devlin carrying his pistols.

Unfortunately for him, he could also see Sophie standing with her hands on her hips in his cave, looking around in wonder at the incredible stalagmites and stalactites, listening to her own voice echoing off the high ceiling, and inquiring politely what he was doing there. He could also see her grinning wildly with the news that smuggled brandy was to arrive in ten minutes.

Damnation. What was wrong with him? There would be no cave visits by Sophie or Roxanne or Devlin; it was absurd to even consider it—Julian realized he was brooding, something he found unacceptable in himself. Brooding was for melancholy poets, not for men who actually accomplished things. When there was a problem, he liked to throw himself on top of it and wrestle it to the ground, not brood about it.

He eyed Sophie, who was now sitting opposite him, calmly swinging her foot and watching him. Beatrice was still sprawled on her lap. She'd said her piece, and now she waited. He liked that in her. She didn't keep talking and talking, in case she found another argument to convince him of something she wanted to have, or repeat the same argument over and over, as most people did.

He said at last, voice remote, "I have a lot of business to conduct."

"Yes, of course you do. What is your point?"

"Some of the things I have to do I simply can't talk about. Also, my business will require most of my time."

Her eyebrow hoisted itself up.

"I must see to my yacht." *Where had that idiocy come from?*

"*Désirée*? I should very much like to see her. Show me a dirty deck and I shall scrub it for you. I am a useful girl, Julian. Use me."

⇌ 35 ⇌

Julian's eyes nearly crossed. If only she knew—yet another sign of her innocence, her damnable youth. He said, "I thought Roxanne was the enthusiast. You also sail, Sophie?"

"Roxanne has never been on a boat in her life. It's true her father, my grandfather, nearly drowned when he was a boy, so there was never any boating for his three daughters. He was simply too afraid to allow it.

"My parents, however, were vastly different. Not that my father, the vicar, likes to sail, mind you; as I think about it, Papa doesn't like to do anything that might make him breathe hard or bring sweat to his brow. But to his credit, he never objected when mother and I were invited to sail with the Caruthers on their yacht. Yes, I enjoy sailing."

"But Roxanne spoke of the gentleman in Brighton who had a yacht, and then she shuddered. With pleasure, I supposed. I thought Devlin would stomp on his hat."

"She said that only to make him want to stomp. She is very good at it. So will you take me out in your yacht, Julian? Will you let me scrub a deck?"

Slowly, he nodded. "Very well, we will remain here, for the time being."

But what of Richard and his father? And mending the breach? Then there is the Dower House, and what of my final smuggling run? He cursed under his breath.

He gave Sophie a look of dislike. "It's amazing what the younger generation gets away with," he said.

"Watch and learn, my lord."

Julian was still brooding when they saw Vicky off some thirty minutes later. He said to her as he handed her into the carriage, "Do thank your father for his hospitality, and tell him I should like to speak to him again. Perhaps he can visit me here."

Vicky nodded, then said, "Should you like to speak to Richard again?"

"Quite possibly."

Vicky took his hand in hers. "I do not know if Papa still believes you killed Lily. Richard does, of course. He loved Lily very much, and he did find you leaning over poor Lily, lying there as dead as one can be. I believe Father wants you to convince him you didn't kill her. As for the Dower House, I do not know if Richard had the fire set. He has become secretive, so I cannot be certain."

"All I can do is tell him the truth, which I have innumerable times, and ask him to his face if he is responsible for the fire."

"It is such a pity," Vicky said.

"What exactly is a pity, Vicky?"

"That you spent only one day at Hardcross Manor."

It seemed more like a year. He said, "Why do you think Lily spent so much time at Hardcross Manor after we married?"

Her eyes darted away. "Why ever do you think I would know that?"

But she knew something, Julian knew it. Baffled, he nodded to the coachman, and he and Sophie stood side by side, watching the carriage roll down the wide drive.

Corinne came up behind them. "I believe Leah is pleased

we are not returning. Now she will have Richard's complete attention."

"Did she have a London Season, Roxanne?"

"No, she did not. She was being courted by Lord Merrick at the time."

Sophie said to Roxanne, who was now looking after Devlin, "Julian is going to take me sailing on his yacht. I believe you and Devlin should join us."

Roxanne gave Sophie a big smile. "I should love to. When do we leave? Now? Oh, dear, I suppose I shouldn't have said that. I know, I must mend my gown."

"Paltry, Miss Radcliffe," Julian said.

Roxanne tapped her toe on the graveled drive. "I see my precious niece has confessed the dreadful truth to you."

Sophie said, "I daresay Devlin already knows about that gentleman in Brighton. I quite liked Lord Ponsonby. He was charming, don't you agree, Roxanne? And ever so accomplished at flirtation and waltzing."

Devlin snorted.

Roxanne stared him down. "I spent many a lovely moonlight evening with him, strolling on the Steyne. I suppose all of your mistresses join you on your sailboat, my lord."

"Roxanne, what a thing to say." Corinne looked torn between embarrassment and amusement. "I know you consider yourself past your last prayers, but really."

Devlin studied her face for a moment, the white flesh, not as white as his but very nearly. "Do you know, dear one, I have never felt the need to invite my score of mistresses to sail? I believe we are always fully occupied in other activities."

Corinne smacked his shoulder. "Devlin!"

Roxanne gave him a look, slammed her fist into his belly, and stalked back into Ravenscar without a backward look.

Sophie said, "Is your liver still intact, Devlin?"

"My liver will survive; as for my guts, they are in upheaval." And he grinned as he rubbed his belly.

"The two of you," Corinne said, "such ill-advised speech. I daresay that you both find each other vastly amusing."

Now, there was an interesting thought.

Two hours later, no one was grinning when Leah's carriage pulled in front of Ravenscar to disgorge not only Leah and her maid but also Richard Langworth.

"It is a case of the mountain and Mohammed," Richard said to Julian, who stood silent and stiff.

"I don't believe I wish to be either a prophet or a mound of land," Leah said, and hugged his arm to her. "What I wish is a lovely cup of tea."

"I wonder if the baron will be the next to show himself," Julian said, as he walked next to Roxanne back into Ravenscar.

⇥ 36 ⇤

Leah Cosgrove, Lady Merrick, saw only Sophie when she glided into the drawing room, gowned for the evening in her favorite pale blue, her lovely white shoulders bare, diamonds at her throat. Her niece was singing a Scottish ballad, accompanying herself on the pianoforte. She wished the idiot girl were twenty years older and didn't carry her mother's beautiful face and all that rich dark brown hair, and—*well, no matter.* She said, "How can you bear sitting there with your shoulders uncovered? Can you not feel the awful draft?"

Sophie broke off her song, sighed, and turned to look at her aunt. Leah was always stylish, and this evening was no exception. "I am very comfortable, Aunt Leah. Your shoulders are as bare as mine. Are you chilled?"

Leah walked to the pianoforte, drummed her fingers on the mahogany lid. "Richard decided I should see Ravenscar, since he spent so much of his time here as a child. I cannot believe he was not warmly welcomed. I thought it a disgrace the way Mr. Monroe—"

Sophie smoothly interrupted her. "He is a duke's son, Aunt Leah, and thus he is Lord Julian."

"That's as may be, but he treated Richard like he was some sort of ruffian bent on mischief. Thankfully, he had enough manners to invite him to stay."

"Do you so quickly forget someone burned the Dower House, Leah? People could have been hurt or killed."

Leah was scandalized. "No one was. It was a simple accident, or a servant's carelessness, nothing more. Don't tell me he believes Richard to blame for that? I know there are misunderstandings between Richard and Julian, but it is not Richard's fault. Julian murdered Richard's sister, so how is he supposed to feel?"

"I assure you Julian did not murder his wife."

"You know nothing about it, so I think it best you keep your opinions to yourself."

"You don't know anything, either, Aunt Leah."

"Of course I do. Richard confided to me that he wanted to believe Julian hadn't murdered Lily, but he saw—do you hear me, Sophie?—Richard actually saw Julian kneeling over her body. He said he still didn't want to believe it, but there was no reason for her to have killed herself, none at all, despite talk of her having a lover. So there."

"Did Richard also tell you he burned down the Dower House, a sort of stupid revenge, since if he killed Julian he would be hung?"

"You are a silly girl, Sophie. As I said, it was an accident. Richard was with me the entire time." Leah eyed her for a moment longer, then turned and flung out her arms. "I must say I cannot like this pile of stone. So many steps and frigid rooms. I have never seen such disorder in a house's design. I cannot imagine living here in the winter—your bones would freeze, and you would crack apart."

Sophie said, "Whilst you are in this house, Leah, I strongly advise you against accusing Julian of murder. For myself, I very much like Ravenscar; it seems to bridge the past to the present and promises it will be here in a distant future. It has a sort of grandeur that quite moves me. You might consider not speaking so badly of his home."

"Ah, I am polite, you know. But this house—no wonder Lily kept escaping back to her home at Hardcross Manor. I wager I would have wanted to leave this monstrous pile of rock, too."

Sophie kept her voice even, but it required a good deal of effort. "Did you know the old duke had six water closets installed in the family wing, Leah? You must visit them, you will revise your opinion."

"Oh, those ridiculous water closets—my maid couldn't stop heaping on glowing praise when she told me about each and every one of them, over and over again. I wanted to slap her. So what is a water closet, anyway?"

There came a rustling from behind Leah, the clearing of a throat, and Leah whirled about to see Corinne looking at her, the *London Gazette* lying open on her lap. Corinne said very gently, "Surely you wish to revisit that statement, Lady Merrick. It sounded so very absurd, you know."

It wasn't fair, Leah thought, staring at the dowager duchess. She hadn't noticed her at all, sitting so quietly, quite rude of her, really, not to announce her presence when Leah had come into the drawing room. No, Leah had seen only Sophie, heard that pitiful little voice of hers, her fingers butchering the simple tune she was trying to play. She wondered if the dowager duchess had been purposefully quiet, urging Leah to say what she thought, wanting to hear her honest opinion, only she hadn't liked it. And now the old bat was angry because she'd disdained a few paltry water closets?

If only Richard hadn't insisted he and Leah visit the cliffs to gaze worshipfully over the channel, lightly touching his fingertips to her mouth, stroking her bottom lip, something that both delighted and alarmed. However, the wind was violent, the air chilled, and she'd hated it.

She cleared her own throat. "Your grace, Ravenscar—where ever did that name come from?—it is surely impressive."

To give the devil her due, it was an excellent distraction, Corinne thought, rising and shaking out her satin skirts. "I have no idea where the name Ravenscar came from. We will ask Julian. Ah, there you are, dearest. Since you are the Prince of Ravenscar, you must know the origin of the name of your kingdom."

"Prince?" Leah snorted as she turned to face him. "Prince? She called you *Prince*? Richard said nothing of a title of prince for you. What sort of affectation is this?"

"Affectation? I prefer to think of it as an old amusement, nothing more," Julian said pleasantly. "My solicitor told me the third Baron Horsly actually selected Ravenscar for the name of his destrier. He decided the name had grit, perhaps even some magical power, since he believed his horse somehow saved him from certain death at the hands of a French knight, and thus, he decided to bestow the same magic on his new house, to bring luck.

"Actually, the solicitor said the baron named everything in sight Ravenscar, including, I believe, his wife at the time."

"Imagine," Sophie said, grinning, "waking up to hear your husband call you Ravenscar."

Julian arched a dark brow. "I believe he must have shortened it to Raven in moments of closeness. As a lady, don't you think that rather romantic, Sophie?"

Leah wanted to shout that it was ridiculous, but she wasn't stupid. She held her tongue. Perhaps she should be more conciliatory, encourage their confidences. Perhaps she could find proof that Julian Monroe was nothing but an upstart murderer.

Both Richard and Devlin came into the drawing room, each garbed in evening black, each looking extraordinarily fine indeed. It was obvious, though, that there had been words between them. *What?* Julian wondered.

Sophie said, "Devlin, where is Roxanne?"

He cocked his head to one side. "I hear her tinkling voice now; she's trilling laughter at Pouffer, I believe. She quite enjoys the old man. Do you know he tells her stories about Cornish pixies?" He bowed to Corinne. "Your grace. May

I say you are looking lovely this evening? The dark blue is very charming. It is a pleasure to behold you."

"I thank you, dear boy," Corinne said. "Leah was telling us you made her come here, Richard. I will admit to surprise, since you believe my son to have murdered your sister. Tell me, where were you this afternoon, when the Dower House was set afire?"

R ichard said easily, "You have known me all my life. Surely you do not believe I would take a torch to the Dower House. Why, Julian and I used to play inside, hiding in the various rooms, shouting taunts and challenges to each other."

"I wouldn't have believed you would turn on him, either," Corinne said.

Julian said, "My mother is right. Given how inseparable we were as boys, how could you possibly believe I killed Lily?"

There was hot silence. Then Sophie sat herself down on the piano stool again and began to play a French ballad, her French accent quite perfect, Julian thought, her voice not very robust but sweet and true.

Richard said, "A man must believe what he sees with his own eyes. I should like a brandy, if you decide to treat me as a guest." He paused for a moment, then said, "As my father treated you very well, indeed, yet you picked up and came to Ravenscar."

Sophie said, raising her fingers from the piano keys, "I

would like to commend Baron Horsly's sense of humor. I cannot believe he named his home after his horse, much less his wife. Do you think he really called his wife Raven, Julian?"

"Perhaps."

"I hope she was charmed and not appalled. Could I please have a glass of champagne, Julian?"

Julian nodded, and rang for Pouffer. After the old man shuffled out, Julian turned to Corinne. "Would you care for something to drink, Mother?"

"Sherry for me, dearest," Corinne said. "All of it is nasty, but I find sherry the least noxious. After all, Mrs. Coltrak prepares dishes with sherry, so how bad can it be? One must adapt, your father told me. But perhaps champagne would be nicer." She looked over at Leah, standing close to Richard Langworth, her white hand on his forearm, nearly on her tiptoes, looking up at him, at his mouth, if Corinne wasn't mistaken. What did he feel for this foul-tempered witch? she wondered.

Julian looked at the assembled company. It appeared that Ravenscar was now to be the new battleground. The kettle would boil merrily here in his home, not at Hardcross Manor, where it more rightfully belonged.

Julian said, "Roxanne? Devlin? What would you like to drink?"

Once there was champagne and filled brandy snifters, each raised a glass, but there were no toasts. There was only tense silence, each eyeing the others, both gentlemen and ladies.

Oh, joy, Roxanne thought, as she sipped her brandy. It was excellent. "Julian, I don't suppose this is smuggled French brandy?"

He stiffened, she saw it, only a second, no more, and then he was all easy and smiling again, but she was certain. What had bothered him? Smuggling? What was this? She saw Richard was nearly *en pointe,* and said quickly, smiling, "I always think my brandy must be smuggled, since it tastes so good. Now, Sophie, as you can all see, is a lover of champagne."

Pouffer didn't announce dinner for another fifteen minutes, which allowed the party to keep drinking.

Dinner passed off well, with Mrs. Coltrak hovering as Pouffer himself brought in her specialty, squab pie, as well as mutton. There was also pilchard and leek pie, stewed watercress served with boiled chicken, and black cake for dessert. Corinne said, after a bite, "I do adore the currants and the raisins and the almonds." She didn't want to remove with the ladies from the dining room, a dark-paneled room with a score of paintings showing dead animals strung up in a kitchen. It had forward-facing windows covered with golden draperies, and for all its heaviness, was nonetheless elegant and warm. She didn't wish to leave the men alone. Only the heavenly father knew what would happen.

Pouffer asked Devlin as he poured port, "My lord, I understand your father is a leader in the House of Lords."

The old man was quite the diplomat, Julian thought, and sat back to listen to Devlin talk about his father, Julian's half brother.

When silence fell again, Julian said, "I fear you and I will not be able to speak civilly to each other, Richard. Therefore, I suggest we join the ladies." He added after a brief moment, "Richard, I daresay you know what you're doing with Roxanne's sister. She obviously does not wish to be here. Perhaps you wish to return to Hardcross Manor with her in tow?"

"Oh, no," Richard said easily, stretched out in his chair, his hands clasped over his lean belly. "I fancy it amusing to see Leah's sister and her niece try not to slap her."

Devlin set down his port, leaned back in his chair, and swung his leg over the armchair. "Have you ever seen her unpleasant before?"

Richard was thoughtful, then shook his head. "I must make it a point to tell her to admire Ravenscar, not despise it, for I myself have always admired this vast pile of stone. Surely she would wish to be of one mind with me. Also, I will remind her she is to admire the water closets."

Devlin said, "You can never count on ladies to do the expected thing. Do you know my mother?"

Richard shook his head.

"I have, needless to say, known her all my life. At home, I have never seen her agree with my father, not one single time, but in company she is so compliant, agreeing with everything that comes out his mouth, it makes me stare. I find myself wondering—are all ladies like this? Do none of them even like their husbands? Is their behavior in polite society a sham?"

Richard never looked away from Devlin's face. He said slowly, "It appears I must think about this."

When they joined the ladies a scant ten minutes later, Leah was seated, silent and docile as a lamb, next to the dowager duchess, admiring her needlework. Roxanne and Sophie were off by themselves, obviously arguing about something.

What was it? Julian wondered.

⟿ *38* ⟿

Ravenscar
THE FOLLOWING MORNING

Julian wasn't surprised when he heard Sophie's light foot-steps behind him. He sighed as he turned to her. "I had hoped you would not notice my leaving. It did not enter my mind that you would follow me." Well, it had, but he wasn't about to tell her that.

She smiled at him as she stepped into the low-hanging cave entrance. "You were clever, asking Pouffer to say you were riding to Ravenscar Village to hire men to clean up the Dower House and begin the rebuilding. However, Cannon was still in his stall. Then I saw you walking this way, looking shifty and secretive, so I followed you."

There was a touch of humor in his voice as he said, "I should have waited until midnight."

"I am a light sleeper. I would have heard you pass by my bedchamber and followed." She paused, then stepped in farther and stared. He was standing not six feet away from her, holding a lantern. "Goodness, this is amazing. Where is the ceiling? How big is the cave? Oh, my, look at all those formations. What are they called?"

He grinned at her, couldn't help it. She'd outwitted him. "Come on in, I'll show you everything."

He pointed out a formation of stalactites that looked like a pipe organ in a church, raised the lantern high so she could see the cave ceiling. "And look over here, I swear it looks like Oliver. One of his ears is longer than the other." He found himself telling her boyhood stories of when he'd protected his cave from the French. "I remember fighting to the death many times."

"You always won?"

"Naturally."

"Do you know, I've only been in one cave before— Roxanne's small cave in Yorkshire. It was quite paltry, really; you had to bend nearly double to walk inside. But this one is grand, indeed. And now . . ." She walked right up to him, came onto her tiptoes, and said an inch from his nose, "Why are you here, Julian?"

Lie. No, give it up. "I'm a smuggler, have been for a very long time. My favorite landing beach and cave are near Chichester, at Saint Osyth. The last time I brought in smuggled goods, I knew someone was watching. It didn't take me long to figure out it was Richard."

"When was this?"

"Not long ago. But I knew I wanted one final run before I retired. I decided it would be safe here, even though Richard lives only a couple of miles away. When I was here yesterday—"

"That's all right. I knew you were lying when you spoke of walking in the home wood. Listen, there is no way Richard could find out."

She gave him a blazing smile, clasped his hands in hers. "It will be our secret. Don't worry, I won't tell anyone, including Roxanne. Does Devlin know about your . . . hobby?"

"Hobby? That makes it sound like a lad collecting seashells. Actually, it is illegal, Sophie, and dangerous. Excisemen are out to catch smugglers. They're a ruthless lot."

"But you're right, no one will know—particularly, Richard."

"I hope you're right. I actually think of smuggling as a service to my fellow countrymen. I make goods available that don't carry the heavy import duties. Ah, but the truth is—it is a lot of fun."

She lightly touched her fingertips to his cheek. "It is also something that is yours, isn't it, Julian? Just yours."

He said, "You asked about Devlin. I took him along with me some five years ago, after he'd come down from Oxford. I told him no more, since the future Duke of Brabante couldn't very well take the chance of being deported to Botany Bay if caught. He's argued with me, but I've held firm. He quite liked landing the boats, trading midnight jests with his men, and unloading the goods." Julian didn't mention the profits, which were usually quite substantial.

Sophie said, "Do you know, Devlin is particularly well suited to smuggling, since it always happens in the middle of the night. Add a full moon, and he'd be in heaven. But wait, you wouldn't want a full moon; the darker the better."

He laughed. She joined him, their laughter echoing all around them. She thought she sounded like a braying donkey and quickly shut her mouth. Julian thought it a shame he could no longer hear the sweet sparkling bells. He said, "It isn't a lark, Sophie; one must be very careful. I never bribed any of the excisemen before. Why let them dip their hands in my pockets?"

"I shouldn't want them in my pockets, either," she said. "It sounds very exciting, but I will tell you I am relieved this is your final time."

He watched her. He was coming to know her so well, since now he knew exactly what she was thinking. He lightly tapped his fingers to her nose. "No, you may not come with me. I mean it, Sophie, it is simply too dangerous. No."

She looked like she would argue with him, then, suddenly, she gave him a fat smile. "Very well, Julian, whatever you say. Can we explore?"

"There isn't anything more, only this one huge room."

"When is your last shipment coming in?"

"I must contact my man in Portsmouth, give him instructions. I'm thinking ten days from now. There will be no moon, and given we are in Cornwall, it is likely to be very overcast. No, my girl, you will not even consider trying to sneak here."

Sophie gave him a beatific smile, rubbed her hands together. "Of course not. Now, I know smuggling is dishonest, but goodness, Julian, what adventures you've had."

"Usually, everything goes very smoothly. The goods are moved days later to London, and my man Harlan Whittaker sells to our particular buyers." He studied her face. "You're lying to me, Sophie. I can see that clever brain of yours working out how to sneak to the beach."

"Do you know, I've never had a single full-bodied adventure before in my life? I am twenty years old, Julian. Think of all the adventures you had before you were my age. You were in the battle at Waterloo! Come, one time, that's all I ask. There won't be any danger, you said so yourself. One real adventure for me and I shall be content for the rest of my days. It will be safe. No excisemen know about this cave. Richard won't find out about any of it."

She saw he was wavering.

"I am so tired of reading about other people's adventures. Just one for me."

He didn't believe it, but he actually nodded.

"Yes! You are wonderful; nothing will happen." She threw her arms around him.

Julian remained frozen to the spot. He felt her warm and soft against the length of him. "No," he said, and took a step back, but Sophie didn't release him, she simply stepped with him. She looked up at him, smiled. "You are not my uncle, Julian. You are my partner."

Partner? Well, that sounded better than—what? Lover? Husband?

"A partner, Sophie?" he asked carefully.

"Yes, I will help direct in the boats, perhaps help unload contraband. Or if you prefer, I could keep a watch for excisemen. I can do it all, Julian; you will see how very useful I am."

She still hadn't released him. He felt the excitement in her. She was so young, so protected. She was a lady; she wasn't meant to have dangerous adventures like men—well, maybe men weren't, either. He took her arms in his hands, intending to set her away from him, but his hands didn't obey him. His hands, attached to his arms, went around her and drew her in close, too close, so close, in fact, he could feel her heart pounding against him. She was tall, and that was quite fine, every bit of her against every bit of him, a perfect fit.

He lowered his head, but not all that far. "No," he said, even as he lightly touched his mouth to hers. "No, I can't do this. It isn't right. You are far too young, you—"

"Be quiet, Julian," Sophie said against his mouth, and this time she kissed him, her warm breath feathering over him. His mouth opened, something he hadn't planned, but she didn't jump back, horrified, as surely an innocent maid should do. No, Sophie let out a little sound of surprise, then opened her own mouth. Not all that wide, but a little bit, enough to make him forget he should be running out of this cave as fast as he could. But he said the words, and they actually hurt. "Listen to me, Sophie, this will stop now. Keep your tongue in your mouth. Move back three steps. Maybe four."

She drew back three inches, stared at him. "My heart is pounding rather loudly. Can you hear it? Can you feel it?" And she moved back in, nearly as close as his shirt.

He could feel her heart. He lowered his forehead to hers. "Keep your tongue in your mouth." He made the mistake of looking down at her mouth, her lips slightly parted, soft.

She said, "If your tongue doesn't stay in your mouth, then why should mine? Shouldn't our tongues be together? I mean, I've never thought about tongues before—doing this—I suppose it is considered a magical addition to a regular kiss?"

Magical? She didn't know the half of it.

"You know, Julian, I think I would like to do it again. Can we perhaps try a little bit?"

"Be quiet. It is not a good idea. No, obey me on this."
And he raised a finger and placed it over her mouth. "Don't
argue with me about this tongue business. It is always a
prelude to other sorts of things—"

"Like what?"

"Be quiet."

"But how will I learn anything if these other sorts of
things aren't explained to me?"

"It will be up to your future husband to explain other
things to you. It is time we left here."

He sounded like a pompous disapproving parent.

Disappointment bloomed in her, and a dollop of nice cold
anger. She wanted to kick him, then she wanted to throw
herself at him and take him down to the sandy cave floor.
Then she didn't know what she wanted to do, but she did
know she'd make sure tongues were involved. *What other
sorts of things?*

But it was not to be. Julian held firm. He took her hand
and dragged her to the cave entrance. When they walked
out into the overcast morning, rain hovering over the next
rise, Sophie said, "The cave is fairly well hidden, and only
a dozen feet from the river shore. I believe its destiny was
to be a smuggling cave."

He was a moron to let her be a part of his final hoorah.
Her first and last adventure. She'd be safe enough, he'd make
sure of that. No one knew about this cave, no one—well,
Richard did, but there was no way Richard would find out
what he planned. He nodded and led her to the edge of the
River Horvath. "A boat can swing into the river and be here
in fifteen minutes." He looked back at the cave. If one wasn't
really looking for it, it couldn't be seen, what with the vines
hanging over the entrance and the bushes growing wildly
around it. *One last time,* he thought, *one last time.*

But what if something did go wrong? No, nothing could
happen. Nothing.

⇌ *39* ⇌

Roxanne walked into the drawing room to find Sophie seated in a wing chair, smiling. "Whatever are you so pleased about, Sophie?"

Sophie, who had Cletus and Oliver on her lap, stroking their silky, long ears, looked up. "Pleased? Well, it is a lovely day, now, isn't it? It hasn't begun raining yet."

"I know you. You were humming. You've been humming since this morning. And now that I really look at you, I realize you look different. I can't tell what it is about you, exactly, but—"

Sophie lifted Cletus under one arm, Oliver under the other, and rose. "Do you know, I fancy I like Ravenscar." *And its master, the prince.* She gave Roxanne a brilliant smile and walked from the drawing room.

"Are you going to feed them?"

Sophie shook her head. "It's a walk for these cute fellows. I've got to go to the estate room and fetch Beatrice and Hortense, unless they're with Julian, then I shall have to find him. Have you seen him?"

Roxanne frowned at her niece. Something was going on

here, but what? "I believe both Devlin and Julian left to see to the Dower House."

"What are Leah and Richard Langworth doing?"

"I fear to know."

Not a half-hour later, when Sophie was standing near the cliff in the spaniel run, watching the spaniels chase one another around, she felt him. She didn't actually hear him over the wind, but she somehow felt him near. How very odd that was, this knowing when another was present. It occurred to her then: ten days until her first foray into smuggling. Would they spend the next ten days at Ravenscar, or would everyone wish to return to London? How would Julian manage coming back? With her?

She turned slowly, the four spaniels racing away from her to Julian. He went down on his haunches and gathered all four of them into his arms and talked to them even as they licked every bit of skin their tongues could reach. He laughed, trying to duck his head, but it was no use. Slowly, even as he continued petting them, he looked up at her.

What he saw was a woman with her back to the channel, the wind whipping her skirts about, jerking her hair out of its heavy plaits.

No, he thought, *no,* she was too young, too innocent, she had no experience with men. Ah, his ridiculous litany. But he knew he had to keep that litany in the front of his brain— a score of years between him and Sophie. He pictured himself a doddering old man with few teeth in his mouth and little hair on his head—*my father, my bloody father*—and *he* was kissing a girl even younger than Sophie. His mother, he knew.

Their marriage had been a travesty, even though Julian wouldn't have ever drawn breath if they hadn't married. Then he heard Baron Purley's words about his father clear in his head, and his image of the doddering old man fell out of his mind to be replaced by a strong, vigorous man, fierce and proud, with a mouthful of teeth and abundant hair. But he had no face. Were there portraits of his father at Mount Burney?

"What are you thinking, Julian?"

He rose to his feet. Again, the words simply poured out of his mouth. "Baron Purley told me about my father when he was a younger man. He told me things I'd never before heard. He told me my father had great physical strength. He was known for his fairness, and he loved"—Julian swallowed—"he loved me, the baron said, loved me more than Constantine, his first son and heir. He said I would do great things. The baron said my father knew his life couldn't simply continue on forever, and it saddened him that he would never know me as a man. So he died, and I never knew him."

Sophie said nothing until she stood only a foot from his nose. The spaniels began jumping on her until Julian ordered, "Sit, all of you!"

The spaniels sat, their tails wagging madly. Then a seagull flew close and they were off, yipping, trying to catch it.

She lightly laid her hands on his shoulders. "I am very glad you have found someone to tell you about your father. He sounds an estimable man."

"I asked the baron to tell me all his memories of my father."

"Why, then, don't you invite him and Vicky to dinner this evening? I should love to hear stories about your father as well. I'll wager your mother can add her own."

"No, she can't. He died when she was your age. She knew only the old man."

Julian took Sophie's hands and gently lifted them from his shoulders. "It will rain soon."

"Yes. You can taste the rain in the wind. Roxanne asked me what was going on, since she said I looked different and she'd heard me humming all morning, a sure sign something was up. I wonder if I should tell her I kissed you and there were tongues involved in this kissing, and it was very fine indeed. I wonder if Roxanne has ever been kissed with tongues."

He stared down at her, mesmerized. "She's twenty-seven. Surely she has."

"Ladies are not like gentlemen, Julian. A lady can be one hundred and untouched, a virgin still. There are no societal dictates that allow an unmarried lady any sort of freedom at all."

"Surely she has been kissed."

"I do know there was a gentleman a long time ago, but her father, my grandfather, Baron Roche, discovered he wanted her money, and so Roxanne kicked him out. There hasn't been any gentleman since. I am afraid she will start wearing caps any day now." Sophie tightened her hold on him, then gave him a brilliant smile. "There is no one about save us, Julian." And she went on her tiptoes and kissed him, her skirts whipping madly about his legs.

The spaniels forgot the seagull and barked and leapt around them.

When Julian raised his head, he felt lust roiling thick and hot in his blood. He wanted to kiss every beautiful inch of her, listen to her moan, laugh when he kissed her toes— instead, he stood very still. Sophie lightly patted his cheek. "It will be all right, Julian, you'll see." She whistled for the spaniels and strode like a young boy toward Ravenscar, not looking back. To Julian's surprise, his dogs left him to race after her. How had she gained their loyalty so quickly?

He walked to the cliff and looked out over the vast expanse of turbulent water. *Rain,* he thought, *any minute now.* What the devil was he going to do? He could still taste her in his mouth.

40

If Richard was surprised to see his father and sister when he escorted Leah into the drawing room early that evening, he gave no outward sign of it. He stood for a moment in the doorway, looking toward the windows, listening as the rain slapped loud against the glass, the wind whipping up in a mad fever, lashing the trees sideways. Leah, however, said, "Goodness, my lord, how very nice to see you. And such a surprise. Good evening to you, Vicky. What a dreadful night to travel."

The baron lifted Leah's hand, lightly touched his lips to her wrist. "It was a very short trip, my dear, and the rain wasn't coming down quite so fiercely. I'm sure the horses are happy to be cozy in your stable, Julian."

He crossed to where Corinne sat, resplendent in a black gown, Julian's beautiful pearls in three loops around her neck, and eased himself into a chair opposite her.

"We are quite a party this evening," Corinne said, brow raised as she surveyed her guests. "Despite this hideous storm, Cook was singing, a sure sign her pickled salmon will be ambrosia."

"I did not know you intended to visit, Father," Richard said, his voice stark.

"Julian sent me an invitation," the baron said easily. "Truth be told, it is rather quiet at the manor, and Vicky gave one or two very deep sighs, so I decided, despite the weather, this would be a welcome diversion."

Richard wasn't happy, it was clear to everyone in the room. Why, Julian wondered. Had Richard intended to try to gullet him this evening, at least verbally, and now he couldn't in his father's presence? Or didn't he want his father to know he was bedding Sophie's aunt?

He heard Devlin laugh, turned to smile at him. He was talking to Vicky and Roxanne, and if Julian wasn't mistaken, it seemed Vicky bloomed under his attention. He watched Roxanne take a small step back, turn, and speak to Sophie.

He'd tried to avoid looking at her, but now he looked his fill. She looked amazing in a cream satin gown, and her breasts—no, he wouldn't remark upon her breasts. Julian turned back to the baron, drew him aside.

Pouffer appeared in the doorway, bowed to Corinne. "Dinner is served, your grace."

The old man looked natty, Julian thought, his linen as white as Julian's, his black suit shining, his black boots a mirror. His shoulders were ramrod straight, his head thrown back. He was obviously enjoying himself immensely. Julian felt a stab of guilt. He'd been gone for three years. And Pouffer could have died. Thank God he hadn't. And now everything was different. He wasn't at all certain why it was different, but it was. This was his father's home, and now it was his, and Ravenscar deserved more than a part-time master. No, not a master, a prince. The Prince of Ravenscar. It was his kingdom. His father had ordained it so.

"I have brought you something, Julian," Rupert said. "I had it well wrapped against our inclement weather."

Julian smiled at the baron, his head cocked to one side.

"Come, Rupert, what did you bring Julian?" Corinne asked, coming to her feet. "Ah, I see, you wish to surprise him, to have him stew about it over dinner. Well done. Do tell me as we walk to the dining room." The baron took her arm and led her away, his head lowered to hers.

After a dinner of excellent pickled salmon, buttered grouse, squab pie, and a mélange of peas and carrots and onions, Cook presented her own special Banbury cakes for dessert. Julian watched his guests, wondered what the baron had brought him, and kept wondering, but he knew he wouldn't ask, just as, he suspected, the baron did. Julian had always loved surprises, even as a small boy. He would never forget the morning his mother had awakened him and told him to follow her. He had skipped and run all the way to the stables, where a chestnut pony stood, eating oats from the bin. He'd never forgotten the joy that had welled up in him. Clancy had died only four years earlier, old and content. What had the baron brought him?

Everyone else at the table was also curious, and guesses abounded, but Julian offered none at all. Roxanne said thoughtfully, "Perhaps it is another spaniel, Julian. What shall you name him? Wait, the baron wouldn't have bundled him up like a package, would he?"

"No spaniel, Miss Radcliffe," Rupert said, and toasted her with his wineglass.

Richard said, "You gave him something that belonged to Lily, perhaps? Some token for him to ponder throughout what time he has left?"

His father frowned at him. "No, I have nothing that belonged to your sister, save her small portrait."

Vicky said, her voice firm and adult, "I think it must be one of your valued books, Father. About animal husbandry, perhaps?"

The guesses continued, the baron shaking his head with each one, a small smile playing over his mouth.

Julian held his peace until the ladies rose to leave the gentlemen to their port.

Not an instant after they'd passed out of the dining room, he rose as well. "I am ready for my surprise, sir."

Rupert laughed. "You have been so restrained, my boy, I shan't tease you any longer. Come with me."

Julian walked into the drawing room, nodded to the ladies, then stared as Baron Purley pointed. Hanging over the mantel was a portrait of a man. Julian's heart started to pound. It was his father, he knew it to the soles of his feet. He was young, Julian's own age. He stood tall and lean, radiating as much power as the beautiful black stallion beside him. His large hand lay on the animal's sleek neck. A wry smile played over his mouth. He was an eighteenth-century gentleman, his black hair powdered, his eyebrows as black as a sinner's dreams. He looked like a king, a magnificent being in control of everything in his universe.

Julian was his image. He walked numbly to stand in front of the portrait, simply stared up at it, saying nothing at all. He was scarcely aware that everyone had stilled; there was no sound at all now in the drawing room, as if everyone was holding his breath, waiting, watching him.

Julian swallowed. He didn't turn, merely asked, "Sir, where did this portrait come from? I have never seen it. Indeed, I have never before seen a painting of my father. He—he is a young man."

Corinne said quietly, beside him, her hand on his forearm, "I have never seen it, either, Rupert. Oh, my, had I known him then, I should have flown through the vilest storm to get to him. Even old, he was formidable." She paused, swallowed. "You are his image, dearest. I had not realized—" She swallowed again and turned. "Where did you get this painting, Rupert?"

"Actually, his grace gave it to me not long before he died. He said since we were close, he hoped that I would also be close to you, his son. He asked me to guard it until you were a man grown, Julian. He said that once you were a man, perhaps you would see yourself in him.

"I had forgotten it, truth be told, until I was telling you about your father. It is about time you had it, don't you think?"

Julian felt swamped with feelings so intense they were nearly unfathomable, and they ebbed and flowed through his racing blood. He turned to face the baron. He said simply, "Thank you, sir. I thank you very much."

Corinne said, "I thank you, too, Rupert." She threw out her arms. "Do you know, I believe this grand surprise calls for dancing. Shall we?" She raised her voice and called out, "Pouffer, we need a waltz!"

The old man must have been standing outside the door, because he was in the drawing room and seated at the pianoforte in an instant. Soon the strains of a waltz bounded throughout the room. Julian had always wondered how those arthritic old fingers made such beautiful music.

Julian found himself turning toward Sophie. She wasn't moving, merely smiling at him.

He cocked an eyebrow at her and held out his hand.

His mother looked toward him, smiling, before she accepted the baron's hand. "That was very well done of you, Rupert."

He said, as he waltzed Corinne slowly in wide circles, barely missing Devlin and Roxanne, "Julian—the prince—is special, as his father told me he would be so long ago. Perhaps it is best I forgot the painting until now. They are of the same age, and Julian can now understand who and what his father really was when he was young."

Corinne said, "It is such a pity so many die so very young. His grace was very lucky. You and I are lucky as well. I have found that one seems to come to understand what one is really made of as the years pass and experience brands us. But there seems too little time to make use of what we learn, since the time simply disappears from one thought to the next, and then one is dead. But another's experiences, do they really teach us anything at all?"

Rupert said, "I agree that we all travel alone. I think another's experiences may touch us, maybe even teach us about ourselves."

Corinne said, "I remember well your precious wife, Lydia. Such a dear lady she was. She surely touched you deeply, made you more aware of who and what you were."

The baron said nothing. He began humming.

Richard paused by them for a moment. "I believe years do change one, but not at the core, never at the core."

Vicky tapped her slippered foot until Pouffer finished the first waltz and immediately broke into another, this one more exuberant. The old man seemed to bounce on the piano seat. Vicky danced with Julian, and she laughed, a sane, focused laugh, Roxanne thought, as she watched them.

Devlin said to Roxanne, as he watched Sophie waltz with the baron, "Who knew Pouffer had such talents? Her grace, I have found, usually has fine ideas."

"I think Corinne wished to give Julian time to settle. Seeing his father as a young man, seeing himself so clearly in his father, it must touch him deeply."

Devlin said slowly, "Julian holds what he feels deep inside, so I do not know how profoundly it touches him. I believe I heard Richard laugh at something your sister said. How can you be enemies with a person when you are dancing? Have I ever told you your name sings on my tongue?" He grabbed her and brought her into his arms. She was laughing as he whirled her about, barely missing Leah, who was so happy she didn't even frown at her.

After all of them drank their tea and were off to bed, Julian found himself returning to the drawing room. To his surprise, his mother was there, a candle held high in her hand, staring up at his father's portrait.

He said quietly, "I wonder why Lord Purley never showed it to you?"

Corinne turned slowly to face her son. "I'll tell you why, Julian. I never showed any interest, and so he simply forgot, as he said." She looked at the portrait again. "When I met your father, I was seventeen years old. Your father was old, beyond old, to my girl's eyes. Even when I married him, I never thought of him as any other than what he was when I met him. Do you know, looking at him quite terrifies me."

"I am the image of him, Mother. It is like I am looking in a mirror. Do I terrify you?"

Corinne looked at her son, lightly patted his forearm. "It is not the same thing, dearest. No, not at all."

"Do you have a portrait of yourself as a young girl,

Mother? Hidden away? Perhaps there is something about my face that resembles you?"

She only shook her head.

"I shall have a portrait done of you now. I should like to see the two of you side by side above the mantel." He paused for a moment. "Why did you never remarry, Mother? You were twenty when you became a widow, were you not?"

"It was a very long time ago, Julian, and if you do not mind, I have no wish to speak of it."

He wondered why she'd had no wish to speak of it as he walked to his master's bedchamber. He knew a portrait of her now would please him very much. Odd, but she would look like his father's mother now, not wife. Sometimes life was Byzantine.

He paused in the wide corridor, listening, but he didn't hear rain or wind. The storm had passed out to sea. It was now utterly still. Then he heard whispers. They came from Leah's bedchamber.

Richard was in Leah's bedchamber. Julian hoped she knew what she was doing.

⊶ *41* ⊷

Roxanne was dreaming of her mother. She couldn't see her, but she knew she was close; she could smell her scent—jasmine, her mother always wore jasmine. Her mother said something, a muffled sound, as if behind closed hands, but Roxanne heard it. She was still half asleep when the sound came again, a sort of scratching sound, coming from against her door; someone was there, someone meant to hurt her—she snapped awake. She jerked up and stared toward her bedchamber door.

It was quiet. Again, that slight sound—perhaps it was a mouse, perhaps a branch slapping lightly against her window. *What drivel.* Again, she had the mad thought that someone was outside her door, maybe talking low, someone who wanted to come in. But the door was locked. If they were up to good, why didn't they simply knock? *That's because they're not up to good.* Her heart started pounding. She stared at the large brass key in the keyhole. She'd turned it after she'd sent Tansy off to bed, surely she had, but she couldn't be certain.

This was ridiculous. Put her in a dark room by herself

and watch her begin to foam at the mouth. Why couldn't Sophie have come to sleep with her again tonight? Roxanne swung her legs off the bed, slid her feet into her slippers. She grabbed up her wrap, pulled it around her shoulders, and tightened the sash at her waist. She walked very quietly to the door, pressed her ear against it. And listened.

Nothing at all.

She watched her own hand turn the brass key to unlock the door. She was witless, she thought, no other explanation for it, as she watched her hand pause on the knob. Then before she could talk herself out of it, she pulled open the door and stepped out. The corridor was dark, silent. She had no candle, but her eyes began to accustom themselves to the darkness. She began to make out shapes—a table set against the wall with a marble bowl atop it, a marble bust of some long-ago Monroe inset in a small alcove. But no one was lurking about to make those small sounds.

Not fifteen feet down the corridor, a door creaked open. Roxanne's heart stopped. Was that what she'd heard? She saw a shadow—it was a man—and he stepped out into the corridor, a candle held in front of him.

She heard his voice, quiet, a bit peeved. "Who is there?"

Roxanne's breath whooshed out, and without a thought, she ran toward the man, her slippers clipping on the wooden floor. She threw herself against him.

"*What?* Who—Roxanne?"

He cursed, grabbed her with one arm while with the other he held out the candle so he couldn't catch either of them on fire. "Roxanne, what the devil are you doing out of bed? What—"

"I heard something or someone out here, Devlin." Roxanne realized she was pressed against him. She also realized there were only three items of clothing separating them. Devlin's hand pulled her closer, and suddenly he was kissing her hair, all wild around her head, spilling over her shoulders, his brain filled with her scent, the feel of her, the softness of her hair against his mouth.

Was he mad? He forced his brain to step back, since his

body wasn't about to. He was panting, surely not at all the thing for a man of his sophistication to do, but she was standing so close, and perhaps her breasts were heaving a bit beneath those two thin layers of nightclothes, and he *felt* them.

Devlin nearly stumbled out of his own slippers. He brought the candle closer so it made a barrier of sorts between them. "I heard something, and came to investigate."

"Yes, yes, I did, too. Then your door opened, and you were here, and I was so relieved—" Her voice dropped right off the cliff. She stared at him. Her tongue was on her bottom lip, worrying, tasting, and he wanted—he shook. He opened his mouth, shut it, then it burst right out of him: "Your hair is incredible." He raised his hand to touch it, then quickly dropped his hand to his side.

My hair is incredible? It was the middle of the night, and they were swallowed in shadows so deep perhaps Devlin wasn't seeing things the way they really were. Maybe he was overset because he'd fancied someone or something was out here—but no, he'd said what he'd said. It was all about her and her incredible hair. She beamed at him in the darkness. "I am so glad it's you, Devlin. I was alarmed, silly of me, I know, because who could be skulking about in the middle of the night? Who could be making noises to jerk me out of a very nice dream?"

"Richard Langworth, for one. He was with your sister earlier; I heard them whispering. Maybe they were finished with—never mind that. They were probably speaking at her bedchamber door before he left."

"Whispering? Leah and Richard? That's what I heard? But that would mean that—how could she do such a thing? They are not married, they are very nearly strangers, they—"

Devlin raised a finger, laid it against her lips. She opened her mouth beneath his finger, closed it again. Merciful Lord, he wanted his mouth against hers, not his bloody finger. Still, he forced himself not to lower the candle to the floor; that would surely bring him everything he wanted—perhaps Roxanne wanted it, too—but the consequences?

Roxanne gulped. "Are you wearing only your dressing gown, Devlin?"

"You should not remark upon that, Roxanne. Yes."

"That is not much barrier between thee and me."

"You are quoting Shakespeare to me?"

"It does sound like something Oberon would say to Titania, doesn't it? No, no, don't answer that. I should go back to my bedchamber. I should lock my bedchamber door again. And I should shove the key through to the other side."

"I can see you clearly now, Roxanne. You are framed by black, it halos your face. You are so very white, do you know? Perhaps you have vampire leanings yourself. Perhaps you should eschew the sun as I do."

She nodded, stilled. "I wonder which of us is the whiter?"

I think if we were naked together, we would blend into a perfect single whiteness. Where had that ridiculous thought come from? Because he wasn't a complete dolt, he managed to keep that madness behind his teeth.

He merely smiled at her.

"Do you prefer your mistresses be as white as you are, Devlin?" *As white-skinned as I am?*

He could but stare at her over the arc of candlelight. "No, you are the first to be as white as I am. Is the rest of you as white as your face?"

She didn't mean to, she truly didn't, but she parted his dressing gown. He didn't move, scarcely breathed.

She said, "Even the soles of my feet are white. Are you smooth as white marble, or do you have hair on your chest?"

"Yes, I do have lots of hair. So does my father. And Julian, too. You cannot imagine what picturing all of you is doing to my brain, Roxanne." Now she was tangling her fingers in the hair and he was leaning into her fingers.

Her fingers flattened on his chest. She was closer now, and he could feel her breath sighing through the warm air between them. She said, "Your heart is galloping, Devlin, as fast as Eglette, my prized childhood pony. He was faster than a storm rolling right at you. Your heart is pounding so hard and fast that if you were an old man, I would fear for apoplexy."

He raised his free hand. His fingers, light as a shadow, pressed against her breast. "Your heart is drumming as well, Roxanne."

"Once, it was a very long time ago, I remember feeling quite strange when John kissed me, but it didn't make me want to bound to the heavens and shout with joy at the same time; it didn't make my heart want to leap out of my chest."

"It is lust," he said.

"Lust? It is lust that is making me warm all over and my heart race like a flying arrow?"

"It is. Listen to me. Lust is a simple thing that freely roams the land, pops up in unlikely places, like in a castle's dark corridor, between a man and a woman who shouldn't even be in the bloody corridor together, maybe even in the bloody castle together."

"No, Ravenscar is a palace," she said. "Sophie said a prince could only live in a palace."

Devlin watched his own hand drop from her breast. The loss of her nearly broke him. He forced himself to step back in his mind, one step, another. He said, "Do you know, I am a very content man?"

Roxanne was silent for a long moment, then she managed a sneer she knew he couldn't appreciate despite the candlelight. "Naturally, you are content. You are rich, you are a duke's heir, an earl in your own right, and you have three mistresses. I am given to understand if a man were to enjoy three mistresses—three *different* mistresses at the *same* time—he would be very content even without money, without a title. Mayhap he'd be whistling all the time. Do not forget, you excel at being a vampire. You have played the role so long every woman who meets you is immediately fascinated. You represent the danger of the unknown."

"Do I fascinate you?"

"I shall not answer that. Now, I have said too much, and I have said it at great length. I began by insulting you . . ." She paused. "I suppose I ended with the insult intact."

He nodded. "Very fluent you were, too. But you know, you said so much I can ignore what I wish to. Yes, I much enjoy whistling, particularly when the moon is high and I can raise my face and see the clarity of it piercing through the shadows surrounding me, and no, it will not fry me like the sun. If you had three lovers, I wonder if you would be as content as I, Roxanne?"

"Where would a lady find the time to juggle three lovers, Devlin? I mean, can you imagine having to change your gown for three different gentlemen? And your hair, brushing it into a new style for each lover? It would be exhausting, don't you think?"

He wanted to laugh, but he didn't. He had to stop, he had to.

She said, "Do you know I am twenty-seven?"

He nodded. "When is your birthday?"

"August the third."

"Then I am three months older than you."

"Are you older than your mistresses?"

He shook his head. "Only one of them, and she is nearly twenty-five. I have never cared for ingénues; they are not so, well, they are not so polished, I suppose one could say, and their conversation isn't what—" His brain seized. "Even though you are wearing only two thin layers of clothes and standing not six inches from me, your heart flying so fast it could split the air like an arrow, you are a lady. I thank the good lord for the candle between us, else I might have you against the wall. Do you know what that would lead to?"

"I am a spinster, Devlin. I am so high on the shelf it would require a ladder to pull me down. Perhaps it is time I understood a bit more about this lust business. I think the wall sounds like a fine idea."

He laughed this time, couldn't help it. He lightly touched his fingers to her smooth cheek. "What you are, Roxanne, is you, and that is a very fine thing. Good night." He lightly kissed her mouth, turned quickly, and disappeared back into his bedchamber.

She sighed and ached and wondered. She stood in the

dark corridor for a moment longer, then turned resolutely toward her bedchamber. As she locked her door, she thought of Leah and Richard Langworth. Should she tell her sister Richard was using her to get to Julian? She couldn't begin to imagine what Leah would have to say to that. Well, she could, and it made her stomach hurt. She would have to make certain there was no weapon within sight.

She refused to think about Devlin Monroe. But there, blossoming full in her mind, was a lovely image of their two very white selves naked, blending perfectly together.

Roxanne fell asleep aching and smiling.

⟿ 42 ⟾

When Julian stepped into the drawing room the following morning, it was to see his mother, her brow furrowed, holding a piece of paper in her hand, Pouffer hovering over her.

"Good morning. What is this?"

He watched her close her hand over the paper, open it again. "Rupert told me when he first showed me the portrait yesterday that he'd noticed the brown paper had peeled loose on the back of your father's painting. Pouffer and I decided to see to it. Look what I found stuck inside. It is a letter, written to you, from your father."

She handed him the letter. It was yellowed with age, the creases set deep in the paper. Julian unfolded it and read the bold black handwriting, firm and vigorous, penned more than thirty years earlier.

To the Prince of Ravenscar

A jewel beyond understanding awaits you.
It is flat and ugly and can feel

its magic pulse to your bones.
It lies beneath spears of stone.
I could not use the magic, since it is for you,
if your brain is tuned to find it.
You are now a man. Do you look like me?
I wonder—

Your father, Maximilian Monroe,
5th Duke of Brabante

His father's black scrawled name filled the rest of the single sheet of paper, letters thick and firm, though faded by the thirty years that had passed. Julian read it through again, and once more, then raised his head. "You read this, Mother?"

"Yes, but it makes no sense to me. Never did your father mention leaving a jewel for you—and a magic jewel? Flat and ugly? What sort of jewel is flat and ugly? You find it beneath spears of stone? What stone spears?"

Pouffer was unable to contain himself. His voice was deep and awed. "I had forgot how fanciful your father was, Prince, how he adored mysteries and puzzles. Your father tells you the jewel is for you, that it awaits you. Only you."

Julian nearly laughed. Didn't that sound like fine melodrama?

He made his excuses and walked to the stables. Ten minutes later, when he was saddling Cannon, he looked up to see Sophie striding like a boy toward him. *Long legs,* he thought, momentarily distracted.

"Your mother told me about the note, but she couldn't remember it exactly. May I see it?"

"Do you walk a lot, Sophie?"

She blinked at him. "Walk? Well, certainly, all my life."

Long, strong legs. He wanted to see her legs, the whole length of them, wanted to kiss them, draw them around his flanks.

"Julian, what is wrong with you? Why are you looking at me that way? Why do you want to know if I walk a lot? Come, let me see your father's note to you."

He settled the saddle on Cannon's broad back, not looking at her. "My father must have been long lapsed into his dotage when he devised this elaborate word puzzle. I fear it is a story spun by his aged brain."

"Your mother said your father was lucid until he closed his eyes in death. May I copy the letter for you?"

He gave one last yank to the saddle girth, swatted Cannon's neck when he turned to nip him, and said, "Come, Sophie, do you honestly believe there is something hidden away for me—something magic that didn't work for my father but will for me if my brain is *tuned* to it? And what does 'tuned' mean?"

"Yes, I believe there is a hidden ring. Magic? We will see when we find it." She held out her hand. "I will copy it." He handed her the small square of paper.

"Where are you going?"

"I'm meeting Devlin at the Brazen Crow in Ravenscar Village. It has been owned and run by Mrs. Casper for thirty years."

"May I come with you? I haven't seen the village yet."

Julian smiled at her. "No, not this time. It is none of your affair. Both of us will be back soon enough." He frowned. "Keep yourself safe, and my father's note as well." He swung onto Cannon's back and was gone.

Safe? What was the matter?

She walked thoughtfully back to the house to climb the wide stone steps, glistening like soft gold in the morning light, the night's storm gone by dawn, the old duke's letter in her hand.

She passed Pouffer, who gave her an absent bow, muttering to himself all the while. She smiled at Tansy, who held a pressed gown over her arm, and nodded to two maids and to a footman dressed in Ravenscar's colors—royal blue and gold.

She went up the wide staircase, down the long corridor to her bedchamber, only to stop at the sound of two women's voices—Roxanne and Leah. If God himself had ordered her to keep walking, she doubted she could have done it.

She pressed her ear to the crack in the doorway. She heard Roxanne say, "I hope you slept well, Leah."

"Naturally. Why should I not have slept well?" And she began humming to herself. "Isn't it a lovely day, Roxanne? Would you look at that brilliant sunlight pouring through the windows? Richard and I are having a picnic beside the river. The sun is so brilliant it should dry the ground quickly, so Richard tells me. I believe he is speaking with Mrs. Coltrak at this very moment. He told me she'll make us a wonderful lunch, since she always liked him, even as a little boy." She picked up her skirts and began twirling around her bedchamber.

Better to spit it out. "I must speak with you, Leah."

Leah stopped twirling, turned, and eyed her sister, her *younger* sister, with that roof thatch of common red hair piled atop her head that most people were stupid enough to admire. "What do you have to say, Roxanne?"

"I know about you and Richard Langworth. I know he was with you last night."

A lovely blond brow shot upward. "I don't know how you know about Richard and me last night, but I don't really care. It is none of your business. Don't you dare turn up your common little prude's nose at me! I am a widow, unlike you, who will probably remain a virgin until you die. Unlike you, I have no father to order me about. I am independent; I can do exactly as I please."

Meaty insults, every one of them, but that wasn't important. Roxanne said calmly, "Father has never ordered me around. He never ordered you around, either."

"He certainly didn't want you to leave, did he? I know how he drove away John Singleton. He wanted to keep you under his thumb, and you, you weak little ninny, you cast off the only man who wanted you."

Defensive words nearly popped right out of Roxanne's mouth. No, it was absurd to argue with Leah. It wouldn't gain her anything at all. She said calmly, "It's very possible Richard Langworth is using you, Leah, to get to Julian. You know he believes Julian murdered Lily. I had to tell you. There was no choice."

Leah merely shrugged. "Julian very probably did murder her, why not? Richard disagrees with me, but I believe Lily did have a lover. Richard has told me Julian has always been very possessive of anything he sees as his. He would certainly see Lily as belonging to him. Julian wouldn't tolerate a lover, and so he shot his wife dead."

"You are wrong about that, Leah. Lily had no lover. No one believes she did, because there was no other man about to fill the role. Not a single one."

The sneer in Leah's voice matched the sneer on her mouth. "Both you and Sophie, you think Julian a hero. He is only a man, as they are all only men. And tell me, how would Julian be so certain she had no lover? Few men see what is under their noses. Precious Julian didn't, either. What is this? You want Julian? You want a murderer? Beware, Roxanne, if he murdered one wife, he could easily murder another. He got away with it, after all."

"Julian is not a murderer."

Leah laughed. "So his wife killed herself? A stranger wandered into the Hardcross gardens and shot her? Why, I ask you? She was so miserable she killed herself to escape her husband? Any possible explanation is unsavory, isn't it? Go away, Roxanne. You bore me with your pathetic defense."

"Richard is using you, I tell you, Leah. He has this obsession with Julian; it consumes him. He would do anything to get back at him. Do you know Richard tried to kill him in London? When you were there?"

"That is a fine tale, indeed. Tell me, Roxanne, will you still think he's using me when I marry him?"

Leah ran to the door, her laughter floating after her. She jerked it open, and Sophie nearly fell into her.

43

"Well, isn't this charming." Leah smacked Sophie's shoulder, nearly sending her to the floor. "Look at you, your ear pressed to the door like a silly little girl. You are a disgrace, Sophie Colette Wilkie. What would Bethanne say, were she here? I hope she would be appalled as I am. She didn't raise you well, that is certain."

Rage overrode guilt. "My mother was the best mother in the whole world, Leah. Look at you, all mean in the mouth, so miserable at having to live with yourself that you must make everyone else miserable, including your poor dead husband, which is why he never stayed at home. I should run away, too, if I had to live with you. My innards fair to shrivel to think of you as my mother."

"You ridiculous girl, I am too young, far too young, to be your mother. I look like your sister, your *beautiful* sister. My husband did not run away. He had to leave to do his duty. Naturally, I was unhappy. You would be, too, if your husband was bound to duty and couldn't spend time with his very young wife. I did not chase him away. He had the gall to get himself drowned.

"How dare you call me mean! I always speak only the truth, something you are too mealymouthed to do. But that isn't important now, because there is Richard. He is everything Lord Merrick was not. He is honorable and amusing and very handsome. He doesn't have those ridiculous whiskers on his face. He adores me, but I will tell you, Julian will never adore you. He will never marry you, either, even though his mother has begged him to. He thinks you're a useless little girl. He sees you as you really are, Sophie—a spoiled child prancing around in a lady's gown."

I don't prance, Aunt Leah, and I am not spoiled. But Sophie swallowed the useless denials. She said with a smile, "You don't think I, your niece, deserve to be adored like you, Aunt Leah?"

It left Leah with her mouth open, so frustrated she wanted to slap Sophie. She got herself back together and attacked. "You don't really want Julian, though, do you? Oh, yes, it's Devlin you want, the future duke, not the paltry second son. Oh, yes, now I see clearly. Well, my girl, that is shooting for the stars, now, isn't it? If anything, Devlin Monroe will dally with you until you bore him, then he'll move on to his next conquest. Your only chance to get yourself a husband is to return to London and try to snag some unsuspecting baron's son. Maybe he will adore you."

"That is a lovely thought, Aunt Leah. Thank you for making everything so very clear. What should also be clear to you is that Roxanne told you the truth. Richard Langworth sought you out purposefully so he could get himself close to Julian. If you do not see that, you are a dolt."

"Roxanne has been jealous of me all her life. What I had, she wanted. Does she want Richard? Come, now, Sophie, think. How could he even know to purposefully seek me out? He was in York on business for his father, he told me. He did not know I was related to you. He had no reason to suspect you, of all girls, would be sent to London to try to attach Julian Monroe."

Sophie said, "He found out about all of us from his father, who was undoubtedly told the particulars by the duchess.

She had no reason not to confide in Baron Purley, since she had known him all her adult life. You have been taken in, Leah. Richard Langworth does not care about you; you are merely a means to an end."

"You little bitch!" Leah slapped Sophie hard.

She heard a noise and whirled around to see Roxanne standing behind her. "You, too, Roxanne. That I should have to be related to the two of you. It quite turns my stomach!"

Roxanne and Sophie stood side by side, Sophie rubbing her cheek, watching Leah race down the long corridor away from them.

"Did she really bring Richard Langworth into her bedchamber last night, Roxanne?"

Roxanne nodded. "I knew what would happen if I warned her, I *knew,* yet some perverse devil inside me told me it was my duty to tell her. I wish you had not been close by, Sophie."

Sophie shrugged. "She hates both of us, what does it matter? Did she also hate my mother? What is *wrong* with her, Roxanne?"

"When we were children, Leah and I made a pact to cut each other's hair. I snipped off one of her small golden curls that was sticking out. She cut off all my hair, stood back, and laughed. She said now I wouldn't look so common. She was only nine years old. You were right, she has a mean mouth. But I don't think she hates any of us, your mother included."

"You're wrong. I wonder if Richard Langworth will come to realize that whatever revenge he is planning is not worth the misery once he gets to know her. Once she turns her mean mouth on him. Once she's netted him. Do you really think she will marry him?"

"Maybe they deserve each other. Sophie, am I a prude?"

"You? Oh, indeed, you are so prudish I fear you will attend Methodist meetings and wear only black to your throat. I fear you will denounce all those who dance the waltz."

Sophie laughed at Roxanne, patted her cheek, and danced

away. She called out over her shoulder, still laughing, "A prude!"

＊═➣　◆═＊

Leah slowly straightened and made her way down the wide staircase. What did those two twits know about anything? Her palm still tingled from the slap she'd given Sophie. It was about time someone disciplined the chit.

Richard was using *her*? If only they knew.

⤙ 44 ⤚

Julian pulled Cannon up in front of the Brazen Crow, handed the reins to Homer, an ancient stump of a man. "Prince," Homer said, and tried a sketchy bow. "Ah, dear old Cannon. Ye come wit' me and I'll stuff yer gullet with nice big carrots, fresh picked from Mrs. Casper's garden."

Julian pressed coins in Homer's hand and asked, "Is the earl here, Homer?"

"Yes, the lad is drinking Mr. McGurdy's cider, hard enough to make 'is liver shout and sing."

Julian was still grinning when he saw Devlin seated in the taproom, one leg draped over a chair arm, laughing at something the barmaid, Briggie, was telling him. She was bending low as she spoke, her lovely eighteen-year-old breasts nearly spilling onto Devlin's chest. Odd, Devlin wasn't eyeing those breasts of hers, he was looking directly into her face. He would have normally, wouldn't he? He'd bedded Briggie before, Julian knew. What was different now?

Julian said, "Hello, Briggie. May I have some of Mr. McGurdy's cider?"

"Aye, Prince, I'll fetch ye an even newer batch than 'is vampireship 'ere."

Julian watched Briggie walk out of the room, along with another half dozen local men. He turned to Devlin, a black eyebrow arched. "His vampireship?"

Devlin took a drink of Mr. McGurdy's cider, wiped his hand over his mouth, and grinned up at Julian. "Briggie is a clever girl, don't you think? Vampireship—it has a lovely terrifying ring to it."

"I wonder what my half brother, your esteemed father, would think of it?"

"My father would laugh his head off," Devlin said. "It is mother who would hiss and crab and want to skewer Briggie for her gross impertinence."

"You scarce noticed Briggie."

"Yes, well, now that you point it out, I suppose I must agree. It is not what I'm used to, is it?"

"Whatever that means," Julian said, as he sat down across from Devlin at the small scarred table.

Devlin began swinging his leg. "I keep forgetting to call you Prince."

"You'd think I'd be used to it by now, and maybe I will be after I'm home for a while. When I was a lad, I thought myself quite important—a prince, that's what I was—the most important boy in the land. But now?" Julian shuddered. "What could my father have been thinking?"

"Since he quickly bred a male child in his advanced years, I think he was so pleased with himself, so proud, he couldn't help himself. He believed himself a king, so what else could you be?"

Julian laughed. "How many glasses of Mr. McGurdy's cider have you poured down your throat?"

Devlin gave him a beatific smile. "Only two. It fair to makes my throat sing."

"You rarely drink, Devlin. Come, what is the matter?"

Devlin brooded for a moment, swirling the incredible Cornish cider around in his glass. "I kissed Roxanne's hair in the corridor in the middle of the night. It is beautiful stuff, Julian. I wanted to wrap it around my hands and pull her closer and closer, until I felt it rippling over my face, you know?"

Julian looked up as Briggie set his own glass in front of him. "Is there aught else ye wish, Prince?"

He shook his head. "Thank you, Briggie." He took a drink, then said to Devlin, "No, I don't know."

"Well, there was nothing more to it than that, really. Other than the fact I wanted desperately to yank up that bedrobe of hers and take her right there, holding her against the wall." He took a drink, then looked at his uncle. "Do you know, what near to knocked me on my heels was that she wasn't at all averse to the wall idea."

Julian laughed. "Well, my lad, this leaves me blank-brained. Roxanne? I trust you know what you're doing."

"I haven't a clue," Devlin said. "She is a virgin. She is twenty-seven years old, and she is a virgin. That would be an awesome responsibility, Julian. I heard you telling Pouffer you were off to Plymouth, that it was time you looked over the *Blue Star*. You've already had assurances from your captain that all is well, that your goods are on their way to your warehouses in London. Why, Julian, why travel there now?"

"I wish to question all my men, see if there was a new man among them on this voyage, get his name and direction. Richard Langworth tried to sabotage the ship, and I intend to find proof of it. Would you like to come with me? Mayhap all the ladies would like to come as well? We could be there in three hours. There are some fine sights in Plymouth. What do you think?"

"What will you do with Richard and Leah?"

Julian shrugged. "They can leave or remain, I really don't care."

"Richard and Leah slept together last night. I heard them. Roxanne knows as well. Knowing her, she will try to warn her sister."

"That will not have a good ending. Leah will blight her."

"Very probably." Devlin raised his glass. "She seems to have made a hobby of it all her life—especially Roxanne. Drink up, Uncle. We have an offer to make the ladies. You're going also to arrange for a final shipment, aren't you?"

How did Devlin find these things out? Well, since Sophie was now going to be part of the endeavor, why not Devlin? "Yes. I checked the cave twice. It will do nicely. Sophie followed me. She wishes to be a part of it all. An adventure, she says. I am thinking I should tie her up. Actually, I am thinking of tying you both up."

"And Roxanne, for she knows, as well. Forget tying Sophie up, Julian; she would retaliate, probably something quite fierce. Nothing will happen, in any case. I hear there are no excisemen around these parts in the past decade. There will be no danger. For any of us."

⋆⇒ ⇐⋆

After lunch, the three ladies were settled into the Ravenscar carriage, along with Tansy, who'd had tears in her eyes at the joyous thought of visiting Plymouth, Julian and Devlin riding beside them, leaving their respective valets to kick up their heels at Ravenscar and try to avoid Richard and Leah.

⇒ 45 ⇐

Plymouth Docks

Julian stood on the deck of the *Blue Star,* a sturdy brigantine he'd purchased five years before from Thomas Malcombe, the Earl of Lancaster, a man he admired and trusted. It was indeed a small world, he thought, what with Meggie, Malcombe's countess, being a Sherbrooke, and that surely made him shake his head. He remembered well the dinner in the Malcombes' lovely pink stucco house in Genoa, Meggie telling him about racing cats. Thomas told him how his own racer, Keevil, a black tube of a cat with a chewed-up ear, was the current champion, and did that ever burn his wife to her heels. He thought of James and Corrie Sherbrooke, Meggie Malcombe's cousins. Sometimes the world really was too small, dishing up so many lives that overlapped. He wondered if Keevil was still the racing-cat champion of all Ireland.

The *Blue Star* captain, Cowan Cleaves, ruddy-faced from a lifetime spent on the sea, not a humorous bone in his big body, and steady as a rock, raced along the dock, up the gangplank, out of breath. "My lord, you are here, thank the heavens. I sent you a messenger."

"What happened, Cowan?"

"Everything is all right, but it was close, my lord. A man I hired on at Gibraltar—his name is Orvald Manners—he set a fire in the cargo hold as we were docking. My cabin boy, Ira, managed to put out the fire before there was any damage, but Manners was gone. None have seen him. I've sent out my first mate, Abel Rowe, to try to locate him. You know Abel, if he finds him, he'll break his head."

The first thing Julian did was to go into the cargo hold. The timbers were charred but cooling. Ira had come to smoke a pipe, Cowan told him, something he was forbidden to do, and saw Manners set the fire. Ira was a smart boy; he waited until Manners had left the hold, then put out the fire.

"Give the lad a sovereign, Cowan."

"Perhaps, my lord, I won't tan his hide for trying to smoke, the little blighter."

Julian had to laugh, easy now that his ship was safe and the valuable goods safe as well.

"Tell me about this Orvald Manners."

"Abel hired him on as a new man at Gibraltar because one of our sailors simply disappeared. I think now Manners is responsible."

"Oh, yes," Julian said.

"Manners didn't have any friends, not really, kept to himself. According to Abel, though, he was always willing to do whatever was needed, always had a nice word for the galley cook, Old Tubbs. Still, it was as plain as a pikestaff the fellow didn't have much experience."

Julian knew to his bones none of the sailors would know anything about Manners, particularly where he'd hared off to. He got Manners's description. His name—Orvald Manners—mayhap that was the key to tracking him down. But, of course, it was likely a fiction as surely as Manners had signed on the *Blue Star* in good faith.

Manners couldn't have conjured up the storm, and that must have frightened the man to death, Julian thought. But he'd tried to burn the *Blue Star* right here at the dock, in Plymouth. How much had Richard paid him?

He set a half dozen sailors to the task of finding Manners, but he had little hope. The man had failed. There wasn't any way he would stay around. No, he would go report his failure to Richard.

Julian wanted to join the sailors in the search, but first he toured his ship, saw the repairs to the damage caused by the storm were nearly complete. Within a sennight, thank the good Lord, Indian tea, materials of all kinds made in Manchester mills, farm equipment, and myriad household items gathered by Harlan and warehoused over the past three months in Plymouth would be loaded aboard the *Blue Star,* and she would make her way to Boston. Without storms. Without sabotage in Boston Harbor. The return trip would bring dozens of barrels of whale oil.

When he was finished checking the repairs, Julian shook Captain Cleaves's hand and wandered around the dock area, stopping various men, giving them Manners's description. He had no luck. He paid out coin for information on Manners. He wanted him badly. He was his only connection to Richard Langworth.

When he saw Devlin standing in front of a milliner's shop on High Street, Parisian Feathers, all three ladies clustered around him, Julian grinned. He'd been so intent on sabotage and mayhem, finding Manners, and kicking both him and Richard into the channel. But now here was Devlin, his hat brim pulled down to protect him from the bright sun overhead, laughing, quite enjoying himself, looking at bonnets.

"That one," Julian heard him say, and saw him point to a high-brimmed straw bonnet with at least a dozen pieces of fruit decorating its high poke, nests of ribbons holding them, and a thick, long red ribbon to tie beneath a lady's chin. "Roxanne, you would look a treat with those peaches all over your head. If I ever was hungry, I could simply pluck one off. You would be my private orchard."

Roxanne poked him in the belly. "All those peaches, that bonnet must weigh a stone, Devlin. I would have a bowed back by the end of morning wearing that bushel of fruit."

As for the bonnet Roxanne was wearing, Devlin found it very charming, only two small finches perched beside the crown, the bonnet as wide-brimmed as Devlin's black hat. Should he offer to provide her birdseed?

"Ah, dearest, there you are," Julian's mother called to him. "Do come here, I require your opinion. Devlin simply will not be serious. Tell me what you think of these bonnets. They are newly arrived from Paris, and I am in need."

Julian obligingly looked more closely and surveyed the bonnets in the window, each of them decorated with bows, ribbons, and flowers, and occasional fauna. "That one," he said, pointing to a pink straw that was in the corner of the window. "That one would look splendid on you, Mother."

"Do you not think it very plain?"

"Not at all. It is perfect for you."

A half-hour later, they all emerged from Parisian Feathers, the pale pink leghorn hat, with a line of braided darker pink ribbons encircling the crown, set atop her grace's head, tied rakishly beneath her chin.

Roxanne said, "Do you know, Devlin, even with your hat, your nose is becoming red. I think it best we go into the Golden Goose Inn and plant you in a dim corner."

He quickly pulled his hat down farther over his eyes. He looked at her closely, lightly touched his fingertips to her nose. "I believe I see some freckles coming out to march over your lovely white self."

Julian, still on the lookout for Manners, realized he was striding a good distance in front of their group, eyeing every man he saw. He slowed his step and placed his mother's hand on one arm and Sophie's on the other. His mother was speaking of the fine weather and her new bonnet. Sophie, however, was quiet. Sophie was never quiet, she was always laughing, talking, always doing something. He leaned close when his mother stopped to look into a shop window. "What is this? You're mute as a tree. Did Leah blight you that badly?"

"What? Oh, yes, I suppose she did. Leah is a master blighter. She is going to marry Richard Langworth, Julian, and that really makes me wonder what he could possibly be up to."

It made him wonder as well. Their attention was diverted by a young boy who came running up to Julian, saying he "knowed the name of the sot wot set the fire on the *Blue Star.*"

The sod turned out to be Orvald Manners, but he was gone.

That evening's dinner was served in the small private dining room, where lavish gold curtains were drawn over the windows. Mr. Knatter, owner of the Plymouth Heights Inn, served them Mrs. Knatter's special deviled whitebait. "The secret be in the hot oil, my missus tells me; it's gots to be hot enough to burn the hair off a man's tongue," he whispered to her grace. "And here be the Norfolk dumplings; 'tis the quality of the castor sugar, that's the key, says my missus."

Sophie was quiet again. Julian imagined she was thinking about all the trouble, so why not share it? He ordered a bottle of Mr. Knatter's best champagne.

That perked her right up.

"Now, Sophie," he said, toasting his champagne glass toward her, "tell us more about Leah and Richard's upcoming nuptials."

That drew everyone's attention.

"Well, as I said, Roxanne told her Richard had attached her purposefully to get to you. Leah told Roxanne and me we were idiots, that there was simply no way Richard could have even known about our connection to you. That's when she hurled her bolt—and announced she was going to marry him."

Julian said, "There isn't really much of a connection, though I myself have wondered. But despite all the complexity involved, I know it is something Richard would do. Even as a boy, Richard enjoyed making things complicated, enjoyed intrigue, the game, so to speak." He sighed. "Once Richard made up his mind about something, nothing could change it, even a stone tablet with God's commandments on it. He hasn't changed."

Sophie sipped her champagne. "It is helpful to understand your enemy. Come, Julian, don't shake your head. Richard hired that Orvald Manners to burn your ship, after, of course, he was safely on land. Richard himself tried to kill you in London. He is no longer your boyhood friend; he hasn't been since Lily's death. Of course he planned the meeting with Leah, and that means this Orvald Manners has to be somewhere nearby. Richard wouldn't hire him, then let him walk away after he failed."

Sophie turned to Corinne. "Your grace, did you happen to mention to Baron Purley that you wished Julian and me to wed?"

His mother nodded. "I believe I did indeed express to Rupert my devout desire for the two of you to marry." She sighed. "Evidently, he told his son. It would seem Richard has great confidence in my power over you, Julian, to execute such an involved plan. I am sorry if it led to Leah and Richard both being under Ravenscar's roof. Why do you think they came?"

Devlin said, "To learn more about what we were doing, what we were thinking and planning."

This led to more questions and possibilities until Sophie announced, "Julian, I wish you would select a bonnet for me. I think I should like to have a pair of geese perched on the crown. What do you think?"

"Red roses," Julian said, "a lovely line of them across the crown."

"Hmmm," said her grace.

After Julian and Devlin escorted the ladies to their bed-chambers, they returned to the taproom to settle in with brandy. The air was heavy and sweet, the conversations around them low and easy.

Devlin said, "Have you made arrangements for a final shipment to the cave?"

Julian nodded. "Yes, the night of the twenty-fourth, there will be no moon. As for storms, it is late spring, so perhaps we will be lucky."

"It makes no sense for us to return to London. I am not even tempted to settle into London intrigue again. I am quite enjoying myself in the wilds of Cornwall."

"Your mistresses will languish, Devlin, and perhaps even give up on you, and White's is surely bereft without your presence."

"I do enjoy the Season, always have. It is odd of me, isn't it? Well, the bonnet you selected for your mother becomes her very nicely. I had no idea my uncle had such excellent taste in bonnets."

"A man must be accomplished at many things," Julian said, and lifted his brandy snifter in a toast to Devlin's.

"I see you are worried. Is it about Sophie playing smuggler? Come, Julian, you know there won't be any problems."

"I'm worried about Orvald Manners. I must find him, Devlin. He's the only one who can point to Richard. As I told you, the lad who hunted me down took me right to where Manners was staying, only he was gone. Where to, I wonder?"

"Probably to see Richard and report his failure. At least no one will get aboard the *Blue Star* now. Captain Cleaves had two men on duty all night."

An hour later, Julian lay on his back, his head pillowed on his arms, staring up at the inn's sloping ceiling. It was a warm night, and utterly silent. There was not a sound of a single carriage or horse outside his window, no drunken voices, no yelling or singing. He was tired, but his brain wouldn't close itself down. He found himself thinking not about Orvald Manners but about an ugly black jewel that was magic. But the magic would work only for him, not for his father. And this magic lay beneath stone spears. His mind went round and round with the absurd idea of magic itself until he thought he'd drive himself mad. He finally rose, pulled on his clothes, and made his way downstairs to the taproom.

He'd hoped Mr. Knatter was still about, but the taproom was dark and empty. He wanted a brandy, anything to make his mind stop racing. He heard a small noise, whirled around to see an apparition all in white standing in the shadows before him, a candle cupped by a hand.

He smoothly pulled the knife out of his boot. Then he smelled her unique scent.

"Julian, what are you doing here? Before you blight me like Leah did, let me explain. I heard you walk by our chamber and followed you. Are you all right? It is very late."

He slid the knife back into his boot and straightened. "Sophie, it is well after midnight, and there is no one about. You should not have come down after me."

She merely smiled and glided toward him. "I saw you pull your knife out of your boot. You were fast, Julian. Had I been a villain, you would have brought me down between one breath and the next."

"Come, I will walk you back to your room. Hopefully you did not awaken Roxanne."

But she didn't move. "If I awoke anyone, it would be Tansy. She starts at the sound of a curtain moving at the window. I heard Devlin telling Roxanne about Mr. McGurdy's hardfisted cider. I should like to try it."

"Only if you wish to lose your virginity by the second glass. Forget I said that." Julian scraped his fingers through his hair, making it stand on end.

She held the candle higher. "You have whiskers."

He nodded, said, "Yes. By morning, I look like a pirate."

"So does my grandfather. Once when I was visiting Allegra Hall with my mother, I chanced to see him early one morning. He had black whiskers all over his face. I asked him if I had to walk the plank, and he came down on his haunches, told me in all seriousness that his whiskers meant he was a Russian czar, not a pirate, and I was to bow to him."

It was on the tip of his tongue to ask her if she'd bowed, but he got his brain back on track. "Come, back to bed with you."

"What do you think about this puzzle from your father?"

"Not much."

"I believe I know what he means by spears of stone."

They both whirled about at the sound of a man's angry voice. "What nasty piece of work is trying to steal my ale in the middle of the bloody night?"

Julian took the candle from Sophie, held it high. There stood Mr. Knatter, his bulk wrapped in a lovely Scottish plaid dressing gown.

"We aren't nasty pieces of work, sir," Sophie said. "We're works of art."

Julian laughed, couldn't help himself.

⇚ 47 ⇛

It was to everyone's collective relief when Pouffer announced that Richard and Leah had returned to Hardcross Manor during their three-day trip to Plymouth.

Pouffer was rubbing his gnarly hands together, grinning widely. "It's peaceful now, Prince, very peaceful, no more harangues from Lady Merrick. Master Richard was polite as can be, but then he's been in and out of Ravenscar all his life, and everyone knows him, so why would he become ill-mannered? However, I did not regard his good manners with any approval at all."

"Why?" Roxanne asked him.

"Because Master Richard believes our prince killed her poor ladyship. He is naturally quite wrong. It fair to curdles my liver to show him politeness even when he is so very polite to me."

Corinne said as she stripped off her gloves, "Now they're gone, we can quite enjoy ourselves."

She gave a sloe-eyed look at her son, then looked purposefully toward Sophie, who was removing her bonnet.

Julian rolled his eyes. He said, "Sophie, aren't you due in the schoolroom for your geography lesson?"

Sophie said thoughtfully, "Indeed, I wish to chart the *Blue Star*'s course to Boston. I wonder, are there any ice floes to batter a vessel in the North Atlantic?"

Julian said, "There are ice floes everywhere to batter the unwary."

"I wonder who is about to instruct me?" Sophie gave him a blazing smile, and walked up the staircase, dangling her bonnet by its blue ribbons.

Julian stared after her. She hadn't yet told him what she knew about any spears of stone. He supposed she'd been jesting with him. However, not ten minutes later, he looked up to Sophie striding toward him, making her bonnet ribbons dance in the stiff breeze. He stood in the dog run, surrounded by all four spaniels, all yipping and leaping about, trying to bite one another, vying for his attention. When they heard Sophie's voice, they left him flat and raced back to dance around her, barking their heads off, their tails wild metronomes. He turned again to face the channel, breathing in the wondrous smell of brine and fish and sun, when she said from behind him, "If you will come with me, I will show you spears of stone."

When he turned to face her, she was on her knees, staring up at him, trying to duck the dogs' tongues licking at her face and hair.

"Heel!"

The spaniels eyed him, then, one after the other, heeled.

"They obey you."

"Occasionally. I keep telling them they should do whatever I command, since I am their master. Let's give them another ten minutes—Cletus, no, don't try to bite Beatrice's belly. Ah, so you really do think you know where we'll find these spears of stone?"

Sophie was petting each spaniel's head, one after the other. She said, not looking at him, "I'm really not such a silly girl with air between her ears, as much as you would like to think so."

"No, there's barely any room in your head for air, you've got so many brains tucked in there. I'm afraid you know all too much—for a girl your age."

She grinned up at him now. "You should have known me when I was five years old. I was a right proper little whip, according to our gardener."

The thing was, he couldn't really see her as a little girl, not now, dammit.

When they brought the spaniels back into his estate room, Sophie realized she liked the smell—dog and leather and the scent of the sea from just beyond the glass door. And man.

"We're going to the cave," she said.

As they walked side by side to the banks of the River Horvath, he said, "Spears of stone, that could very well be it. How came you to think of it?"

She raised her skirts a bit to avoid a tangled bush.

"Sophie?"

"All those brains in my head have to be good for something." Fifteen minutes later, they slipped behind the thick brush that hid the entrance and stepped into the cave. Julian raised the lantern high. "I've never thought of stalactites being made of stone, yet they are. There are so many of them."

"You're right, I hadn't realized. Very well, we must concentrate only on those that look exactly like a spear."

Unfortunately, most of them were spears.

She faced Julian, shaking her head. "I imagined it would be so simple. I would bring you here, point to the only spear, we would scrape away sand, and there it would be, this ugly black jewel, perhaps wrapped in seal cloth. But instead . . ." She waved her arms around her.

"I had thought to impress you, to make you see me as a grown-up lady, to make you see me as, well, never mind." She sighed. "I had thought to be a heroine, but I am not. I am not even a right proper little whip anymore."

"Don't say that."

His voice was deep and harsh. Sophie stared at him. "But it is true, Julian. We could spend the next ten years digging beneath every single limestone spear in this dratted cave."

"Your deduction was excellent. We must try to think like my father when he was writing out his blasted clues. *Spears of stone*—it has to have meant something special to him, something he perhaps mentioned to my mother. We will ask her to think on it."

"Or perhaps it is here." Sophie fell to her knees beside a particularly long sharp stalactite and dug her fingers into the smooth sand. After several minutes, she stopped and looked up at him. "Well, this probably isn't the right one."

He laughed, hauled her to her feet. He used too much strength, he knew it, and yet he still did it. She came flying up hard against him, every bit of her hard against him, and he felt a bolt of lust so powerful he nearly fell over.

"No," he said, pushed her away, grabbed the lantern, and left the cave, pausing only to hold the branches out of the way for her to pass.

"I'm not a right little whip anymore, Julian. I'm a right big whip."

He said not a word to her on their walk back to Ravenscar.

Pouffer told them Baron Purley was in the drawing room with her grace, drinking tea.

"Like Pouffer, I shan't pay much attention to his lordship's politeness, either," he said.

As they drew near, Julian heard his mother say, "I found a folded note beneath the tear, Rupert. Let me show it to you. Sophie made several copies of it."

He and Sophie came into the room even as his mother opened a small Chinese box atop a marquetry table, retrieved the paper, and handed it to the baron.

Julian said nothing, merely watched the baron's face, aware of Sophie's every breath. The baron looked interested, then excited. "Good Lord, Corinne, I had no idea. I mean, I saw the backing paper had torn away, but I didn't wish to take the time to repair it, I only wanted to give it to Julian. Come, my dear, this puzzle from his grace, what does it mean?"

"None of us knows," she said. "Julian, Sophie, do come in. I have shown Rupert the puzzle from your father."

"Do you have any ideas what this can mean, Julian? Do you know where these spears of stone could be? Or what they are? Or what this magic jewel could be?"

"No, sir, I have no idea where this so-called magic jewel can be, or its purported magic. It will work for me but not my father? Did my father ever speak to you of this?"

"You're speaking of thirty years ago, my boy. But I imagine I would remember if your father spoke of a magic jewel."

Julian shrugged. "I understand Richard has escorted Lady Merrick back to Hardcross Manor."

"Yes," the baron said, smiling. "She is a charming lady. I believe my son has perhaps found his future wife."

Sophie opened her mouth, then shut it.

"Would you care for tea, dearest?" Corinne asked, her voice carefully neutral.

"I must see to business, Mother, and Sophie and Roxanne have planned an outing. Sir, good luck with your houseguest."

They heard the baron say, "Why would Julian wish me luck with Lady Merrick? She is Roxanne's sister, is she not? Sophie's aunt? A charming young woman, and I must say her husband left her very well situated, indeed."

"Oh, dear," Sophie said to Julian, as they walked from the drawing room. "I wonder what Leah is up to at this very moment?"

⇒ *48* ⇐

Julian was walking from the stables, flicking his whip against his boot, when he heard shouting. It was Sophie, and she was running to him, her riding skirts pulled above her ankles, calling his name over and over. He felt an awful fear. He grabbed her arms. "What's wrong? What's the matter? Are you all right?"

"She's gone!"

"What? Who is gone, Sophie?"

"Roxanne. She is not in her bedchamber, she is nowhere, I've asked everyone. No one has seen her. Everyone is looking for her. Do you know where she is?"

He took her hands in his, rubbed his thumbs over her palms to calm her. "No, I don't know. Here's Devlin. Surely he knows where she is."

"No, he doesn't. He and I are riding to Hardcross Manor. I know Richard Langworth took her, I know it; so does Devlin. Now that you're back, we can all go."

"Wait a moment—you've looked here?"

"Yes, yes. Tansy came to me at seven o'clock this morning and said Roxanne wasn't in her bed. At first I wasn't worried. Ravenscar is huge, and Roxanne loves to explore, but I couldn't find her. I asked everyone, then Pouffer told me Devlin was in the billiards room. He was losing to himself, and cursing, really quite mad about it. Oh, who cares if he or himself was winning?"

"I usually lose to myself, Sophie," Devlin said, trying for calm even as cold fear nearly bowed him over. "Julian, we must go now to Hardcross Manor. I agree with Sophie, Langworth took her. It makes no sense to me, but he must be the one to have taken her. After his failure to burn Julian's goods on the *Blue Star,* he must be getting desperate."

In the nine years Julian had known Devlin, he'd never before seen him so afraid.

Devlin said again, "I know Langworth took her, I know it. He has gone too far. I fully intend to kill him."

"Devlin, you said it makes no sense, and it doesn't. Why would he take Roxanne when you are the one she—" Sophie stalled.

The two men exchanged a look that said clearly, *If he wanted you to suffer all the way to your soul, he would not have taken Roxanne, he'd have taken Sophie.*

"What?" Sophie turned from one to the other. "What are you thinking? What don't you think I should know?"

Julian said, "If Richard wanted me to suffer, he should have taken my mother."

Devlin rolled his eyes. Julian ignored him.

Sophie said, "Maybe he did try to take her grace but couldn't manage it. So he took Roxanne instead. But why? She is Leah's sister, and he supposedly is going to marry Leah. Why would he take his future sister-in-law?"

Devlin said, "Leah carries a great deal of dislike in her, some of it toward her sister. Once we have Richard, he will tell me. He has hidden her, probably on manor property. Do you know of a storage house, an old barn, a gazebo, any ancient ruin where he could hide her?"

"There is an old barn on the edge of the property, where Richard and I played as boys, though I don't know if it is still standing."

"Let's go," Sophie said, and raced into the stable.

"I'm going to pound the bastard into the dirt, Julian, so don't try to talk me out of it."

"When we find Roxanne, I'll help you."

"And then I'm going to kill him."

⟡ ⟡

Thirty minutes later, the three of them pulled up their horses in front of Hardcross Manor to see Victoria Langworth standing on the deep steps, hands on her hips, yelling and waving her finger at a man they'd never seen before.

She looked up at them, then continued to shout as she waved her fist in the man's face. "This villain was supposed to fix my saddle! But did he? No, he patched it with some cheap leather that looked like it was taken from a dog collar. You, sir, you are an poltroon, and I shall see you ruined!"

The man managed to get in, "But miss, it is my brother who was to fix your saddle. He's a feckless lad, and I'll—"

Victoria actually growled. "You will take my saddle back to your feckless brother and see that he does it right or I will come at night and chew off his cheek when he's asleep!"

"Goodness," Sophie said, "that's a powerful threat."

Evidently, it sounded fairly powerful to the man as well. He grabbed the saddle from the ground, hoisted it onto his back, and nearly ran toward the stables.

Victoria turned to them, frowned. "You are all here. It isn't even noon yet. What is the matter?"

Julian stopped one step below hers. "Where is your brother, Vicky?"

"However should I know? He is probably nuzzling that dreadful woman's neck. Do you know she actually coos at him?" She looked at Sophie. "That woman is your aunt, which makes no sense to me, since I find you quite likable. Why is she so nasty?"

"Well, that is an excellent question, and I will tell you, Vicky, I have wondered that myself many times, particularly during the past three weeks. Where do you think they're nuzzling and cooing?"

Victoria Langworth flicked a glance toward Devlin, sketched him a curtsy. "My lord, it is very sunny today, unusual, but still—being of a vampire's persuasion, are you all right?"

It was then they all noticed Devlin wasn't wearing a hat. "I want to know where the nuzzling place is, Miss Langworth. I will worry about burning up under the sun after we have found your brother."

"But why do you wish to find Richard so badly?"

"He took Roxanne," Sophie said. "Truly, Victoria, we must find her. I am afraid for her."

"It is Roxanne's sister you should fear, not my poor blind brother. Do you know, I happened to tell Lady Merrick how I missed my sister, Lily, and how I believed she was so lucky to have her sister Roxanne still living. I told her how very charming and beautiful I thought Roxanne, and I wished she would marry Julian so she would be close by, and we could be friends.

"I was surprised when she puffed herself up and blasted Roxanne. She said Roxanne had fooled all of us, that she was malicious, you couldn't trust a word she said. She said Roxanne hated her because a score of gentlemen had proposed to her, Leah, and she'd been married and was considered the most beautiful of the Radcliffe sisters. She said Roxanne was jealous of her because she was a failed woman—a *spinster*—and barely passable-looking, what with her common red hair.

"Then she turned her fire on you, Sophie, her very own niece. She dismissed you, saying you were only a brat who needed to be smacked. I stood there, my mouth open, and marveled at her."

Julian said, "I don't suppose Leah said this in anyone else's hearing? Like your brother's or your father's?"

"Of course not. Lady Merrick isn't stupid. Do you know, she asked me several times to call her Leah, and she patted my hand in this intimate way that quite made me want to bolt. She charms both Richard and my father. As for me, she has to be endlessly kind to me, and so she is."

She turned her beautiful faraway eyes to Sophie. "Is she right, Sophie? Are you really only a little schoolgirl who is a spoiled brat?"

"What do you think?"

Victoria sighed. "Who knows? My brother and Leah rode off an hour ago. I think Richard wanted to show her the river. It is possible they are having a picnic on the banks of the Hovarth. But it is rather early, don't you think? I wonder if they are nuzzling and other things as well? Won't you come in, Julian? I know Richard hates you, but he isn't here. I don't hate you, and neither does Father, at least I don't believe he does. He told me about the magic jewel. I would like to discuss these spears of stone. I have some ideas about that."

"Thank you, Vicky, but I believe we will ride to the river ourselves, see what's for luncheon."

Ten minutes later, they heard a horse whinny.

"That is Beamis, Richard's gelding," Julian said. They rode down to the river's edge to see Richard and Leah sitting decorously on a spread blanket beneath a willow tree, food between them. Leah was laughing at something Richard said. She looked up, saw them, and called out, "Richard, I do believe we have unexpected company. Alas, we have only two apples left."

Richard pulled his knife from his boot as he leapt to his feet.

Julian realized they'd both carried a boot knife since they were ten years old, when an old gin-sodden varmint had tried to pound them, for what reason, Julian couldn't re- member. He watched Richard slowly straighten, the knife still held in his hand. Then he gave a grunt, resheathed the knife, and pulled on his riding coat.

"What are you three doing here, uninvited?" Leah asked lazily, sitting back on her elbows, watching them closely.

Richard said, "I should like to know as well."

Sophie jumped off her mare and strode up to him like a

boy. She grabbed his coat collar and shook him. "Where is Roxanne?"

"Roxanne?" He repeated her name slowly, his head cocked to one side, then lightly laid his own hands over hers. "What is this? You have managed to lose your aunt?"

Sophie looked him right in the eyes. "Where is she? You took her; you've got her hidden somewhere. Where?"

"Another drama you're enacting for us, Sophie?" Leah gathered her lovely sea-foam-green shawl around her shoulders and came up to her knees. "All three of you—what is happening here? You have somehow lost Roxanne? Perhaps she returned to Plymouth? Perhaps she met a gentleman there who pleased her?"

Devlin said, "How do you know we went to Plymouth?"

Richard said, "You know as well as I do you cannot change your coat without it being known throughout the county. I believe my man mentioned it to me."

Sophie said, rage bubbling up, "She is missing, sir. You took her, I know you did, to get back at Julian for your sister's death. Look at him—Julian wouldn't ever hurt a woman, ever. I have known him only a month, whereas you have known him all your life. How could you ever believe such an awful thing? You, sir, must be an idiot." She smacked her knuckles to her cheek. "Why am I repeating myself? Where is Roxanne?"

Richard said, "Julian is so guilty it shines from his eyes, hard, brutal. He ceased being the boy I knew years ago. Go away, all of you. I know nothing of Roxanne."

⇥ *49* ⇤

Leah jumped to her feet. "Listen to me, Richard and I have been together for hours now. Go back to Ravenscar; I'll wager Roxanne has been there all the time, teasing you. She's always wanted attention, you know, and now she's got it."

Sophie yelled, "How can you say that about your own sister, Aunt Leah? She was kidnapped right out of her bed. Don't you care? Don't you care that this man you believe so very gallant is behind it?"

"That is absurd. Roxanne wouldn't allow anyone to kidnap her. She's back at Ravenscar, laughing her head off, you'll see."

Julian said quietly, "Come, let's go."

"Where?" Richard asked.

"Since you are so innocent, I don't believe that is any of your business," Devlin said.

Julian said, "We will be back, once we have Roxanne. Then you and I will finish this. It will be over, once and for all."

"No," Devlin said, "I shall finish it."

They rode through a long, narrow field. Julian watched Sophie close her eyes when her mare jumped a fence, and smiled. She had guts.

Julian pointed, clucked Cannon forward. "There is the barn," he said, over his shoulder.

A wreck of a barn sat crumbling in a clearing in the middle of a maple forest, its wide door hanging drunkenly on its rusted hinges and its roof caved in in several places. Maple trees crowded close. The barn looked deserted, as though it had been deserted for more years than any of them had been on the earth.

Julian put his finger to his lips, dismounted Cannon, and tethered him to a low-hanging maple tree branch some twenty feet away. "Let's go quietly. Sophie, you stay—"

She stopped him with a look.

"Stay close." They heard a horse whinny and stopped dead in their tracks, waiting. No one said a word. A moment passed, another. Finally, Julian whispered, "Devlin, you and Sophie go around the front, make sure no one leaves. I'm going to the back. I remember a window there. If I see anything, I will give an owl call. Then you, Devlin, can come in through the front door." He crouched down, walking swiftly toward the back of the barn, nearly swallowed up in the trees.

Julian kept crouched down as he ran lightly to the one window, the shutters long gone. He looked inside.

At first he didn't see anything, but when his eyes adjusted, he saw a movement in the shadowed end of the barn. Was it Roxanne?

He put his hands to his mouth and gave a credible owl hoot. He had but a moment—Julian jumped up, grabbed the sill, and threw himself through the window. He felt his shirt rip from a stray shard as he flew headfirst into the barn, a moment of pain in his arm. He rolled and came up, his knife in his hand. Why the devil hadn't he brought his pistol?

He saw Devlin crash through the front door, heard the crumbling wood crash to the ground, heard him shout, "Roxanne!"

Julian raced to the shadowed end of the barn and stopped, Devlin and Sophie beside him, to stare at the white specter.

"Roxanne?" Without thought, with no hesitation whatsoever, Devlin grabbed her, cupped her face between his palms, and kissed her. He pulled back. "You have scared the wickedness right out of me, you abominable girl." Then he was kissing her all over her face, only to push her back again, his hands feeling her arms, roving over her chest, her hips, finally, her legs. "You're not hurt, thank the Lord. What the hell happened?"

"Hello, I am very glad you've come. I was wondering what to do." She pulled away from Devlin and pointed. "Look," she said.

Six feet away from them, a man lay on his side, huddled in on himself, his wrists bound together with his own belt, his legs tied together with the remnants of his shirt, and he was groaning.

"Roxanne!" Sophie was in her arms, both of them turning to watch Devlin and Julian kneel beside the man.

Devlin turned him onto his back. His eyes were closed, his jaws whiskered, his clothes filthy. Devlin slapped him hard as Julian lightly kicked his leg. "Open your eyes, you puling bastard."

The man's lashes fluttered, and finally he opened his eyes to look up at the men. "She near to kilt me."

Julian said slowly, "I believe we have found Orvald Manners." He turned to Roxanne. "All right, Roxanne, tell us what happened."

"I wish to kill him first," Devlin said, and aimed his pistol at the man's head.

Roxanne lightly laid her hand on his arm. "Not yet, my lord. Let him tell us who paid him to kidnap me first. Then we can both carry him to the local magistrate."

"Which would be me," Julian said, with a ferocious smile. "I wonder what I shall decide to do with you."

"I don't have a gun," Sophie said, "but if he doesn't tell us, I have my hands, and I will squeeze his neck until the words pop right out."

50

It was so very easy for him, Roxanne told them, and she kicked Orvald Manners in the ribs. He groaned and tried to spit up at her, not a smart thing for him to do, since he couldn't move and the spittle landed back on his face.

"I don't know how he got into my bedchamber, but somehow he did. I came awake with a cloth pressed over my mouth and nose. It smelled sweet, sickeningly sweet. I tried to fight him, but I didn't have any strength left, and the world turned black.

"When I awoke, I was lying in this filthy hay, all tied up and wearing only my nightgown."

Devlin hadn't noticed she was wearing only a ripped, dirty white nightgown, but now he did. He took off his riding jacket and helped her shrug it on. "Thank you, Devlin. Oh, goodness"—she touched her fingers to his face—"you're sunburned. Are you feeling ill from the sun? Wherever is your hat?"

He laughed, couldn't help himself. "A little red won't hurt me. Come on, how did you get away from this idiot?"

"He didn't believe I could hurt him," she said, frowning

down at Manners, and kicked him again. He groaned, whispered, "Ye shouldn't oughtta do that, miss, iffen ye break my ribs, I won't be able to talk, me air'll be all clogged off."

"Oh, yes, you will talk," Sophie said, and kicked him in the leg. She looked back at Roxanne, whose hair hung in wild tangles around her dirty face, wearing Devlin's riding coat. She looked ridiculous and, oddly, valiant.

"First tell us who hired you," Devlin said.

"I don't know. I niver saw 'is face, only 'eard 'is voice. Maybe it were a female, I swears I really don't know."

"Of course he knows," Roxanne said calmly. "I've been asking him over and over, but he won't spill out the truth."

Sophie came down on her knees beside Manners. She grabbed his face and jerked him around to face her. "Look at me. That's right. Do you know what I will do to you if you don't tell us the truth? You are looking at a demon, Mr. Manners, a female demon, the worst sort. I am called a succubus, known for my cruelty, known for devouring men's souls. If you don't tell us the truth, I will have the gentlemen knock you unconscious and then I will chew off your cheek, and then I will lay my palm over your heart and your soul will fly right out into my hand. When you wake up, I will hand you a mirror and show you the blood running down your face; then you can look at your own blood on my mouth, and then you can realize you're nothing but a deaf, empty husk, your soul gone."

The silence was thick and heavy. Manners gasped out, "That's worse than anything I could ever do, and ye a lady. You ain't, yer a foul demon, who oughtta be tied to rocks and drowned in the Thames. I don't know who the bloke was wot paid me, I swears it! I ain't niver 'eard o' no suckeybus; ye made that up."

"That's all he says. Do you know, he was going to rape me?" For a moment, the awful fear nearly choked off Roxanne's voice. She'd never been so afraid in her life.

She heard Devlin's harsh fast breathing, saw him raise his fist. "No," she said. "No, not yet. He didn't succeed, Devlin."

"Tell me," Devlin said. He looked ready to commit murder.

Roxanne looked down at Manners, then drew a deep steadying breath. "He stood over me, his thumbs in his belt loops, and he was singing a sailor's ditty, singing like he didn't have a care in the world, and he was talking aloud to himself, going on and on about what a pretty little thing I was with all my sinful red harlot's hair. He said he bet I craved a bonny gentleman, that I'd love what he was going to do to me. Then he was arguing with himself, saying things like who cared, nobody said anything about not having fun with me." Roxanne realized she was nearly panting with anger and fear. She growled deep in her throat, and kicked Manners in the stomach. He moaned and cursed at her. She smiled. "He wondered if maybe he'd return me pregnant, 'a brat in my belly,' he so charmingly put it. Then he wondered if he would even be sending me back, and since he didn't know what the gentleman had in mind for me, he'd best take his chance now.

"He saw I was awake, and he gave me a big smile. I remember he said, 'Aye, ye gots yer brain back, that's good. I likes to 'ear a woman moan for me while I sticks my manhood in 'er.'"

She could feel Devlin's rage pumping off him in black waves. She had to get a grip on herself. She'd won. Manners lay at her feet. Roxanne said, her voice stronger now, "When he dropped his britches, jerked up my nightgown, and came down over me, I really didn't think, I simply reacted—I kicked up as hard as I could, just as my father taught me, and he screamed and cursed and fell back, holding his stomach. He fell, and he rolled around a bit, moaning and crying. I got loose, hit him on the head as hard as I could with that plowshare, and tied him up." She stopped, smiled at all of them. "And waited for you. I knew you'd come, you see."

It sounded so simple, so very easy, but how could she tell them she'd been so terrified she was whimpering even as she kicked him, that she nearly vomited when she finally had him tied up. And she'd hit him again on his head with the plowshare.

Devlin growled deep in his throat, fell to his knees, and grabbed Manners's neck. "You puking little sod, say your prayers, because the Devil's waiting for you."

It took all three of them to pull Devlin off him.

Roxanne said to Manners, "I will make you a promise, sir. If you tell us who hired you, I won't let his lordship kill you, nor will I let her chew off your cheek and steal your soul."

"Wait a minute, it ain't this fellow wot's supposed to want ye, it's this other one, this 'ere high-and-mighty prince wot's got 'is ship back wit' all 'is bloody goods jest fine an' dandy. I 'eard that demmed bloody little gnat, Ira, got the fire out, quick as a flash and none o' the goods was burnt. It weren't fair, none of it were my fault.

"Ah, I sees now, this fellow wot wants to murder me is the prince's little bullyboy. Don't want to dirty up yer 'ands, do ye, yer princeship?" Manners spat, turned his head quickly so his spittle landed on rotted hay and not back on his own face.

Sophie crossed her arms over her chest. "What a moron you are, Mr. Manners. This high-and-mighty princeship here always does his own dirty work. As for his bullyboy, why, he might not be a prince, but he's a lordship, and one of these years he'll be a duke, only one step down from a prince. He really, really wants to kill you. Now, sir, if both Roxanne and I guarantee your miserable life, will you tell us who hired you?"

Manners looked mournful, saw it didn't sway any of them, then looked philosophical. "Iffen I tells ye, I'm dead anyways, probably worse than 'avin' the little girl chew off me cheek, though I can't really imagine anythun' bein' worse than that. As fer drawing out me soul, I doesn't know what that'd be like."

Sophie was tapping her foot, her arms crossed over her chest. *Tap, tap, tap.* "Let's take Mr. Manners back to Hard-cross Manor. Let's see what Richard has to say when he's faced with this fool."

"See 'ere, I ain't no fool, I gots rotten luck, thass all. Wot's 'ardcross Manor?"

51

R oxanne liked Manners's horse, a big brute of a gelding they found tied next to the barn, who whipped around his great head when Julian lifted Sophie behind Roxanne, and whinnied up at her. She patted his neck. "This proud fellow holds both of us easily, Sophie. I think I shall keep him. That sod doesn't deserve him."

"He probably stole him," Sophie said.

"I think I shall call him Luther."

"I can't wait to see Richard's face," Sophie said, a good deal of satisfaction in her voice. "If you like, I will hold him while you punch him in the nose. Are you all right, Roxanne?"

Roxanne started to assure her niece she was fine, an automatic reflex of an adult to a child. But Sophie wasn't a child. She was a grown woman. She deserved the truth. Roxanne stared straight ahead as she spoke. "I no longer want to cry and shake myself to death, and that's a relief, but the terror, Sophie—it's still clogging my throat, threatening to choke me. Truth is, I've never been so frightened in my life. Then to see all of you there—" Her voice broke, and she shook her head, steadying herself. "I was naming a bloody horse. Am I mad?"

"No, it took your mind away from what that horrible man put you through." Sophie hugged herself tightly against Roxanne's back. "You were so brave and so smart, you saved yourself. We weren't in time, and I'm so sorry, but we tried. We had to hunt down Richard—he and Leah were having a picnic, if you can believe that—and it was only ten o'clock in the morning. Who wants a picnic at ten o'clock in the morning?"

"They wanted to be occupied with each other while Manners was holding Roxanne," Devlin said, "so he could pretend innocence."

Sophie drew in a deep breath. "Yes, that is why. Oh, Roxanne, I am so glad you're my aunt, even though it means I have to put up with Leah. I hope she does marry Richard and the two of them can make each other miserable."

Roxanne laughed. She was surprised there could be anything at this moment that could make her laugh, but then she realized that in her twenty-seven years there was usually something unexpected and quite absurd lurking around the next corner to rocket one's spirits to the sky. She felt Sophie's warm body pressed against her back, felt her arms tight around her waist, and was immensely grateful. For life and for Sophie. She looked over at Devlin, who was staring thoughtfully at her, as if he was considering a very knotty problem. *Were you really so scared you forgot your hat?* She grinned at him. "I shan't fall over, I promise. Nor shall I faint. I should not want to dirty up your fine coat."

"There is straw in your hair," he said, and watched her hand automatically go to her tangled hair, then drop. He said, "Don't worry about it. When we return to Ravenscar, I will tidy you up."

"Do you like the name Luther?"

"Were I a horse, I would prance about with my tail flicking if I had that name."

Roxanne laughed again, felt more of the terror ease out of her. She said, "Sophie, I cannot believe you told Manners you would chew off his cheek."

"That exquisite threat is compliments of Vicky. Our villain here certainly didn't like it."

Orvald Manners, tied facedown over the back of Sophie's sidesaddle, was cursing nonstop as the mare's gait made him bounce up and down, pulverizing his liver. Suddenly, Manners reared up, cried out, and flopped down, unconscious.

Devlin cursed—a ripe one featuring animal parts.

They pulled up and lifted Manners out of the saddle. "Here," Roxanne said, "put him under this tree. Not for him but for you, Devlin, to keep you out of the sun."

"He appears to be unconscious," Devlin said, shifting to look up at Julian.

Julian leaned down, felt the pulse in the man's neck. "I wonder, is he trying to fool us?" and he slapped him hard.

Manners didn't move.

Roxanne said, "Do you think he's having a reaction from my blows with the plowshare? I did hit him as hard as I could."

Devlin said, "I suppose it's possible."

"When I kicked him, I thought he was going to scream himself to death, so maybe that's what he's reacting to now—"

"No," Julian said. "Kicking him there wouldn't send him unconscious an hour later. He'd want to die immediately, but he wouldn't."

"Why?" Sophie asked, coming down on her knees beside the unconscious Manners.

"It's not important," Julian said.

Roxanne said matter-of-factly, "Papa told me I should always kick a man low in his belly before he works himself up to violence. He said it is guaranteed to focus a man's brain elsewhere instantly. I will teach you what to do, Sophie, but Julian is right, it's not important right now."

Devlin rose, dusted off his britches. "Let's haul him back on the mare's back. By the time we arrive at Hardcross Manor, he should be awake again and cursing at the top of his lungs. I want to see Richard face-to-face with this miscreant."

"Let's do it," Roxanne said. "I'm dressed a bit strangely, but who cares? At last maybe we can get this resolved."

A smile blazed on Devlin's sunburned face. "You look like a queen. My coat has never looked more stylish."

She returned his smile, adding more power to hers. "And you, sir, look like a bullyboy, your sleeves rolled up and your shirt collar open, ready to take on any villain. I hope one of the gentlemen of the house can lend you a hat, Devlin. Also, some cream for your face."

"Do you know," Devlin said, after he'd finished tying Manners back across the mare's sidesaddle, "a cream might be just the thing. I am feeling very warm; mayhap I can even feel my flesh beginning to crisp."

"That is horrible," Sophie said.

But when they reached Hardcross Manor, none were laughing nor smiling.

Manners hadn't regained consciousness.

Devlin hefted Manners over his shoulder and walked to the front door. Julian slammed down the lion's-head knocker, once, twice.

Victoria opened the door. "Goodness, what is this? I see you found Roxanne, but who—"

"We want to see your brother," Devlin said. "Now."

"He isn't here. He and Lady Merrick came back rather quickly from their picnic, then decided, quite on the spur of the moment, to visit Saint Austell, and wasn't it fun to be spontaneous, said she, all twittery and laughing, a quaint place her darling Richard had told her about, and since it wasn't raining, she was perfectly prepared to enjoy herself.

"If you really want to speak to him, my lord, you could catch them, or perhaps not. Lady Merrick allowed they might take country roads, to admire the scenery, not the direct road. If you ask me, I think she wanted to admire Richard's scenery—well, that is vulgar, isn't it? Roxanne, I believe you should have the gentlemen chase after them, since you really aren't dressed for it."

"What is going on here? Who is this man? Is he dead?"

Baron Purley strode into the entrance hall, eyeing the man slung over Devlin's shoulder.

"Well, here, put the fellow down before you break your back, boy. This is the man who kidnapped you, Miss Radcliffe? You appear to be unharmed. Does he need a physician? Victoria, tell Elmer to have Dr. Crutchfield fetched."

"No, thank you, sir," Julian said. "I think we should take the fellow on to Ravenscar. Did Richard say when he and Lady Merrick would return?"

"No, he did not," the baron said. "I am hopeful, however, that they do not spend the night in Saint Austell, since they are not yet wed."

Victoria said, "Papa, Richard is a man. He can do what he wants, and Lady Merrick is a widow. You've seen the way she looks at him, like she wants to lick him like an ice."

The baron huffed out a breath but kept further thoughts to himself.

⇥ *52* ⇤

Victoria went down on her knees next to Manners, her pale yellow muslin skirts fanning out around her. She lifted one eyelid and examined Manners's pupil. She muttered something to herself, let his eyelid drop, and looked up at them. "Leah said they were planning a wedding in June. I doubt they'll come back, mayhap not until the day of the wedding. If this man kidnapped you, Roxanne, he didn't prove very competent, did he?"

The baron said, "Richard did not ask his valet to accompany him, so I know he will be back. He and his valet cannot long be parted; both suffer. Leave that creature alone, Vicky, you might catch a putrid disease from touching him."

"If Richard returns, tell him I will see him," Julian said. "Once and for all. My apologies for disturbing you."

This time he hefted Manners over his shoulder and walked out the front door.

He said to Devlin as they tied Manners onto the mare's saddle again, "I don't wish to risk this fellow's health by leaving him in this house alone to fend for himself, nor do I have any desire to remain here with him."

Sophie asked, "You think the baron might throttle him to save his son?"

"That's right," Julian said.

⊷⇒ ⇐⊷

Back at Ravenscar, Pouffer ignored the unconscious man hanging over the prince's shoulder and stared at Roxanne, whose red hair was wild and tangled, ancient straws sticking up here and there around her head, her gown filthy and ripped beneath the arm, her feet bare, his lordship's black coat around her shoulders. "Oh, my dear young Miss Roxanne, thanks to all the beneficent gods who reside somewhere above our heads, you are returned to us. I see a great deal of dirt but no blood, a great relief. I am grateful the prince saved you, or perhaps it was his lordship here."

"She saved herself, Pouffer," Sophie said. "She didn't need the gentlemen to do the job."

"That is not a notion that reassures, Miss Sophie. A gentleman must be useful, else what good is he? Now, her grace has been wringing her hands, something she rarely has cause to do." He looked back to Roxanne. "You are certain you are fit enough, Miss Roxanne?"

"I am fine, Pouffer," Roxanne said, lightly patting his arm. "I will remove myself upstairs. Please tell her grace all is well again. As you see, we even have the miscreant who kidnapped me. Unfortunately, I hit him on the head—only two times—and he had the gall to fall unconscious." She paused on the stairs, looked down to see Devlin staring up at her. "Thank you all again for coming after me so quickly."

"Even though you didn't need us."

"Didn't need you, Devlin? I fancy needing you will become something of a daily occurrence." She searched his face. "But we will see, won't we?"

Not thirty minutes later, Sophie and Roxanne walked into the drawing room. "Is our villain awake, Julian?"

"No, he hasn't moved, not even moaned. Pouffer sent one of the footmen to fetch Dr. Crutchfield. He's old, and his hands shake a bit—the doctor, not the footman. He doesn't see too well, but he normally doesn't kill his patients. He brought me into the world, and I survived the experience."

Corinne said, "I remember when you were three years old, dearest, you had a dreadful putrid throat. I am convinced his special tonic saved you."

Sophie said, "I don't believe a tonic is going to help this time, ma'am. I really don't want this villain to die until after he tells us who hired him." Sophie rubbed her hands together, smiled at Julian, and made her way to the lovely Georgian teapot. Roxanne stared after her. She looked at Julian. He was looking down at his boots. Now, this was very interesting.

Corinne rose and walked to Roxanne, cupped her face between her white hands, then, with a sigh, she clasped her to her bosom. "You are quite recovered, my dear?"

"Yes, ma'am. Well, maybe still a bit shaky, but the man didn't have a chance to hurt me. I am glad to be back. Ah, Devlin, you have rubbed cream into your face. Do you feel less crispy?"

He was once again wearing his coat, quickly brushed by Pouffer himself. His face didn't have his usual vampire pallor, it was white with cream. He touched a finger to his cheek. "Should you care to rub the cream in for me while I try to find any straws you missed and pick them out?"

Sophie laughed. "It took me five minutes, but I think I got them all."

"I have been wondering," the duchess said slowly, "how this man managed to get into Ravenscar. Pouffer makes his rounds every evening at ten o'clock sharp. So how did this scoundrel manage to slither in? But the bigger question is this: How did he know which was Roxanne's bedchamber?"

Devlin said, "An excellent point, ma'am, which rather proves it had to be Richard who hired him, since he did know exactly which bedchamber Roxanne was in."

Julian said, "Since Richard has been in and out of Ravenscar for years, he'd know every way to get into the house."

Sophie was pacing, a frown on her face. "There is

something wrong here. I don't think Richard is a fool. Why would he do something so utterly outrageous, knowing he would be suspected? Doesn't he have a brain?" She smacked the side of her own head. "What am I talking about? He is evidently going to marry Leah. He must not only be a moron, he must hate himself."

Roxanne said, "Don't forget Manners set fire to the cargo on the *Blue Star,* on Richard's orders. That could have worked, I suppose, but our wonderful cabin boy saved the day."

They looked up to see Pouffer clearing his throat at the door. "Prince, Baron Purley is here with Dr. Crutchfield."

"Show the baron in here, Pouffer, and please take Dr. Crutchfield to Manners."

The baron said from the doorway, "I wish to visit this man with Dr. Crutchfield, Julian, examine him more closely. I think now that I have seen him before."

Everyone accompanied Dr. Crutchfield to a small sewing room at the end of the west corridor. It held only one narrow bed, a washbasin, and a large work table. Tom, the beefiest footman in Julian's employ, stood against the wall, arms crossed over his chest, standing guard and taking it seriously.

"I wonder where Baron Purley saw Manners?" Sophie whispered to Julian, as they stood near the door, watching Dr. Crutchfield examine him.

Dr. Crutchfield straightened, turned to Julian. "Prince, I see two large lumps on his head. How was he struck?"

Roxanne said, "I hit him twice on his head, sir, with a plowshare. As hard as I could."

"I trust he deserved it, for the lumps are of a great size. Now I believe he has fallen into a deep coma. I honestly do not know if he will awaken, Prince. I'm very sorry."

Baron Purley said, "I was wrong, Julian, I haven't seen him before." He paused for a moment. "I know you think Richard to be responsible for Roxanne's kidnapping, but I do not honestly believe Richard is behind this. He is a gentleman, when all is said and done."

53

"You said I belonged to you."

Julian had closed the door to the sewing room, leaving Tom to keep watch over Manners. At her words, he stiffened straight as a shot, gave her a harassed look.

She was standing not six feet from him, dressed in a lavender muslin gown, belted with a darker lavender sash. The color made her skin glow. Her dark brown hair shone in the dim hallway light. She looked like she was willing to stand exactly where she was until he spoke. "You aren't remembering correctly. It was Devlin who said that about Roxanne."

He realized he knew very well Devin had said that to Roxanne. She shouldn't ever gamble, she would surely lose every groat she had.

She took a light step forward. "Ah, yes, I remember now. I wonder, would you say the same about me, Julian? Do I belong to you?"

"You are close to my mother, are you not? And thus you are like my family. It is my responsibility to guard my family, since my family is part of me, and thus belongs to me."

"You could not repeat that if you tried with all your might, since it is so very convoluted and at its core means nothing. You know as well as I do that isn't at all what Devlin meant."

She struck a pose, her fingertips tapping her chin. "But wait, I rather think now I like being considered simply one of your family. Yes, that is fine. A powerful family at your back is a very good thing. Do you know what I'm going to do? After we go on our smuggling adventure and you have taken care of Richard, I am going to return to London to finish my first Season. Goodness, how many more balls are there? Dozens, don't you think? I won't have missed all that many. I do love dancing, and gossiping with all the other girls about this and that gentleman, comparing their faces, their forms, how much money they have to lay on the marital block, wondering which one will propose to which girl—ah, so many days I must wait until my future can begin again." She turned away, whistling, and strode off down the corridor like an arrogant boy.

Julian went to his estate room. He tried to focus on accounts, but within ten minutes he was leaning his head back on the sofa cushions, asleep, his four spaniels hunkered in close.

He awoke with a start, bounded to his feet, dumping the spaniels on the carpet, when he heard Pouffer shouting, "No! You cannot go in there, sir! That is the prince's private room he shares only with the dogs and Miss Sophie. No, sir!"

The door flew open, and there stood Richard Langworth, his face pale with rage.

"I see you came quickly back from Saint Austell. What happened? Did Lady Merrick decide the lovely scenery wasn't to her taste after all?"

"No, it began to rain. Damn you, how dare you order me here to deal with me 'once and for all'?"

"Did I say that?"

"That is what my father told me. He said you wanted to end it. Damn you, I did not hire anyone to kidnap Roxanne!"

"That is very difficult to believe, since you already hired

Mr. Manners to burn my goods aboard the *Blue Star*. You can't deny it, since you gave it away in London."

"All right, yes, I did hire him to cause a bit of damage. He wasn't going to burn all your goods, that would be fool-hardy, he was going to keep the blaze well under control, bring about just enough damage so your goods would be worth nothing much at all, but the blighter failed, damn his eyes. You know you deserve that I try to ruin you. You bastard, you murdered my sister! You shot her dead. I think you believed she had a lover, and that's why you killed her."

Julian said very quietly, "Do you believe Lily was un-faithful to me, Richard?"

Richard drew a deep breath. He stuffed his hands into his pockets. "No, I don't know, but I've never known you to act in your life without a good reason. Lily having a lover is the only reason that makes sense, the only thing that would anger you sufficiently. Why won't you admit it? Why? There is no one here to hear you confess, you won't be hung, dammit."

"Do you know, if Lily had taken a lover, I wouldn't ever have considered killing her. How could I? I loved her. I would have set her free."

"I have seen you in a rage before."

"And did I kill anyone?"

"No, you beat the fellow to his knees."

"Ah, that one. Well, he was a bully, and he insulted Lily. What was I to do?"

"Beat him to his knees, damn you."

"Richard, let me be honest here. I wouldn't have killed Lily if she were unfaithful, that is quite true. The man, however, I might very well have killed. But I wouldn't have been in a rage. I would have been as smart as I could, killed him, and buried him and gotten away with it.

"Now, I will tell you yet again. I didn't shoot her. When I came into the garden, she was already dead. Listen to me, Richard. I will say this once more, then never again, for I begin to bore even myself. I swear my innocence to you on my father's honor, since you obviously don't believe I have any honor."

"You had honor once."

"As did you."

Richard picked up a brass candlestick and hurled it against the fireplace. Both men stared as the candlestick bounced off the marble, then rolled across the wooden floor, coming to rest on the Aubusson carpet.

"You frightened my spaniels."

Julian sat down again, gathering the four dogs to him. "It's all right. Just an accident. Cletus, don't you forget your manners." He calmed the dogs, then looked over at Richard, who stood, white-faced, leaning against his desk.

Julian said, "You have spent the past three years of your life plotting my downfall. You have thought of nothing else. It has become an obsession with you, your father is quite right about that. You have stopped moving forward, Richard, you have stopped living your life."

"I owe it to my sister to bring her murderer to justice. Until you are dead, I will continue to owe it to her."

Julian eyed his boyhood friend, saw his hands clench and unclench at his sides, felt the heat of his bubbling rage writhing about just below the surface. He said, "I would ask you to believe—but for a moment—that I am not guilty of her murder. If you believe my innocence—for a moment only—then tell me, Richard, what do you think happened?"

"What is this nonsense?"

"I ask you to humor me—for but a moment. If I didn't shoot Lily, then what do you think happened?"

"She didn't commit suicide, as you were claiming. I know Lily; she would never kill herself, never. It would mean that someone else killed her and tried to make it look like suicide. And the someone else saw you coming and hoped you would be blamed, that is what I would think if I were not certain in my own mind that you were guilty."

"All right. I ask that you consider for yet another moment that I did not kill Lily. Let me ask you, did you kill her, Richard?"

"I? Kill my own sister? I loved her; I would never have harmed her."

"Even if she did something so reprehensible it destroyed all feeling for her?"

"No, there is nothing that would make me feel that way, even if she took a dozen lovers and flaunted them about the neighborhood."

"Very well. I ask you to keep thinking that I am innocent. If Lily didn't kill herself, then who put a pistol to her heart and pulled the trigger? Who left it in her hand? Do you remember who was in the house that day?"

Richard shoved his fingers through his hair. He began pacing the estate room. The spaniels were pressed tightly against Julian, watching first him and then Richard.

Richard whirled about. "My father was in the house. So was Vicky. She had tried on a new white gown, I remember that clearly. When she came running into the garden, you were crouched over Lily, bloody, looking down at her. Vicky fell to her knees and hugged her sister tightly, began rocking her. When my father lifted her off, there was blood all over her white gown. I remember thinking it looked like she was shot."

Julian nodded. "Yes, now I remember you yelled at her to go burn the damned gown. I remember, too, that I simply couldn't accept Lily's death, couldn't accept that she wasn't breathing and I couldn't bring her back, that she was gone. I remember there was so much blood. I had her blood all over my hands."

"You were shaking her, yelling at her, pleading with her, pouring your breath into her mouth—all of it an act to convince everyone of your despair. You were crying—yet another act."

Julian was seeing it all clearly again, and it nearly bowed him to his knees. He said, his voice thick, "The pain of it has lessened over time, but speaking of it brings it all back again. I can hear Vicky screaming; I can see your father's bloodless face, see his lips moving, but nothing came out.

"Richard, consider that nothing I did was an act. That what you saw was a husband who was devastated by his wife's violent death. Do you remember anyone else who was about that day?"

"No. You asked everyone, you questioned every servant, every gardener, every stable lad, but none of them saw anyone else. So if we are to continue your game, it means you want me to believe one of Lily's family murdered her, either my sister or my father."

"If you didn't kill her and you swear to me she wouldn't have killed herself, then yes, who else is there to consider?"

"Damn you, no, it is impossible."

Julian said slowly, "You wish to believe me guilty because you can't bear it to be either Vicky or your father. Blaming me has kept them safe from your scrutiny for three years. Making your focus on me as the killer has kept that awful fear buried deep inside you, the fear that one of them was responsible." He waited a beat. "Or the only other possibility is that she did indeed kill herself. But like you, I would swear there was no lover, so the question is: Why would she kill herself? We'd only been married six months. It's true, I was gone a lot in those days, so much to be done. Mayhap she was lonely, mayhap she did meet a man, but I don't think so, nor does my mother.

"I still feel the guilt of it now, leaving her at Ravenscar by herself. My mother said she spent a great deal of time at Hardcross Manor. And I remember well she still went back and forth most days even when I was home.

"So why, Richard, why would she kill herself? Can you think of anything that happened, anything that could have sent her into such despair that she no longer wanted to live?"

Richard gave him a blind look, kicked a chair leg, and said, "She didn't have a lover, damn you, I know it to my soul. I can't remember that anything out of the ordinary happened. It could not have been either our father or our sister, that is quite absurd. So your moment is over, Julian. You are the only one left. It was you who killed her, no matter your continuous protestations of innocence. So leave it, Julian, for I will never believe you, ever.

"About Roxanne. I did not take her. You must have enemies other than myself; look at the wealth you've gained in a short amount of time.

"Since I cannot believe Roxanne somehow brought this down on herself, then it is you who are responsible. What sort of ruthless bastard are you, Julian?"

Julian said, his voice emotionless, "All right, let us move on to Roxanne. I will consider—for a moment only—that you are innocent of this. Then who hired Manners to drug her in her bed and haul her out of Ravenscar?"

Richard was silent.

"You see how difficult it is for me to believe you innocent? I mean, no one else even knew about Manners, did they? Mayhap your father and your sister, but no one else. Who else knows their way around Ravenscar the way you do? Except perhaps your father and your sister?

"I'm very much afraid there is something in your household, Richard, something right under your nose, that you are refusing to see."

"There is nothing untoward going on at Hardcross Manor!"

"Do you know Manners was going to rape her? He did not succeed, because her father had taught her to kick a man in the groin to bring him down, and so she kept her wits about her and kicked him hard. She saved herself. We arrived at the old barn when she'd already tied him up. She'll have nightmares, Richard, probably as long as she lives."

"I did not hire Manners to take her."

"You see my dilemma, do you not? I must believe you as guilty of taking Roxanne as you believe me guilty of shooting Lily. Tell me, Richard, are you really going to marry Roxanne's sister, Lady Merrick?"

"That is none of your business."

Richard was pacing again. Julian didn't move, merely watched him.

He said, "I believe you searched Leah out on purpose, to use her to get at me. Such an outlandish scheme, Richard, more complicated than any other I have seen you concoct over the years. Did your father tell you my mother wished me to marry Sophie, but all came to believe it was Roxanne I wanted, and that is why you decided to roll the dice? Tell me, what has winning her affection gained you?"

"Don't be stupid. Knowing Leah has made me aware of your plans, has given me entrance to this house. Damn you, you hate me, call me out, let's end this like gentlemen."

"Hate you? I do not hate you, Richard. What I hate is the boyhood friend now lost to me because he simply can't force himself to look beyond me.

"Do you really intend to marry her? Or will you simply make her—a lady—into your mistress until you have no more use for her?"

"You don't know what you're talking about." Richard kicked the sofa, sending the spaniels into a frenzy, and slammed out of the estate room. He shouted over his shoulder, "I did not hire Manners to take Roxanne. If I'd wanted to destroy you, I would have hired him to take Sophie, not Roxanne. I like Roxanne; I would never hurt her. I do not know who hired Manners to do it; surely neither my father nor my sister, that is ridiculous. There has to be someone else, there has to be. Wake the blighter up, he'll have to tell you."

Julian listened to Richard's boots clicking on the marble floor, receding into the distance. Sophie said from the doorway, "What a very hurt man he is." She walked to Julian, ignoring the spaniels leaping at her. "You did excellently with him. He's been angry for so long, he doesn't know anything else. But now you have forced him to think. Perhaps he will realize something he hasn't wished to see these past three years."

"You eavesdropped."

"Don't sound so horrified. It is the best way to gain needful information. I'm sorry Lily is dead, Julian, but I am also very glad she isn't here to be married to you." She kissed his cheek. "What a fine forbearing sort of uncle you are." She turned quickly to scoop up Cletus and Beatrice, leaving the other two to howl at her. She laughed, and said, "I'm taking them out to run. Come, Oliver, Hortense. You two stop complaining, I can't carry all of you." And she was through the French doors, and walking in her long-legged stride toward the cliff at the end of the dog run, the spaniels skipping and dancing beside her.

⟪ *54* ⟫

"I think I should like to take you away from Ravenscar, Roxanne."

"Exactly why do you think that?"

Devlin was leaning back on his elbows, no hat on his head, looking at her intently. "I suppose I'm thinking aloud. My heart's finally slowed a bit now that I've convinced myself you are really all right. You scared me out of a good ten years."

"Add us together and we've twenty less years on this earth." They sat on a blanket in the shade of an immense willow tree on the banks of the Horvath. Devlin sat up next to Roxanne to lean against the tree. She lifted her hand to touch him, then dropped it back to her side. She smiled, then cocked her head. "I don't know what I think of your having a tanned face, Devlin."

"It will fade if I am careful. Should you like to leave here, Roxanne? Sophie told me your maid Tansy told her you had a nightmare last night."

Roxanne picked up a small pebble and gave it an expert flick into the water. "Blast Tansy." She watched the pebble skip three times. "She means well, but she cannot keep a single thought to herself. What am I saying? She is only sixteen years old, and she is very protective of me. I fear she might regard me as a sort of mother figure, which depresses my spirits." She sighed. "I was an idiot to say anything about it to her."

"It wouldn't have mattered. It was the major topic of conversation at the servants' table last night, I wager. Now, I can see for myself that your eyes are shadowed, and you are more pale than you usually are. Thus you're not sleeping well. I think perhaps a change of scenery might do you good. Perhaps you should like to visit my home, Holly Hill. Did I tell you, it was finished the year Henry VII removed himself from this earth? That Tudor king was a great friend of my ancestor; the two of them, it is told, hunted often together, my ancestor singing all the while. It was said his deep baritone voice brought out the deer."

"A charming tale. Did you make that up, Devlin, to distract me?"

"I? Not a word of it. I can show you three-hundred-year-old papers, recounting the history.

"If not Holly Hill, perhaps you would wish to come with me to my parents' home near Colchester? You will like Mount Burney, it's in the Palladian style, all big columns, huge high-ceilinged rooms. It looks more like a real palace than Ravenscar. I would like you to meet my parents, Roxanne."

"I have met them, Devlin."

His voice deepened, grew austere. "You would meet them in a different way now." He drew a deep breath. "The thing is, I'm thinking I quite like having you around. And if you agree to be around, then I want you happy and laughing, not having your eyes shadowed, not enduring nightmares that scare the sin out of you."

She said, "I like having you around as well."

He looked at her now, studying her face for a long moment. Then he wound a loose curl around his finger, leaning forward as he did so, until he fancied he could hear her heartbeat. He closed his eyes and breathed her in. "You are magnificent. Marry me, Roxanne."

She was magnificent? He wanted to marry her? She was something of an heiress, that was true enough, but she was only a baron's daughter. He was the Earl of Convers, heir to the Duke of Brabante. She was a spinster, long accepted as such and well settled in her nest on the shelf, wherever that was. They were the same age. She didn't move, scarcely breathed. He was always elusive, always saying something she didn't expect. But, she realized, since she'd been kidnapped, he'd changed.

She said slowly, "You haven't let me out of your sight since you came bursting through that barn door."

He was chewing again on a water reed, looking at the river, fingering a flat stone. "I fancy I won't until I cock up my toes."

"Last night, you even insisted on walking me to my room. You checked the keyhole and the key itself very carefully, then bade me lock the door, then check it to make certain it was locked. Then you turned and eyed the corridor wall for the longest time."

"You know exactly what I was thinking whilst I was looking at that wall."

"Well, it was only three nights ago when voices awoke me and I came out to find you, and you kissed me and brought me against you and I felt all of you and you felt all of me." She paused for a moment, flicked another pebble into the water, this one gaining only two jumps. "I know I probably should not say this, Devlin, but I have come to realize I could so easily have died yesterday. Manners could have killed me, or the person who hired him could have taken me away and killed me. And if I were dead, it would mean that I'd left something important unsaid. And now that seems rather ridiculous to me.

"So I shall say it aloud. When you kissed me, when you held me tight against you, I was aware of things I've never really thought of before, I was aware of you as a man, a man who wanted me, a man who could take me against the wall, and I will be honest here, I was certainly willing. To solve that final mystery, to understand what you and I could be together—" She drew a deep breath and looked him straight in the eye. "I have never felt feelings like those in my life. I wanted more, and you knew it. And you, the man who keeps more mistresses than most men have shirts, was the one to stop, not the prim on-the-shelf virgin spinster."

He was silent. He leaned forward and again began wrapping and unwrapping the hank of hair between his long fingers.

"I should say pulling away from you makes me sound vastly honorable. Or, more likely, a great fool."

"Devlin, do you really wish to marry me?"

"Yes."

"If I become your wife, you can no longer visit your mistresses."

He wanted to make light of it, tell her she shouldn't listen to gossip, but he didn't. He looked at her straight on, leaned forward, not touching her, and kissed her lightly. Then he cupped her face in his palm. "You could have died, you're right about that. I have realized as well that I am keeping things inside me that should be spoken. I will be honest here. I was not looking for a wife. I believed myself too young, even though my parents have been hinting that it is time I set up my nursery. I liked my life, liked the way one day flowed into the next. I was happy, I was content, the days were full, usually quite pleasant—racing, gaming, loving, dancing—I sound like a worthless sot, don't I? A man with no substance, a spoiled man who's always played at life, never burrowed in and tried to do anything worthwhile, not like my uncle, who works very hard.

"Let me tell you, Roxanne, Julian is a power. I think he's that way because he was the second son, the son who never knew his father, the son who believed he had to prove himself to gain worth. But I'm probably spouting nonsense."

"No, it sounds very reasonable, in Julian's case. But what is wrong with enjoying your life if you are able? You are not worthless, Devlin, you have a fine brain, and yes, you are quite honorable. I know you read a lot—so why didn't you add that to your list of amusements? Are you ashamed to have something worthwhile in your assessment of yourself? And I have never heard you be malicious or cruel. The fact is, I think you an estimable man. And an estimable vampire. I like vampires.

"You criticize yourself. Well, what about me? What have I ever done that has helped the world? I have been content, as well, enjoying life as much as any mortal can. But what have I done?"

"You are a shining light," he said simply.

"What? What did you say?" She stared at him, but he only shook his head, a slight smile on his mouth.

"Well, if I am indeed a shining light, I should like to know what it is I light up."

"You light up everyone's life, Roxanne. You are kind and good, and you give all of yourself to those you love. I believe if you accepted me as your husband, you would be loyal to me until I left this world. You would defend me, you would honor me, not to mention you would be a wonderful mother. You would birth the future Duke of Brabante, and perhaps five sisters and brothers to keep him company."

Roxanne cleared her throat. "That is a lot of children, Devlin."

"I quite like children. Do you?"

She nodded, mute.

"In all fairness, to give you your just due, I shall also add that I admire your pallor. You are nearly as white as I am. You are the vampire's perfect mate."

Her mouth opened, but nothing came out. He laughed, lightly kissed her. He felt the leap of pleasure in her, felt her leaning into him, but he couldn't allow it, not yet.

"About my mistresses," he began.

"Yes," Roxanne said, leaning away from him. "About your mistresses."

He sat back again on his elbows. He looked out over the water. "Do you know I found one of my many mistresses in an alley, huddled in refuse, unconscious, nearly dead? Her name was Madelyn, she was thirty-two years old, she'd lost her baby, and she wanted to die."

She could but stare at him. "What did you do?"

"I was afraid she would bleed to death. I carried her home with me, fetched my physician, and cared for her. She did not speak for nearly two weeks. When she finally spoke, she said very clearly, 'I wish you had let me die.' She turned her face away from me and refused to say anything more.

"I didn't know what to do, so I simply let her be, instructed my housekeeper, Mrs. Sampson, to stick close to her, but Mrs. Sampson did more than that. She fetched a needle and thread and a large swatch of fine muslin and left it on a chair beside her bed.

"When I came to visit her two days later, she was sitting in a chair, wearing one of my dressing gowns, and she was humming as she sewed a gown. Beautiful stitching, I saw."

He paused, looked at Roxanne, smiled. "Her full name is Madelyn Halifax. She'd been a seamstress who was raped by some toughs who broke into the shop when she was there working alone. Her employer blamed her, dismissed her without a reference, something that commonly happens, I am told, but who could do such a thing? She survived only to lose her babe, and so she chose to bleed to death in an alley."

"She isn't your mistress, Devlin."

"No, of course not. She is a seamstress again, owns her own shop on Bramble Lane, off Bond Street. She sews all my shirts. She is quite excellent. I, well, I am very proud of her. What's even better is that she's forgiven herself—for what, I asked her, and she said, 'I should have killed myself after he raped me once, but I was selfish and wanted to live.' I grabbed her, held her head under water in the bedside basin for a moment, then lifted her out, shook her, and told her not to be a damned idiot. Do you know she laughed? She actually laughed."

It was in that moment Roxanne realized how much she loved this man, loved him so much she wanted to both cry and sing. She also realized what she felt for him bore little resemblance to the tepid feelings she'd had for the long-ago John Singleton. "So that is one supposed mistress down. Tell me about the others, or are they really not your mistresses at all, and this is all a fiction you've created to gain you other men's esteem and keep people from realizing what an excellent man you are?"

"I am not a saint, Roxanne. I have always loved women, loved to smell them, loved to touch them, and—well, never mind.

"I am not a philanderer. I have been with these two women for nearly five years now. They enjoy me, they tell me, as much as I enjoy them. They don't wish to be married, either of them, but they enjoy having me in their lives. They are friends, and we enjoy ourselves together."

"In bed."

He nodded. "And out of it."

She slowly got to her feet, smoothed down her skirts. "The wind is rising. Do you think it will storm?"

He leapt to his feet as well. "I asked you to marry me, yet you want to talk about the storm? What of all your fine words about spitting out what you felt rather than keeping it inside you?"

"This is quite different."

He grabbed her arms, shook her. "I have spilled my innards to you as I have to no other woman in my adult life. But now you wish to ignore me and talk about the coming storm? A *bloody* coming storm?" He shook her again.

She took his face between her palms and kissed him, a loud smacking kiss. "Ah, Devlin, I find you delightful. No, I have no wish to talk about the storm, but to be honest here, I am afraid about what this all means. You see, I've never felt like this before, and I don't know, I simply don't know, what to do or what to think. But there is one fact I will admit to you. I have always had a soft spot for vampires."

"You are a baggage. When I don't want to throttle you, I want to kiss you." She raised her face. He kissed her again, and this time, he didn't stop. When he was on top of her, kissing her all over her face, as his hands tangled in her hair, she whispered, "I'm a virgin."

He said between kisses, "Of course you are. You're also mine. You really do belong to me, Roxanne. Now and until I am naught more than a shadow in the corner."

"I hope that will be a very long time from now." She gazed up at him, felt his strength, the hardness of him against her belly through all the petticoats, and surely that was amazing, and she couldn't help herself, she lifted her hips.

He groaned, closing his eyes against the immense pleasure of it.

"I cannot share you, Devlin, even with these two women I fancy I should quite like, were you not bedding them."

"They shall become friends, to both of us, if you wish, and nothing more."

"I do not know much of anything, you will quickly come to dislike me, and you will be miserable."

He looked down at her beloved face. "I will enjoy teaching you endlessly throughout the years of our lives. Should you like your first lesson now, Roxanne?"

"Since I am a spinster, it would be nice to get started with the business before I am any older."

He gave a shout of laughter and kissed her, nudging her mouth open. She felt his hand on her breast, kneading her through her gown. "I can feel you, the outline of you, but it is not enough. I want you naked. I know you will be white and soft, and your taste will make me howl at the moon."

"No, that is a werewolf."

"Be quiet. I will do my best to see that both of us howl together at the moon. The moon at midnight."

She raised her hand and stroked his face. "Do you know, I cannot wait to see you, and us, together."

Devlin realized, even though she didn't, that the air had grown chill and the sun was now behind dark clouds. Having her naked wouldn't be pleasant here by the river at this moment, even with lust pounding through both of them, particularly when it started to rain, as it most assuredly would at any time now. He sighed, lifted himself off her. "We must wait. I will fetch you tonight, if it pleases you. Or, if you would prefer, we can wait until we are married." Those words nearly made him stutter, he hated speaking them so much.

"Perhaps you are right," she said, and he loved that she sounded so disappointed. He straightened his own clothes, then hers, patted her hair. He kissed her once more.

"We must go."

As they ran hand in hand back toward Ravenscar, the rain clouds nearly upon them, Roxanne shouted, "Perhaps I shall see you at midnight, perhaps we will dance together, and I shall present you my neck."

They beat the storm by exactly four minutes. She said to him when he left her at her bedchamber door, "This is different, Devlin. This is forever."

⊶⊸ ⊶⊶

He did not realize until he was drinking a brandy after an excellent dinner that evening with Julian that she had not agreed to marry him. He also realized he hadn't told her he loved her. *I quite like having you around.* That was certainly true, but he should still be clouted. Where was his damned brain? He looked at Julian and said slowly, "I am an idiot. Impale me on a pole and throw me into the Thames at low tide."

Julian said, "I know this has something to do with Roxanne. Why are you an idiot?"

"I'm not at liberty to speak of it."

"Of course you are. I'm your uncle."

Devlin balled up his napkin and threw it across the dining room. "I did not tell her I loved her. Can you believe this? I told her I liked having her around."

"Yes, that was remiss of you. However, you have a fluent tongue, Devlin. You will fix it.

"Do you know, I believe Beatrice is going to have puppies? Cletus is the proud father. He is hovering over her, not letting her out of his sight."

"I would like two of the litter. Cletus is very possessive. He will not easily give them up. As for Beatrice, she will lick them endlessly until they have no hair at all. Do you think it reprehensible to sleep with a woman before you marry her?"

"Yes, I fear I do."

Devlin cursed into his brandy. "She is eager, Julian, mayhap as eager as I. Only four nights until we have our last smuggling run—damn, it is an eternity. I am certain my mother will wish to plan an elaborate wedding. How many months will that take?"

"Tell your mother you will wait no longer than August. Surely you can control yourself until then. After all, you do have two mistresses to ease you through it."

Devlin was shaking his head. "I must begin this fidelity

business right now. She will make a perfect duchess, don't you think, Julian?"

"Yes, I do. I suggest you live at Holly Hill, Devlin, perhaps only visit Mount Burney, say, at Christmas. But don't worry, she will deal well enough with your mother. Roxanne is made of stern stuff."

Devlin raised his snifter, clicked it to Julian's. "She will enjoy putting her mark on Holly Hill. Do you know Roxanne smells of jasmine with a hint of lemon?"

⇒ 56 ⇐

Julian stared down at Orvald Manners, who still lay in endless sleep. What held him unconscious? Julian knew he would die soon if he didn't wake up, from starvation and thirst.

He felt his pulse, found it slow.

"No movement of any kind?"

Julian looked up to see Sophie standing in the doorway. "No, none. He merely lies there, like a dead man who happens still to be breathing."

She walked to the bed, stood silently beside him, looking down at Manners. "Do you think Richard hopes Manners will never wake up?"

Julian sighed. "I don't know, Richard seemed very sincere in his denial."

"There is no one else, Julian."

That was true enough. *Just as there was no one else but you to kill Lily.* He would have to think about this. "It is difficult to believe that even Manners had a mother who must have loved him, at least at one time."

Orvald Manners suddenly opened his eyes, blinked, and whispered in a scratchy voice, "I've a powerful thirst."

Sophie quickly poured him a glass of water and held it to his lips. He drank and drank until, exhausted, his head fell back against the pillow.

"It is about time you woke up, Mr. Manners," Julian said. "Are you hungry?"

He was silent for a moment, and finally nodded. "Aye, I could eat a broiled eel. What'd ye call me?"

What was this? Julian said, "Your name is Orvald Manners."

"Orvald, ye says? I don't knows as I like no *Orvald,* sounds furin, like I'm French, or something nasty like that. Where am I? Who's the purty young missis wot's starin' at me as if I 'ad two 'eads?"

Sophie leaned over him. "I'm the purty young missis who is going to pound your head when you are well again, Mr. Manners."

His eyes lit up. "Oh, aye, ye're welcome to 'ave a go at me, little one. I likes 'em feisty, leastwises I thinks I do. Are ye come to feed me?"

After Mr. Manners had eaten his fill, not boiled eels but stargazy pie, he fell to sleep. This time, Dr. Crutchfield assured them, shaking his head at the miracle, it was a simple sleep. Whatever had held him from consciousness was gone. "Mayhap it was hearing you speak, Prince. On some level, he heard your voice and it brought him back. I daresay I can't ask for my fee, since in all honesty, I didn't do anything for him."

Julian laughed, paid Dr. Crutchfield a pound note, watching the old man's veiny hand shake a bit as he accepted it.

Sophie said, "Mr. Manners appears not to remember who he is. Dr. Crutchfield, do you have any experience in this sort of thing?"

"Head wounds—you never know what mischief they will cause inside a man's skull. Some never remember how they were injured in the first place. Some never remember anything at all. What to expect from this fellow? I don't know.

Good day to you, Prince, Miss Wilkie. I will be interested to hear what happens to the man."

"So will I," Julian said, as he turned back to Sophie.

"Devlin told me Beatrice is pregnant."

"Yes. This will be her first litter."

"What are we to do now, Julian?"

"I fancy there isn't a lot we can do. She will grow fat and lazy and—"

She poked his arm.

"All right. About which of our villains? Manners? Richard Langworth? Don't leave out your aunt Leah, who could be lurking out in the corridor at this very moment." Julian said to Manners's guard, Tom, "Do not tell anyone that Mr. Manners doesn't know who he is, all right?"

Tom said, "You wish to confound the guilty one."

"That's right."

Tom made a sewing motion across his mouth.

Sophie was studying Manners's face. "When he awakens again, I think I should question him, you know, ease him back into himself; maybe I'll jostle loose some memories."

"It can't hurt. I suppose all of us could take turns with him. But first I think Roxanne should see him. What he did to her, what she did to him, mayhap simply seeing her will trigger his memory. We'll give him another hour of sleep."

❖⇒ ⇐❖

When Roxanne stood over Orvald Manners, she didn't think he looked particularly brutish. Indeed, he looked quite benign, lying there, light little snorts ruffling the air. The top of his head was bald, and the hair he did have was a mix of gray and brown. His skin was leathery from time spent in the sun. Well, he had been aboard Julian's ship. He was perhaps forty years old.

"He looks harmless, doesn't he?"

She touched her fingers to her clean hair, her scalp still tingly from Tansy's famous head rub. "You know, Leah will find out about this; something this fascinating always gets out." She lightly slapped Manners's face. "Well, wake up, you sot, it's time to face me."

He moaned, finally opening his eyes to stare up at her.

"Would ye looks at all that beauteous 'air, purtier than any bloomin' peacock's feathers. Where'd ye get 'air like that, little girl?"

"From my mother, who was a powerful witch. She taught me, her witch daughter, how to blight evil men, such as yourself. My name is Roxanne Radcliffe."

"That's a powerful fancy name ye gots there; sounds kinda uppity."

"It is fine alliteration. It isn't uppity at all; what it has is style."

"Be ye really a witch wot curses off men's parts?"

"Yes. You, in particular, should be worried."

"Why? I ain't done nuthin' to ye." He frowned. "Well, 'as I?"

Roxanne told him exactly what he'd done to her. "You smashed this sweet-smelling cloth over my mouth, then once I was unconscious, you took me to this ancient old barn; you were told to take me there by the man who hired you to kidnap me. You were going to rape me." Manners listened with an air of great concentration. Toward the end of it, despite the fact that Manners kept his face perfectly blank, as if she were reciting a wild tale to him, Roxanne realized there was a good deal of cunning behind his eyes. She paused for a moment, sighed, leaned close to his face, whispered, "Do you know, sir, you didn't have to rape me. You scared me, and that is why I kicked you. But then I realized I acted too swiftly. I realized I quite fancied you, your wit, your charm, and wondered—" She paused, gave a delicate shudder.

"Ye really wanted me? Then why'd ye kick me in me privates? An' then ye coshed me on the 'ead. Why?"

"I told you, you frightened me. I am a lady, sir. You didn't have any finesse."

"I 'as this finesse—wot's finesse?"

She smiled at him.

"I didn't think ye wanted me. Ye were acting wild and

yellin' at me. I'll tells ye, purty 'un, it fair to locked my chops I wanted ye so much. Why, I remember—"

"Yes, Mr. Manners?"

His brain overcame his remembered lust. "Well, beat me on me noggin for bein' an idjut."

Roxanne pulled a pistol from her pocket and laid the muzzle against his unshaven cheek. "Yes, you are indeed an idiot. Now, you will tell me who hired you to kidnap me or I will shoot your head off."

"But ye said ye wanted me—"

"I lied."

"Yer a lady; a lady don't lie and she don't shoot men in their cheek, leastwise not the cheek that resides on their faces."

"Don't you remember, Mr. Manners? I kicked you in your groin, I struck you twice on your head with the plowshare. I will shoot you twice, to make certain you will never bedevil anyone again, if you don't tell me the truth. Now, who hired you?"

"Awright! It were the 'igh-an'-mighty king!"

"King William hired you to kidnap me?"

"No, no, I meant it were the prince. No one goes against the prince and lives to tell about it."

"I see. So Lord Julian Monroe, the Prince of Ravenscar, hired you to kidnap me?"

"Aye, it were, the prince be a downy one, none disobeys him, ever, iffen they wants to keep their 'earts beatin' in their chests." Manners grabbed his hair in his fists and pulled. "Ah, me bleedin' 'ead, I fair to feel like pukin' up me guts."

Manners had the gall to throw up. At least he missed her slippers.

Roxanne, Sophie, Devlin, and Julian left poor Tom to deal with him. They stepped outside and listened to Manners alternately vomit and groan.

"He'd better not dare go unconscious again," Sophie said, and shook her fist in his direction. "Poor Tom, having to hold the chamber pot for him."

"I don't suppose you hired Manners, Julian? For some

nefarious reason that eludes me? You are the only prince I know."

"He isn't altogether stupid," Julian said slowly. "I wonder if he's used this ploy before?"

When the sounds of vomiting stopped, they all trooped back into the small room. It smelled vile. Tom raised the single small window, fanned the air with his coat.

Orvald Manners turned his face to the wall and refused to say any more.

Julian said, "Let's leave him be for a while. Tom, tie him down to the bed, so he won't be able to do anything, save think about his long list of sins."

Tom set to work with a good deal of relish.

Roxanne said, "To accuse you, Julian, it makes me quite froth at the mouth."

Devlin patted Roxanne's cheek. "It makes me froth more. Calm yourself; Manners will come around, once we make it perfectly clear Julian will send him to Botany Bay if he doesn't tell us the truth."

"Botany Bay?" Julian's eyebrow shot up. "I fancy that is a believable threat, Devlin. I can contact a naval captain I know. He can tell me what to do, give me specifics to scare the sin out of him."

"Would you really send him there?"

"Oh, yes, Sophie. At the very least, we wouldn't have to worry about him anymore. But he'll talk, then we'll see."

⇥ 57 ⇤

Julian looked up when Pouffer cleared his throat.

"Yes, Pouffer? What is it?"

"It is Lady Merrick, Prince. She is in the drawing room. She brought several valises with her, and her maid, who smiled at me until Lady Merrick saw her smiling, and I tell you, it fell right off her face, poor lass."

"What?" Roxanne was on her feet. "Leah is here? But—"

"That's quite all right, Roxanne," Corinne said, as she allowed August, a footman more slight than she, to help her to rise, something she was perfectly capable of doing all by herself, but it seemed it was a sacred requirement of both her and August. "Shall we take a vote? Who would like me to clout Leah?"

"I vote yes. Clout her," Sophie said.

Julian tossed down his napkin. "No, Mother, not you. If there's any clouting to be done, I shall see to it. Everyone continue with luncheon."

But no one ate another bite. All rose silently and followed Julian to the drawing room, where Leah, dressed in a dark blue traveling gown, a clever bonnet set atop her blond hair, stood by the fireplace, holding a beaded reticule in her white hands, staring up at Julian's father's portrait.

"Leah, what are you doing here?" Roxanne asked. "Have you decided Richard Langworth no longer suits you? What happened to make you come back?"

Leah gave a gay laugh, smiled at all of them, graciousness oozing out of every pore. "Oh, nothing has happened. Richard was forced to go to London to attend to some business, so I decided to return here to rejoin my sister and my niece." She smiled. "You are both looking quite well, as are you, your grace. If I may impose on your kindness yet again, I should be very grateful if you would let me stay with you until Richard returns to Hardcross Manor." Her words wafted through the warm air, embracing all of them.

Before Corinne could open her mouth, Julian said, "Did Richard go to London to hire another thug to abduct your sister, since Orvald Manners failed so spectacularly?"

Leah splayed her hands and looked at them sadly. "You know Richard was distraught when you told us about Roxanne being kidnapped. As was I. Both of us are vastly relieved she is back safely. Richard told me he quite liked Roxanne, and it smote him that you thought he'd done such a thing. He is hoping that man, Manners, regains consciousness so he can clear his name." She turned to Roxanne. "My dear, I do hope you are recovered. What a dreadful experience for you."

Roxanne thought, *Why are you really here, Leah? Do you want to try to discover more of our plans, and inform Richard? Don't you realize no one in this house would even tell you if it was going to rain? Not anymore.*

Then it hit her. *No, it's about Manners, isn't it, Leah? You're afraid what he'll say if he comes around. You want to warn Richard if he does. You'll never know he already has regained consciousness.*

"Yes," Roxanne said pleasantly, "dreadful."

Corinne saw no hope for it. She cleared her throat. "I hope you will enjoy this stay more than your last one. How long does Richard plan to be gone? A week? Two, perhaps?"

"Oh, I quite enjoyed my last visit, your grace. It was Richard, you see. He is so bitterly unhappy with you, Julian. But Roxanne's kidnapping, that concerns him greatly. A week? I don't know, your grace. Such a charming house this is. A palace it's called hereabouts, isn't it?"

Leah continued to charm, to spread gaiety around, and she laughed whenever any of the party said something even mildly amusing.

Later, when Roxanne offered to escort her to her bed-chamber, not a single insult slithered out of her mouth. Roxanne lightly laid her hand on Leah's arm. She had to know the depths of her sister's treachery, and she knew how to do it. "A moment. I am worried, Leah, I will admit it to you. You are my sister, you have my best interests at heart. This man, Manners, he woke up a while ago. He wants to kidnap me again, Leah, he said he had a taste for me now. He says the prince hired him. That cannot be true, you know it cannot. I don't know what to do."

Leah, eyes bright, squeezed her hand. "The prince? Why don't we go speak to Manners together, Roxanne? I can be very persuasive. I don't wish you to be afraid anymore. He is only a bad man, and bad men can be dealt with. Now, where is this creature?"

Roxanne led her down the long corridor to the small sewing room. She nodded to Tom, who was sitting on a chair, a cup of tea balanced on his knee. "Please leave us, Tom. It will be fine."

"Excuse me, Miss Roxanne, but the prince said it was all right for you to be here? With that foul sot?"

"The prince said a lady's touch might be the thing," Leah said easily.

Once Tom was gone, Leah said, "It smells dreadful in here."

"Not nearly as bad as it did." Roxanne looked down at Manners, who, at the sound of Leah's voice, slowly opened his eyes. "Another beautiful angel wot's come to flutter 'er wings about me."

Leah said nothing at all. She leaned over Manners, studied him for a moment, then slapped him hard.

Manners gasped, then said, sputtering, "But why'd ye do that fer? I ain't niver done anything to ye!"

Leah leaned close. "You smell vile. You are vile, I doubt not. Now tell me who hired you to kidnap Roxanne."

Roxanne couldn't move. What would Manners say? What would Leah do?

"It were the prince, I already told the red-'eaded witch wot's standing right aside ye that it were the prince wot paid me the groats."

Leah straightened. "I don't know, Roxanne. There is defeat in his voice, but if it is the prince—what a ridiculous appellation that is—listen, Julian Monroe is nothing more than a merchant, running his string of ships, doing accounts, like any clerk. He may be the son of a duke, but he has the heart of a merchant." She eyed her sister and leaned down again over Manners. "No, it is not the prince. I am sick of your lies, you filthy varmint. The prince wants her, he wouldn't have someone do away with her, unless—" Leah broke off, looked over her shoulder at Roxanne. "Did something happen between you and the prince? I know you seduced him. Is he now refusing to marry you?"

"No, he isn't refusing to marry me," Roxanne said. "We really haven't discussed it, you know."

"Are you pregnant?"

"No." *What would happen,* Roxanne thought dispassionately, *if I slapped her, as she did Manners? She still thinks Julian wants me and I want him?*

"Ye shut yer chops, missis, that ain't a nice thing to say to the little witch. Actually, ye said a whole lot of not nice things to 'er." He stopped cold, reevaluated, then gave them both a toothy grin. "Aye, 'twere the prince, 'e don't want ye in 'is bed anymore, but I'll take ye, make ye scream wit' 'appiness."

Leah slapped him again. "Are you telling me the truth? Was it really the prince who hired you?"

"Oh, aye, missis, 'tis the truth, I swears it on me ma's grave."

Roxanne looked from Manners to Leah. She began to

laugh. "You were pleasant for perhaps twenty minutes, Leah. I believe that might be a record. It was difficult for you, wasn't it? Have you got what you wanted? Manners is blaming the prince? For kidnapping me, his one true love? Such a puzzle that is, don't you think? Will you leave us alone now? Will you leave Ravenscar, filled with news for Richard?"

Leah turned on her. "How dare you say—"

Still laughing, Roxanne turned on her heel and left the room, sending Tom back to protect Manners from Leah. It was certain Leah did not believe Richard had hired Manners to kidnap her, else she wouldn't have slapped him. So who had? At the moment, it didn't matter.

Roxanne was hiccupping when Devlin caught her at the top of the stairs.

He took both arms in his hands, shook her slightly. "What is this? Pouffer told me you went off with Leah. What happened? Why are you laughing like this, like you feel so much pain you can't help but laugh because there's nothing to be done?"

She said on a sigh, "It is Leah. She believes the prince is enamored of me, and yet Manners claims the prince had me kidnapped. It is all so ridiculous, you know." She swallowed another laugh, looked him right in his dark eyes. He knew her well, and in such a short time, and he accepted her, loved her. Roxanne took his face between her hands and kissed him hard.

Devlin said, "Open your mouth, sweetheart."

She opened her mouth and poured herself into a kiss that nearly made her teeter herself off her heeled slippers with delight.

"That's better," he said into her mouth, his hands stroking up and down her back, then bringing her closer.

He pressed his forehead against hers. At the sound of Leah's voice, he said, "Do you think that voice comes from a stray nightmare?"

"I now understand why the prince hired Manners to kidnap you, Roxanne. You have played him false with his nephew. His *nephew*! The prince is proud, I have been told, and he is well used to violence, all know it. Did he not kill his first wife because she betrayed him?"

Roxanne smiled at him.

"I counsel you to take care, Roxanne. It appears the prince doesn't wish to have you around, either. Who knows what he'll do to rid himself of you."

She waved at Devlin. "I think I would prefer to have this one, since he's the heir to a dukedom, not a miserable merchant."

"You'd best take care, Roxanne. After he tosses up your skirts, he'll leave you. He keeps a score of mistresses, all know it. You have no morals at all. I am ashamed to be your sister."

Before Roxanne could leap on her, Leah brushed past her and went down the stairs, never looking back.

"Am I deceived in you, Roxanne? Are you a lady of low moral disposition?"

His voice, his words, calmed her instantly. She smiled at him. "Well, how can I be certain when I have never before had to examine my moral disposition?"

He kissed her again. "Perhaps you are skilled at deception? Is your sister right? Have you decided to leave Julian and come to me? Ah, imagine his rage." He kissed her again, then once more.

"I fear," Roxanne managed, when he raised his head for a moment, "that my sister is again herself. What's sad is that it is not a surprise."

"No, her display of finer feelings did not last very long. A pity, but in the long scheme of things, who cares? I daresay we shall never have to see her again. Do you mind if she is not invited to our wedding?" Devlin kissed Roxanne again, picked her up, and carried her down the corridor to his bedchamber.

He stopped cold, cursed. "There are servants everywhere, probably behind every door and around every corner. No, I'm not jesting. Haven't you noticed that Julian has more servants than he knows what to do with? You want to know why? I'll tell you. If anyone is in trouble, if anyone can't find a way to feed himself, or his family, Julian hires him, and when he is not here, Pouffer is to hire those in dire straits." Devlin touched his forehead to hers. "Do you think her grace is behind that door to my right? Is she tapping her foot, wondering if I am a dishonorable sot because we are not yet married and I want to strip you naked and kiss every white inch of you?"

He cursed. "I suppose Julian is right. We must wait, that is, if you agree to wed me. Get me out of my misery, Roxanne, agree to marry me, or shoot me. Before you answer, allow me to tell you the reason I want you around me is that I love you to the breadth and length of me. You fill me with joy, Roxanne. My life is yours, and my happiness. Ah, the children we will have. Say you will be my wife, my countess."

58

Sophie was sitting on the carpet in Julian's estate room, laughing as she lightly rubbed Oliver's soft ears. She looked up at Roxanne, who was pacing. "Married to Devlin—this is wonderful. I am so pleased for you. Who would have guessed, since you've been a self-proclaimed spinster whose only goal was to see me well placed, so filled with common sense I feared you would collapse under the weight of it. But no longer."

Roxanne said, "No more mistresses for him. He fancies we can all be friends. That is something I must consider carefully, and probably with a great deal of humor. Yes, he's all mine." She paused, frowned, and sank down on the carpet beside Sophie and began to lightly pat Beatrice's belly. "I suppose we will take one of her pups, too. No, don't growl at me, Cletus, I'm not hurting your one and only love. Oliver, why are you growling? Are you jealous?"

Sophie smiled. "Julian is convinced Cletus is the father, but I wonder. Oliver has been prancing about lately, looking quite proud of himself. Both he and Cletus are very possessive. Would you look at Hortense, all by herself in the corner." Sophie rose to fetch Hortense and held her on her lap.

Roxanne said, "Devlin told me the plans for our smuggling adventure. He believes I will quite enjoy myself. He insists we both cover ourselves with black and wear masks."

"I only wish Julian would stop worrying that something will go wrong. Nothing can go wrong, I have told him over and over. I mean, the dastardly Richard knows nothing about it, nor does anyone else, save the four of us." She frowned. "Still, everyone hears everything in the palace."

Roxanne said, "There won't be a moon, so that is good. You're right, what could possibly go wrong?"

⟡

There was a storm coming, Julian could taste it, but he wasn't going to call off this last smuggling run. A storm kept curious men in their homes, huddled near a fire. It was past midnight, the wind was high, black clouds scuttled across a black sky, obscuring the stars. Sophie strode like a boy at his side, wearing a black cloak over a dark gown with no petticoats beneath. She was not, however, wearing a mask.

Julian, too, was wearing a thick black cloak. He took her hand, guiding her toward the cave.

"Don't worry about Roxanne, Devlin will take care of her. They will meet the boat on the beach and direct my men onto the river route to the cave. You and I will wait here for them and direct the unloading."

He looked at her shadowed face. "You are grinning, I know it, Sophie. If there were any moon at all, I would see your face glowing with excitement."

"Do you know me so well, Julian?"

"Well enough. You have been my constant companion for—how long is it now, Sophie?"

"All my life?"

"I could have fathered you."

"You were that precocious?"

"Perhaps not quite, but still—"

She dropped his hand and stopped. When he turned to her, Sophie sent her fist into his belly. He whooshed out a breath, grabbed for her, but she danced out of his reach.

"No, don't you touch me, you baboon. If you ever again mention the years between us—the *great* number of years that separate us—I will hurt you so badly you will be on your knees, moaning. Do you understand me?"

He stared at her, and Sophie knew he was staring, even though she could barely see the outline of his face.

"Did you really tell Devlin you wouldn't bed a woman until you were married to her?"

If he was surprised she knew this, he didn't let on. He supposed he was getting quite used to there being no secrets between Roxanne and Sophie, as there were no secrets between him and Devlin. "Yes, I said that."

"Why?"

"Because a lady, a virgin lady, deserves more than a clandestine mauling."

'Well, that is something. On the other hand, you wouldn't conduct this mauling in public."

"Don't you make sport of me, Sophie Wilkie, you know very well what I mean."

"Why do you call it mauling? When you kiss me, I never think of mauling."

"Very well, an unwed lady doesn't wish to have her purity in question before she is wed."

"Purity," she said slowly, savoring the word. "Is that why a lady shouldn't seduce a gentleman before marriage? She doesn't wish to soil his purity?"

He had the insane desire to laugh, to kiss her silly, and perhaps teach her a little bit about lovemaking, but the wind was whipping about outside, it was cold, and his men would be coming soon with the smuggled goods.

"Come," he said.

She began walking toward the cave, aware he was right behind her. She could hear his steady, calm breathing. She intended to seduce him tonight, in the cave, not that she knew the first thing about seducing a man, but she was her mother's daughter, with her rich and devious imagination. Yes, she would spread her black cloak on the sandy ground. Once all the goods had been stored, all his men had rowed back down the river to the channel and back to the ship, Devlin and Roxanne were safely away back to Ravenscar, she would jump on him, and—*hmmm*. She was so excited she wanted to shout with it.

They heard the loud report of a gun and froze. Julian cursed, shoved her down, whispered against her mouth even as he held her down, "Don't move."

He left her on her knees, her head down, her black cloak wrapped around her, her heart pounding hard, suddenly scared to her toes. The adventure had turned into something else.

Julian made his way, silent as a shadow, weaving in and out of the thick maple and oak trees, to the river's edge. They were only twenty yards from the mouth of the cave. He stood in the shadows, staring downriver.

Another shot, then half a dozen more. He heard a man shout something, then another several shots.

How had anyone found out about this?

He saw her running lightly toward him, a black shadow weaving in and out of all the other shadows. She was at his side in the next second, breathing hard. He leaned close. "We're going back to the cave. You will stay in there, safe, and I'll try to find out what's happening."

He led her to the entrance, pulled aside the branches. "Get inside. Don't make any noise, all right? I'll come to you as soon as I can. You know where the lantern is. If you light it, make certain you keep it partially covered. Everything will be all right."

"Of course it will be all right, because you will make sure that it is," she said, and the certainty in her voice made something deep inside him expand with pleasure. He touched his fingers to her face, then he was gone.

Sophie heard him piling more branches to cover the cave opening. She quickly lit the lantern and placed it beneath a narrow ledge to hide most of the light.

She straightened, looked around, crept to the entrance of the cave, and listened. She heard more shots. Was that a man yelling? Had someone been hit? One of his men? Julian?

Her blood ran cold. She desperately wanted to run out of the bloody cave and see what was happening, but she wasn't an idiot. If she left the cave, she might cause more danger for Julian or Roxanne and Devlin.

She waited, the hardest thing she'd ever had to do in her life. Time passed, but how much, she didn't know.

It had to be excisemen, and they'd been told about tonight's smuggling run. But who had informed on them? Had Leah somehow overheard them? She didn't think so. But who?

She thought of Roxanne and Devlin down at the beach. She closed her eyes and prayed with all her might, promising God more good works than a single person could accomplish in a lifetime.

Her heart jumped into her throat when she heard a man's voice outside. It was Julian, whispering for her not to worry. When he came into the cave, she ran to him, stroked her hands down his arms, his chest. She dropped to her knees, her hands on his legs. He grabbed her hands, hauled her back to her feet. "Sophie, I'm all right. Now, listen to me."

"Roxanne, is she all right? It is excisemen, isn't it? Someone told them."

"Yes. There are at least a half dozen, not planted down at the beach where Devlin and Roxanne were supposed to meet the boat but near the mouth of the river, maybe a hundred steps away. My men know if there is ever trouble they are not to fight, they are to row back to the ship. Devlin and Roxanne weren't to come with them to the cave, only guide them to the river entrance. They're all right."

There was more gunfire.

Julian quickly put out the lantern. He gathered Sophie to him and eased down to the cave floor and pulled her close. "They won't find the cave. Don't worry. Now we have to wait."

59

Roxanne and Devlin greeted the men on the large boat at the entrance of the river. A dark-coated man stepped forward. He said quietly, "Jake doesn't like the way things smell. I don't like it, either. We want to get this done. Where is his lordship's cave?"

Devlin whispered the instructions. The man nodded, but no more words were spoken, and they were off, rowing up the river.

Roxanne said, "I wonder what doesn't smell right to Jake. This worries me, Devlin. Sophie and Julian are at the cave. What if—"

He placed a finger over her mouth. "I don't smell anything. It will be all right. Who could possibly know about tonight? You're thinking about Richard—but he is in London."

"So Leah told us. All right, no one at Ravenscar, even if they knew about tonight, would betray the prince. I wish there had been room in the boat. I should have liked to help unload the goods and carry them into the cave. Do you know what they were bringing in?"

Devlin shook his head. "The storm will hit very soon now. Come along, our part is played. Let's go back to Ravenscar."

They'd only taken three steps when they heard gunfire, sharp and terrifyingly loud. Devlin grabbed her hand, and they ran up the cliff path. A bullet struck a rock a foot from Roxanne's boot.

All Roxanne could think was that their marvelous adventure had turned into a nightmare.

She never broke stride. "I'm worried about Sophie. We must do something, Devlin."

"The best thing we can do is get to safety. Trust Julian to take care of Sophie."

Three men leapt out of the darkness, blocking the path, each holding a gun. "That's enough," the man said when Devlin would have gone after him. "Now, it's the lady we wish, not you."

Devlin heard a whoosh of sound. He whirled around, his derringer in his hand, but he wasn't fast enough. Roxanne screamed. A gun butt cracked down hard over his temple, and he collapsed where he stood.

"Ye're to come wi' us, Miss Radcliffe." She kicked him, hoping for his groin, but her foot struck hard against his thigh. He grunted, jumped back.

Another man yelled, "She's only a woman, get 'er, ye fools."

But Roxanne didn't go easily. Her fingernails scored down a man's face, she managed to kick one man in the groin, and he dropped to his knees, groaning and holding himself. One of them clouted her in the jaw, and she went spinning to the ground, only to be caught by another man and thrown over his shoulder. Before she passed out, she heard one of the men say, "Wot were she doin' wit' this bloody duke's son? Ain't she supposed to be wi' the prince?"

Another man said, his voice sharp, clear, his English excellent, "I don't know. Make sure the bloody duke's son is still breathing. I don't want him dead."

"Aye, he's breathin' nice 'n strong."

"Good. Let's go, lads. I want to be off the moment she wakes up."

Roxanne thought the man's voice sounded familiar to her, but she didn't know, nor did it matter now, nothing mattered. She knew nothing more.

⟐ *60* ⟐

The gunfire abruptly stopped.

Julian lightly patted Sophie's cheek. "I'm going to see if I can make out anything in the darkness. Don't move, Sophie."

"Not this time," she said, and stood beside him.

He gave her a look that didn't sway her at all. He was looking at his future, and he couldn't help it, he both grinned and cursed. "At least stay behind me." Julian eased out through the pile of branches that covered the cave entrance. He listened, didn't hear anything. She came up to stand beside him. "Do you believe your men are all right?"

"They rowed back to the ship. Those are the standing orders. Since we don't hear any more gunfire, no shouting, I think they made their escape."

"Let's go see. I want to make sure Roxanne and Devlin are all right. What if the excisemen got them, Julian?"

He had no answer to that. He didn't want to put her in any more danger, but he knew a set jaw when he saw one. He took her hand and led her through the woods, staying close to the river's edge. They didn't see anyone—no excisemen, no smugglers, no Devlin or Roxanne. When they reached the beach, Julian could make out the boat in the distance nearly back to his ship. His men and goods were safe.

Sophie said, "Where are Roxanne and Devlin?"

Julian didn't answer. He didn't like this, didn't like it at all.

They found Devlin unconscious on the path leading up the cliff. There was no sign of Roxanne.

⇒ *61* ⇐

Devlin wasn't about to move. He knew if he did, his brain would fall out of his head, roll about on the ground, and he'd be dead, naught but an empty husk. On the other hand, his suffering would be over.

Slowly, the pounding hammer began to lighten, thank the munificent Lord. A memory came into his head—a long-ago night at Oxford when a group of friends had drunk six bottles of French brandy stolen from one of their father's wine cellars. He'd awakened by himself the next morning in an alley, the agony in his head unbearable. That day he'd sworn never to drink himself insensible again, and he hadn't.

He hadn't broken his vow, had he? He hadn't gotten drunk; surely he wasn't that great a fool. He didn't want to open his eyes, knew it would bring him low. He couldn't remember what happened, couldn't—*dear God, Roxanne.*

His eyes flew open to see Julian leaning over him, Dr. Crutchfield at his side, Sophie standing at the foot of his bed, her hair tangled around her face, her face haloed by candlelight. "Devlin, thank goodness you're awake. Where's Roxanne?"

"Roxanne." Devlin could only manage a whisper, and even that hurt.

"You've a grand lump on your head, my lord. Hold yourself still, that's right. The pain will ease. I'll give you some laudanum as soon as you can tell me how many fingers I'm holding up."

Devlin counted twelve fingers.

"Not quite yet," said Dr. Crutchfield. "Keep yourself awake, my lord. Your brains are still a bit scrambled."

Julian said, voice pitched low, "Do you remember what happened, Devlin?"

Devlin started to say no, but then everything came rushing back. "The boat came in. I told your head man where to find the cave, and they were off. I remember your head man, Jake, said he didn't like the way things smelled. I suppose he somehow sensed danger? Still, they left, and Roxanne and I went back up the cliff path. Then there was gunfire and three men came out of nowhere. One of them struck me down." He closed his eyes, felt curses fall out of his mouth. "Dear sweet Lord in Heaven, I don't know what happened to Roxanne."

Sophie said, "They took her. Richard hired them to take her. But how did he know where you would be? Who betrayed us?"

"There can be only one person to betray us," Julian said. "And that is why Leah came back here. Somehow, she overheard our plan. Devlin, you hold still until you have yourself together. The laudanum will help."

Since it was near dawn, Julian and Sophie expected to find Leah in bed, but she wasn't. Pouffer, so frightened he could barely speak, pointed to the drawing-room door. They found Leah reading a book by candlelight. But she wasn't reading it at all, Sophie saw; the pages weren't cut.

She looked up. "What is this? What is going on? Was there a fire?"

Sophie stared dispassionately at her aunt. *Did you send your own sister to her death at Richard's hands because you still believe Julian loves her?*

She felt anger, clean and pure, wash through her. "Why

aren't you in bed, Leah?" Sophie strode toward her. She still hadn't donned all her petticoats again, and she felt a stone lighter.

Leah shrugged. "I heard all the commotion and woke my maid. I saw Dr. Crutchfield hurrying past my bedchamber, as fast as an old man can move. I heard the servants talking about bad things happening, and his lordship was gravely wounded. What happened?"

"Devlin was struck down. Tell us how you knew about the smuggling adventure this evening."

"I assume Devlin will be all right?"

"It appears so."

"Well, that will relieve his family. What did you say? Smuggling operation? What is this?"

Julian said, "Have you seen Roxanne?"

"No, I have not. Is she still abed? What is going on here, my lord? Where is my sister?"

Leah looked suddenly alarmed; Julian would swear it was genuine. "Your sister was taken when Devlin was struck down."

"Taken? What do you mean Roxanne was taken?" Leah jumped to her feet, sending the book sliding to the carpet. "What is this about a smuggling operation?"

Julian walked to the fireplace, leaned against the mantel, his arms crossed over his chest. "How did you find out about the smuggling run tonight, Leah?"

Leah rose, smoothed out her skirts. "I have no idea what you're talking about, Prince. Smuggling? There is no such thing anymore. All know that, but if there is, if you are a smuggler, then you should be sent to Botany Bay. Were you all involved? My sister as well as a future duke of the realm?"

Sophie said, "Don't sound so disbelieving and outraged, Leah. You overheard us making plans for the smuggling, and you told Richard. Where is he? Where did he take Roxanne? What does he plan to do with her this time? Rape her? Kill her?"

"That is utter nonsense, and you well know it."

Sophie walked up to her aunt, grabbed her arms, hauled

her up, and shook her hard. "You will tell us the truth, you malicious witch, all of it, or I swear I'll hurt you. I'm bigger than you are; you know I can do it. I can start with your face. How would you look with no eyebrows? Aye, I could hold you down and shave them right off."

Leah grabbed her wrist. "Stop it, you stupid girl! What is this? You are accusing me of willingly harming my own sister? Are you mad?"

Sophie shook her again. "We don't have time to do this ridiculous dance, Leah. Stop lying. Where is Roxanne?"

Leah began to cry. Disgusted, Sophie pushed her away. She landed on the sofa, bowed her face in her hands, and continued to weep.

Sophie stood in front of her, hands on her hips. "You will listen to me, you viper-tongued harpy. You have made Roxanne's life a misery with your spite, your malicious comments, your outright insults. *She is gone, do you hear me?* Your sister is gone, kidnapped—again. You are the only one who would betray her, who would betray us. You are a disgrace, madam, a miserable human being with so little heart and feeling you should dry up and disappear." Sophie paused for a moment, drew herself up very straight. She pointed her finger. "You are no longer related to me. I disown you."

Sophie was breathing hard. She couldn't think of anything more to say. She looked over to see Julian staring at her.

"What?"

He said quietly, "Come here."

Sophie, frowning at him, her heart still pounding with rage, walked to him. He took her arms in his big hands, and very slowly, he drew her to him. He said against her cheek, "You are magnificent. I will thank God every day for the rest of my life if you will marry me," and he kissed her.

Sophie's arms went around him, and she hugged him hard as she felt him kissing her mouth, her chin, her nose. Everything was chaos and fear, endless fear for Roxanne. She was so afraid she wanted to choke on it. And she was magnificent?

She leaned back in his arms. "Yes, I will marry you. I

love you so much I will willingly cut your meat for you when you are old and have no teeth. What are we to do now?"

"What is this?"

Sophie didn't release him, merely turned slightly to see Leah now on her feet, staring at them.

"What is what, you foul-tongued fishwife?"

"Don't you dare speak to me that way, you ignorant spoiled brat! You are betraying your aunt just as I saw her betraying the prince yesterday, kissing Devlin Monroe at the top of the stairs. All know your precious aunt is to wed the prince, no one else, certainly not the future Duke of Brabante, whose family would not allow her through the door.

"Yes, all know you want the prince, but he doesn't want you. He wants Roxanne. So what are you doing kissing him? Marry him? What the devil is going on here?"

Sophie said slowly, "Roxanne told me about your tirade yesterday when she was with Devlin. She laughed and laughed, said you didn't understand, and it was really quite funny. But it isn't funny, is it, Leah?"

Julian, never releasing Sophie, said quietly, "This is why Richard had Roxanne kidnapped yet again. He thought I was going to marry her, and he wanted me to know the pain he knew when Lily died."

"Your precious Lily didn't simply die. Richard swore to me that you murdered her, you shot your very own wife!"

"Richard is quite wrong," Sophie said. "And you are a credulous fool, Leah."

"What do you know, you ignorant little twit?"

"I am not a twit, nor will I be ignorant for much longer. I am magnificent."

Leah waved her fist at them. "What is this, Prince? You can't make me believe you will wed this pathetic little girl."

"I am not a little girl. I am twenty years old."

Julian laughed. "She will be my wife. I quite like the sound of that, Sophie. My *wife*."

"That is not possible." Leah stared hard at Julian. "Not Roxanne?"

"No, not Roxanne. She and Devlin are going to wed."

"She is not worthy to marry a duke's heir! She is only a baron's daughter."

"She is an heiress, Aunt Leah."

"She is no more an heiress than I am!"

Sophie smiled up at Julian. "When she was only seventeen, her father, Lord Roche, realized she had a knack for selecting profitable investments. He gave her her entire dowry, and she tripled it by the time she was my age. My grandfather told me of this himself. He is so very proud of her. So, yes, I know she is an heiress."

Leah shouted, "I don't believe that. I never heard of such a thing. Father simply said that to make her sound more important than she is. An heiress? Impossible."

"I wonder why your own father did not tell you, ex-relative."

Leah paused, regrouped. "Even if she is an heiress, it makes no difference, the Monroe family will never accept her. She will be spat upon, turned away; she will probably become his mistress. She should excel at that role, what with her wicked red hair.

"Of the three Radcliffe sisters, I am the most beautiful, the one most sought after and admired. I am Lady Merrick. Why, look at who Bethanne married—that ridiculous vicar who proses on and on, boring everyone senseless. And he only managed to produce you, a simpleton girl with no pretensions to anything at all. Your mother was a fool."

Sophie felt violence brim to overflowing, rising up to choke her. She tried to jerk away from Julian, but he held her tight. She shook her fist at Leah. "Don't you talk about my mother like that. She was magic, my mother, and she was good and kind and loving. She never said a bad word about you, even when you deserved to have your rear end kicked."

Leah's breasts were heaving with anger. "Be quiet, you idiot. *Magnificent?* You're nothing but a bad jest; the prince will see the truth of you soon enough, hopefully before he weds you." She whirled away from them and began pacing the drawing room, muttering to herself over and over, "Everything is wrong, everything. What am I to do?"

⇒ *62* ⇐

Roxanne gingerly touched her fingers to her jaw, and that made her realize she wasn't bound, much to her relief. Her jaw wasn't broken, thank God, but it hurt. She realized she was lying on a dirty narrow cot, shoved up against a wall. She slowly sat up, felt the room spin a bit, and held perfectly still until it passed. She swung her legs over the edge of the cot, rose, weaved like a drunkard for a moment, then the punch of dizziness passed.

She was in a small room, with only one old slatted chair and a filthy chamber pot in the corner. There was a single window, so dirty she couldn't see clearly through it, could see only that it was daylight. Nothing else. Where was she?

She walked across the narrow space to the single door. She turned the handle, but it didn't move. The door was locked.

She remembered very well what had happened. One of the men had struck Devlin on the head. She closed her eyes for a moment and prayed. *Please let him be all right, please, he has to be all right*. She drew a deep breath. If he was all right, she knew he'd be frantic for her, Julian and Sophie as well. They'd be searching for her. But who was there to tell them where she was? No one, and that meant getting away from this place was up to her.

Three men had taken her: two sounded like copies of Orvald Manners, and the third, he'd sounded like a gentleman.

None of them had sounded the least bit like Richard, even if he'd tried to disguise his voice. No, it was someone else, and she vaguely remembered he had sounded familiar to her.

Still, didn't Richard have to be behind her kidnapping? There was simply no one else, was there? She remembered the man had said he wanted to leave as soon as she woke up. Leave for where? This couldn't be good. Her mouth went as dry as sand. Fear froze her to the dirty floor. She started shaking. *No, no, stop it.* There was a way out of here, and all she had to do was find it. Wherever here was. It didn't take long to realize there was nothing to use as a weapon. If there'd been anything of use in here, the men had removed it when they'd brought her here.

That left the window. It was narrow, but she could get through it. It was too high so she picked up the chair and placed it against the wall. She climbed up and tried to shove the window up, but it didn't move. She looked very closely. It was very narrow, indeed. Well, she wasn't all that grand a size; she'd fit through it, she had to. Why wouldn't it open?

How many years had it been since anyone had opened it? Probably not since the turn of the century.

She heard men's voices outside. She quickly moved the chair back and threw herself down on the cot and closed her eyes.

The door opened. She heard heavy footsteps, men's footsteps, coming closer. She held herself perfectly still. Could they hear her heart pounding? *Breathe easily, slowly.*

"Looks like she's still dreamin' of fine gowns and waltzin' wi' dukes."

"Ye struck 'er purty 'ard, Crannie."

"Come on, Vic, I only gives 'er a little tap. Jest look wot

she did to me face, scratched me up good. I'll have no end o' problems gettin' the ladies to admire me now."

"As if any female worth 'er salt would ever toss up 'er skirts for ye. Now, what she did to me, that was bad—kickin' me in me ballocks, it fair to made me puke up me guts."

"Shut up, both of you," said the third man. His voice was perfectly pleasant and cold as ice. He was coming toward her.

Don't sneeze, don't sneeze.

She felt his warm breath, he was that close to her face. It was so difficult not to move, to keep her breathing slow, barely there, as if still unconscious. She very nearly flinched when his fingers lightly touched her face.

Don't sneeze, don't sneeze.

But she wanted to. There was something one of the men was wearing, or maybe it was too much accumulated dirt. She wanted to laugh. *What's wrong with you? Now, hold perfectly still.*

She heard him say from above her, his voice meditative now, "She is quite beautiful." It wasn't the words he said but that thoughtful way he'd said them, like he was considering carving her up like meat for his dinner. It scared her to her toes. Somehow she didn't think he'd be like Orvald Manners, all rough and dirty and stupid. Who was he? "All that white flesh," he said, "I wonder."

"Aye, a purty little thing," said Crannie.

"Yer too ugly fer 'er to admire," Vic said, and she heard him buffet Crannie, on the shoulder or on his head?

"Ey! Wot's ye do that fer?"

"Be quiet," said their leader. "She should be waking up soon. Her jaw is turning an ugly purple. You did strike her too hard, Crannie." Again, she felt his fingers touch her jaw, and the sharp pain nearly made her cry out. "At least you didn't break her jaw."

Hold still, keep quiet.

She could feel the weight of his stare on her face. Who was he?

The man said in that same thoughtful voice, "The prince loves his mother, enjoys pleasing her, yet he chose this one, not the tender little pullet his mother served up to him on a platter. I believe he thought this one was filled with joy and laughter, everything a man dreamed about."

"A man niver does wot 'is ma wants 'im to," said Crannie, sadly.

Vic said, "Once she wakes up, wot's ye goin' to do wi' our little bird?"

She felt his attention shift from her. *Thank you, God.* Where had she heard his voice? She felt stupid, her head fuzzy.

"That is none of your business."

She heard him stride from the room.

"Somethin' not good, I'll wagers," said Vic. "Poor little pigeon." And the two of them left her alone. She heard the door lock.

They believe the prince wants me and not Sophie? Who are these men?

She forced herself to lie quietly for several more minutes until the silence weighed so heavy she couldn't bear it anymore.

She set the chair very quietly against the wall beneath the window and climbed up. She shoved and pushed, but the window wouldn't move.

She sneezed, froze, her eyes darting to the door, so afraid she whimpered, deep in her throat. But they didn't come back.

What to do?

She fetched the chamber pot, prayed, and slammed it against the dirty glass. It sounded like a cannon firing. The glass shattered, shards flying everywhere.

She didn't hear any shouts, any running feet.

She dug out shards of glass from the window frame, cut herself, but it didn't matter. Once the window opening was clear, she jumped. She was praying hard when she managed to grab the outside of the window frame and hoist herself through the opening.

Hurry, hurry.

The opening was narrow. No, no, she could do this,

because she wasn't wearing any petticoats. She jerked and heaved, and at last her hips went through. She fell headfirst but managed to turn before she landed on the ground below. She hit hard on her shoulder and grunted.

She didn't even consider being hurt. She jumped up and ran toward the thick forest, never looking over her shoulder, concentrating only on reaching the trees. She stopped once under cover of the maples, breathing fast and hard. *Which way to go?*

She didn't realize it was raining until drops splatted on her face through the leaves, heavy, hard rain. Within seconds, she was wet to her skin. Who cared? She ran. She pushed her sodden hair off her face but didn't slow. It was a pity there was no sun to give her any clues as to where she was. She shivered, stopped for a moment, crouched down, and listened. She could see through the waving tree branches back across the open clearing to where she'd been held—a dilapidated old cottage, set by itself in a small clearing, smoke belching from its stone chimney.

There was still no sound coming from the cottage. The rainfall was heavy, so perhaps they hadn't heard the glass shattering. Could she possibly be so lucky?

No, she couldn't.

She heard a yell. They'd discovered she'd escaped. She turned and ran to her left, weaving between the trees, ducking the branches. She stumbled over some tree roots and went down to her hands and knees. Head down and panting like a dog, she stayed where she was until she could breathe more easily again. Then she jumped to her feet and ran.

She ran until she was hugging her side, the pain was so great. She didn't know if she could keep going, but she did, even though she feared her body was going to rattle apart, that or the ghastly pain in her side would make her heart stop beating and she'd be dead and nothing would matter anymore.

She heard several gunshots and more men's shouts.

Surely they didn't know which way she'd run.

The rain was coming down even harder, slashing through

the thick tree branches with their spring leaves, and she shuddered with the numbing cold.

She crept behind a huge oak tree, went down on her haunches, and pressed herself against the trunk. She had to determine where they were. She tried not to pant, to breathe lightly, and she listened.

She heard crashing feet off to her left. *How close?* Then she realized they were coming toward her. No, that wasn't possible, her luck couldn't be that rotten.

Well, yes, it could.

She waited, still breathing so hard and fast it hurt her stomach. The pain in her side lessened a bit, but it still pulled and throbbed. She knew the longer she remained motionless, straining to hear, the more her arms and legs would cramp up. And the longer she stayed motionless, the more she knew the fear would grind her down, the fear would settle into her very bones. She couldn't let it. She wasn't helpless, she wasn't.

She jumped to her feet, staggered because she was so cold, and realized the last thing she should do now was run— they'd somehow been able to follow her through the forest because they'd seen signs of her mad passage. So be it. She began to walk, making her way very slowly, even though her legs cramped with cold. She tried to move silently, tried not to leave a trail.

She changed her direction several times, zigzagging until she stopped dead in her tracks—the trees were beginning to thin. No choice, she had to keep going.

In another twenty yards she stood at the edge of the forest and looked at the open expanse in front of her. Directly ahead, not fifty feet distant, was the channel, a thick curtain of rain blending with the gray turbulent water, making the world look like an endless filthy gray curtain.

She swore the rain slackened. Was that a sliver of light on the horizon, the sun trying to show through? She slapped her arms, trying to keep the numbness from turning her into a block of ice. *Which way to go?* She stared up the coast and down, but she didn't see anything familiar. No village, no houses, not a single cow, nothing. She couldn't remain in the cover of trees. No, she had to find her way down to the beach. She'd be safer there than running in the open.

She pictured Ravenscar in her mind and turned south. *You think you can outrace monsters? Prove it.* She ran as fast as she could across the open expanse to the edge of the cliff, and skidded to a stop, felt the earth breaking off beneath her feet, and frantically windmilled her arms. She got her balance and crawled to the cliff edge and looked down. It was a sheer drop to the beach below. She wanted to cry. Then she saw it—a narrow snaking path tracing back and forth across the cliff wall all the way down to the beach. She was so grateful, she nearly cried.

She heard a loud cracking gun report, but she didn't hesitate. She dashed down that path, tripped and fell to her knees, rocks digging into her hands and knees as she scrabbled wildly for purchase. She grabbed the branch of a scraggly bush and managed to pull herself flat against the cliff. And waited.

Another gunshot. Was it closer? She simply couldn't tell. Had they seen her running toward the cliff? And on this, the worst day of her life, she knew they had.

She heard a man's shout.

She looked down to the beach, sucked in her breath, and ran, trusting her balance and her feet.

63

R oxanne is smart."

Devlin knew he was saying this aloud more for his benefit than for Julian's and Sophie's. Like the others, he was hunched forward, the hat on his head giving him some protection from the rain. Sophie had a scarf tied around her head.

"It's true," Sophie said, "she is smart. She'll do something, I know she will. Devlin, you shouldn't even be out of bed." Sophie leaned close to his horse to poke him lightly in the arm. "And it's raining, you could get sick—oh, very well, that doesn't make sense, does it? Please, don't fall off your horse."

He wasn't listening. His head felt like it was going to split open, and he was so scared for Roxanne he wanted to vomit. But Roxanne was smart. She would figure out something. She would keep herself alive until—dear God, he just wanted her to be whole and safe.

Julian said even as he kept scanning all around them, "A pity we couldn't get Leah to confess anything. All she did was defend Richard, claiming he was in London."

Sophie snorted. "I could have gotten everything out of her if you'd only let me chew off her cheek."

Julian laughed. He didn't know where it had come from, but he was becoming quite used to laughing, even at strange times, like now.

"Perhaps we should split up," Devlin said.

"No." Julian shook his head. "One alone could become a victim as well. We stay together."

Sophie frowned. "We've looked everywhere. Wait, what about the cliffs?"

"The cliffs?" Julian turned to face her. "What would she be doing at the cliffs? There's no place to hide there."

"I don't know why, but it feels right."

They said nothing more, each of them intent on searching the countryside, blurred and indistinct through the pounding rain.

At least a dozen men were out, searching southward. Mayhap they'd found her, but, oddly, Julian didn't think so. He looked over at Sophie. She looked fierce.

It pleased him. They rode through a small forest of trees and out on the open land that led to the cliffs.

They dismounted a dozen feet from the cliff edge, since the heavy rain was turning the ground to mud, and walked carefully to the edge to look down.

They could see nothing through the rain, it was that thick. Then, suddenly, the rain lessened. Sophie pointed to the distant horizon. The sun was trying to come out behind a black cloud. Devlin shouted, "There's Roxanne. Look, there are men after her."

64

Ravenscar

Leah didn't know what to do. She paced the drawing room, thankful the duchess had left her finally to go to breakfast, since she'd politely refused to say anything more. What could she have said, in any case?

Surely Richard wouldn't have taken Roxanne. Surely. He certainly hadn't taken her the first time, because she and Richard had been together, not ready to eat their picnic luncheon but to make love beneath that lovely old willow tree, when Julian, Sophie, and Devlin had burst upon them.

But he could have hired some men to take her. She couldn't believe it, wouldn't believe it. And she'd kept insisting that Julian was taken with Roxanne, not Sophie. Had Richard believed her? Had he acted?

How had it come about that the prince wanted Sophie? Leah suddenly saw her as a little girl, eager, delighting in everything. Bethanne, her mother, so in love with her own child, petting her, laughing with her in pure joy. But she wasn't a little girl now. She was twenty years old. Old enough to marry, old enough to marry a man twelve years her senior, and she'd been selected by his own mother. Leah had heard Julian say Sophie was too young for him, more like a niece, and she'd believed him. That claim had fallen by the wayside, hadn't it?

Leah couldn't stand it. She had to discover if Richard was behind this madness. She quickly ran upstairs to her bedchamber, donned a riding habit and boots, and rushed to the stables. No one tried to stop her. No one even spoke to her, but she saw some of their looks, shot at her from nearly averted faces, dislike radiating from all of them.

They all hated her. They all believed she was guilty of allowing the kidnapping of her own sister.

She wanted to scream that she hadn't even known about it until Sophie and Julian had told her.

The stable lad whose name she didn't know blocked her way. "I must have a horse. Now. Saddle a mare for me."

"No, missis, I daren't. Only the prince can tell me to saddle a mare for ye." The stable lad paused, and he looked beyond her left shoulder. "As ye know, milady, the prince is searching for Miss Roxanne. Yer sister."

Leah was so scared, so furious, she shoved the lad aside, marched into the stables, found herself what looked like a sweet-tempered mare, led her out, managed to saddle her, something she hadn't done for a good ten years, but she hadn't forgotten how. She pulled over a mounting block. She was panting when she was finally on the mare's back.

"Ye shouldn't oughtta steal the mare," the stable lad shouted at her, wringing his hands. She would have ridden him down if he hadn't quickly moved out of the way.

She rode toward Hardcross Manor.

But how could Richard be at Hardcross Manor? *He left for London only yesterday; he hasn't even arrived in London yet.*

The sky, black clouds hanging low, opened up, and rain poured down. She cursed, urged the mare to go faster.

But what if he never planned to go to London? He didn't tell me what this important business was, now, did he? What if he was planning all along to take Roxanne? Again. But why?

The rain beat down, soaking through her skirts, her petticoats. She'd not even thought about a riding hat.

There were no trees, only open country. She clucked the mare faster, leaned down to press against the mare's neck, and hung on.

She smelled horse sweat, and, oddly, it smelled good, and she saw herself as a young girl, riding across the countryside. She remembered once when Roxanne had ridden with her and had been thrown when a crow spooked her mare. And Leah had pulled her free of the briars, where she'd luckily landed, and taken her home, praying as hard as she could.

So very long ago.

Would Richard be at Hardcross Manor?

65

Roxanne looked over her shoulder to see all three men running after her. No use in trying to hide now.

She was exhausted, but so were they. She wasn't a weak female. Unlike those bullyboys who'd probably spent all their time in a town, she'd spent her life walking all over the Belthorpe moors.

She had no intention of letting them catch her.

But they can shoot you.

She wouldn't let them get close enough. She felt good, her heart pumping. Thankfully, the pain in her side was gone. Since they didn't have their bloody horses, it was a footrace now, and she was going to win.

As she ran, she kept searching for another path upward. There had to be one. She saw absolutely no one, saw no sign of a house on the cliff. But then again, who would build near a cliff?

She held her skirts up higher and continued to run, her pace steady. She didn't look back again. She heard an occasional shout, a gunshot, but nothing near her. What were they shooting at? Did the fools expect her to stop and raise her arms in surrender? Did they think her so stupid?

She was wearing boots, a good thing for welcoming a bunch of smugglers to the beach but not so good for running, since they were heavy and growing heavier by the minute.

She kept her pace steady, tried to keep her breathing steady.

She looked upward when she saw a sign of movement. There, on top of the cliff. What was up there? What had she seen?

It didn't matter if she'd seen only the play of shadows against the sky, because right ahead, she saw a narrow path snaking back and forth up the cliff.

The path was steep and slippery from all the rain. She was heaving now. She couldn't help it, she took a quick look back. The three men were only twenty yards behind her. Two of them were flagging, but one of the men, their leader, she thought, was running hard. Another minute and he would be close enough to shoot her.

She leaned nearly to the ground and moved as quickly as she could up the winding path.

She looked up at the sound of a shout.

It was the most precious voice she'd ever heard in her life. It was Devlin's voice, and he was there, on top of the cliffs, waiting for her, and she pressed forward, trying desperately not to slip, climbing for all she was worth toward his voice.

She heard the man climbing up below her. Hadn't he heard Devlin's voice? Didn't he know he was now the prey?

She threw back her head and yelled, "Devlin, you're wearing your hat!" When she felt his strong hand pull her up, she laughed and threw herself against him. "Their leader, he's behind me. It's not Richard. His voice sounded familiar to me, but I can't place it. He's still coming. Give me a gun, Devlin, I want to shoot him."

66

Hardcross Manor

Leah threw the mare's reins at the gaping stable boy.
"Is Master Richard here?"

The boy quickly tugged on his forelock. "No, milady, 'e
went to Lunnon, don't ye recall? Ye was 'ere when 'e left."

"Of course I remember, you idiot." She didn't wait for
him to assist her down. She jumped, nearly fell, but straightened and ran toward the manor.

The front door opened before she made it to the top of
the stone steps. It was Vicky.

"Leah! Goodness, whatever is the matter? What are
you doing here? Oh, my, you're wet to your skin. Come in,
come in."

Thank God for Vicky. She was leading her inside the
manor, bemoaning how wet she was, and asking her over
and over what had happened.

Leah grabbed her arm. "Vicky, none of that matters. Is
Richard here? Has he returned?"

"Richard?" Vicky cocked her head to the side. "You
know he went to London. He was going to perform some
task for our father."

Some task for Lord Purley? Richard had said it was business, and she'd assumed it was his own private affairs.

"Take me to your father; I must speak to him now."

"He isn't here, Leah. He went riding, even knowing it was going to rain. I don't know when he'll be back. I do hope he does not return ill. What has happened? What is wrong?"

Leah didn't want to scare Vicky. She had to get hold of herself. She drew in one deep breath, then another and yet another. "All right, everything is all right. Yes, I'm very wet. May I borrow some dry clothes?"

Vicky took Leah to her bedchamber and clucked over her as Leah stripped off her clothes behind an ornate Japanese screen and put on dry ones. She accepted only two petticoats—who needed a dozen petticoats?—and pulled the lovely gown over her head. Vicky hooked the buttons up her back.

"Here are slippers." The slippers, naturally, matched the green of the gown, a lovely soft Pomona green. Then Vicky sat her in front of the dressing-table mirror and began toweling her hair dry. If Leah wasn't mistaken, Vicky was humming, very intent on what she was doing.

Leah said, "Roxanne was kidnapped again. Last night. She was taking part in Julian's final smuggling operation."

Vicky stared at her. "Smuggling? Goodness, there hasn't been any smuggling in Cornwall forever. Well, not much that I've ever heard about. The prince—he's a smuggler? How very romantic that is. However do you know this?"

"No one told me. I overheard Julian and Devlin speaking of it. Romantic? Well, it didn't turn out that way. Devlin was with Roxanne, and he was struck down. When he awoke, Roxanne was gone. Everyone is out looking for her. I had to know—" Her voice fell dead. She looked mutely in the mirror at Vicky, who was working loose a tangle in her damp hair.

"You have beautiful hair, Leah."

"That's not important now. Didn't you hear what I said? Roxanne is missing. Someone took her."

"It appears someone is always taking her. Are you certain she didn't whisk herself away this time? Mayhap because she likes the attention?"

That is something I would say. "Vicky, that makes no sense. Roxanne is sensible."

Vicky shrugged. "Who knows what another will do and why? Is Devlin all right?"

"Yes, yes, a minor head injury, no more than that."

"That's good. I shouldn't want to hear his lordship had died. Such a treat he is to the senses, don't you think? And to watch him laugh and play the vampire, I find it quite amusing. He is so tall and lean, and so very white, such a contrast to his dark eyes and hair. I have wondered what it would be like to kiss him."

"Please, Vicky, do you know if Richard indeed went to London?"

"Richard? No, I don't know for sure if he went to London, how could I? He is a man, he can do as he pleases, he can strew lies where he pleases. All I know is that he isn't here, so that means he had to go somewhere, doesn't it?"

"Where is your maid, Vicky?"

"Oh, Whipple is doubtless in the village, having tea with her sister."

"But why would you send her away? It's raining."

Vicky paused with her brushing, met Leah's wild eyes in the mirror. "I don't know why you should care, Leah. Am I not doing a fine job assisting you?" Leah's hair tangled in the brush, and she yelped.

"How clumsy of me. Do forgive me." Vicky worked Leah's hair free and continued to brush until it was nearly dry.

"Do you know, the gown fits you very well. We are nearly of a size, isn't that fortunate, since you will be my new sister?"

Who cares?

"I had another sister, you know. Her name was Lily. She was very nearly my size as well. The gown you're wearing belonged to Lily. It was one of her favorites. It has been hanging in my wardrobe for three years now. I haven't worn it, but I thought it would be perfect for you. I'm glad, since it seems you will replace Lily."

Leah met her eyes in the mirror. Something was wrong

here, something she didn't understand. She said, never looking away from Vicky's face, "I do not wish to replace Lily. She was your real sister, as Roxanne is mine. Do you know where Roxanne is, Vicky?"

"I? However could I know where your sister is? Could she be hiding from the prince? Perhaps she no longer wishes to wed him? He has asked her, has he not?"

Leah shook her head. "We were all quite wrong about that. It isn't Roxanne Julian prefers, it is Sophie."

"Sophie? How can that be possible? I've seen him treat her as one would a precocious child but nothing else. Surely it is Roxanne."

Leah shook her head. She watched Vicky reach into a small jewelry box and pull out a small golden heart on a delicate gold chain. "This also belonged to Lily. She wore it always." Vicky flicked open the locket and showed it to Leah.

She saw a small painting of a young woman with black hair and eyes so dark they looked opaque. A small portrait of Julian was opposite hers, and she saw Lily's eyes were even darker than his. They both looked very young and very proud. Why had she thought that?

Leah smelled Vicky's light rose scent as she leaned close and pointed. "Isn't she beautiful? More beautiful than you, but again, surely Richard would not agree. That sort of thing depends on who is doing the looking, doesn't it? The prince loved Lily; he treated her like a princess—fitting, since he is, after all, the Prince of Ravenscar."

"Her portrait—Lily doesn't look particularly happy to me."

"Do you know, I believe you are right. I do wonder what she is thinking. She posed for this miniature for two whole days. Father was rather upset that the young man demanded so much of her time. What do you believe she's thinking, Leah?"

"I could have no idea, since I didn't know your sister."

"And now she is dead, so what would it matter what she was thinking so long ago? Did you know, Lily was wearing the pendant the day she died? When all the women were removing her clothes to wash her, I took it off her and put it in this beautiful jewelry box. The jewelry box was hers as well. She never took it with her to Ravenscar. I asked her why she hadn't, but she only shook her head and wouldn't answer. It is much nicer than mine, and I enjoy looking at it. I have never wanted to wear any of her jewelry. I do look at the locket occasionally, when I can't remember what she looked like."

"Why didn't you give the locket to Julian?"

Vicky shrugged. "Julian—how odd that name sounds. He is the prince, everyone calls him that." Leah watched Vicky carefully remove the small portraits from the locket, close it, then slip it back onto the chain and over Leah's head before she could stop her.

She clutched the locket. It felt like a heavy stone in her hand. She hated it. "No, no, Vicky, I don't wish to wear it."

"Why not? It looks perfect with this gown, don't you think? Both yours and Richard's miniatures can be painted and put in the locket. Yes, that looks quite fine. You do not believe Richard will mind, do you?"

Leah dropped her hand from the locket. She shook her head, stared at herself in the mirror, then at Vicky, standing behind her. Their eyes met in the mirror. Vicky smiled, lifted a mass of her hair. "Very nearly dry now. I shall arrange your hair for you."

Leah said, "I can twist it up, do not concern yourself."

"Hold still, Leah. I occasionally arranged Lily's hair. She said I had a special talent for it. No, don't try to move away. You will see how very fine you will look."

Leah sat frozen, not knowing what to do. Neither Lord Purley nor Richard was here. Vicky's maid wasn't here. She was alone—no, she was being absurd. This was Vicky, a bit on the odd side, but surely that had nothing to do with anything.

It stopped raining. A sliver of sun burst through the window into the bedchamber.

"Vicky, have you been to London? Did you have a Season?"

Vicky was humming again. She grew still, then said,

"No, I have never been there. Lily teased Father, begged him to let her have a Season, and finally he agreed. She went to London to stay in a fine house my father rented for three months. He even brought our aunt Elaine down from Gatenby to be her chaperone.

"What happened is strange indeed. She hadn't seen the prince in a very long time, since he was always out of the country, in Italy, I believe, working on building up his shipping empire. A prince should have an empire, don't you think? When she went to her first ball, he was there. When they saw each other, Aunt Elaine told my father, they both began to laugh. To meet after so long, and in London, of all places. It was fate, they both believed.

"Two months later, she married the prince, and Lily moved in to Ravenscar. Her grace, if I recall aright, was always very kind to Lily, just as I'm certain she's also kind to you. Do you know what I mean?"

"No. What do you mean?"

"I know for a fact her grace didn't want the prince to marry Lily. Why, I don't know. Perhaps she'd heard something about her. I understand she really quite detests you."

"Why would you say such a thing to me?"

"Oh, it is something I fancy I must have heard. I don't remember. Am I wrong? Well, no matter. What I say doesn't count for anything, now, does it?"

Leah heard herself say, "Surely Lily called him Julian, not the prince."

"No, she always called him prince, all her life, like everyone else—*my prince*. I know he didn't used to like being called prince, but he certainly liked the way Lily said it. I heard him tell Lily he loved to hear her whisper *prince* to him once, and then he was kissing her, pressing her up against the wall.

"Three years ago, I turned eighteen and I asked my father if I could go to London for a Season. Maybe, I told him, I could find a prince as well.

"But you see, Lily had died two months before the Season began, and Richard said we all had to mourn her for a year.

I thought that rather foolish, since wearing black had nothing at all to do with the grief we all felt, but I was told there was no choice and I had to wear black gowns. I have always hated black; it makes me look rather sallow."

"So did you go to London for your Season when you were nineteen?"

She saw Vicky was plaiting her hair. Leah had never worn braids, even as a little girl; she'd always loved to wear her beautiful hair loose and flying about her head when she ran. She started to say something when Vicky said, "No, I decided I wished to stay here in Cornwall. This is my home. I decided I didn't want a prince any longer."

Vicky kept plaiting. Leah stared at her in the mirror. "But why?"

Vicky shrugged. "Richard and Father believe the prince murdered Lily. I don't know what happened, no one does, even though Richard swears the prince is guilty. When I found her, I remember I kissed her and she felt so very cold. It was quite horrible. Her eyes were staring up at me, but she wasn't there any longer. I remember I rubbed and rubbed my mouth to wipe the cold away. It took a very long time.

"No, if I went to London, I might find a prince, too, and he might kill me, and I'd be dead just like Lily."

"You do not believe she killed herself, or perhaps she had a lover?"

"Oh, no, she had no lover. Well, not exactly what you would call a lover."

Leah said, "What do you mean?"

"I mean I have no need of London, seeing everyone trying to be something they're not, or trying to make everyone believe they're better than everyone else. It must be fatiguing. I am happy right here at Hardcross Manor. I do miss Lily, though. But soon I will have you. Look at yourself, Leah. Don't you look grand?"

Leah stared at herself in the mirror, then looked down at the small miniature of Lily that lay on the dressing table. Vicky had fashioned her hair in exactly the same style—hair pulled away from her face and braided high on her head, no loose dangling curls. A severe look, too severe, and identical to Lily's. But on Lily, it didn't look at all severe, it made her look somehow regal. Like a princess.

Leah again looked at Vicky in the mirror, smiling like a proud mother, patting her hair here and there. "Here," she said, and handed Leah a pair of small pearl earrings. "Lily always wore these earrings with this gown."

Without saying a word, Leah fastened the delicate pearl earrings onto her ears.

She looked once again down at the portrait of the long-dead Lily. Despite her blond hair and her light eyes, she still looked too much like the dead woman, and for the first time, she felt alarm.

She turned slowly on the dressing stool. "What happened to Aunt Elaine? Did she return to live here at Hardcross Manor?"

"Yes, she did. Her son no longer wanted her about in his house, you see. I rather liked her."

"What do you mean? What happened to her?"

"Oh, didn't I tell you? She caught a putrid inflammation of the lung and died. I believe it was soon after Lily died. There is so much death in the world, don't you think? I'm very glad I'm not dead."

Leah nodded numbly. She couldn't look away from the pale-faced woman in the mirror. She again met Vicky's eyes in the mirror. "It must have hurt Richard very much to believe his best friend killed his sister."

Vicky shrugged, lightly tugged a small curl out of the braid to pull it down along Leah's cheek. Then she studied the braid, pulled down another bit of hair on her other cheek. "That softens your face, but it is a pity you don't look as fine as Lily did without the dangling curls. What did Richard really think of the prince? They were close, I suppose, but it was Lily who held Richard's heart."

Vicky leaned close. "Do you know, Richard always believed Lily the most beautiful girl in the world? And perhaps that is why he never allowed himself to really see other ladies, you know? But now here you are. You are the first."

⟺ 67 ⟺

The two women stood atop the cliff, watching Julian and Devlin make their way down the path. The rain had stopped, but the footing was treacherous.

"It's not really a path," Roxanne said. "It's so dangerous, and Devlin is still hurt."

"I don't care if we have guns or not," Sophie said. "Those men chasing you—surely they must realize they can't get to you now." They saw the men's indecision, then all three of them turned and ran back up the beach toward the upward path.

"I don't think Julian and Devlin can catch them. Oh, no, Devlin slipped. Thank goodness Julian caught him."

Sophie turned and pulled Roxanne close. "We were so worried, so scared, but Devlin said you were smart. He said it over and over, he knew you would manage to get yourself free. But how did you get up that path when it isn't a path at all?"

"I prayed," Roxanne said. She kissed Sophie's cheek and pulled away to look down at Julian and Devlin. They'd stopped halfway down the cliff, staring after the retreating men. Then they turned and began the climb back up.

Roxanne said, "I know where the cottage is. I think we can beat them back because that's where they'll return, since they left their horses there."

Julian helped Devlin to the top of the cliff. He threw back his head and laughed. "I heard you, Roxanne. Let's end this, ladies, once and for all." Then he stopped cold, saw they were all soaking wet, Roxanne's hair in wet ropes down her back. She was shivering, so pale he thought she'd surely drop into a dead faint. Sophie looked drowned as well, her heavy clothes weighing her down, her hair straggling down her back from beneath her scarf. But there was such fury and determination on her face, he knew if he said anything, she'd very likely try to hurl him off the cliff.

Devlin was looking even paler than Roxanne, yet he was shrugging out of his cloak, wrapping it around her.

Roxanne looked at him even as she felt the warmth from his cloak sink through the wet material to her skin. "No, this isn't right. You were hurt, Devlin, you must—"

Devlin lightly laid his fingertips over her mouth. "Hush, dear one. Do you wish to show us the cottage, or do you wish to stand here arguing with me?"

"Let's go."

It was only a ten-minute ride back to the cottage. How could that be, Roxanne wondered, when she had run for so very long?

"It looks as if we've beaten them back," Julian said. "Roxanne, you and Sophie see if there are any more weapons inside. Devlin, let's take care of their horses. We must hurry."

It required only five minutes to walk the three horses, one of them a very fine Thoroughbred, a goodly distance away from the cottage and tether them in a copse of maple trees.

"I found this," Sophie said, and showed them a pistol.

Julian took it, saw it was loaded.

Roxanne said, "There was nothing else. Listen, I hear them coming. I still can't remember where I've heard the one man's voice, but he is educated, unlike the other two."

They raced across the clearing to huddle down behind some thick yew bushes.

"It ain't fair, jest ain't fair."

"Shut yer trap, Crannie, if only ye'd tapped the little pigeon 'arder, she wouldn't 'ave escaped."

"Ye were saying I 'it the littl' gal too 'ard!"

"I can't believe she gots 'erself through that window, thin as a sliver of ice that window is. I saw ye looking at that window."

"Both of you, be quiet." Roxanne saw the third man was well dressed, unlike his compatriots, in buckskins and a long cloak, and he carried a gun in one hand, a riding crop in the other. All of them were soaked to their bones.

"Yes, I did look at the window, and yes, I deemed it too small for her, yet she still managed to get through. You were supposed to be sitting outside her door, Crannie. Why didn't you hear her break the glass?"

Roxanne whispered to Devlin, "Where have I heard his voice? Why won't he turn around so we can see him?"

"I don't need to," Julian said quietly.

All three of them stared at him, but he shook his head.

Crannie didn't say a word.

Vic said, "Tell the truth, Crannie. Ye were drinkin', yer brain fuddled, that's why, ain't it?"

The man whirled about. "You drunken lout!" He back-handed Crannie across his face, sending him sprawling to the rocky ground. "You stupid sot, I should have known." He raised his pistol and shot Crannie through the heart.

Crannie didn't make a sound. He looked surprised, then fell back and didn't move.

Vic said, "Crannie! Ye shot Crannie dead! I'll kill ye fer that, ye bastid!" And Vic rushed at him.

"You are both incompetent fools," and he shot Vic in the head. Vic grabbed his head and lurched forward, but then he dropped to the ground beside Crannie.

"Good riddance to both of you."

Devlin said quietly, "I'm sorry, Julian."

Julian only nodded. "Stay here, all of you." He strode around the side of the cottage to see Harlan standing there, his pistol at his side, anger radiating off him, slapping his riding crop against his thigh.

"Hello, Harlan. I suppose I'm not really surprised," Julian said. "When Roxanne told us she believed your voice was familiar to her, I didn't have the time to pick my way through to you, but I should have. If only I'd really opened my eyes, I would have realized Richard couldn't have been the one hiding in the shadows, watching our smuggling run that night in Saint Osyth. It was you, wasn't it?"

Harlan Whittaker whirled around, bringing his gun up.

"No," Julian said very precisely, his own gun aimed at Harlan's chest. "No, Harlan, this is the end of it. Drop that gun to the ground or I will shoot you between your eyes."

Julian watched the other man's eyes, knew he was considering what to do. Finally, Harlan nodded, dropped the gun to the ground.

"Kick it over to me."

Harlan kicked the gun toward him. It stopped several feet short.

"It was you that night, wasn't it, Harlan?"

Harlan was breathing hard. "Yes, it was. How did you know to come here?"

Julian said, "You must have seen his lordship and me coming down the cliff after the three of you, but evidently you didn't see us run back up. It is always faster to ride than to run. You still don't understand, do you?"

Devlin said from behind him, "Harlan didn't realize Roxanne would remember the location of this cottage and bring us here."

"Prince, Julian—"

Julian said, his voice emotionless, "You and I have worked together for five years, Harlan. I trusted you until— well, I did wonder how anyone could have known about my final smuggling run here at Ravenscar. Who was there to tell?" He said over his shoulder to Roxanne and Sophie, "I never believed Leah knew; we were too careful. And that meant Richard could not have known. Why did you do this, Harlan?"

Harlan's mouth twisted in a sneer. "You were so trusting, Julian, and you told me everything. I even remember you told me what your long-ago Sergeant Lambert told you, something you lived by but hated, you told me, but it made me smile."

Julian nodded slowly. "I asked Lambert why men couldn't ever be content with what they had, and he told me that greed and envy and jealousy were sewn into the very fabric of a man's body. Evidently, he was right, at least about you, Harlan. Was it greed and envy and jealousy?"

Harlan smiled at him. "That sounds rather damning, doesn't it? But yes, I suppose that is close enough."

"I know Richard Langworth took Roxanne that first time, but that was because he believed I loved her. Why did you take her, Harlan?"

"Do you know, I was certain you'd allow the ladies to accompany you on this harmless little adventure. And I was right. Why did I take her? The moment I saw her in your drawing room, I knew I wanted her, more than you wanted her, and because you wanted her as well. I took her because I was going to leave England with all your money and marry her in France. I have enjoyed basking in the irony of it."

Harlan looked at Roxanne, standing beside Devlin, clutching his cloak around her. "When I first met you, I knew you were different, I knew you saw more than you should see. You fascinated me. You were too good for him. I wanted you."

Roxanne said, "I certainly didn't see you for what you are, Mr. Whittaker. Did you kidnap me that first time as well? And not Richard Langworth?"

"I had nothing to do with the first time. Julian has doubtless told you Langworth hired Manners to damage the goods on the *Blue Star*. He did manage to light a fire, only to have it put out by that cabin boy. Then Langworth hired Manners to kidnap Roxanne. Why he imagined Manners could do anything right, I do not know. I was not at all surprised to hear you did him in and escaped. Manners is an incompetent sod."

Sophie said, "It seems to me you also hired incompetent sods, sir."

Harlan rounded on her. "You crass little fortune hunter, no one cares what you think."

"I care," Julian said.

"So do I," Roxanne said. "I fancy all of us care."

Sophie said, "You are grossly misinformed, Mr. Whittaker. It is not Roxanne who is going to marry the prince. I am."

Harlan's sneer became more pronounced. "He wouldn't have you, he's far too proud."

Sophie merely smiled at him. "You really believe I'm crass? A fortune hunter? I doubt that would sit well with my father, a vicar, you know. You needn't worry, though, since it won't be your problem, sir, but rather my future husband's, and let me tell you, the prince believes me an angel. How did you know Roxanne knocked Manners unconscious and he never woke up?"

"Everyone talks in a village." Harlan shrugged. "Everyone knows about your misadventures."

He drew a deep breath and said to Julian, "Well, you've won. You always win, don't you, Prince? You're renowned in the city for your luck. But I've always recognized it was more skill than luck. I've admired you, Julian, but alas, when it came to the sticking point, I chose the groats.

"Do you know it was my plan to have excisemen on the beach, waiting for you? But not one of them came, because, to put it simply, they refused, to the man. Not the prince, they said, not the prince. One of them said you should have your fun, and God bless you."

Harlan gave Roxanne a brooding look. "When you came to his house, you were alone. I saw how you acted with each other. I saw you were taken with her, Julian, and she with you. Will you tell me what happened? Why did you turn to this one?" He gave a negligent nod toward Sophie.

Roxanne said, "It appears things sorted themselves out the way they were meant to be sorted. Actually, Julian and Sophie are quite perfect together."

"You lost him to this little girl?" Harlan said. "Will you be the maiden aunt to your niece and her husband, mayhap tend their children for them, Miss Radcliffe?"

"Occasionally," Roxanne said.

Devlin said, "Miss Radcliffe will be my wife and the future Duchess of Brabante. She will tend her own children."

Harlan was shaking his head, staring back and forth from Sophie to Roxanne. He threw back his head and laughed. "It is really too much. How very blind I was. Do you know, Miss Radcliffe, my mother had red hair, not flaming red like yours but red enough. I always hated red hair, as I hated her, the witch, until I met you. You could have been my wife, not his."

Roxanne looked at him from head to toe. "Do you think I would marry you, sir? I would stick a knife in your ribs the first chance I got."

Julian said, "Of course, this wasn't your only betrayal, Harlan. How long have you been stealing from me?"

Harlan shrugged. "You've gathered so much money, Julian. And you were always traveling, and I was in charge of everything, since you trusted me. I haven't taken that much over the years, though. I'm not a fool." He began tapping his riding crop against his thigh. "What are you going to do, Julian?"

"I believe I should kill you. That would end it."

"It would."

Sophie took a step forward. "The prince is too honorable. I wish to kill you."

Harlan looked over at her. "You?" Harlan watched her move closer to Julian, watched her lay her hand on his forearm. He said slowly, "Did you seduce him to make him turn from your aunt?"

"I tried," Sophie said, "but he refuses to allow any seduction at all until we are married."

Harlan whirled about to Roxanne, who had moved closer to Devlin. "Let me tell you, the Duke of Brabante will never allow his precious heir to wed a mere baron's daughter. I wager your dowry is nothing out of the ordinary."

Roxanne said, "It appears you haven't seen anything clearly, Mr. Whittaker. You have made one mistake after the other. And you had the nerve to shoot those poor men for being incompetent? What about shooting yourself?"

She took Devlin's hand. "Do look at his lordship and me, sir. We complete each other. He is an excellent man, and I am the luckiest of women."

In an instant of time, Harlan pulled a stiletto out of his sleeve and hurled it at Julian.

Devlin fired.

⊷ *68* ⊶

Ravenscar

Roxanne, Corinne, and Devlin stood at the end of Julian's gigantic bed, one of his ancestors' beds, mayhap even the very first Duke of Brabante's bed, as Corinne had endlessly repeated while Dr. Crutchfield, so very ancient and rheumy, worked to save her son's life.

Sophie sat on the bed beside Julian, watching every move Dr. Crutchfield made. She hated that his old hands shook, but hadn't he been a doctor for decades? What was a little unsteadiness, since surely he knew what he was doing by now.

Dr. Crutchfield looked at her. "The knife missed his organs, blessed be his famed luck. Ah, he's stirring, more's the pity. Hold him down, missy, don't let him jerk around."

Devlin stepped forward, but Sophie frowned him away. "I can do it." She leaned over Julian, her palms flat on his shoulders. She whispered down to him, "You mustn't move, Prince. Dr. Crutchfield is going to set stitches now in your side. Hold still, all right? Can you understand me?"

Julian was swimming in laudanum and pain from the knife that had sunk deep into his flesh. He didn't really understand what Sophie said, but he smelled her, a wonderful smell that was surely lessening the pain. He breathed in deeply, felt her smell reach deep inside him. He felt the needle jab into his flesh, but he didn't move.

He looked up at her face. "I love the way you smell, Sophie."

She wanted to weep. She leaned close. "You will be able to smell me until the next century, Prince. I'm sorry the pain is so bad." She leaned down and kissed him. He lurched up, nearly knocking her backward. But she came down over him hard. "No, you can't move." Her gentle voice changed abruptly. "Dr. Crutchfield, you will kindly go more easily! Surely you are nearly done?"

He gave her an evil smile. "Don't let him move again, or I just might jab the needle into his manhood, and surely that would not be a good thing for you." Left unsaid was *You'd best mind your manners, missy.*

Julian had the insane desire to laugh, but he didn't move. "Listen to me, Sophie, this is important. And Devlin, Roxanne, Mother, are you there?"

"We're all here, dearest," Corinne said.

"Devlin, if I die, you will see to it Sophie is taken care of. Do you swear it?"

"If you have the nerve to die on me," Sophie said, her nose nearly touching his, "I will have Devlin bite your neck."

Julian laughed, and the rip of pain made his jaw lock. He closed his eyes and concentrated on Sophie's smell. What was it exactly? He didn't know, he only knew he wanted to breathe her in the rest of his life, he hoped a life that extended beyond this torture.

"Promise me," he said, teeth gritted.

"Oh, aye, I'll promise you anything to make you calm," Devlin said. "I'll also look after your mother, and don't forget Pouffer. Now be quiet and let Dr. Crutchfield set his last stitches."

"Aye, all done now," Dr. Crutchfield said. "I'm old, Prince, too old for this nonsense. You getting yourself stuck with a knife—it could have struck an organ and done you in. I don't like it. Avoid villains in the future. Now, this young missy crouching over you like a tigress, I can tell you from experience she needs a firm hand. However, I doubt there is a single part of you that is firm enough to do the job anytime soon, and even then, I'd say it's questionable.

"Now, let me wash away all your blood, sprinkle basilicum powder on my very fine stitches, and get you bandaged up. Missy, you will see the prince keeps to his bed."

"I will tie him down, if necessary," Sophie said.

Julian groaned, wondered if Dr. Crutchfield was right, nothing firm about him, at all. "You are too young to be a shrew."

She leaned down and kissed him again, stroking her hand over his beloved face.

"I am the queen of shrews, dearest," Corinne said, from the bottom of the bed. "Even with lessons, Sophie will never gain my stature. But we can try."

"Thank you, your grace." Sophie smiled down at Julian, kissed him again, kneeled back on her heels, and laughed.

"Heal yourself, Prince, do you hear me? Then you may be as firm as you like with me."

"If you only knew," he said.

"We also have a wedding to attend."

The prince gave her a twisted smile. "We have two weddings to attend, and isn't that a fine thing?"

Wʜat are you doing on my bed? We're not married yet."
Julian wondered if any part of him was firm again.
He cleared his throat, cast about his brain, but simply
couldn't sort through much of anything. "Are we?"

Sophie, who'd been lying beside him, her palm over his
heart, came up onto her knees and leaned over him. "Thank
heavens you're finally awake. It's been hours." She closed
her eyes for a moment. "Too many of them."

"Sophie, I will not die, all right? I have a very big
problem."

"You're thirsty? I know you've got to be hungrier than
our pregnant Beatrice."

"Sophie, I must use the chamber pot. Immediately."

She said nothing at all, jumped off the bed, brought the
chamber pot to him.

"Thank you. Go away."

She went. Fortunately, Devlin was in the hallway outside.
"Go to him. He needs assistance. With the chamber pot."

Devlin shut the door firmly in her face. Sophie devoutly
prayed for Devlin's sake that he take very good care of

Julian. She was tempted to wait, but she heard voices coming from Corinne's sitting room down the corridor.

She should go back—

Roxanne called out, "Sophie, come in here. Corinne and I are having tea. Devlin can take care of my soon-to-be uncle-in-law. Come visit us. Goodness, Sophie, you will be my aunt now."

That stopped her in her tracks. "Good heavens, the prince will be your uncle-in-law. I will be your aunt? That sounds rather illegal, mayhap even immoral."

"Since I'm your aunt as well, I would rather consider it interesting."

"Do you know, Roxanne, Papa will be very surprised indeed when I present him with Julian, a prince. I'm sure he never expected anything at all to come from my Season. A waste of groats, he always said."

Corinne said, "You are marrying my son, Sophie, surely only one single small step from attaining heavenly rewards. Ah, how very pleased I am. The two of you are doing exactly as your mama and I wished."

"Mama would be very happy, indeed," Sophie said, and felt the blurring of tears. She swallowed and sat down on a plush settee.

"Devlin, is our patient showing improvement?"

Devlin smiled at Corinne from the doorway and said to Sophie, "My dear auntie-in-law, Julian asked me whether the two of you were married. What could I say?"

"Devlin," Roxanne said very slowly, "have you been making mischief?"

"You mean I told him he was indeed married, and why didn't he remember it? Surely a gallon of laudanum could be no excuse for forgetting your wife."

Laughter burst out, but no one had a chance to say anything, because Pouffer glided into the room, a Meissen teapot in his hand. "Your grace, Richard Langworth is here. Lady Merrick is here as well.

"As you know, Lady Merrick has sent several messages, which none of you have answered. May I congratulate you on your oversight? As for Richard Langworth, if he had sent a message wishing the prince well, I fancy I should have burned it myself. I have brought very hot tea. It is entirely your decision what to do with it."

Devlin rubbed his hands together as he rose. "What a fine day this has become. Show them in, Pouffer. Ah, wait a moment." He walked to Pouffer and spoke low into his ear. Pouffer gave him a long assessing look, nodded. "I shall show in Mr. Langworth."

"And my sister, please," Roxanne said. She looked around the room at the sudden silence, at the suddenly long faces. "Stop it, all of you. We enjoyed a few minutes of laughter. Don't feel guilty about it, any of you. Now that two of our principals are here, we can deal with business. The prince is safe; he will not know what is going on."

"Actually, I will, Roxanne. No, don't look appalled. I will not fall over. However, I will be seated."

He was wearing a dark blue velvet dressing gown, his big feet bare. Sophie didn't make a move toward him. She searched his face. "You know what you're doing, my lord?"

He smiled at her as Devlin helped ease him down in a large brocade wing chair. "Yes. Don't fret."

"Dearest," said Corinne. She rushed over to examine his eyes, lightly trace her fingertips over his whiskers, pat his shoulder. "You look much better than yesterday. I shall give you a cup of oolong tea. It will strengthen your stitches."

Pouffer cleared his throat from the doorway. "Your visitors are here, Prince, your grace."

When Richard and Leah entered Corinne's sitting room, Richard's eyes immediately went to Julian.

"Here you are having tea when I had believed you near death's door."

"Not quite. But forgive me if I don't rise," Julian said.

Richard didn't answer. Instead, he was staring at Leah. "You look different today."

"I am wearing one of Lily's gowns."

Richard grew very still.

"Your hair is fashioned like Lily's," Corinne said. "All

the braids atop the head, but with you, Leah, there are some softening curls over your ears. It's a distinctive look. Why, Leah? What is this all about?"

Leah said, "I like it, nothing more than that."

Julian said, "You're wearing Lily's locket. I had thought she was—"

"You thought she was buried in it? No, Vicky evidently kept it," Richard said, then turned to Leah. "Did she give it to you?"

Leah nodded. "She said since I would be her sister, she believed I should have it. You do not like that I am wearing it, Richard?"

He said slowly, "I suppose our portraits can be set in the locket."

Julian felt the pain building in his side. He ignored it. He said, "Orvald Manners finally told us you were behind Roxanne's first kidnapping."

Richard glanced from face to face. "I regret that. I shouldn't have done it. Forgive me, Roxanne."

"Of course I shan't forgive you. You're a putrid slug, Richard."

Julian said softly, "I wonder at the depths of your regret if Manners had raped Roxanne."

"I would expect to fight you to the death in a duel."

"No, you would not have fought Julian, you would have fought me," Devlin said. "I am even a better shot than Julian, so I would have killed you. Such a chance you took, knowing if your plan had succeeded, you would be a dead man. I cannot believe you hired that idiot to take her—and the wrong lady, too."

Richard turned to the prince. "So you will marry Sophie."

"If we are not already wed, then yes."

"We are not yet wed, Prince," Sophie said, "but as soon as you are well, then the Prince of Ravenscar will be married in the village church to a worthy maiden—namely, myself. We will invite everyone. It will be grand."

Leah said, a sneer marring her mouth, "You will be rich,

Sophie, but it is Roxanne who will be the future Duchess of Brabante."

Sophie said, "This is very true. It would seem to me you should endeavor to be a bit more conciliating, Aunt Leah. No, I disowned you, didn't I? Well, no matter. Remember we will be neighbors."

"I really don't care what you do, Sophie. I do wonder, however, what your dear mother would think of all this."

"My mother would wonder why you, her sister, treat me like—I am even boring myself repeating this very old business. You are what you are.

"Richard, evidently Devlin isn't going to kill you, since Roxanne managed to save herself from Manners. A great pity, I think, since you have proved that you are a nasty piece of goods and a danger not only to the prince but to Roxanne and me." She cocked her head at him. "Do you know, Richard, I must say this again—it amazes me that you have known the prince all your life and yet you do not immediately accept his word that he did not kill Lily. Yet I, who have known him for perhaps a month, recognize his integrity, his innate goodness and fierce honor, all the way to my bones."

⊸⊷ 70 ⊶⊷

There was dead silence.

Richard jerked away and began pacing. "This is all damnable," he said over his shoulder, and continued his pacing. He turned back to Julian. "All have heard that Harlan Whittaker, your own man of business, betrayed you. Why did he take Roxanne?"

Julian shook his head. "He fancied himself in love with her and planned to steal her away, to wed her, which, naturally, she wouldn't have allowed. That leaves you and your feeble attempts, Richard. What should I do with you?"

Richard stood mute, his hands clenched at his sides. Julian saw the misery and pain in his eyes. For a moment, he also saw the boy he'd known so many years before, full of laughter, ready for any adventure, no deceit in him at all. But Richard was no longer a boy, and Lily was dead three long years. Julian didn't think he could bear it. He waved a hand toward the settee. "Both of you, sit down."

Leah, who'd stood ramrod straight and stiff, her eyes down, sat, smoothing her skirts around her. Richard, however, remained standing. Alone.

Corinne said, "I shan't ask either of you to enjoy a cup of tea. Now, Richard, answer my son."

But Richard remained silent.

"What does your father say about this, Richard?" Roxanne asked him.

"He is very upset about these—attacks. He is spending most of his time in the library, alone."

As you are alone, Julian thought.

Sophie moved close to Julian now, placed her hand on his shoulder, and her fingers began to lightly massage him.

His side was aching fiercely, the stitches pulling whenever he moved, but he knew he had to finish this. He said, "I remember when Lily died your father's grief was deep and hard. However, he told me he didn't believe that I'd shot her, and he held me close, sharing his grief with me.

"When he asked me to come to Hardcross Manor, I believed he wanted to heal the rift between us."

Richard said, "I was surprised and angry when he told me you were coming, that you were bringing all of them with you. As protection? I remember he smiled and said something about your finally finding yourself another wife—her." He pointed to Roxanne. "I had written to him about her, you see, told him how your feelings were engaged—with her.

"I'll admit it, when I realized the opportunity presented to me, I knew I could finally make you suffer as my family has suffered, only Roxanne got away from Manners. Bloody hell, she nearly killed him." He smacked his fist into his palm. "I wish she'd shot him. I didn't know what he intended, I didn't . . ." He shrugged.

Julian said, "When we arrived at the manor, your father called me into his library and spoke to me about my own father, what a fine man he was. I was moved, Richard, since I'd always thought of my father as a foolish, doddering old man, not a man worthy to be loved and respected and admired. I was so very grateful to your father for making my own father come alive for me, showing me the man I had never known. I sensed great caring of your father for mine, and thus for me. I sat down to dinner with you with hope in my heart, but that was my mistake."

Richard said, "Do you know what he said to me, his only son? He said he'd asked you to Hardcross Manor for me. He said it was time for me to get on with my life, he said I was growing too alone, that I had become obsessed."

Leah spoke, the first time since coming into the room, her voice flat. "Why did you never marry, Richard? You are thirty-two, are you not?"

Richard said nothing, didn't look at her.

She said quietly, "Your father is right. You never even let yourself get close to another lady because of your obsession with your dead sister—with Lily. And me? Roxanne was right, you searched me out in Yorkshire, and I fell right into your net. You must have believed yourself very smart indeed when I came flying after you to London, moved in with my sister and niece, and told you everything that was said in that household, everything you wanted and needed to know.

"Vicky told me how you'd adored Lily, how you still did, and how if I wore her gown, arranged my hair like hers, even wore the bloody locket, you would admire me more. She knew your supposed affection for me was all an act on your part, didn't she?" When he only shook his head, Leah laughed, a harsh, grating sound that held no amusement at all. "All the drama in this room, the mysteries that should have been uncovered years ago, and a score of crushing memories that eat into your hearts, and so much blame. I fancy all this blame can be spread around.

"But there is only one fool in this room." She laughed again, pointed to herself. "Look at me, Richard! Am I the image of your long-dead sister?"

He gave her a long look. "I never liked that gown on Lily."

Leah stared at him. "So you admit it?"

He said nothing.

"Yes, if I were you I'd keep quiet as well. Here's some

truth for you—all you did was use me, Richard. Why, then, do you want to marry me? I could give you no more information. Why, Richard? Or was your proposal all part of your elaborate ruse, to ensure I was fully secured and tied to you, that I would do whatever it was you wished me to do?"

The silence stretched endlessly. Leah laughed, a wrenching laugh that made Roxanne want to leap up and strangle Richard Langworth, but she knew what happened was her sister's decision. Leah said, "Well, I see you won't wish to answer me. You're not entirely stupid, are you? I hate this gown, too, and my hair?" She laughed again. "My hair looks absurd."

Roxanne said, "Richard, would Lily have applauded you for your actions? Or would she be horrified at what you've tried to do, at how you've stopped living your life and wallowed in a grief so corrosive it poisons the very air you breathe? Would she say your actions no longer have anything to do with your grief for her? That you know nothing else, and thus you are trapped in your hatred and it has become you?"

Richard began pacing again. "Lily would understand. She always understood; she loved her family more than she ever loved you, Julian. I am not obsessed, damn you, Roxanne, I am not."

"Were you going to kill me, Richard?" Roxanne asked.

"No. Manners would have taken you to the Continent, left you there. I swear to you, there was nothing about rape."

Roxanne walked to him, stared him in the face, drew back her fist, and slammed it hard in his belly. He whooshed out breath, staggered a bit. "I don't think you would have cared what Manners did to me. You are a coward, and you don't deserve anything good in your miserable life. My sister asked you a good question: Why do you still wish to wed her after using her so abominably?"

Leah jumped to her feet. She looked at each of them, then her eyes came to rest on Julian. "It is all your fault. If you hadn't murdered Lily, none of this would have happened." She turned to Richard, her hands on her hips. "I find I agree with Roxanne. You are a coward, Richard, and you have no honor. Your father is right. You have grown twisted in your grief. As for Vicky, who knows what she is really thinking about anything. You are not a healthy man, Richard. What you are is pathetic."

Leah walked out of the room, not looking back.

Julian looked at Richard. "I believe, finally, I know what happened to Lily."

❧ *72* ❧

Hardcross Manor
THAT EVENING

Julian said quietly from the doorway of the drawing room, "Vicky."

She looked up from the book she was reading. She didn't move, merely regarded him without expression. "You should not be here, Prince. Surely you are still too weak from your injury. You were stabbed only two days ago."

He had to keep standing, he thought, despite the vicious gnawing in his side. He *would* keep standing. He had to finish this. Now. He said, "I am well enough."

"Why is Richard standing behind you? He might have a gun, you know; he might shoot you and bury you near to where you shot Lily. Don't you think that fitting? You're here as well, Papa. What is this?"

Baron Purley walked into the drawing room and sat down next to his daughter. He picked up her hand. It lay limp between his strong ones. He studied her long fingers, so much like Lily's. "Would you like to have a Season in London, Vicky?"

"I? Now? Why should I?"

The baron said, "Did you not tell Leah you didn't wish

to have a Season because you might meet a prince and he would kill you, like Lily was killed? But you know, Vicky, you know the prince did not kill Lily. You know it."

Vicky grew very still. She stared at each man's face.

Julian said, "I know, Vicky. I know."

She looked from her father's face to her brother's, both set and still. She looked down at her father's big hands. She shook her head.

Julian said, "I know Lily never had a lover, Vicky. It simply wasn't in her, not the girl I knew all my life, not the girl I married. I also could see no guilt in anyone else. So I was forced to face it—she either killed herself for some reason I simply could not fathom, or something else entirely happened. For the life of me, I couldn't find my way to the truth. Until Leah came into the room today wearing Lily's grown, her hair dressed like Lily's hair. By you, Vicky.

"Tell us, Vicky. Tell us what happened that afternoon in the garden. Tell us what happened between you and Lily."

Vicky never looked away from him, but Julian knew she wasn't seeing him, she was seeing her sister on that hot, long-ago afternoon in the wildly blooming garden.

She said, her voice far away, as if reciting a story she'd read, "You still don't know anything, Prince—particularly, the truth. The fact is Lily was going to leave me."

"What do you mean she was going to leave you?" Baron Purley squeezed her white limp hand, but there seemed to be no life in that hand. He said gently, "Vicky, Lily was here nearly every day after she married the prince. When he was gone from Ravenscar on his shipping business, she spent entire days here; she even slept here in her old bedroom. I saw very little change. What do you mean she was going to leave you?"

There was no pain in Vicky's simple words as she spoke them, her voice utterly without feeling. "I killed her. I killed my own sister."

Julian clutched the back of a wing chair. He felt nausea and pain, and couldn't think. Then the sickness passed, leaving only the pain. "Tell us why you killed her, Vicky." He walked slowly to sit on her other side. He raised his hand and cupped her cheek. "It's time, you know, time to understand what happened, so all of us can place it in the past, where it belongs."

Richard was still standing by the open doorway, his face deathly white. He said, "Please, Vicky, tell us."

Vicky looked again at her hand held between her father's big ones. She raised her eyes to Julian's face. "Lily loved you, Prince, she loved you too much, more than I wanted her to, but since I knew you all my life, knew you liked me, I wasn't all that upset when she married you. She would live at Ravenscar. If you went to London, I would go with you. Everything would continue on the way it always had.

"I don't think you realized it, but our souls were one, Lily and I, and we both knew it, even though Lily never said the words to me. From the very beginning I recognized I was part of her, and she was the very best part of me. She was my mother, my sister, my very best friend, and she loved me without reservation. But then it happened."

"What happened?" the baron asked.

"I came to her in the garden. Her hands were dirty from pulling up weeds, and she was smiling, wildly happy, and it burst right out of her. 'I am going to have a baby, Vicky. The Prince and I are going to be parents.'

"She'd come to tell me she was letting me go, that it was time I matured, that I spread my wings and became my own woman.

"I couldn't believe these words came from her mouth. She nearly sang the words, she was so happy. She told me it was time for me to leave my home, time to get away from her, time for me to go to London and have a Season, as she had. She told me I would find a gentleman who would please me, that I would marry, and have my own children. She told me I didn't need a mother any longer—namely, her—that since our own mother had died so long before, she had played that role to me, but now I was grown, I was my own woman. She would now be my sister, and I would soon become an aunt.

"I knew to my soul I didn't want that, knew that I wanted only her, and I wanted her forever, but I saw she was resolute. I knew she'd made up her mind. And so I finally agreed and left her. I fetched one of your pistols, Papa, and I found her still in the garden, humming, happier now because she'd done her duty by me and set me free. I still remember her face—how very radiant she looked.

"I told her we belonged together, that I wouldn't let this child in her womb continue to grow and come out of her and make her leave me. She tried to grab the gun, to protect her babe, and the gun went off." Vicky stared down at her hand, still held in her father's. "She looked up at me in the instant before she died. She smiled and told me it would be all right. Then she was gone."

Julian felt the past whip into the present and crush him. Lily was pregnant with his child, and Vicky had killed her, killed his babe. He felt such pain he wanted to yell. This damnable girl had been responsible for all the pain and death and misery. He wanted to kill her, to take her white neck between his hands and choke the life out of her, as she had killed Lily, as she had killed his child. *His child, dead with its mother, never to know life, to know him, his father, or Lily, his mother—*

Julian had believed he'd understood, but he hadn't. He'd thought of the obsession in father and son but had not considered Vicky, not really, until he realized obsession was part of her as well, and he'd believed Vicky had considered her sister marrying him as betrayal. But she hadn't. No, it was all about their unborn child.

He hadn't realized how profoundly Lily had affected Vicky's life. But he did now, only it was too late. And what would he do? Accuse Vicky of murder and see her hanged?

No justice, he thought, for Lily, for him, for Richard, or for Vicky's father. He wanted only to lie in bed and sleep away the pain in his body and the pain in his heart.

There was not a single sound in the room except for Vicky's sobs and her low strangled words, "I wanted to die, too, but there was only one bullet in your gun, Papa, only one bullet." Lily's father drew her against him. Lily's brother stood, again utterly alone, in the center of the drawing room.

Julian looked from the baron to Richard to Vicky, now lying limp against her father's chest, her father's hand lightly stroking her hair.

Julian knew the truth would remain in this room. He also knew that what Richard had done, what his father had done, that all of it would remain in this room as well. None of it would ever be spoken of again.

Such misery, he thought, *such utter waste,* and he thought again of his unborn child and wanted to weep.

Ravenscar
FOUR WEEKS LATER

Corinne sat in the Ravenscar pew at the front of the beautiful Norman church, built by the conqueror's own hands. The church had been protected by the long line of Brabante dukes throughout years of interminable wars and destruction. Ravenscar was large for a local church, and most villagers were able to cram inside. Those not able to be seated in the row upon row of wooden benches lined up against all the walls. There were even those who stood outside the open doors, listening to the service. All the Ravenscar servants, Pouffer at their head, were seated directly behind Corinne. She knew the moment the service was over they would scramble madly back to Ravenscar to set out enough food to feed the entire village. It would be a fine celebration, and Julian's wine cellar would be severely depleted by the end of the day.

Corinne looked at the two couples standing tall and proud before the Reverend Hubbard, known as the Young Vicar, having attained only his sixty-fifth year. He was so happy he looked fit to bursting with it. She listened to his words, beautiful, rich words that flowed smoothly out of his mouth, words that would bind these beautiful young people together. The four of them were so happy the air seemed to glow around them.

She listened to her son's strong voice, to Sophie's sweet one, so pure and happy, and saw dear Roxanne looking at Devlin through her veil, and who knew what she was thinking? When she spoke her vows, her voice was resonant and calm, reaching to every ear in the church, and to Corinne's ear, she already sounded like a duchess, and she smiled, thinking, *You will surely set Lorelei back on her heels, Roxanne.* Devlin, so vampire-white he was today, he'd announced to them all, and wasn't it perfect for his wedding? He was so obviously pleased with himself that it fairly burst from him, sounded arrogant and happy; *odd,* she thought, *but true.*

Both uncle and nephew were dressed in stark black. Roxanne wore a pale yellow gown, her glorious red hair piled atop her head, lazy curls drifting down to touch her shoulders. As for Corinne's soon-to-be daughter-in-law, Sophie wore a gown of pure white. She looked very young and innocent, yet, Corinne remembered, she was older than Corinne had been when she'd wedded Julian's father. *Ah, it was so long ago. How was one to remember what one felt so many years before?* But these two, they were right for each other, their bond deep and abiding.

Corinne heard a slight sniff, and looked from the corner of her eye toward Devlin's parents, the Duke and Duchess of Brabante. Both were sitting straight and proud, the duke obviously content, but Lorelei, dressed in blazing purple, mouth pursed, was not at all pleased the ceremony wasn't in Saint Paul's Cathedral in London so all who counted could see her son's nuptials. And what, Corinne wondered, did the old besom really think about Roxanne taking her place one of these days? She could imagine Lorelei bursting her corset stays with rage. Julian had told her Devlin had confided to his father that Roxanne was gifted with financial matters, and everything had changed. Devlin said his mother had actually bestowed one stingy smile upon Roxanne. Corinne didn't believe it, but still she'd wager the old bat was deliriously happy the Monroe coffers would overflow, and who cared if she was only a baron's daughter and her hair was the color of sin? But she'd carped and carped about Saint Paul's, where she and Devlin's father had pledged their troth so many years before. Devlin had patted his mother's hand. "It is all right, Mother, you will be a radiant star shining amongst low-lying clouds." Whatever that meant. To Corinne's surprise, Devlin had told Roxanne his mother had shut her mouth. *A radiant star shining amongst low-lying clouds?*

As for Roxanne's father, Baron Roche, he towered over those who sat next to him, his eyes—Roxanne's green eyes—glittering with pleasure. His hair was a rich burnished copper color, threaded only lightly with white at his temples, a beautiful man, a kind man, filled with humor and the sheer pleasure of being alive, and she wondered, had Leah become a shrew because the father had preferred Roxanne? Who knew why people were like they were? Sophie had told Corinne, laughing, that Roxanne promised to continue dealing with her father's financial investments. She'd added that Julian was giving it consideration as well.

As for Leah, Lady Merrick, she sat three rows behind Corinne, alone, silent, contained. Had she changed a bit since Richard Langworth? She appeared more aloof, perhaps, more measured in her speech to her sister and niece. Was she really less of a viper now? Corinne was surprised to see Richard Langworth standing against one of the nave pillars at the back of the church. She hadn't seen him come in. Was he looking fixedly at Leah? What was he thinking? She thought again about what Julian had said—Vicky had accidentally shot Lily while showing her their father's new pistol, and then she'd been too paralyzed with fear to say anything. Somehow, Corinne thought, deep down, she knew there was more, but she would never know.

But what did it matter? Lily was long dead; there was no more strife between the Langworths and her beloved son. As for Baron Purley and Vicky, they'd left two weeks before for America, to Washington, the colonists' capital, but

Richard had remained, the master of Hardcross Manor. What would happen, she wondered, between Richard and her son?

She heard a slight cough and looked over to see Lord and Lady Hammersmith—James and Corrie Sherbrooke—sitting next to Sophie's father, the Reverend Wilkie, who'd acted when he'd arrived at Ravenscar three days before like he'd been shot in the gut, so disbelieving he'd been of his daughter's "uncalled for" good fortune, the obnoxious bore. Corrie actually looked pregnant now, and as lovely as could be, gowned in pale blue, her husband holding her hand, never, it seemed to Corinne, letting his wife out of his sight, and wasn't that lovely?

The service was over. Reverend Hubbard beamed as he gave the two grooms permission to kiss their brides. Corinne watched Julian lift Sophie's veil off her face. He looked down at her, but not all that far down, laughed, picked her up, and twirled her around. When he lowered her, he gave her a smacking kiss that brought laughter and cheering from the crowd. There was even more laughter when Sophie grabbed his face between her mittened hands and kissed him back.

The crowd seemed to hold its collective breath as they watched Devlin and Roxanne. Devlin slowly lifted his bride's veil, looked at her for a very long moment, then slowly brought her against him. He kissed her gently, then rested his white cheek against her equally white cheek. He closed his eyes as they stood silent together.

Corinne found herself looking up at the beautiful stained-glass window her husband had commissioned for the church back before the turn of the century. A sudden beam of sunlight speared through. Corinne lifted her face to the warmth. *Our children are joined, Bethanne, as we wished them to be. I know you can see them and know you are smiling along with me. I miss you, dear friend, but know I will keep watch over our beautiful daughter.* Corinne felt the warmth deepen, felt it all the way to her bones, felt a peace flow through the air itself, and she thought of Julian's father, an old man who'd worshipped her all those years ago, and the gift he'd given her, a prince.

⇥ 74 ⇤

The Shapewick Inn
THAT NIGHT IN PLYMOUTH

Roxanne paced back and forth in front of her new husband, who was lying at his ease on the huge tester bed in the center of the corner room that looked out over Plymouth Harbor. He was naked, a single sheet pulled to his waist, and he was harder, he thought, than the floorboards beneath the bed. He eyed her with amusement mixed with lust. She was wearing a sinful pale pink peignoir, sheer as a veil, over her equally sinful pale pink nightgown, striding back and forth in front of him, the long-legged stride of a young Amazon. *His* Amazon. He wanted to grab her and consign that pale pink to the ether, but he knew her—and prepared to enjoy himself. She whirled about to face him, her hands on her hips, the firelight behind her outlining her long legs, haloing her glorious hair, hanging all loose down her back. He thought of those long legs of hers around his flanks and shook with it.

"It's true, I tell you, Devlin. It's true! The little hussy was laughing just now in the hallway, telling me how the prince was helpless to say no to her, how she seduced him in his estate room surrounded by all four spaniels—two full days *before* the wedding. She all but danced off to their bedchamber after she whispered to me she knew *everything* now, and I didn't know spit, and here I was, her *elderly* aunt. She laughed and laughed, telling me how much fun I was going to have if you were but half the lover the prince was. Then she looked mournful and said she couldn't imagine any man being a more superb lover than the prince, but doubtless you and I could admire our mutual whiteness if you weren't all that certain what to do. I could have smacked her, Devlin.

"And then I could have smacked you. You want to know why?"

He nodded, trying not to laugh.

"I could have smacked you because I remembered that night in the hallway and you wanted me against the wall, and I was eager, I'll admit it, Devlin, I was excited and feeling things I've never felt before. I wanted to learn what this lovemaking business was all about. But *nooooo*—you became all saintly and noble, and sent me back to my bedchamber with a pat on the cheek. But the prince didn't send Sophie on her way, did he? No, he did not wait." She waved her fist at him.

Devlin was laughing so hard he nearly fell off the bed, aware that his bride was standing, watching him, tapping her foot on the carpet. When he was finally able to speak, he said, still grinning like a fool, "Sophie is a wonderful actress to convince you so completely. She made fine sport with you." He laughed again. "My darling, listen to me. When Julian told me a man shouldn't take a woman until she was his wife, he meant it. Julian has so much honor, it sometimes makes me want to punch him, like this time, since I wanted you so very much. But you see, I took what he said to heart. I believed him. I know he would never take Sophie until"—Devlin looked at the ormolu clock on the mantel—"until about now."

Roxanne's eyes were narrowed on his face. "She could not fool me; surely, she could not. Did she?"

He nodded, laughed, then choked.

Roxanne waited until he got himself together again,

wiped his eyes, then said, her own eyes even more narrowed now, "How I wish you'd never asked him anything at all. What prompted you to ask him? Who cares what he thinks? Look at the result. We missed our wall opportunity at midnight because he'd already told you his damnable marriage rule, and you believed he was right, damn both of you.

"And there you were, kissing me until I was mad for you, but you kept saying over and over you wouldn't dishonor me, wouldn't have me naked until our wedding night."

"Would you believe I suffered more than you did?"

"No."

"Well, I did, since I knew exactly what I was missing. Do you know, dearest one, I shall congratulate Sophie in the morning for pulling such an amazing stunt on her aunt. However, Roxanne, very soon you will be naked and beautiful, your cheeks all rosy with delight from the pleasure I will give you. Forget making love against the wall at midnight. This is much better. I think our wedding night has been perfect so far, don't you? Come here, Roxanne."

She frowned down at him, her voice snide. "I assume you know how to continue this business, since you've had simply *scores* of mistresses. That wasn't a lie, was it?"

He grinned, patted the side of the bed. "No more than two score, but you know, I suppose it's possible I could have forgotten how one accomplishes this business in the past four weeks of sainthood. Come here, let's see what happens."

When she was stretched out beside him, Devlin leaned down, kissed her, and kept kissing her as he stripped her naked. He leaned up and stared down at her. Slowly, his hand cupped her beautiful white breast. His leg moved to press hers apart. "Now you are as naked as I am. *Hmmm,* what is next, I wonder?"

"That feels rather nice. Whatever you're doing, don't stop."

"I shan't, my darling, I shan't. Ah, look at us, Roxanne. I believe I am the whiter."

She studied them for a moment, pressed together, then, "No, I am the whiter."

"No matter, we blend perfectly together, just as I knew we would."

Roxanne kissed his chin, his nose, his eyebrows. "Thee and me," she whispered against his mouth. "Have I told you how much I love you, Devlin?"

"Not since this morning, after I kissed you in the church. I believe I told you I loved you more. As we'll blend our whiteness, let's blend our love. Come, let me show you pleasure now."

⋙ ⋘

In the other corner bedchamber of the Shapewick Inn, Julian was grinning down at his new wife. "I cannot believe you told such an outrageous tale to your poor aged aunt. Don't worry, Devlin will make her realize you were pulling both her legs and her arms as well. Seducing me two full days before our wedding? Beware, Roxanne is liable to clout you once she realizes what you did."

Sophie giggled. "I got her," she said between giggles. "She was red with rage at me—her little niece—learning things she didn't know *before* she did."

He was laughing with her until she began kissing him all over his face, her hands stroking over him, his chest, his belly, and lower, until he moaned. Finally, he came over her, stretched out on top of her, pressed her into the soft mattress, and soon she was panting between her kisses. She whispered against his throat, "Tell me again you love me, Prince."

"I love you, and my four dogs love you."

"And the unborn pups?"

"Yes, the pups, too."

She touched her fingertips to his beautiful mouth, his chin, stroked her thumbs over his black eyebrows. "I am the only woman in the world for you. Because you are a smart man, it did not take you all that long to realize it."

"I did but what my mother wished me to do."

"And my mother. How I miss her, Prince. If only she had not died, if only—"

"I know, sweetheart. But I have this belief deep inside me that your mother was there in the church with us, and she was happy, Sophie.

"Now, my noble self is brimming with lust that needs to be requited." And he kissed her, his mouth going down her body as her hand had his. In the next minute, Sophie burst with pleasure, and she screamed with the power of it. She would swear she heard Cletus barking his head off when the prince threw back his head and yelled to the ceiling.

Epilogue

Ravenscar
FEBRUARY 2, 1832

Julian read the letter from Baron Purley once again.

Dear Prince:

It is snowing today in Washington, and the winds gust through the trees and make the windows rattle. Vicky and I are just returned to our home only one short mile from where the American president Andrew Jackson resides. We attended his New Year's reception, a wild affair given to much drink, immoderate jollity, and dancing. Withal, I find President Andrew Jackson a magnificent man.

Two nights ago, we attended a ball at Straithberry House, and Vicky laughed. She danced with two gentlemen. I believe she is healing. The past will never be forgot, but perhaps she will learn to deal with it. I doubt, however, there will ever be forgiveness; that is too much to ask.

I wish to tell you, Prince, that I betrayed your father because of my greed. When he gave me his portrait to hold for you, he also entrusted to me a sealed envelope to give to you as well, when you reached manhood. I opened it and read it. It was the clues to the magic jewel. I could not find the spears of stone, and I searched and searched. When I remembered your father's portrait, I tore free some paper from the back of the frame and slipped your father's letter inside, hoping you would find the hiding place. I planned to retrieve the treasure before you could.

But you didn't know where these spears of stone were, no one knew, including Corinne. Sophie guessed the stalactites in the cave, but I had dug beneath those spears, probably all of them over the years. Nothing.

Before Vicky left me this evening to go to bed, she said she remembered something, and she told me she knew where the spears of stone were.

Vicky says you are to go down to the beach below the promontory. There are three rocks there; you will recognize them, since you and Richard always played there as boys. She said the middle one is shaped particularly like a spear, the other two not so much, really. She said that beneath the middle rock must be the flat and ugly jewel, whatever it is.

Can it be so simple? So mundane? In any case, I hope you find it, Prince, whatever it is. Is it magic, like your father believed? If so, where, I wonder, did your father obtain it? Does it come from an ancient time? Perhaps it belonged to Merlin? Like your father, I wonder if it, whatever it is, will work for you, his son. I pray you will forgive me for my deceit.

Your father told me once he wished he could know you as a man grown, but he knew his time was running short. I told him I knew to my bones you would be a man he would be proud of, a man who would make his way well in this world, that you would conduct yourself fairly and honorably, and you would love your family to the fullest of your heart. He died two days later.

*I wish, too, you could have known your father.
Before I left with Vicky for America, I visited his grave
once more, a very fine resting place your mother
keeps covered with flowers. I told him he now had a
fine daughter to birth sons to carry on his line.*

*I think of Lily and know in my heart there would be
no blame in her against her sister. My own regret is
deep for not seeing what Vicky was becoming. I begin
to believe pain has become an old friend, but perhaps,
in time, the pain will lessen, if only this bitter winter
weather will go away.*

*You should know Richard writes he is attempting
to court Leah again. I do not know if she will forgive
him. We will see. He also wrote he is having the
Dower House rebuilt. Do you believe it possible the
two of you might become friends again?*

*I thank you for telling Vicky you forgave her, that
you didn't blame her. Mayhap you will even come to
forgive her, for you have great kindness.*

My regards to your wife,

*Your respectful servant,
Rupert Langworth,
Baron Purley*

Ravenscar
THE NEXT DAY

Cletus barked, butted Julian's leg with his nose. "What
is it? You wish me to admire your pups? They'll be as
big as you are within the year."

He walked outside to see two spaniels, Tynley and
Maude, rolling over and over, barking, yipping, trying to
bite each other's necks. Their two siblings lived currently

in London with Devlin and Roxanne, city dogs, Sophie snorted, and wouldn't they be spoiled rotten, used to sitting on pillows, waited on hand and paw, not knowing what it was like to face death, racing toward a cliff on a dare?

Roxanne was pregnant, Devlin had written to him, and they were looking forward to bringing a new vampling into the world, and Julian could see the two of them laughing as they sampled this new word.

Sophie came out through the estate-room doorway. It was blowing hard today, and the wind whipped her hair around her head, plastered her skirts to her legs. She waved at him, and he saw she was wearing the damnably ugly ring they'd found in a lead box wrapped in oilskin some two feet under the beach sand, beneath that middle stone Vicky had described. Odd that it fit her perfectly. Odd as well, she said wearing it made her feel blessed. Blessed how? She didn't know, simply blessed. As for any magic in the thing, they'd both played with it, trying to evoke some sort of power. But there didn't seem to be any.

She was striding to him, all beautiful long legs. There was something different about her lately, something different about the way she moved and how she sometimes sat, simply smiling at nothing in particular. But what was it? When he asked, she merely smiled and waved away his words.

Life, he thought; it was a chain of miracles that sometimes gave you a glimpse of Heaven.

Keep reading for an excerpt from

THE VALCOURT HEIRESS

by Catherine Coulter.
Now available from Jove Books.

$\Longrightarrow$ *I* $\Longleftarrow$

Valcourt Castle
MAY 1278

She knew she had to do something. If she did nothing, her mother would force her to wed Jason of Brennan.

Her mother, Abbess Helen of Meizerling Abbey, had swooped in before nightfall, surrounded by her own contingent of soldiers, imperious and arrogant, recent widow of the Earl of Valcourt, and taken charge. Men stared at her beautiful face, at her white skin and golden hair untouched by gray, heard her velvety voice carry to every corner in the great hall, and quickly obeyed every command that flowed from her lovely mouth. As for her grief-stricken daughter, Helen informed her that she would wed in two days.

She'd stared at the woman who was her mother, a woman she didn't know, but knew what she was—a witch with unimagined powers, people said. They spoke of her behind their hands, their voices low, their fear pulsing in the air.

She'd never seen her mother do anything magick the three times she'd been in her presence. Ah, but the stories— the neighbor's wife choking to death because Lady Helen had wanted to buy her mare and had been refused; the plague striking down a village where Lady Helen had been insulted by the local monk; and now her own father, lying dead, no reason for it that their healer could see, hale and hearty but two days before. Now he lay stretched out on his bed, his hands folded over his chest, dressed in his finest tunic and hose, his beautiful sword strapped to his waist, his men below in the great hall drinking themselves insensible. What would happen now? There was no heir, only a daughter who had no power, and her newly arrived mother, a witch who could smite them all with but a wave of her hand, and the soldiers who surrounded her.

She had to do something or she would be sold to Jason of Brennan, a man she'd seen only once, just an hour before, well-made and young, but something deep inside her had recoiled when he'd turned his dark eyes on her. There were black secrets in those eyes of his. Her mother's eyes were the light gray of storm clouds, and she feared her more than the Devil.

She slipped out of Valcourt's great hall, pulling her cloak about her, for rain-bloated clouds hung low in the sky, obscuring the few stars, and the chill night wind howled. It occurred to her only after she'd crept across the inner bailey to the stables that she had no idea where she'd go. It didn't matter, she would think of something. She usually did. When she heard a man's voice, she nearly screamed. It was coming closer. What to do?

2

They rode single file on the narrow rutted path through the Clandor Forest, a place of ancient magick, it was said, and wicked magick. Thick pines, oaks, and maples crowded in on them, canopying overhead. The leaves would tangle together in another month. Warm afternoon sunlight speared through the rustling leaves.

Garron lifted his face to the sunlight, felt the soft breeze against his skin. It was a day a man was pleased to be alive, a day that gave optimism to the days to come. And God had also wrought a miracle—no rain for three straight days. Aye, a holy miracle, Aleric said to all the men, and told them how his grandsire had once bragged about a two-day trek with no rain. But three days without the heavens pouring buckets of rain down your neck? It was unheard of. They were blessed, surely it was a good omen. Everyone was quiet, thinking his own thoughts. Garron thought of his brother Arthur, and wondered how he'd died; he'd been a young man, only thirty years of age. The king hadn't known. As for his men, Garron imagined most were probably wondering what their lives would become now that he was Lord

Garron, Earl of Wareham, a nobleman with land and a castle, and income from farms, two small towns, and two keeps. And mayhap they were thinking of their visit to Lord Severin and Lady Hastings, wondering if Wareham would be as impressive as Oxborough.

"It will not delay you overmuch, Garron," King Edward had told him. Then those famous Plantagenet blue eyes had sparkled cajolery and a bit of humor to leaven the effect. "Before you travel to Wareham, you can deliver this request to Severin from his king." He nodded toward his secretary and the Chancellor of England, Robert Burnell, who handed Garron a tightly rolled parchment tied with a thin black cord. Even at the most inconvenient of times, which this most assuredly was, a man never turned down his king's request, and so the king's parchment, carefully wrapped in oilskin, rested safe against Garron's chest all the way from London to East Anglia, to Oxborough, the seat of the Earl of Oxborough, Lord Severin of Langthorne-Trent.

He didn't have the slightest wish to read the king's missive, and only sighed, thinking of the three days added to his journey to his new home. On the other hand, Garron hadn't seen Severin since the king had sent him to Oxborough nearly a year and a half before, to become the dying Fawke of Trent's heir and son-in-law. He'd become a husband and the Earl of Oxborough in a span of three hours. And now Severin had an infant son.

Garron smiled to himself as he remembered the look of utter contentment on his friend's hard face when he'd held his babe, Fawke, named after the former earl, and remarked in the most foolish way that he was surely the handsomest babe in all Christendom. And Lady Hastings watched, smiling, sitting in her countess's chair, humming as she sewed clothes for the future earl.

Near midnight, when all had retired, Garron and Severin sat alone in Oxborough's great hall, in front of the massive fireplace, a chess board between them. Severin moved his king's knight, sat back in his chair, laced his fingers over his hard belly, and sighed. "Do you know I find myself missing de Lucy, the madman who poisoned his own wife so he could have Hastings?" He studied Garron's pawn move, quickly slid his queen's bishop to a safe square, and again sat back in his chair. "There are no more unruly neighbors, no French mercenaries to harass my fishing boats, no smugglers of any account at all. Well, there are always malcontents, an occasional villain, but they are nothing, really."

Garron laughed. "You have your heir, Severin, the handsomest babe in the world, so you yourself told me. You have a comely wife who sees well to your needs, Oxborough prospers. Be content." Garron paused a moment, his fingers hovering over a pawn. "Did you read the king's missive? Surely what he wants would relieve your boredom. Does he not want you to execute some daring commission for him?"

Severin moved his queen, and announced, "Checkmate, Garron."

"Hmmm." He studied the board, gave Severin a twisted smile, and gently laid his king on his side. "The game is yours. Come, tell me, what does the king wish of you?"

"He wishes to breed one of his favorite stallions, a gift from Philip of France, to Lady Hastings's mare, Marella. He wishes me to send Marella to London when she is next in season."

The king had sent him here for *this?*

"Ah, Trist, come and bid welcome to Lord Garron. You spent all your time watching over Fawke this evening, ignoring me, the one who has fed you and saved your furry head more times than you can count, and I know you can count, since I've seen you equally divide acorns among your own babes."

The marten climbed up Severin's arm, settled himself on his shoulder, bathed while he watched Garron.

"Hello, Trist. I am not a bad fellow. If I had a bit of pork, I would give it to you. I did not know you ate acorns."

"He doesn't. He is, I believe, teaching his own babes how to count, though they're very nearly grown now and ready to leave us for the forest. Why would they count anything, I wonder?"

Garron laughed.

Trist appeared to consider the laughter and the acorns. After a moment, he extended a paw. Garron lightly ran his fingertips over the marten's paw, then up his back.

"He spends most of his time guarding Fawke. I have told him it is not necessary, but he doesn't heed me."

Trist mewled and wrapped himself around Severin's neck.

"Ah, Garron, the king made other requests. He does not write it in so many words, but he sent you here to ensure we will support each other against mutual enemies since Oxborough and Wareham are not too far distant from each other. 'Tis true that he encourages some strife between his barons and earls, not wanting to have too much complicity brew up between his vassals, but since we are both known by Lord Graelam de Moreton and approved by him, the king wants us strong, should he need us."

"Need our soldiers at his back and our money in his coffers, you mean."

Severin's mouth twisted in a grin. "Aye, that's it." Trist mewled.

Garron raised his goblet, fashioned of a beautiful dark green glass from the Rhineland, and saluted Severin. "I am ready for your friendship and I willingly offer you my assistance should you ever need it."

"I, too," said Severin, and raised his own goblet.

The men drank. Garron said, "But you know, I am tired of fighting. I am also tired of men's duplicity, something that abounds at court. I believe I should enjoy boredom, Severin, mayhap a good six months of it."

The men drank more of Severin's precious wine, and Garron lost another game of chess.

Garron was jerked back at the loud yell just ahead. He held up his hand to keep his four men in place. He patted his destrier's neck, calming him, and Damocles immediately quieted. They heard another yell, men cursing, arguing, horses whinnying and thrashing about.

Garron said low to his man Aleric, "Stay. I will see what's happening ahead."

He dismounted and drew his sword as he walked quietly through the thick trees and the tangled undergrowth toward the men's voices, louder now, curses filling the air. Through the branches of an ancient oak tree, he stared into a small clearing. A huge man, surely the size of a sixteen-hand stallion, his face covered with a filthy black beard, was trying to hold a struggling boy who was slamming his fist into the man's face, his neck, his chest, whatever part he could reach. The man tried to avoid the blows, not retaliating. So, he didn't want to break the boy's neck. He tried to grab his hands, but the boy lurched back and slammed him in the belly. Garron was impressed. The boy wasn't about to go down without a fight. The boy yelled, his voice shrill with fear, "Let me go, or I will kill the lot of you! You fools, this man, your leader, he lies to you! I will bring you no gold, I will bring you nothing but misfortune. Let me go!"

The boy had bravado, Garron would give him that. As for this villainous lot setting the boy free, that didn't seem likely. There were two other men, both hard looking as the man mountain, ready to jump into the fray, their clenched fists holding thick-bladed knives.

"Don't kill him! No, the rest of you stay back."

This was from their leader, who looked like a king surrounded by beggars. He was richly dressed in a red wool tunic, a fine sword strapped at his lean waist, his armor well made. One of the men stepped toward the struggling boy, and their leader raised a gauntleted hand and called for him to stop.

Garron watched the boy suddenly free himself, rear up, and clout the big man in his nose. He heard the bone crack from where he was standing. Blood gushed everywhere. The man bellowed, jerked the boy up by his collar, and flung him three feet away from him, against a pile of rocks. "Ye little cockshead! Damn ye to hell and back for busting me nose, you puling little sprat!" He charged the boy, flinging out ribbons of blood in all directions.

3

Their leader yelled, "Stop, Berm! You idiot, I told you not to harm the boy! Look what you've done. My lord will kill all of us if his head's broken open. You'll be without your liver before the night falls if you've killed him."

Berm swiped his hand over his nose, and looked with loathing at the boy, now lying unconscious on his back. "He bain't be dead, the little bastid." But his fists smoothed out as he bent down to pull him upright. Fast as a snake, the boy struck up with his legs into Berm's groin and sent him pedaling backward, yelling as he grabbed himself. "My manhood is dead! The little spittlecock kilt it!"

Good blow, Garron thought, and now was the time to intervene before the others fell on him like a pack of wolves. He shouted, "Aleric, *á moi.*" He leapt out from the trees into a small clearing, his sword held high.

He yelled, "That will be quite enough, lads!"

Garron felt their surprise, their terrifying joy when they saw him, prey more meaty than this scrawny boy.

Their leader shouted at Garron, "This is none of your affair, sirrah! Get you gone now and we will not kill you!"

Garron glanced at the three villains, then over at the boy, who was scooting away from them as fast as he could move. He came up and pressed against a tree, drew his knees to his chest. Garron saw the wild hope in his eyes. Garron smiled at him.

Berm was bent over, still holding himself and moaning while blood gushed from his nose. Garron couldn't make out his features what with the filthy woolen cap pulled over his forehead and the huge tangled black beard that covered his face and neck. He looked back at the man in the rich red tunic, and said easily, "I've a fancy to save the boy. Would you like to tell me what you're doing with him?"

Red Tunic said, "He is my nephew, a spoiled and heedless boy, and disobedient. I was merely taking him back to his father."

The boy yelled, "You're a mangy liar! I never saw you before in my life until you and these nasty louts kidnapped me!"

Red Tunic took two steps toward the boy. Garron stopped him with a raised hand. He said, his voice cold as the winter solstice, "I suggest you and your men leave at once. If you do not, then Saint Peter may find himself judging you this day. Given what you've done, I doubt you would like the outcome."

One of the men growled as he slashed out with his knife, "'Tis nay likely, ye cockhead. I can send ye to hell meself. Saint Peter will never have a whiff of ye."

"Look behind you," Garron said, as he leapt backward.

Aleric called out, "Aye, fill your eyes, you fool! We are here, my lord."

Garron said easily as he slashed his sword before him, "Either you leave now or you will die. It is your choice."

Red Tunic shouted as he pulled his sword from its scabbard, "Kill them!" He ran straight at Garron. Garron saw furious concentration and intelligence in the man's dark eyes, unlike his men, who were all violence and no brains. This man was a formidable opponent, single-minded in purpose, and filled with pride. Was there desperation as well? No, he didn't think so. He was a good fighter and he knew it. Garron saw one of the men run toward the boy. He jumped back from Red Tunic's sword, pulled his own knife from his belt, and released it all in one smooth motion, so fast it was a blur. The man grabbed at the knife that stuck out the back of his neck. He whirled around, stared at Garron, and crumbled to the ground. There was an instant of frozen silence, then Red Tunic yelled, fury lacing his voice, "Bastard! I'm going to kill you now!"

You're still not afraid of me. Garron smiled, then yelled like a berserker as he ran toward Red Tunic, his sword directly in front of him like a lance. He heard the horses scatter into the forest.

"Aleric, dispatch the others," he shouted over his shoulder. "Protect the boy!" He saw the man wasn't so cocky now. He paused, stroking his chin a moment, goading his opponent. "If you weren't so meager, I would take your rich red tunic after I slit your throat. Mayhap I'll spare you if you offer it to me on your knees. I'll give it to the boy."

"I am not meager, you whoreson!"

"If you are not meager, then just who and what are you?"

"I am— It is none of your affair. There is no reason for you to interfere. You have killed one of my men. You will pay for that." He slashed his sword in front of him. "You'll not have my tunic, damn you."

"I'm thinking if the boy doesn't want it, I will use it to wipe down my horse after I have sent my sword through your belly. Why are you afraid to tell me who you are? Who is your master? If I don't kill you, mayhap he'll relieve you of your tunic when you return to him empty-handed. You are so scrawny, mayhap he'll use your tunic to rub down his horse."

The man squared his shoulders and cursed, loud and fluent.

Garron said over him, "Four men with a struggling boy. You stole him, didn't you?" His smile was ferocious. "What are you, a pederast? Or is your master a pederast?"

Red Tunic growled deep in his throat and lunged. He was well trained and agile, Garron thought dispassionately as he sidestepped, watching how the man moved, watching for a weakness. Then he saw it. The man was furious, not thinking hard and cold, as a warrior should. Garron knew the man didn't have his strength, but he didn't want to kill him yet. He wanted to know who he was first, and who the boy was, and so he contented himself with hacking a wide circle in front of him, keeping him back, wearing him down. He knew the moment the man realized he wouldn't survive this fight. He chose to run, shouting over his shoulder as he jumped a tree root, "You'll die for this!"

Garron was after him in an instant, but Red Tunic had a stout warhorse nearby, and Damocles was back in the forest, tethered with his men's horses. He was mounted and away before Garron could catch up to him. He stood there panting, watching the bright red disappear into the thick of the trees. He wondered again who the man was as he slid his sword back into its scabbard. He knew if he chanced upon the man again, he would certainly recognize his thin face, his dark, hot eyes beneath heavy black brows. He'd also recognize his warhorse, a bay with four white fetlocks, a horse he would take after he'd dispatched the man to hell.

Garron flexed his hand as he walked back to the clearing only to see Pali, his eyes red and watery, stick his sword in a man's chest, then kick him onto his back.

It was dead silent now in the clearing.

Garron said, "Where is the boy?"

Aleric looked around. "He was—well, the ungrateful little bittle's gone. He must have been frightened and run to hide in the forest."

"No wonder," Garron said. "What were they going to do with him? Ransom, I suppose, and that would mean he's of some importance to someone."

Aleric asked, "Shall I send Pali to search for the boy? With those long legs of his, he can cover more ground than the four of us put together. Or Hobbs, he can see better than an eagle."

Gilpin, Garron's squire of nearly two years, laughed. "Aye, Hobbs can see a worm hiding under a leaf."

Garron looked at the dying afternoon sun overhead through

the thick trees. It was growing late. Still, he couldn't simply leave the boy alone. He and his men searched, kept assuring him they wouldn't hurt him, that they would protect him.

They didn't find the boy, even though Garron called again and again to him.

Finally, Garron said, "We have only another hour or two of daylight. I wish to be at Wareham before night falls. I wish to sleep in my own bed this night." How odd that sounded—his own bed, the lord's bed, not the small narrow cot he'd shared with his younger brother, Kalen, years before, a younger brother long dead.

He kicked the boot of one of the dead men as he said, "We have no tools to dig graves, so we will leave them." He looked again at the sun, wondering if he should search more for the boy. How far from home was he? And that damned man in his red tunic who'd kidnapped him, who was he? Garron shouted yet again, "Boy! We mean you no harm. We have killed your captors. I promise you safety. Come out now!"

After a few minutes of silence, Garron realized there was no hope for it. "We've done our best—either he'll survive or he won't. Let's go home."

As they walked back to their horses, Garron asked, "Did any of you recognize their leader, the man in the red tunic? He would not tell me his name or that of his master."

"Nay, but he's an old hound," Gilpin said, and spat on the ground.

"You are but fifteen years old," Garron said, and buffeted his squire's shoulder, nearly sending him to the ground to land on his own spit. "I am an old hound to you, and Aleric yon is a veritable graybeard."

"No graybeard there," said Gilpin, his voice cocky, his hands on his narrow hips, "since Aleric is bald as a river rock and his chin as smooth as a pebble."

Aleric waved a fist at the boy. "Well, puppy? Think you I'm an old hound? With my bald river rock head?"

Gilpin gave Aleric a singularly sweet smile. "Oh, nay. My lord is nearly my own age and you, Aleric, you are a wise and generous protector, of no particular age at all. Your head is a beacon to all those who seek justice and hope."

Aleric shouted with laughter.

Garron shook his head at the two of them. "I shall surely puke."

Gilpin said, "Nay, my lord, do not since I should have to clean your boots. Methinks the boy is afraid to come out because he saw Pali's red leaky eyes and believed him the Devil."

Pali, those long legs of his making him even taller than Garron, gave Gilpin a terrifying smile. "If the boy saw me, Little Nothing, he'd fall on his knees before me."

"What?" Gilpin said. "You are God, not the Devil?"

Garron said, "Were I you, Gilpin, I'd shut my mouth. It might save you a hiding."

"Or Pali would wrap one leg around me and squeeze the life right out of my heart."

"Half a leg," said Pali, and scrubbed his fists over his eyes. "I can do nothing about my eyes, they turn red with the coming of spring."

Garron said, "Stop rubbing them, Pali, it just makes it worse. Pour water on your eyes. Now, enough. Let's leave this place." His voice deepened. "Let's go home."

Gilpin looked around, and said, "I hope the boy will be all right. He had guts. Did you see him kick that hulking brute and bloody his nose?" And he threw back his head and shouted, "Boy! Come here, we'll take care of you! I'm a boy too, like you, come out."

A horse whinnied, making Garron smile. "Hobbs, get the villains' horses. We've just increased our stables." Horses loved Hobbs; he had only to speak in his low musical voice and they came trotting eagerly to him, legs high, heads tossing. In minutes, three horses were blowing into Hobbs's big hands.

An hour later, Garron pulled Damocles to a halt. He raised his hand to stop his men behind him and looked toward his home. Wareham Castle, just shy of two hundred years of age, sat like a great fist of gray granite in front of them, a massive sentinel atop the end of a desolate promontory that stuck out into the North Sea. From the sea, Wareham was impregnable; black basalt rocks surrounded the promontory, spearing up twenty feet into the air, and the tide would do the rest, ripping boats apart.

Garron felt an odd surge of satisfaction as he looked at the stark fortress that now belonged to him. It would be his line to call Wareham home, not his brother's. This was the first time he'd been back in eight long, gritty years.

It was a beautiful spring evening, not yet dark, an early, nearly full moon beginning to climb into the sky beyond the castle walls. Stars would stud the sky tonight, another hour, no more. An evening breeze was warm and soft against his flesh. It was completely unlike that night eight years before when a storm from the sea had raged hard, hurling heavy rain, frigid winds, and a thick curtain of cold fog on anyone unlucky enough to be outside. He'd been sixteen the night he and his best friend, Bari, the armorer's son, had ridden into the storm, not waiting for morning, only two days after they'd buried Garron's father, his brother's words sounding stark in his ears: "There is nothing for you here, Garron. You are strong and you have a brain. 'Tis time you made your own way." He'd never forget the moment he'd turned in his saddle for a final look at Wareham. The black clouds had suddenly parted, the swirling fog had lifted, and he'd seen the castle outlined by a hit of lightning, stark against the black sky, an eternal beacon, and he'd wondered bleakly if he'd ever see his home again in his life.

Well, he was here now, but Bari wasn't with him, hadn't been since he'd choked to death, coughing up wads of blood so many years before. Wareham Castle and all its surrounding towns and farms were his, his legacy, his future, his responsibility.

Catherine Coulter is the *New York Times* bestselling author of more than sixty-five books, including historical and contemporary romances, and the FBI thriller series featuring Dillon Savich and Lacey Sherlock. She lives in Northern California.

CONNECT ONLINE

www.catherinecoulter.com
facebook.com/catherinecoulterbooks

ISBN 978-0-515-15115-2

The #1 *New York Times* bestselling author presents a Sherbrooke novel featuring a cast of witty and outrageous characters and two wonderfully complex mysteries.

www.catherinecoulter.com
www.penguin.com

ISBN 978-0-515-15115-2

$7.99 U.S.
$8.99 CAN